Optimistic Oath

also by Chelsey Blue Spicer

Paramour Promise
Requited Rivalry
Learning Late

Optimistic Oath

Chelsey Blue Spicer

To the ones who dared to embrace
imperfections, acknowledge the fractures
in the mosaic of their connection, yet find
beauty in the broken spaces.

1

The almost brawl began because Charleigh deep down had always been a liar—a good enough liar to fool even herself half of the time. Charleigh and Mona were late for tip-off because of a tug-of-war match over a purple jersey with Lexa Jenson's name on it. Thirty minutes of arguing about whether wearing the jersey was a crime against womanhood.

"Lexa Jenson is a womanizer and a cheater," Mona yelled, her fist tightened around the purple mesh material.

Her evidence was TikTok videos where Jenson was shown holding on to a woman who wasn't her wife. A blonde half Jenson's size had tried her best to keep her face covered as she pulled and pushed her way free from Jenson's drunken grip.

Mona had a very strong argument, and if Charleigh was grading it like one of her student's essays, then she would have to give Mona an A. However, Mona wasn't Charleigh's student. The tattooed taller woman was basically her sister and had once been her girlfriend. A once upon a time type of story that did not end in a happily ever after. Their story was a fractured fairytale, and the almost brawl ended with the blonde's decision that being told what she could not wear by the girl who dumped her was a battle worth winning.

Charleigh jerked the jersey from Mona's hand. She'd worn it to every game since Mona gifted it to her three years earlier. The other woman had to know that. Three years of supporting the Devils and Lexa Jenson in that jersey. And they hadn't lost a home game all season while she wore it. A win streak that brought them to the playoff game the two women were late for.

The real question was: how could she not wear it?

She didn't ask though. It would mean the topic was up for debate.

She pulled it over the top of her. Got her head briefly stuck in the armhole before she fixed herself. She always fixed herself.

"You stopped being allowed to lecture me when you decided to dump me," Charleigh hissed. "It's supposed to be my birthday present, so I'm going to wear what I want."

They left Charleigh's house without talking to each other. The music played while Mona huffed at every red light on the trip across town. The gravel lot across from the arena was filled, but Mona made her own parking space. She navigated the truck with ease, while Charleigh's mind ran through their argument once more.

With arms folded over Jenson's number on her chest, Charleigh convinced herself she was right to wear the jersey. Reminded herself that Mona didn't even know what happened at the bar the night Lexa Jenson was arrested. Mona didn't even watch basketball enough to care that this was the Devil's shot at the first championship in seven years. Or to care about what Lexa was going through.

Charleigh understood what it was like to have someone come between her and the girl she loved. Mona had just never loved Charleigh enough to understand, which is why Charleigh could forgive Jenson. She had to forgive. After all, she'd done worse things in her life.

The cracked soles of her orange Converse Chucks slapped against the wet concrete. Charleigh dragged Mona through the mostly vacant courtyard outside of the basketball arena's doors. At least there wasn't a line to move through the metal detectors.

The court was visible from the lobby, but the teams looked like ants fighting over a Cheeto crumb. Luckily, the big screen was focused on Lexa Jenson in possession of the ball. Charleigh stopped and stood on her toes. She watched the woman drive toward the center, fake left, then slip around the opponent on the right for an easy lay-up.

The ball sank, but the behemoth in blue hit Jenson's face. Jenson's body twisted while she was still in the air before hitting the wooden floor with a slight bounce. She curled into a ball, holding her nose. Her dark hair came loose from her standard bun.

The footage replayed the thick elbow smashing Jenson in the cheek and nose in slow motion. Then from a different angle.

"About time someone decked her," Mona grumbled. "If I had known you're still obsessed with that bitch, I never would have brought you here for your birthday."

Charleigh swatted Mona for thinking it was a good thing the Devil's MVP and highest scorer lay on the floor.

"We need her," Charleigh explained. "If she's out, then we're fucked. Tanzon is only averaging sixteen points a game and her field goal average has dropped over the last four weeks. She is only good if she gets a clear shot, and Jenson is the one who clears the lane for her to shoot. So, you know what that means?"

"They lose," Mona stated.

"We lose," Charleigh corrected. Her hands moved in the air but contributed nothing as she explained. "We would have to come from behind in the series, and the blue team has never lost a series where they started on top. Winning tonight means we take the first round."

Mona laughed at Charleigh bouncing on her toes, trying to see the court where ant-like Lexa Jenson lay surrounded by a few other black ants with miniature red bags. She tugged on Charleigh's arm, but the blonde shook away the grip. Her eyes had returned to the now live action of the medic's prodding Lexa's face. It didn't look like it was bleeding.

Mona called to her, but Charleigh waved her off. "Not now. I need to know if she is okay."

Lips pressed a kiss to Charleigh's cheek. A hand was shoved into Charleigh's front pocket, then the rear one. The right side produced nothing but an old gum wrapper, so Mona tried the other side.

"I need your ID, Princess," Mona said.

Charleigh disregarded the stupid name and pressed her face into Mona's lips to get another kiss. Seven years as sisters instead of lovers still broke Charleigh's heart, but she knew Mona was seeing someone else. She knew she'd never be anything more than what she was, and she was learning to accept that.

She reached down the neck of her shirt. Her ID was a little sweaty when she put it in the other woman's hand. Whether Mona cared or not went unnoticed when the screen switched to a view of the Devils in a huddle. Their coach danced his fingers over the palm of his other hand. His lips curled over his teeth as he snarled at the players. Spittle flew from his lips toward the woman not looking at him from the bench.

Charleigh felt something slip over her head and glanced down to see the purple lanyard with a plastic holder in it. The ticket was huge with foiled lettering. Lexa Jenson in 2D went up for a layup across the cardstock.

She held it for a moment and just looked at the woman. Even after everything that happened, she wished it would have been different. She wished for the woman who'd fumbled through a Shakespeare sonnet in the overcrowded lecture hall they'd shared once upon a time. Or the one who'd stood smiling while she held up the Devil's jersey. Number 1 draft pick for the NWBA before she'd even finished four years of college.

Mona hooked an arm through Charleigh's and pulled her toward the glass doors to a little old man in the oversized orange jersey just as the Devils went back out onto the floor. Without the screen to distract her, Charleigh smiled at him and held out her ticket.

"Hiya, Charleigh." His voice was tired, but Charleigh could hear the happiness in it.

"Hey, Hank," she said. She held up her ticket so he could scan it. The scanner let out the three little beeps of approval.

"VIP tonight. Must be a special occasion," he said with a wink.

Charleigh nodded her head and felt her hair flop side-to-side. "Next week's my birthday."

The old man's bushy gray eyebrows rose. "Your birthday! Well, early happy birthday, Charleigh. How old you gonna be?"

Charleigh ducked her head and smiled, "Twenty-three on Thursday."

"Good for you," Hank offered. He scanned Mona's ticket. "I still remember you coming every summer with your pop. Good man. He'd be proud to see how big you got."

She forced the smile on her face not to waiver. Her father, the one to always make friends with the people he passed by, had brought them to games since Charleigh was a child. Their seats were always too high to see anything, but they'd share popcorn and a soda as he reminded her to always root for the home team.

"You have a good time. And be safe!" Hank called after her as Mona dragged her from her thoughts and the doorway.

When Charleigh turned back to smile at him once more, Hank waved. He'd been working the door for as long as she could remember. She worried each time he wouldn't be there the next time she came, and the last piece of her life before she was alone would disappear.

Mona abandoned Charleigh without a word in front of another television screen for food fifteen feet later. As play stopped for a commercial break, Charleigh's impatience began to set in. She tapped her foot, watching her sister move like a snail through the line. She'd already missed the first four minutes of the first quarter.

With the screen alongside the concession stand on a commercial, Charleigh glanced down at the ticket around her neck. She checked Mona's position in line, then decided seeing the game was her birthday present and she was done waiting.

She followed the instructions to entry point 101. With step one done, she studied the next set of information. She'd never had a ticket like this before, because the row was a letter, and the letter was A. The first letter in the alphabet, which meant the first row. Her eyes scanned the seats along the floor, landing on the only two open. Two padded folding chairs sat unoccupied, directly next to the Devils' bench.

Her heart beat the air out of her lungs. Mona hadn't just gotten her tickets to a playoff game; she'd gotten her courtside seats. She was going to be right next to the bench. Next to Lexa Jenson and the rest of the Devils.

Watching from the stands was her plan. She would blend in with the crowd. Be far from Jenson's gaze, like in the lecture hall. Squished between older lesbians and soccer moms. Screaming with others where she couldn't be heard, and she wouldn't be seen.

Mona sidled up alongside Charleigh standing at the top of the stairs with her hands overflowing with snacks and a drink in the crook of her arm. She hip-checked Charleigh before leading the way down. Her dark hair swayed, the scarlet red tips peeking out from under the sharp cut.

Charleigh found Jenson on the court. The woman led by a stride, running the ball down the court with two guards in blue closing in around her. She sucked in her lower lip, then chewed on the peeling skin. The ball pounded into the wood with each step she took, but before she was up, she tossed the ball to the left where number 27, Danaya Tanzon had come up. The defenders couldn't redirect the motion to block Lexa, leaving 27 completely open for the corner three.

With hands above her head, Charleigh jumped up and down while yelling, "Yeahhhh!" Her cheers joined the roar of the rest of the crowd, and she felt at ease with her people. Remembering that Jenson had no reason to care she was sitting in the front row of the game. There were hundreds of people there to see the MVP. Plus, she didn't even know Charleigh's name.

Checking the scoreboard, Charleigh noted they were up by six. However, in basketball that was only two three-pointers, three lay-ups, or two shots with fouls for a chance of an extra shot. The combinations of scenarios that could lead to her team losing were immeasurable. It didn't stop her from worrying about each one of them.

Mona was already getting comfortable when Charleigh made it down the narrow steps. As she sat, Mona handed over a soda in a red and white cup. It was the perfect combination of syrup and bubbles, and the caramel-colored liquid brought a smile to Charleigh's face with the first sip.

Her sister's arm slung around the back of Charleigh's chair with her legs stretched out. She lounged in the comfort of the luxury game seating, while Charleigh sat up on the edge of the cushion as the teams ran toward them. All of the women on the court were so much bigger than Charleigh was used to thinking about them, and so real. With voices that said words rather than the silent play, she was used to watching from 20 rows up.

Lexa was at the far end of the court flashing two, then five fingers. She called out "Orange slide!"

The chair wobbled with Charleigh's bouncing legs. Her eyes memorized the details knowing this was the closest she'd ever be to a professional court. A sweat droplet ran down the Devil's center, Emma Delango's face. She watched the guard, Danaya Tanzon, get blocked by the screen, but Lexa Jenson moved past the Stars' forward and stripped the ball away. She passed the ball to Delango. Delango took it back down the court only to fake a shot and bounced it back to Jenson who ran into the key. The ball slapped the board and fell into the net.

When Lexa's feet landed, Charleigh felt her heart rattle against her ribs. The familiar eyes looked directly at Charleigh in her jersey. The corners of her dark lips curled into a smile, and she winked at Charleigh.

Jenson pointed at Charleigh and said, "Don't worry. I got more. Just for you."

Charleigh was breathing too fast because she'd been so wrong. The cavity of her chest refused to fill when the memories began to creep back to the forefront of her mind.

A colorful tattooed arm wrapped around Charleigh, pulling her back into her chair. She glared at Lexa, whose brows scrunched for a moment before she turned, running back down the court.

"Hey, Princess," Mona said. "You okay?"

Charleigh stared at the floor, then up at the game where Emma Delango had recovered a rebound. She knew every stat for number 42, Emma Delango. But none of it mattered as Charleigh tried to will away the last time she'd been this close to the woman. The same memory where number 27, Danaya Tanzon, had stood by.

'They were there when...' Charleigh stopped the thought.

She was supposed to be home. If she had just gone home instead of the bar, Lexa Jenson wouldn't have gotten in a fight and been arrested. It was her fault for even going there.

"Did you cream your chonies?" Mona asked as Charleigh stared blankly at the court.

A part of her wanted to leave, it would be easier that way. However, there was nothing at her little house but her dog. Going home meant being alone because Mona would leave again, and Charleigh had exhausted being alone with Mona off living her new life.

She wanted to be here. Needed to be here so she could feed off the energy of the crowd and leave with the drumming of victory in her ears. It would give her something to think about. A win to cherish between the memories of all the loss.

Charleigh shook her head. "No, just in awe," she said. "Thank you for getting the tickets for my birthday. I know they probably cost you a paycheck."

"You're worth it," Mona said. She went back to eating her snacks, basketball being of no interest to her.

Charleigh's heart was still beating too fast, but it raced in step with the fast break that brought 27 back down the court. Charleigh locked away the memory of 27's eyes on her and created a new memory of the woman in this moment. The smile spread across the dark face as she smacked a hand to her chest in pride.

"Welcome to the DEVIL's DEN!" Danaya Tanzon yelled. She held her hand up to her ear, calling for the crowd's cheers. "You know who gets it done!"

As the crowd shouted out the 'Get it Devils' chant, Charleigh created a new memory of 42 to replace the way her eyes had run down Charleigh's pinned body. She replaced it with an open-mouthed laugh at 27 when she helped the woman to her feet after the blue behemoth struck again. Her close-cropped hair shook and sweat showered the younger teammate as they celebrated their lead.

Charleigh couldn't create a new memory of Lexa Jenson, though. She couldn't because every time the Devils came back to defend, the woman's eyes fell on her. Stared at Charleigh as though she could see straight through the jersey hanging off her.

She stopped looking at Jensen. Instead, she spent her one night as a VIP learning the details of the rest of the team and eating the pretzel Mona bought her. She dipped torn chunks of dough into the fake yellow cheese and shoved it into her mouth each time her team played defense on the other end of the court.

Time had moved so quickly with each team seeming to only have a fastbreak offense in their playbook. Charleigh became so engrossed in the game; that she didn't even notice halftime was approaching until the fans began to count down the last ten seconds.

As the team headed her way, Charleigh looked up to find the tired brown eyes standing out against the sweat-sheened skin. They were locked on her once more, and she remembered when she thought it was because she mattered.

Those important eyes had looked at her...

had chosen her to dance with.

had wanted her over the rest of the room.

had looked her over and decided she existed.

Just like they were doing at this moment. Hundreds of people were watching as Lexa walked directly to her.

She turned her body to face Mona. The familiar warmth of Mona's arm wrapped securely around her. She gazed at a different shade of brown. An earthy brown that flitted down to her lips, however, didn't move forward. Their kissing days had passed with their youth. Now in their twenties, Mona had someone she didn't want to know Charleigh.

And Charleigh had her first house. Her dog, Rexa Pawson. And her job.

Charleigh's eyes closed. She thought of the time kisses were stolen between them in their shared bedroom or between classes. But the past was the past, and the present was not a love story between two foster sisters.

"Well, she can't keep her eyes off you," Mona said. "But that's not unusual. You always are the brightest star in the room. Mainly because you're fluorescent."

Charleigh placed her fingers on the red lips. She closed her eyes and locked the door to the past, then pressed a kiss to the flushed cheek. "Thanks for bringing me, even though you hate basketball."

They cheered for the tiny hip-hop team during halftime, then for the Devils as they made their way back to the court. Charleigh pointed out each of the players, taking warm-up shots on their side of the court.

"...and 15 is Denise Forte. She is only 5'6". One of the shortest players in the league so she never really gets to play much."

A ball rolled into Charleigh's feet, and she stooped down to pick it up. She turned to pass the ball back on the court but froze. Lexa Jenson stood in the same spot where she'd missed every attempted shot all season with her hands held out.

With a deep breath, Charleigh thrust the ball back to the woman. A strong chest pass caused Jenson to take a step back. Jenson caught the ball and looked at her. Her eyebrows cinched again. Instead of going back to shooting though, she walked over to Charleigh and Mona. That cocky smile from quarter one was plastered back on her face.

"You want to go out tonight?" Jenson asked with her feet still on the court.

Charleigh swallowed. "Uh, we..."

"Aren't interested in hangin' out with misogynistic assholes like you," Mona snapped. Her arm fell over Charleigh's shoulder. "Anyone ever tell you that you give lesbians a bad rap?"

"Feisty. I like a little fight." Jenson cast her eyes back on Charleigh. Then she asked, "What about you? You busy tonight or is the girlfriend just threatened?"

"I..." Words wouldn't work.

"You know, you could use your hall pass." Jenson's eyebrows rose and fell. "I promise it'll be worth it."

Charleigh studied the way the woman's lips curled at the corners in a self-approved smirk when she spoke this time. And a familiar feeling settled in her chest.

"I... I can't tonight."

Jenson grabbed the Sharpie a fan waved in her face from the row behind them. She scribbled on the ball before handing the marker back to the owner and the ball to Charleigh.

"I'm here all year," Jenson said with another wink.

Charleigh turned to show Mona the birthday prize realizing it was Lexa Jenson's phone number instead of an autograph. There was a point in her life when she would have fought someone over ownership of that ball. However, when the ball came loose from her grasp, Charleigh didn't rush after it. She steadied herself on Mona, then looked back to see what had caused her to lose control of the now-lost ball.

"Don't touch her," Mona barked. Her fingers dug into the ball player's wrist. Jenson's bicep flexed as the chemical compounds tattooed over Mona's wrist seemed to give her superhuman strength. "She's too good to end up like the last girl that thought you were something special."

Lexa Jenson's lips formed a straight line, but her eyes widened in surprise. She pulled her wrist back, but Mona didn't release her.

"Let go of me," Lexa rumbled. The surprise was gone, and the frame of her body rose from the slumped position. Her height loomed over Charleigh's back.

"What?" Mona scoffed. "You don't like it when people put their hands on you?"

Charleigh placed her hand on Mona's, and she released Jenson's hand. She glanced up at Lexa and tried to remember the girl she'd seen in college. With a soft shrug, she explained, "She's just worried you're going to hurt me. You and I have a bad history of touching."

Lexa's glare softened when she looked down at Charleigh. Her brows furrowed, and Charleigh awaited a bitchy comment. Waited for Lexa Jenson to snap like she'd done both times she'd been close to Charleigh.

The music in the arena was getting louder. A buzzer rang when the clock hit zero. The sound seemed to flip a switch in Lexa Jenson. The woman's eyes widened; this time not dilated with lust.

The pale seashell brown irises pulled Charleigh's gaze. Even in a state of shock, Charleigh couldn't help but swoon over how beautiful Lexa Jenson was. How her eyes seemed to be just a shade paler than her skin. Her hair was in a natural curl set, the bun having come undone in the first quarter.

The woman shut her mouth only to open it again. She did this a few times, but no words came out. Emma Delango came up behind Lexa. She shoved the basketball with the phone number back into Charleigh's hands before pulling at Lexa.

"Jenson, let's go," Delango said, but then she looked at Charleigh. Her eyes grew as wide as Lexa's. They were darker and sadder when they stared down at her.

"You're the girl from the bar," she breathed. "I went after you, but you were gone."

Lexa's posture shrunk once more. Her hands gripped the air like bars separating herself from Charleigh. Words began to fall and fail with each breath she took.

"The next day..."

Fans were screaming around them. Called for their team, like sirens.

"I tried to find you..."

Inflatable tubes struck together. Their cracks were as loud as thunder in the cavernous space.

"...to tell you I was...."

Lexa was panicking. She was panicking, but halftime was over.

"I'm so sorry. I wasn't going to..." Lexa's head shook back and forth. Her hand extended to touch Charleigh but hovered just out of reach. "I didn't mean to...."

Charleigh grabbed the dark hand. She squeezed it like a hug instead of a handshake. She told herself not to stutter, but it was hard. It was hard because she was holding the hand that pushed her into the railing. The hand that tried to push its way into her pants because the woman hadn't cared.

"I forgive you," Charleigh yelled over the people screaming around her.

It wasn't the truth, but Lexa wouldn't know Charleigh looked at people's noses when she lied. The woman would feel better about what happened, and the game would go on. Life would go on like it always had without the blonde.

Lexa's eyes blinked. In a single breath, she said, "I'll make it up to you. I'm not the monster they say I am. You'll see. I'll show you. I'll see you after the game."

She turned before Charleigh could agree. Ran down the court as the Stars inbounded the ball with only four Devil's defenders in place.

Once Lexa was on the other side, Charleigh felt the weight lift from her chest. She leaned back into Mona with the ball over her middle, cradling it like a proud mom-to-be. Mona's arms wrapped around her center, pulling the smaller woman flush to her as they waited with the rest of the fans for the Devils to score their first points before taking their seats.

Mona's breath warmed the back of Charleigh's neck. Her chin rested on Charleigh's shoulder as she asked, "Were you the girl in the video at Echo's Escape?"

Charleigh nodded. She nodded because there was no reason left to lie to Mona. There was no reason to try to hide something from Mona she already knew. Because if she tried to deny it was her, then Mona would question the other things she'd said over the years. She'd ask questions Charleigh hoped never to have to answer again.

"Why didn't you tell me?" Mona asked. "Call me to get you? I saw the video. You were scared."

Charleigh lowered her head. Her eyes traced the inconsistent pattern of the floorboards. Taking a deep breath, she confessed, "I shouldn't have been there. I wasn't drinking, but I have said that before... so I figured it was better if no one knew. I just went home and hoped no one would recognize me."

Mona's arms tightened. She pressed another kiss to the honey hair. Her chin made its way to Charleigh's shoulder where she rested the brilliant brain on the smaller woman. The woman had given up so much to stay with Charleigh. The least the blonde could do was not make Mona regret it.

Charleigh could hear the smile in Mona's voice when she said, "Well you have a new ball out of it, and an annoying douche canoe trying to make it up to you. I mean, she could be worse. She could be like Kyle, who used to try and watch you take a shower."

"She could be worse," Charleigh echoed. She tried not to hold her breath when she thought of their oily foster brother. "She could smell like a chicken nugget."

"You really have the worst taste in women. Even Jenson's sweat smelled better than the culinary chick." Mona leaned into Charleigh. "But before you go calling that phone number. I need you to ask yourself. Do you honestly think she is more than her latest catchphrase?"

Charleigh looked over just enough to scan Mona's face. The woman watched the players on the court closer than she'd ever paid attention to a game before. The rich cognac eyes ran over the team, then fell on Charleigh's face.

"What do you mean?"

Mona's arms released her, and she held up her hands as she pretended to yell, "I'm Lexa Fucking Jenson."

Charleigh snorted loudly because even though Mona hadn't screamed, she could hear the exclamation points in the words. Her hands shoved Mona back slightly.

As if on cue, number 1 held up an arm. Her bicep caught the Stars' guard just over the chest. The blue-uniformed player hit the ground hard as Jenson stood over the woman.

"You're going to have to do better than that!" Jenson taunted the girl, who was still trying to catch the air forced out of her. "I'm Lexa Fucking Jenson, not your little school friend!"

Charleigh leaned down and picked up her drink. The tension she'd felt twisting within her began to unravel, and she smiled at the cup of happiness. Her team was going to win, and they would go on to win a championship.

Just as she took a sip, a body slammed into her. Her lower back hit the chair behind her. The stands of people flipped sideways in slow motion. She knew she was falling, but there was nothing she could do to stop it.

2

The pass was off. The Devils were up by eight but there was an opportunity to keep the ball in play. A chance for Lexa to save it, so she launched her body over the line, leaned into the motion, palmed the ball, and tossed it to Danaya. The momentum sent her into the crowd.

She felt the fan crumple to the ground under her, causing the nearby chair to screech. The drink in the fan's hand soaked through Lexa's jersey. The one she was going to give to the blonde after the game. The blonde girl from the bar who now lay under her.

Lexa's legs tangled with the woman. The thin limbs twisted, and her torso pushed against Lexa's weight, keeping the girl pressed to the floor. Pink lips choked for air while a small pale hand grasped the back of the blonde head.

The arena's volume settled to a murmur. She could only hear the sound of feet pounding against the court as the medics made their second trip on camera.

"Fucck!" The single word expelled gave the crowd proof of life.

'Again. Again. Again.' The word echoed in Lexa's head as she stared at the pain etched into the crevices of the woman's face. Tears rolled like rafts on a lazy river down the flushed, freckled cheeks.

Lexa untangled her legs and straddled the woman. Fingers searched the blonde's head. She probed the woman's skull. Felt the soft honey-colored strands wrap around her digits. A bump was already growing.

Stormy eyes shot open. Grey and blue whirlpools twisted up the thoughts in Lexa's head. Eyes begging her to stop.

'Please stop,' the girl had said. Lexa could hear it now even though the woman's lips only trembled in pain.

The bitchy brunette's hands slammed into Lexa's shoulder. Shoved her to the ground, so Lexa couldn't touch the blonde. She was yelling in more than one language, but Lexa couldn't hear while she was trying to see through the medics.

Lexa lay on the ground alongside the blonde with tears running down her face. She reached out and took the hand that tried to slow her down a week before. Lexa needed her to know she wasn't alone when she was in so much pain. Needed to soothe the fear she'd caused not once but twice. Show the girl who'd offered her forgiveness that Lexa wasn't the monster the media made her out to be.

The ball player would prove to the woman she was good. She'd make up for putting her hands on the girl with honey hair. She'd prove she didn't ruin everyone she touched.

'I won't let anyone hurt you,' she promised silently to the girl whose name she still hadn't learned.

The medics flashed a pin light over the blue eyes. They checked her neck and spine before they helped the blonde to her feet, moved her away from the court, and escorted her to the team locker room where she'd have to wait because concussion checks took forever.

The jersey with Lexa's name on it was plastered to her chest. She'd worn her jersey to the game, and to Lexa, it was a sign the woman didn't hate her yet. A chance to make it up to the girl like she'd promised.

"Mona," the blonde said, reaching out for the girlfriend. "Can she come with me?"

She had a girlfriend. She didn't want Lexa last week because she was with someone. That's why she'd pushed Lexa away. She was a good girl, not like the others.

It was hard not to notice that the camera operator had focused on the way the dark-haired girl held the woman during halftime. Held her so perfectly, and Lexa couldn't tear her eyes away from the screen as her coach gave his speech about coming out strong in the locker room.

The voice in her head reminded her, 'You can fix this. You are Lexa Fucking Jenson. There is nothing you can't do if you just set your mind to it.'

"Your girlfriend can come," one of the medics said.

'I'll fix it,' she thought again. 'They call me a monster, but I'm not. They just don't know, but I will show them that I'm not just good. I'm great.'

"Sister," the woman corrected. "She's my sister."

Lexa heard it. She heard it, but it took moments to process. Looking at the brunette who had held the now concussed woman, Lexa watched the smug smile spread over the sharp-angled face. Her dark eyes dared Lexa to step up to her as she pushed herself up from the floor.

"She's your sister?" Lexa asked.

"She's none of your business," the woman growled. "Stay the fuck away from her."

The Latina moved forward, but Lexa was partially blocking her way. She could feel the sweat running down the crevice of her back, and she needed to move. She didn't want to though. She wanted to know the girl's name.

"Get out of my way," the woman barked.

Lexa looked down. Her nails dug into her palms as she reminded herself of her promise. Punching the girl's sister would not prove she was good. She shifted her weight before taking a step to the side. The blonde wanted her sister, and that was fine for now. She had a game to win for the girl, then she would go to her. After the game, she'd find her, and she'd show her. Show her she could be great. Everything she promised that the girl had wanted while their bodies were pressed together on the dance floor.

The ref blew his whistle, and play resumed without Lexa. She looked up to see the coach had put in Tanisha for her, which was okay. She needed a minute, or three. The medics checked her over too as she made a plan in her head.

The rain fell from buckets while she searched the courtyard for the blonde who had been released just before the game ended. Fans congratulated her on the win, but none of those fans mattered to her. Just the one she promised to win for, then made it so the woman couldn't even see it happen.

Lexa's shoes grumbled with each squishy step to the locker room. She could hear the shower calling her name as the wet jersey chilled with each pass under a vent still pumping out cold air. Her teeth were chattering when she pushed open the door to the locker room.

Startled, Emma's dense body flew back half-naked and rolled on the floor. The rookie guard, previously pinned to the ground by the older woman, sat up just as quickly. Her dark eyes ran over every surface that Lexa wasn't on.

Unsure what to say, Lexa stepped over Danaya's legs and grabbed a fresh towel from the bench. She dropped into the seat in front of her locker and wrapped it tightly around herself. She kicked off her shoes, now trashed from running through the gravel lot when she'd thought she saw the honey hair moving between the cars.

The towel wasn't helping, so she pulled the wet jersey off, then her bra. Unclad breasts being a commonality in the room suddenly became not so usual as her brain processed the two teammates who may have been about to fuck on the floor.

A year ago, they probably wouldn't have stopped or tried to pretend they hadn't been about to have sex. Lexa had ruined that for everyone when she'd lost her shit with her wife's trade. No more teammate relationships. Her marriage was declared bad for business.

"Well..." Emma stated as she knelt in front of her duffle bag and pulled out an oversized t-shirt. "Did you catch up with her?"

"No."

Her phone buzzed in her bag, so she pulled it out. The lock screen showed seven texts and two missed calls from her wife's sister. She ignored them all and opened Instagram.

"You good, Lexi?" the rookie asked. The first few syllables the girl had spoken to her since last week. A silence Lexa was fine with since Danaya was the reason her wife was in Chicago.

Lexa's shoulder blades tried to kill the spider crawling under her skin but missed it. The creepy crawly feeling made its way up her neck. She tried to ignore the ick of the name, but when it didn't fade, she growled at the girl, "Don't call me that."

Lexa set the phone down and searched through her bag again until she found the faded Devils sweatshirt. She tugged it over her head. Her hair was now too big to fit easily through the hole, so it took more effort than her tired arms had in her. She left her chin tucked into the overstretched neck. After two inhales, her mind felt less muddy.

She glanced over at the girl she was supposed to mentor. The one they'd replaced her wife with. Danaya had done a shit job so far. The blonde getting hurt would have never happened if Sylvia hadn't been traded for the girl the media claimed would outscore Lexa in the next two years.

"Lexa hates nicknames," Emma said. "But that one most of all. Almost tore a PR person's throat open for printing it one time."

"My mom called me that when she was on a high," she grumbled.

Danaya glanced back at Emma, then at Lexa. She shook her head.

"Sorry. My mom was a drug addict too. Called me all sorts of shit when she couldn't even remember her name," Danaya said.

Lexa cradled the phone in her hands once more. She couldn't swallow the secret she'd kept from everyone, so she spit it out.

"My mom wasn't an addict. She's bipolar and refused to take her meds. She would swing between high and low. I always knew she was on a high when she called me *that*."

She waited for the interrogation that kept her from telling anyone. But Danaya only whispered, "Oh."

"So... you lost the girl. Did you at least tell her you're sorry at halftime?" Emma pressed.

Lexa set the phone down again and leaned back in her chair. She licked, then bit her lower lip, weighing if saying anything was worth the unsolicited feedback. It's not like they were her friends. Well, at least not Danaya. Emma had been there though.

"I told her I was going to make it up to her, but I don't even know her name," Lexa explained.

Emma pulled a pair of Nike slides from her bag and slipped her feet into them. Then she leaned back in the chair and sucked her teeth.

"What?" Lexa asked, now needing the feedback she'd avoided from the woman a season or two away from retirement.

"Nothin'," Emma said.

She studied the woman's lips. The way they moved left to right was as though she was chewing on her sentences. "Naw, you suck your teeth when you suckin' back in your words. So just say it."

Emma's eyes narrowed at Lexa, and she sucked her teeth again. Her head tilted to the side, as she said, "You can't undo what you did."

Her head was heavy, so she let it drop. To the floor, she said, "I know that."

Emma's eyes rolled as her tongue ran over the front of her teeth. "Of course, you know."

"I know I fucked up," Lexa said. "But I can make it up—"

Emma's head snapped as her words slapped Lexa across the face. "You had to physically be pulled off that girl as you tried to rape her."

"I wasn't trying to—"

"You were trying to fuck her in a bar full of people, and she was telling you no, so yes Lexa, you were trying to rape her. You tellin' yourself that you weren't is just you lying to yourself, and you thinking that you can just be around her and it is okay... it can't be okay."

"I told her I would find her after the game and prove to her I'm not the monster everyone thinks I am," Lexa defended. Her hand shot out toward the court. "She said she forgave me."

Emma scoffed. With a shake of her head, she said, "Then you're not the first."

Lexa mulled over the phrase, trying to make sense of what it meant to not be the first. When her mind came up with nothing, she repeated the statement aloud.

"Not the first?"

"You're not the first person to assault her," Emma elaborated. She leaned forward. "And I bet the last person who did was someone she was forced to forgive. Forced to say, 'it's okay'. Probably forced to be around regularly because that's how that shit happens. She doesn't forgive you. She just has to tell herself that because if she doesn't then she has to accept that whoever else hurt her shouldn't have hurt her."

"Damn, Dr. Phil," Danaya said, tapping Emma's knee playfully like Emma was joking, and Lexa wasn't replaying the event in her head for the five-billionth time. "Look at you psychoanalyzing people."

Emma rolled her eyes. "While you got a degree in broadcasting, I studied psychology."

"You're a fucking therapist?" Danaya choked, her eyes growing wide.

Emma shook her head. "No, not yet. Someday. When basketball is over in a season or two. I got a plan next year to stay in state. Gonna open my clinic and work with the police."

She gestured to the room. "This isn't forever. I'm pushing thirty, and these bones are tired of getting beat, so I did a program a few years ago. Didn't go overseas for two seasons, and I got my Masters. When the time comes, I will start my own practice to work with DV victims."

"DV?" Lexa asked.

"Domestic violence. Little girls who are raped by people they live with. Mothers and wives who get beat by their spouses." Emma looked at Lexa. "My sister. She got out of the relationship, but the damage. It was too much for her to handle. She left her kids with my momma and took a bunch of pills. She said she couldn't keep living looking over her shoulder."

"Jesus, Emma." Lexa scanned the floor before she looked up. "When did it happen?"

Danaya turned from Lexa, and her hand rested on Emma's leg. She squeezed it softly.

"The year I was drafted." Emma's arms wrapped around her chest like a shield. She met Lexa's eyes once more. "You were still practicing in your high school swag but Syl..."

The incomplete name of Lexa's wife hung in the air.

Lexa lowered her gaze to the wet shoe lying on its side. Black grime covered the sole and tiny pebbles protruded from the intricate crevices.

"You can say her name," Lexa whispered. "She was your friend."

"Yeah, Sylvia was there," Emma finished.

Lexa rubbed her hands over her tired legs. Quietly, she replied, "She's always there for people. All her good-doer scholarship programs and outreach centers. She even helped open that school."

Danaya got up from the floor and moved into the chair next to Emma. She didn't reach over to hug the larger woman, just resting against her softly.

"Yeah, Via was good people." Emma studied her hands. "No one thought she was shit. Everyone always talked about how she bought her way onto the team. But she was there when I got the call. She packed my bag and flew me home to my momma on her jet. She helped me make the funeral arrangements, and paid for everything, even though I told her not to. I don't know if I could have done it without her."

Lexa knew Emma and Sylvia had been close. She'd just assumed they'd forged a friendship over basketball. It didn't make sense that they were that good of friends though. Emma had been with Lexa all summer. There when Sylvia's sister, Kayla, kissed her. There when she started openly taking women home with her.

"Why did you keep going out with me?" Lexa asked. "If she and you were tight like that."

Emma patted Danaya's hand on her arm. She shook her head, and Lexa realized the action had become synonymous with speaking to her.

"She made me promise to look after you. Even after everything with Kayla, she said you needed someone because you didn't have anyone else." Emma's head shook again like she was back in the moment. "I told her no, but she said that she had been there when I was at my worst, and now she needed me to be there for her by making sure you didn't get yourself in trouble."

Lexa ran through the times they'd been out together. Emma invited her out for dinner. And she'd thought it was because Emma had chosen her. Chosen her over Sylvia's betrayal to just up and leave.

She looked up at the center's chiseled stare. "So, you were never my friend?"

"You want the truth?" Emma asked coldly.

The question was enough, but Lexa needed to hear Emma say it. Needed to hear the words verifying she'd been played this whole time.

"Yes. I want the fucking truth," she snapped.

Emma's hand clenched into a fist. She dropped her weight to her elbows and leaned toward Lexa, as her teeth bared in a snarl.

"I wanted to break your fucking neck when Sylvia showed up at my door after she walked in on you fucking Kayla."

Knuckles cracked as spittle flew from Emma's mouth.

"All the women you cheated on her with. She fucking knew. She knew every time she put your ass on a plane to go make a name for yourself that you would be knuckles deep in a bitch not twenty-four hours after you got off the plane. But your unlimited hall pass wasn't good enough." Emma slapped her hands, punctuating each word that followed. "You. Had. To. Fuck. Her. Baby. Sister. In. Via's. Fucking. Bed."

Emma's hand smacked against her chest. "And I... I had to pick up the pieces of her heart. The heart you broke. And when she superglued them all back together, she fucking made me promise not to say anything to you."

A broken promise, Lexa knew now. Emma didn't break promises, but she was breaking them now.

"So, I didn't say shit."

The rage turned to a growl. The words were less like boulders being launched and more like knives being thrown.

"She's my friend. Sylvia. Not you." Emma sat back. "You weren't my friend then, and since you want honesty, I don't know if I could ever be your friend. I don't know how I'm ever going to forgive myself. Because I let that girl get hurt. I was stupid enough to think you would fucking stop so I wouldn't have to stop you. And all I can think about is how many other girls have you raped, Lexa. How many girls asked you to stop, and you just didn't care?"

They sat in silence as the truth settled in the room. They coated the walls and the lockers with a new coat of varnish that clogged Lexa's airway.

Never in her life had she had a friend. Every single one of them had pretended to like her until they left her. And she began to regret wishing the silent treatment away.

Now there wasn't silence in her head. Her mind played like a porn show. Her brain searched through the women she could remember. Searched for signs of others who'd told her no.

"I could be your friend," Danaya offered in a whisper.

Lexa's brows scrunched, and her mouth opened as she stared at the child next to the faker. She gestured to herself and asked, "Why would you want to be friends with a monster?"

Danaya gave her a one-shoulder shrug. "We all got a past."

She looked at Emma, whose eyes were locked on the ceiling and teeth grinding what Lexa could only assume was another round of ammunition she would shoot at the first opportunity.

The younger woman tapped her legs, then she bounced them like sitting still wasn't something her body was capable of. After a moment of chewing on her words, she said, "What Emi just said is past Lexa. The person in the chair is now Lexa. Now Lexa is... processing. But you know... there's going to be a Tomorrow Lexa. And if Tomorrow Lexa can keep her promise to be a better human, then that's a Lexa that I want to be friends with."

Emma got up. She took a step toward Lexa, whose eyes scrunched up in preparation for the beating Emma stated she wanted to give.

When no hit landed on her skin, she peeked at the area separating them. A large hand extended between them. She reached out and let Emma pull her to her feet.

"I believe in fixing mistakes. But I hope you don't find this girl again," Emma said, still holding on to Lexa. She squeezed Lexa's hand tighter. "I'm going to be here for you because I promised Via. She's never broken her word to me, and I don't plan on letting her down. But you need to know, I won't stand by again."

"Damn, Emma. Chill," Danaya said with a roll of her eyes.

Emma looked back at the kid she'd taken in when the girl showed up to take Sylvia's spot and Lexa slammed the door in her face. Refused the rookie the guest house she'd been promised by the wife who was playing in her place in Chicago.

"No chill, DayDay." Emma dropped Lexa's hand. "She needs to know that she doesn't get to walk away from ground zero if she drops like a bomb on someone's life."

"I'm not a monster."

She'd show them. She'd prove to them all she wasn't a monster.

Especially Sylvia.

And the blonde.

3

Charleigh figured after seven years of Dilynn Greyson pretending to invest in a school with the woman's name on it, she would spend some of her surplus cash to get the plumbing fixed in the girl's bathroom. However, when she'd suggested it at the beginning of the year, Dilynn's solution was installing an automatic air freshener to puff out floral fumes—a typical Greyson Band-Aid to a bullet hole-sized problem.

Charleigh headed directly into a stall as the chocolate cookie churned in her stomach. The shit streak on the back of the porcelain bowl was all it took to send her over the edge. Cookies and coffee spewed from her, reminding her of the mornings she'd spent in this bathroom when she was a student here.

A cookie chunk bounced from the bowl back at her, bringing another wave of sickness. She vowed to never eat cookies for breakfast again as she wiped the splashback from her face.

The stall squeaked as she made her way from the toilet to the sink. Her legs quaked and sweat gathered at her temples. She needed to go back to class, but the cramping in her stomach made her worried she might need to pray to the porcelain gods again. She did offer a silent prayer of gratitude for knowing that even though she was sick, she wasn't pregnant.

Charleigh stood debating if she needed to puke again when the door to the restroom creaked open. She didn't need to look up because Mona dragged every step in the overpriced Jordans on her feet. Her sister must have gotten a higher raise than she did at the start of the year, which wouldn't have surprised Charleigh.

Unable to handle the heat rising in her chest, Charleigh stripped off her sweater and dropped it on the floor. She twisted her hair into a ponytail but let it fall back down when she realized she didn't have a hair tie or pen to fix it in place.

"Not-our-daddy dearest called," Mona said. She wiped a black streak of grease from her cheek with the back of her hand. "I missed the first one because I was under your hood trying to fix the cables, so your car would start again. I think we may need to replace the cables and the battery. Plus, the alternator may be failing."

Her dark hair hung around her face as she scrubbed the dirt and grease from her hands in the sink next to where Charleigh had returned to her previously slumped position.

"Thanks," Charleigh whispered.

Mona gave up on washing, leaving grimy fingerprints on the handle of the tap.

"How's your head?" Mona asked. "You know puking is on the sheet. If it happens again, you need to go to the hospital."

Mona smiled because that's what she did when something went wrong, and it was worse, but Charleigh didn't know how to tell her how much worse.

The woman's sharp elbow dug into Charleigh's side. "You hear me?" she asked.

No words made it to Charleigh's tongue. They twisted in a tangled knot of fragmented sentences and internalized tears in her throat.

"Joey won Student of the Month," Charleigh said. She wiped the tear before it fell. "Casemanager forwarded me a photo. My mom didn't even tell me my kid won her first award. Jesus, I miss every goddamn thing."

"She's not your mom," Mona reminded her. "Just like Marcus ain't our dad. Just another person that doesn't give a fuck."

Mona's hand rubbed Charleigh's back when the blonde turned into the other woman's embrace. Her arms wrapped around Charleigh the way no one else seemed to be able to do or wanted to.

Charleigh choked as the tears started at the reminder of growing up to be just as shitty as both the women who didn't want her. Her chest was still fighting to breathe against the mucus trying to suffocate her. She had to break away from Mona's embrace because she needed something to wipe her nose with.

Getting some half-ply toilet paper from the stall, Charleigh blew hard. The blow horn that was her nose echoed in the small space, pulling a soft chuckle from Mona's lifted lips.

"When's your next court date?" Mona asked. "You have your one-year chip, and Joey has her room. I'm not your roommate anymore. They don't have any reason to not give her back to you."

After a deep breath, Charleigh shook her head. "Not until January. Because she's six, they do the court dates every six months."

Charleigh wrapped her sweater around her waist and tried to wash the red from her face. She stared back at her reflection.

"You look like shit," Mona said.

Charleigh rolled her eyes. "Thanks, asshole. I think... I just need to get out of here."

They heard the rumble of student voices as the second period ended. She'd gotten the new art therapist to cover her class, so she could run to the bathroom when she felt the first wave of nausea hit.

"Well, let's get you out of here," Mona said.

Mona wiped her hands down her jeans before pushing her long hair out of her face. She held the door open, and Charleigh walked back into the crowded courtyard. She avoided looking at any one student as the normally boisterous break time was quelled in a rumbled murmur of whispers and stares.

A dark-haired teen approached cautiously, leaving her clique in the shade of the tree they'd claimed as their territory. When she was close enough so no one else could hear her, she dropped her school formality.

"Hey, Princess. I heard about you getting smashed in the head at the game." She bit her lip. "You going to the hospital?"

"I told you not to call me that, especially here." Charleigh checked to make sure no one was close enough to hear the nickname from hell she'd never been able to shake. "And no, I'm not going to the hospital."

"You look like shit," Kinsley said because hearing it from one sister wasn't enough. "Maybe they need to see if your brain is bleeding or something. It would explain why you're so damn red."

"It's called anger at being told I look like crap repeatedly and called by a name that both of you know I despise." Charleigh took a deep breath. Snapping at either of her foster sisters wasn't going to change the fact that she missed her daughter's big day. "I just need to get out of here. Will you tell Marcus that I'm going to skip family dinner tonight?"

Kinsley nodded, but turned to Mona, "You're coming though, right? Not-our-dad said we're going to Olive Garden because Kyle is coming. He wants to talk to him about his kids because his wife kicked him out."

Mona rolled her eyes before she said, "Yeah, I won't make you sit through dinner with his skeezy ass. I still don't know how Not-our-dad made the biggest douche canoe alive, or why some girl married his stupid ass."

Charleigh felt the need to vomit once more. Any conversation about her foster father's biological son made her skin crawl. Being sick at least was a valid reason to not have to go to dinner, even if it meant missing a real meal. Sitting next to Kyle would ruin her food though.

"She married him because she got pregnant and they are all part of that cult that Not-our-dad left his crazy wife for joining," Kinsley reminded them. "I just can't believe she had two kids with him. Like, she didn't learn after the first time."

Looking up at the sky, she studied the clouds. They were so low and dense that Charleigh couldn't tell they were even moving. Still, she knew a storm was going to hit any minute. Storms weren't unusual for this time of year, and she would have loved to stand there until the rain came in fast and hard. Maybe a flash flood could sweep her away.

A student would probably save her though. Someone like Kinsley's boyfriend, who cared about people. Maybe some of her other juniors too. Or Mona. Mona was always saving her because she hadn't realized it was a lost cause yet.

Kids started to move as the fifteen-minute break between the second and third periods ended. There weren't bells to tell anyone when to go to class, something Charleigh had liked when she first came to Greyson Academy. Simpler days where she didn't have to hide being a lesbian because she'd escaped that same cult Marcus had refused to join. Time had changed everything, and the lessons she'd learned here didn't put her on the path to success like Alex Trikru had promised when they'd given her the tour. Wasn't their fault that they didn't know who she was, or who she would become.

Charleigh pushed Kinsley a little. "Go to class, little sister. And better learn those books like you know those song lyrics because you're not coming back here after college like we did. And no getting pregnant."

As the girl walked away, her boyfriend, Bastian, wrapped a thick arm around her shoulders and tucked her protectively into his side. Even though she'd said it aloud already, Charleigh prayed they were making smarter choices than she did.

"Don't worry. I got her," Mona reassured her sister like she always did when things were bad. "I will stop by the drug store and grab her some Plan B and a box of condoms. You just take care of yourself."

Charleigh glanced back at her classroom as the rain began to fall. Her former foster father, Marcus stood in the doorway to the building, shaking hands with the kids as they came in. The school social worker was the stand-in sub for anyone sick, and she felt bad that she was stealing his day from him.

He must have felt her eyes on him because he looked up. The pit stain was huge when he raised his arm to wave at her. He offered her the same pitiful smile he'd worn since she'd told him she was pregnant, then he nodded toward the exit before adding, "Go home and rest that big brain of yours."

She offered him her own pitiful smile. One that she only wished said she was sorry in a hundred different ways for ruining everything.

The courtyard emptied quickly with the rain. It came down harder than it had the night before, soaking her before she made it to the gate. A few stragglers were coming in from the parking lot from the white van that picked up students who couldn't get a ride to school. Her boss's partner, Alex Trikru hopped out of the driver's seat.

She stopped walking to answer Alex's questions, regretting that decision immediately. There was no way Alex hadn't noticed her white shirt no longer hid the lace-covered bra she wore beneath. She quickly wrapped her arms over her chest as one of the boys from the van smacked his friends and pointed at her.

"Get to class," Alex commanded. They splashed through the puddles, then wordlessly wrapped their tailored suit jacket around her.

She stared at the Doc Martin boots of the human now blocking her path to her temporarily fixed car. She wiped the hair from her face, then squeezed the jacket closed over her chest.

"I didn't mean to give you a free show."

"I wasn't..." they paused and started again, "I saw... uh... I don't want you to think..."

With a soft laugh, Charleigh said, "Don't worry, I know you weren't checking out my chest."

"Are you okay?" they asked like they always asked when they saw her.

A part of Charleigh wanted to believe they cared. However, she'd always be their greatest disappointment. Just like their wife would always be angry the second she laid eyes on her.

"I... uh... I threw up. Ate too many cookies and I just..." she swallowed the rest of the half-truth.

A lie wouldn't cut it this time. Too many witnesses watched her open the message and break down in the middle of class. Her students didn't know she was a shitty mom, but her bosses did.

"That's not the whole truth. I just... I got a message in the middle of second period. The case manager sent me a photo of Joey. She won an award in kindergarten yesterday, and I just... I got really sad, and I cried." She wet her lips. "I was trying to keep it together, but I just got sick, and Parker.... She covered my class because I just couldn't be okay. And I know Greyson is going to be mad, but I didn't mean to make a scene. I actually left because I didn't want the kids to get upset. I just don't want you or Greyson to think that I was—"

"Charleigh, hold on." Alex led her to the small overhang at the front of the office. "First, I'm sorry that you didn't get to go to the assembly. I would have cried if I missed any of my kids' awards assemblies. We can... uh.... I can call my daughter, Sadie. She works for DCS, and I think there are rules about stuff like this."

"There's no point." Charleigh took a deep breath. "My mom... I mean, Grace. She told the new case manager that she thinks I'm injecting heroin between my toes."

Alex sucked in a breath.

"I don't," Charleigh clarified quickly. "I can take off my shoes and show you. I already showed the lady more parts of me than anyone has seen in years, and I went to TASC and peed in a cup and gave them some hair."

"I'm good," Alex said. Their hand hovered above Charleigh's bicep before it dropped back to their side. "They really made you do all that?"

Charleigh sucked in her lower lip, then nodded once.

"I'm sorry."

"It's my own fault." Charleigh tried to wipe the tears from her face, but instantly regretted it as she looked at the expensive jacket now covered in a streak of glistening mucus. "Shoot, I'm so sorry, Trikru. I promise I will pay to get it dry cleaned."

"It's just a jacket. You don't need to worry about it. Just toss it out honestly. I have so many suits because one time I said I wanted to wear a suit and you know my wife. She went on a shopping spree and now I have a walk-in closet full of them." They rubbed over the freshly shaved undercut. "Look, about the whole situation. Is there anything we can do?"

A part of her wanted to tell them the truth so they could maybe talk to their wife. Wanted to ask them to get their wife to stop hating her. Tell their wife Charleigh understood Dilynn Greyson didn't want to be her mother. That she knew the woman gave her up for adoption when she was born because she wasn't any good, and maybe to just ignore her rather than yell at her.

None of those words would come out though. She'd been fall-over drunk and managed to keep Dilynn's teenage pregnancy a secret. The only thing telling Alex would accomplish was to hurt Dilynn, and Charleigh being alive did that enough.

"No." Her chin dropped to her chest, so they wouldn't see she was lying. She tried to regulate her breathing, as she pleaded, "I just don't want Greyson to be disappointed in me again. I can't have her thinking that I... I'm just so close to having everything in order and something like this... she'll think that I am just trying to get attention again. But I'm not. I'm not seeing anyone or going anywhere. I am just coming to work, and I am saving up, and I finished all the classes. I'm going to the meetings... I'm—"

"Hey, hey. It's okay. Dilynn knows how hard you've been working on staying sober. And sometimes we just need a mental health day."

Charleigh shook her head and looked up at them. A gentle concern stared down at her.

"She hates me," Charleigh whispered.

"Who hates you?"

"Your wife." She silently added, 'My mother,' and tried not to let it hurt anymore.

She watched the way their eyes scanned over her face. The dark eyebrows cinched together. "She doesn't hate you. She worries about you and Joey. We both do. No one wants Joey with your mother."

They looked up at the waves of clouds crashing over one another. "I... You have to... Okay, look..." They shook their head, then looked Charleigh dead in the eyes. "You have been through a lot. I get why you started drinking so young, and I know that the pills helped mask a lot of that pain. You were going through so much, and what happened with you having to leave Marcus's so suddenly was too much to ask of anyone. So, you did what a lot of kids do. Just a lot of those choices were really hard to watch for Dilynn and Marcus and even me. But you have come so, so far."

Their smile was a lot like Marcus's.

"You've been sober for over a year now. You know, I am not the one that people typically turn to when they need advice about things, but I guess I am the expert when it comes to my wife." They took a deep breath. "I am just going to say that you should talk with her about how you feel. She wouldn't want you to think that she hates you."

Charleigh's heart tried to believe their words, but her mind reminded her of Alex's need to believe in their words. And Dilynn Greyson, well her mind provided a logical stance on her as well.

'She'd rather I just disappear, which was why she gave me up to begin with,' Charleigh told herself.

Alex reached over, then awkwardly patted Charleigh's shoulder. Three quick taps before their hand dropped once more.

"Get out of here and just think about it. If you want to, I can set up a time for you and Dilynn to talk. I know, she's been gone a lot for the murder trial, but the ADA dropped all charges, so her days are about to open up soon. I'll look at her calendar and schedule something in the next week or two."

"Yeah, okay. Thanks, Trikru."

"You can call me Alex," they reminded her for the thousandth time.

Charleigh sniffed back the snot and smiled at them. With a shrug, she said, "It's just weird. I mean, you were my history teacher."

"I would like to think that I was your favorite history teacher," they prodded.

"You were my only history teacher," she reminded them.

Alex's hand clasped over their chest. "You wound me, Charleigh Marshall."

Tires crunched over the gravel. The posh Audi came to a stop in front of the school and Dilynn Greyson practically leaped from the car with her face fully flushed. Her eyes narrowed at Charleigh immediately. Probably the same look she had when Charleigh was born.

"Sylvia, I get that you are pissed at me. There is more to the story, and we can talk about it when you get back." With her phone clutched in her hand, Dilynn was barely around the vehicle when she started yelling, "What the hell is it this time?"

Alex stepped between Charleigh and the charging woman. They held their hands up. "Dilynn. I already got debriefed on what—"

"I don't want a briefing; I want a goddamn dissertation on why she's leaving in the middle of the damn day again." Dilynn ducked easily under Alex's upheld arms. "And who is watching your class? Parker has her own job to do as does Marcus. And why are you wearing Alex's jacket?"

Dilynn shot a laser-focused glare at her partner. "Jesus, can you stop giving away your clothes? A month ago, it was your boots on Parker's feet. Two weeks ago, it was Zoe wearing your shirt. Today a $400 jacket on her."

Alex choked out, "You spent $400 on a jacket. Why would you spend that on a jacket? And I have six of them!"

Dilynn slapped her hands in the air as though she could smack Alex's words out of existence. "It was a set. And it doesn't matter. You can't keep having these girls walk around in your clothes. People are going to start talking, and the last thing we need is students thinking you're fucking all the young pretty teachers on campus."

They held up their hand, which had some magical power to stop Dilynn's rant.

"I would just like to state that Zoe was only wearing my shirt because you told me to give it to her. And Charleigh needed...." Their words tapered off as Charleigh took the jacket off and handed it back to Alex. She folded her arms over her chest, covering the stiff nipples sticking out from the see-through shirt.

"Jesus Christ! So, you're not just leaving in the middle of the day. You gave the kids a free show as well?" Dilynn's hand waved at Charleigh's waist. "You have a sweater right there. Do you lack all common sense?"

Charleigh's chin dropped as her fingers fumbled with the knot in the sweater she'd forgotten about. She started to explain, "The rain came down as I was trying to leave. It just poured, and I was just trying to get to my car. I tried—"

"You tried to what?" Dilynn's arms folded over her chest as she stepped even closer to Charleigh. "This is your job, Charleigh. I get that this is the only place you've ever worked, but this job matters. These kids matter, and you being here consistently matters. Do you ever stop and think about your actions and what they do to everyone else? As a teacher, as a mother, I know to put my kids first."

'Except the first one you had,' she thought.

Charleigh's hair fell in her eyes, and she wondered if Alex would get it now. She managed to untie the forgotten cover-up and wrapped the drenched material around herself tightly.

"I'm sorry, Greyson." She looked back at the blue door to her classroom. "You're right. I should.... I---"

"Joey got an award at school," Alex said. They held their hand out to Charleigh and waved it slightly. A simple gesture requesting something from her. "Case manager just sent a photo."

Charleigh opened the phone to the picture before handing it to Alex. They smiled at it, then showed Dilynn.

"Remember that day we called out because Sadie's casemanager moved her to my dad's house?"

Dilynn cradled the phone in her hands carefully. The anger seemed to melt from her face as she zoomed into Joey's face.

"She's gotten so big." Dilynn's gaze rose to Charleigh. "Student of the Month?"

"Yeah. It was yesterday," Charleigh whispered.

"When's the next court date?" Dilynn asked.

"January."

Handing the phone back to Charleigh, Dilynn requested, "Please send that to me. And any others that you have gotten since last time. I know, I was only her foster mom, but I want to hang them up with the rest I have."

Charleigh nodded, wishing she dared to just tell the woman Joey was her granddaughter. At least she would know for sure Dilynn knew finally. Then, Dilynn could take Grace Marshall, the woman who unadopted her for getting pregnant in the first place, to court for custody. A part of her knew if she told Dilynn, the woman might fire her, and she'd lose custody forever. After all, Dilynn spent $400 on a jacket, so she would hire a lawyer Charleigh's court-appointed attorney couldn't compete with after she was unemployed. A part of her knew the only reason Dilynn kept giving her a contract was the small hope Joey would come home, so Dilynn would get to see her again.

"Just go home," Dilynn said. "Go home and don't do something stupid. But this shit stops. You're an adult, and she needs a mother. Not some teenager trapped in a woman's body."

Alex stepped between them again. "Dilynn, you need coffee."

"I already had coffee."

"More coffee then." Alex guided Charleigh out of the way gently from the door. "You know, coffee makes everything better. So, let's get you some coffee, Cupcake."

Charleigh didn't wait for another lecture and didn't stop when they heard Alex groan from the slap Dilynn landed against their gut.

The boots she'd bought to look like the woman hissing and growling like a feral cat were tattered from the daily wear. Their time was fading, and their ability to serve their purpose was too as the slick soles gave inward to every slanted rock. She hit the small pools of water, but she dodged the larger puddles. Each left step allowed water to seep through the crack across the ball of her foot.

The gust of wind propelled her back toward the building where Alex and Dilynn had finally retreated. Right when she got to the car, she realized she'd left her keys in the classroom. She couldn't leave without the keys, but there was no way she was walking back into that school with Dilynn as red as a tomato.

She opened the driver's side door that didn't lock and sat down in the cracked seat. The drops splashed against the glass, while dirty water streaked down the window from the top of the car. She'd have to wait until it stopped since the wiper blade detached earlier that morning.

She leaned her head against the steering wheel. Calling Marcus was a lost cause because he never had his phone on him. Mona would be in the middle of her lecture, so she probably wouldn't answer either.

The thunderstruck at the same time there was a knock on her window. Charleigh screamed, holding her chest as she looked through the glass. The art therapist, Parker pulled back her hand to her own chest, apparently scared by Charleigh's scream. Then the painted lips pulled up into a smile as Parker held the faded canvas backpack up with a single finger.

"I saw you forgot this," Parker said when Charleigh opened the door and got out of the car. She looked back at the office. "Sorry, it took me so long. I have been avoiding Dilynn since her daughter broke up with me. And there was no way in hell I was going to get stuck in an interrogation about if I am or am not back together with my ex, so I had to hide behind the copy machine until she went into her office. God, she's on one today. Whoever Sylvia is pissed her off."

"Sylvia Winters," Charleigh offered as a reminder. When Parker didn't seem to register the name, she explained. "Sylvia Winters is the CEO of the Winters Group. She's a billionaire, and she helped open the school, like, nine years ago. She also runs a scholarship program that awards at least one kid from the school each year a full ride to any school they get into."

"Whoa."

With a soft shrug, Charleigh offered, "Sylvia is a big deal around here. When she shows up for a walk-through, Dilynn puts on a big show. Be prepared because Dilynn likes you, which means she will definitely bring Sylvia to see you."

"I saw her losing her crap out here on you." Parker glanced at the office door once more. "Does that happen often?"

"Let's just say that if I dated her daughter, she'd bury me behind her mansion."

Parker studied Charleigh's face, and a fear crept up Charleigh's spine.

"Don't worry. I am not interested in any of the Greyson girls." She laughed as she explained, "They were like the royal family when I went to school here. Mona and I used to make up twisted Grimm-like fairy tales about them."

She didn't explain she'd begun them while wishing to be part of the family. That they'd taken on a whole new meaning when she realized she wasn't just Dilynn Greyson's doppelganger, but the carbon copy of the woman who'd given her to someone else who would grow to hate her as much as Dilynn had while in her womb.

"I have got to hear these someday," Parker said. She tucked a lock of hair behind her ear. "Well, I need to get going, but we should have lunch together someday soon. Preferably out in the courtyard because Alex told me if I didn't start trying to make friends that they would set up weekly staff lunches. I would rather everyone not hate me."

Charleigh chuckled, then held up her hand. "Just wait until Family Fun Day comes around in like a month. Your ex-Greyson will be there with Greyson's perfect police officer daughter and the one who tries to hook up with everyone. Last year, she asked Mona to come back to her place, which is actually Greyson and Trikru's mansion, which is sooo weird."

Parker's eyes grew and her nose scrunched up. "I think I'll pass."

"Good luck with that. They are voluntold responsibilities, and Greyson hands out half of your bonus at the end of it. So, we go for the money and the food is good."

"So, if I don't go to Family Suck Day, I don't get a bonus?"

"Gotta wait a week."

"I think, I can hold off for a week."

"Well, you're doing better than the rest of us." Charleigh held up the bag. "Thanks for bringing out my stuff."

"No problem." Parker glanced at the sky. "You know, the whole offer to have lunch wasn't just a get Alex off my ass thing. Having friends would be nice. If you ever wanna talk or paint or like to draw, I got a room full of stuff that helps release some of the feelings."

"Thanks," Charleigh whispered. "I'm going to go."

"Okay." Parker tapped the hood of the car. "Hey, Echo says hi by the way."

Charleigh's lip fitted between her teeth. "Echo?"

"My sister. Big masc with tree tattoos. Owns the Escape. You danced with her." Parker scanned over Charleigh. "I was there... that night at her bar."

"Oh."

"Don't worry, I won't say anything. I just thought you should know that she said hi. She was worried about you, but I told her you're good."

"Thank you," she whispered. She licked her lips. "And tell your sister I say thank you also for stopping her."

They shared a look. Charleigh had a hundred things she was too scared to say but she tried to tell Parker with her gaze. The therapist seemed to have her own things she wanted to say, but neither of them were able to read each other's mind.

Charleigh nodded to Parker, then tucked herself back into her car. She said a silent prayer to her non-biological mother's god. The one she knew hated her. She pleaded with the entity to ensure Parker did not get back together with the eldest Greyson princess. It would be the only way Dilynn wouldn't find out she'd been at the bar and part of a fight.

Dilynn would never go to court with her to fight for custody like she'd promised if she learned Charleigh was at a bar. No amount of sobriety chips would prove to Dilynn she wasn't drinking again.

The rain slowed to just a few sprinkles. It was possibly the closest thing she would get to a break in the rain, so she turned the key. As she drove home, she tried to think of something good to make today not a complete waste. She'd get to watch her team play game two in New York rather than watch the score on her phone during the fifth and sixth periods.

4

The ball didn't thunk against the backboard, ding off the rim, or swish through the net. It didn't make a sound until it slapped the court on the other side, laughing at Lexa. During a game, and even practice, it was easy for Lexa to blame the missed corner three on an uncalled foul, but standing in the arena with nothing but silence as the ball spun toward the other sideline was inexcusable. But it was her wife's fault.

It was her fault Lexa didn't have any overseas offers.

It was her fault the team was looking for even a terrible trade.

Everything going wrong was her fault.

Lexa retrieved another ball and returned to the same spot. It thunked as it hit the wood. Lexa pushed the ball down again, then again. It needed to know she meant business this time. She stood at the corner of the three-point line. Despite the harsh arena light, she willed her eyes to open wider. The rim faded into a hunk of orange metal until fuzzily transparent and Lexa was able to see where she wanted the ball to go.

She pushed up with her legs and extended her arm. The ball rolled off the tips of her fingers as her arm reached full extension, and her wrist flipped forward. She stood still as she watched the ball miss the target and bounce off the rim.

Her arm dropped and she closed her eyes. She ran through the shot ten times in her head without moving. She set up in her mind and went through each of the movements as she watched the ball sail through the net. Then she moved with her imagination. She pounded the imaginary ball into the ground, and she took the shot. In her head, it went perfectly each time.

But when she tried again with another ball, it missed the basket completely.

She retrieved another ball from the rack.

The sound of the ball slapping against the wood was broken up by the clank of high heels on the concrete, then the click of them on the wood. Lexa didn't look up because there was only one person still talking to her.

"Thursday, you are going to a school for some good PR," her agent said.

Lexa pushed another shot up and missed again.

"I know you heard me, Lexa."

Lexa stared at the net instead of at the disappointment she knew would still be etched into the agent's dark brow. She moved through the motions of the shot again—the money shot that would keep her from getting traded if she could get it to work for the next playoff game.

"You're going to do a meet and greet with a teacher..."

Lexa decided the shot was missing because she used too much leg, and her arm was landing too far forward. She needed to extend more.

When the shot failed again, she knew it was because Phyllis was still speaking.

"The NWBA has invested a lot of money in your face..."

Lexa tried to block her out.

"... she's a fan, and her students are trying to do something nice..."

She retrieved the last ball from the rack.

"...the one who wrote the letter says she is like her savior...."

The shot missed, even though Lexa was sure her form was perfect.

A giant envelope hit Lexa on the head, snapping her back to the conversation where Phyllis was talking like she was the one who signed the paychecks. Lexa's face felt hot enough to cook on. Her hands clenched, and she turned to give Phyllis a piece of her mind.

'I should sue her ass for assault. Yeah, fire her and sue her.'

Then she breathed. She breathed and realized she was doing it again. So, she ran her mental eraser over the idea.

"Thursday, Lexa."

Phyliss turned to leave, but she didn't make it through the doors before she was at it again with a sigh of disappointment.

She turned back to Lexa.

"I did my research. She's not Kayla and she's not crazy. She seems like someone that deserves the old Lexa, not the bitch that puts her hands on women whether they want you or not."

"People ain't stupid, Phyllis," Lexa said since the agent forgot. "Look, I saw the girl from the bar. She said she forgave me, and I just got to move on. In a week, no one is even going to remember because I'm going to bring us home a championship."

Phyllis dropped a box next to the chairs along the sideline. The shape alone told Lexa it was a ball. She tapped the box with the toe of the shoe Lexa knew was paid for with her earnings. "The other girls signed it. Don't forget it."

Lexa grabbed the envelope. What was Phyllis thinking, throwing this at her? It could have sliced her throat, and she could have died of a fucking paper cut. Shaking her head, she knew she was going overboard. It wasn't crazy though. Crazy was only if it came out of her mouth while she was sober. Shitfaced Lexa could say whatever fucktastic crap came to mind, and no one gave a flying fuck; in fact, people usually cheered. They liked drunk Lexa.

She left the balls on the court and walked to the edge of the arena lights. She hated that even though the locker room was just down the walkway the path was swallowed by the darkness. It made the trip terrifying because if anything happened along the way, no one would be there. Not like anyone would be there anyway but Sylvia would be home soon, and she'd put her ring back on. She'd understand and Lexa would go back to her normal life.

When she made it through the doors, she opened the envelope and retrieved a glossy photo of herself. They had done a good job at the shoot. Made her look taller, and the stylist had been hot. Lexa remembered the look on Emma and Danaya's faces when it was their turn to get fixed.

Scanning over the lockers, Lexa tried to remember the stylist's name. The purple and orange reminded her that the girl's hair was purple. But as she pictured the woman, the purple hair faded into blonde. The blonde in the purple shirt who held onto the railing around the bar's dance floor. She wasn't what Lexa would call a slutbag like the girl in the little black skirt she'd fucked in this very locker room. No, the blonde was a woman who had been scared when Lexa didn't stop because she knew she could make the woman feel good.

Lexa told herself again that she didn't hurt the tiny blonde. Scared her, yeah. She could admit that much. But she didn't rape her. She was just a little too handsy and that butch bitch made a scene over nothing. That's all that happened. The girl had known that at the game, and she'd done what she said. She'd won the game and went to look for her.

She pulled a Sharpie from her duffle bag and signed the photo. Only when she tried to put it back in the envelope did she find the crumpled piece of paper. She reached in and pulled it out. She was about to throw it away when the purple print caught her attention.

Dear Ms. Lexa Jenson,

I am writing to you in hopes that you could help me honor my English teacher on her birthday. She is a huge fan of yours and has never missed a game. I know that you are extremely busy, and I know that the playoffs are about to start. (BTW, congratulations on making it to the playoffs.) Marshall is a very special person.

You see she saved my life—

Lexa stopped reading. It was about to get sappy, and Lexa didn't do sappy. She did bitchy and sexy. And if Teacher of the Year was either of those things, then maybe she'd bend her over the little desk and teach her a lesson or five.

As she put the envelope in her bag, she saw the faded hoodie within. Lexa raised the material to her nose and inhaled. It smelled more like her after-game sweat than Sylvia's perfume she'd sprayed on it that morning. It was inappropriate for the Arizona heat, but she still put it on and tried to remember the times before the ground seemed to constantly quake below her.

The walk to the parking garage was as quiet as the trek to the locker room. She put the earbuds in her ears but didn't turn the music on in case she wasn't alone. She was though. She had been since the bar, and she hated it.

She put the phone in her pocket when she reached the only unopened text from Kayla. Sylvia would be back soon with the season ending, and Lexa would have to prove she wasn't going to break the rules again. She'd show Sylvia she stopped answering Kayla's messages. She'd prove to Sylvia she'd changed for the better, and her wife would forgive her like the last time.

Maybe she could even find the girl from the bar. Sylvia would like her, and they could share a night with her. Lexa could keep two promises at once. One to the tiny blonde who she'd said she would prove she'd be better. And one to the blonde she'd married and swore the only other women would be shared between them.

It was a win-win for everyone involved.

5

The key would turn, but not even a light was lit on the dash of the dilapidated Honda Accord. Charleigh tried again, but nothing happened. Her hand smacked against the steering wheel.

Her week hadn't sucked enough with constant head and back aches from being trampled on by Lexa Jenson or missing another big event in Joey's life. No, she had to add showing up late to her court-appointed visit.

Nothing in her life could ever just go the way it should. Nothing was expected of her at the same time as everything was, though. Grace Marshall didn't want her to show up but used her not showing up to prove she wasn't good enough for Joey.

The key turned with ease, but the car still didn't start when Charleigh tried again.

The two windows of the brick bungalow stared at her through the bug-splattered windshield. If she couldn't get the car to start, she'd have to go back inside and listen to the elderly house protest every step she took within. With Joey still so far away, it felt pointless to have a two-bedroom house with a two-seater table and a couch big enough for two.

Charleigh picked up the phone from the center console and dialed the first of the two numbers in her recent calls list. The one constant above the dreaded case manager. Mona would answer. The one thing her sister still offered since their shared lease ended, and Mona had moved into a new phase of her life with someone Charleigh hadn't been asked to meet.

"*I just saw you like an hour ago, Princess,*" Mona groaned as her new life continued around her.

"The car won't start." Charleigh scraped the hair from her face. "And stop calling me that."

"*I don't have time to come get you,*" Mona griped. "*I just got home, and I have plans tonight.*"

Another voice beckoning Mona in the background made Charleigh's skin crawl. The raspy muttering was a little too familiar, even though the blonde couldn't place who it belonged to.

"*Look, I'll look at it later,*" Mona replied. "*I've got to shower and get changed still.*"

Charleigh hit her head against the steering wheel. She swallowed the letdown. Her fingers rubbed a circle around the one-year sobriety token hanging from her keychain.

"Okay," she said, fighting to keep her voice middle-of-the-road. "I'll call the new case manager and tell her I have to cancel."

The line went so quiet that Charleigh had to check to see if Mona had hung up on her without saying goodbye. It was still connected, though, and a moment later the raspy voice was back growling in the background as a deeper one seemed to be playing negotiator.

"*You can't do that,*" Mona said with a huff. A door closed on the other end of the phone where water was already running. "*She'll think you're a flake.*"

The shower that had been turned on, shut off. With a humph, Mona said, "*Okay, let's troubleshoot and if that doesn't work, I'll send an Uber to get you.*"

"That's like a hundred bucks," Charleigh protested.

Mona didn't acknowledge the cost of saving Charleigh's ass. She had shifted gears to save the day by going through Charleigh's previous fuck ups.

"*Did you leave the lights on again?*" Mona asked.

Charleigh checked the switch to the interior light, then the headlights. She double-checked the headlights by switching them on, and then off again. Satisfied that she had turned off the lights, she said, "No."

"*Does it have gas?*"

She searched her memories of the last few days to figure out when she filled up the tank. She knew she'd put in $20 on Monday. She'd only gone to work and back, and it was Wednesday. She couldn't be out already.

"It has at least enough gas to get to my mom's house and work tomorrow," she said.

Mona hummed to herself. Then she asked, "*What happens when you turn the key?*"

Charleigh turned the key again and hoped for a different outcome than the last four times she'd done it. When the car made no sound, she said, "Nothing."

"*No lights?*"

"No."

"*No clicking?*"

"Nothing means nothing," Charleigh snapped.

Mona laughed and a woman's voice grumbled in the background about having to leave in fifteen minutes. She was about to ask who was there when Mona said, "*You wrote that paper for English class. Five pages on how nothing means something because the absence of nothing is a void that is thus a word to describe nothing, making it something.*"

Charleigh shook her head, remembering how she'd woken Mona up to read it before the midnight deadline.

"How do you remember that?" she asked.

She could still remember rambling about nothing being something. The TA had mentioned choosing that word for her paper a few years prior, so Charleigh saw it as a challenge. Her TA hadn't been amused, and left notes along the margins, each countering Charleigh's claims concerning the possibility of nothing being something grander than finite absence.

"*You made me edit it twice, and you sounded like a drunk Dr. Suess, so I doubt I will ever forget it,*" Mona explained. "*Now stop being snappy and open the hood.*"

Charleigh was positive that anything she was going to do under the hood wasn't going to help because she wouldn't know what she was looking for. But she followed Mona's instructions because if anyone was going to get her to her kid, it was Mona.

She held the phone between her face and shoulder, then fiddled with the latch under the hood. The hunk of metal protested as she pushed it up. For as many times as she'd done this in the last two months, she should be faster. But she had to search for the metal arm to hold it in place. Once it was in position, she said, "Okay, what am I looking for?"

"*What does the battery look like?*" Mona asked.

She scanned the dusty engine compartment and found the block she'd replaced last month, only the shiny plastic was dingy. She sighed and prayed it wasn't dead again. That would be another hundred—the same price of a twin mattress still needed for Joey's bedroom.

"*You know what the battery looks like, don't you?*" Mona asked.

Charleigh rolled her eyes, "Yeah, I found it. It looks like a dirty black block."

"*Are the cables attached?*"

Charleigh's eyes opened wider, and she looked at the cables. "How would they become unattached?"

"*The way you drive over potholes, anything is possible,*" Mona poked.

Charleigh leaned down to examine the cables more carefully. They were attached, but they were coated in white crusty-looking stuff. "Is there supposed to be white stuff on the connecting thingy?"

"*No. I just cleaned them two days ago. It's just corrosion, which means the battery is shit already. Wiggle them.*"

Charleigh stood up and stepped back from the car. Shaking her head, she said, "Uh-uh. It's going to electrocute me."

Mona laughed at her again, which only made the feeling of inadequacy bubble in her stomach and burn her throat.

"It would only shock you, and that's only if you are dumb enough to touch the actual connector. Just hold the covered part. Twist it around until the white stuff starts to break up."

Charleigh looked back at the house where the pit bull's face stared at her from the window. She considered just going back inside and cuddling up with the pup. She could binge-watch something on Mona's Netflix account and not be electrocuted. The case manager wouldn't understand, but it wasn't like she was rooting for Charleigh. Her mother had already created a narrative for the woman of a drunk teen mom, who would never choose her kid over a bottle of booze or pills.

"Come on, Chucky. Joey has a certificate to show you," Mona reminded her.

Charleigh filled her lungs with as much air as possible, not sure if that would keep her heart from stopping, then she tapped the red-coated wire. When it didn't send a jolt through her, she tried it again. Satisfied she wasn't dumb enough to touch anything exposed, she grabbed it with two fingers and a thumb and jiggled. Some of the residue broke free, and it gave her hope, so she wiggled more. She wiggled until she could see the top of the connector. Then, she switched to the other side. She jiggled for what felt like an eternity.

"Okay, I think I got it."

She wiped her hand on the floral printed dress her mother would deem modestly heterosexual. The same type of dress all the girls were expected to wear to services where they were told their place was behind a man, no matter what that man did to her.

"Good. Now try to start it again."

Charleigh went back to the driver's seat. She put the phone on speaker and set it in the cup holder. She stroked the steering wheel in the spot she'd assaulted earlier.

"Look, I know I'm a shitty mom," Charleigh told the car. "I promise if you start, I will be better. I will get your oil changed on time and stop waiting until you're past E to put gas in you."

"Stop lying to the car and just turn the damn key," Mona's voice barked from the cup holder.

Charleigh didn't snap back. It was pointless because Mona was right. She'd always come up lacking in the mothering department.

When she turned the key, the car grumbled momentarily and went back to sleep. Charleigh tried again, this time managing to pull the car from its comatose state.

"It worked," she cried out as the engine turned over and the floor below her vibrated to life.

"*Good,*" Mona said. "*Now get your ass to your mom's house.*"

"Thanks."

"*Don't thank me yet. It could still die on your way, so drive carefully.*" Mona laughed. "*Remember to move the wheel so you go around the potholes.*"

Charleigh hung up without saying goodbye. She waved to the dog in the window and headed down the road surrounded by corn fields toward the tree-lined street of the house she'd grown up in. The house she'd sworn she'd never return to when she was loaded into the white van and shipped to Greyson Academy. But that changed like everything else in her life; the court tore Joey from Dilynn and Alex to give Grace Marshall kinship custody.

The six-year-old stood at the window. Her body bounced up and down as Charleigh made it up the walkway with the worn youth-sized basketball tucked under her arm. Joey's braids slapped against her shoulders as the little hand beat against the window.

"Mommy! Mommy!" Joey greeted her from behind the double-paned glass. "Gamma, Mommy's heres for my visits. Shes cames. I tolds yous she's coming."

Charleigh waved and stood just before the steps, so the child wouldn't lose sight of her. When the door opened, the tiny blonde girl shot out from around Grace Marshall at a full-speed run into the arms of her mother. Her entire body slapped against Charleigh's still-bruised chest from when she was tackled at the game.

The ball bounced down the driveway when Charleigh landed on her butt. She wrapped her arms around Joey tightly and hugged her like her father would have.

The little chin dug into Charleigh's shoulder, but the pain didn't matter when the child was in her arms. Charleigh buried her face into the girl's tight braids and inhaled watermelon shampoo. It was different from the normal floral scent, but Charleigh liked it.

"I missed you, Mommy," Joey said with a toothy grin. She opened her mouth wide and wiggled her bottom tooth. "Look, Mommy. It's loose. I's gots a loosed tooth and when it falls out the tooth fairy's gonna comes and shes gonna bring me a money. Dos you thinks it will bes enough moneys to go see Lek-sa Jenison sign my jersey? Yous said yous save yours money so we could go and ges my jersey signed, so I's going to use my tooth money to save too."

Joey pulled back from Charleigh and held her fingers under the hem of the purple t-shirt Charleigh had decorated to look like a Devil's jersey. "I weared my jersey so we can plays the bounceketball. I so excited. I practices my dance move with my wristy flippy and I thinks I going to make a shots today. I goes to makes all the shots today."

"You're late," Grace practically spat.

The woman would never actually spit. That would be unwomanly and crass, just like the mother sitting on the ground.

"Mommy. Mommy, looks at me." Joey's hands tried to pull Charleigh's attention from the grandmother.

Charleigh held Joey's hands in her own. "One second, baby."

She pushed herself up from the concrete and straightened the dress. It was only then she noticed the engine grime streaked down the front.

"Sorry. I had a little car trouble," she explained, gesturing to the proof of her labor.

The creases in Grace's perpetual scowl deepened. She pulled at the dress clinging too tightly to her abdomen. The mandated woman's attire never quite fit Grace Marshall.

"You don't get extra time just because you can't show up on time," Grace stated.

"I'll make sure she's back by six," Charleigh promised with a smile the woman didn't deserve. A smile was given because nothing pissed her mom off more than people who smiled when being scolded.

Joey was already pulling Charleigh toward the park where their visits were scheduled to take place. Her dressy shoes slipped backward as she yanked on Charleigh's arm, but her little legs kept going until Charleigh was walking with her.

"Bye Gamma!" the girl called over her shoulder without looking back at the house or the cankerous woman approaching fifty.

The trees hung over the sidewalk, casting a pleasant shade over them. Joey told Charleigh about the assembly and standing in front of all the Kindergarteners in the whole school. She babbled on and on about how she'd won student of the month because she had been so good. Especially good when the other kids were talking during circle time, which was her favorite time because that's when they listened to the stories about the different families, she learned that some kids have one mommy and a daddy and some live with their Gamma or Gammpa, and some lived with just a mommy, but that today's story was about a girl named Harriet and she had two daddies.

"And Gamma was sos angry," Joey explained. "Shes wents to hers computers and shes typedid with mad fingers."

"Well, your grandma doesn't have to like that Harriet has two daddies," Charleigh informed her daughter. "It doesn't matter what gender they are as long as Harriet is happy. Do you think Harriet was happy?"

Joey's eyes lit up. "Oh yes, shes was very happy and hers daddies let hers dress up in all different outfits. It's better than stupid dresses. I's wants sparkle pants and dinosaurs on mys shirts. I hates stupid flowers. But Gamma likes flowers and shes smiley when I wears the flowers, so I wears the flowers for her like you saids becauses then shes uses her nice words at mes."

The air in Charleigh's lungs exited slowly. She made a mental note to go to the store and pick up some shirts with dinosaurs at the outlet mall before her next visit.

"Joey, I want you to know that I am so proud of you for earning the Student of the Month award," Charleigh praised. "I know being quiet when everyone else is talking can be very hard."

"Yeah. Yeah. But I's can dossss hard things," Joey said, tapping her chest. Charleigh's face hurt from smiling, but hearing her words come out of her daughter's mouth made her feel a little less of a failure.

"I's can dosss the hard things and yous can dosss the hard things." Joey swung their hands as they walked past a mother trailing a little boy on a scooter. "When yous dosss your hard things then I's going to come haves a forever sleepover at yous house, and I don't have to live with Gamma anymore."

Charleigh tucked a stray curl behind Joey's ear. She dropped to her knee just outside the park. "Yes, baby. I am doing all the hard things they are telling me to do, so that you can come home with Mommy."

Joey's eyes widened as they approached the basketball court. But she stopped as a little boy raced to one side of the court with his ball.

"Mommy, do you thinks when I's come home that I's can play the bounceketball on a real team?" Joey looked up at Charleigh. "I's bringdid homes the paper from school and I's askedid Gamma to plays the bounceketball but shes said bounceketball isn't for girls. But I tolds her I's knows girls play the bounceketball causes I met Sylveria Devil whens we went to the game and shes said I could play the bounceketball so whys Gamma tells me a fibbers about girls playing bounceketball?"

Charleigh let out a heavy breath. She didn't have to be there to know the tone the older woman had used when the discussion of basketball came up. She'd listened to the gender normed expectations every year the paper came home for signups. However, her dad disregarded Grace's outcry and filled out the form. He didn't buy into the bullshit that had Grace quit her job to be the woman the pastor told her she needed to be.

"Joey, Grandma doesn't like it when girls play sports," Charleigh tried to explain, not sure her daughter would be able to understand. "Your grandmother was taught that girls are supposed to do some things and boys are supposed to do other things. But I promise you, I will make sure you get to play basketball."

Joey's lips scrunched into her thinking face. "Whys Gamma thinks girls can't do what boys can do? Is it causes meanie Pastor Milkin. He cames to the house and hes tolds Gamma that shes cants lets me wears my sneakie shoes no mores and he says I has to bes in the bigs kids class fors the Sundays schools and thats... and thats... and thats shes needs..."

The rest of Joey's sentences seemed to dissolve on her tongue. Whatever the man, who'd convinced her mother to send her away, had said lay heavy on the girl's heart.

"I don't know, baby. I don't know why Pastor Milkin tells people that they have to be only one way." Charleigh sighed. "I don't think that is true though. You can do whatever you want when you're a grown-up, and you can like whatever you like."

Joey took the ball from Charleigh and ran to the court. Her little hand slapped against the ball, and it bounced back to her several times before she chased after it. She smiled when she caught up to it, and cried out, "I's goings to play the bounceketball like Lek-sa Jenison when I's a grows-up."

They played until the alarm on Charleigh's phone went off. Saying goodbye was the hardest part, but they said it the entire time they walked back to the house so there were fewer tears when they gave their last hug, and then their last, last hug.

6

The tires of Lexa's Range Rover hit every rock, rattling the vehicle in a manner that was probably very detrimental to the suspension—all because Phyllis decided to send Lexa off-roading to the middle of nowhere because some kid wanted to tell her teacher Happy Birthday.

Lexa screamed at the car, "How much longer on this fucking road?!"

Another equally shitty road passed by with nothing but cornfields surrounding it. She couldn't see a building anywhere in sight.

'Satellite twat must have gotten me lost,' she told herself.

Lexa stopped the car, not even bothering to pull off the road. Getting out, she hopped on the door frame and looked out over the fields, rippling in the early morning breeze like waves of yellow water.

Crunching tires pulled Lexa's attention from her search. A dented and peeling, yellow pick-up approached and stopped a careful distance behind her car.

'Great some hillbilly going to stop and help my black ass. Probably already calling the cops, thinking I stole a car,' Lexa growled.

Pulling her shit together, Lexa waited for an old white dude to get out with a shotgun. She breathed a little easier when she saw the balloons bopping around in the cab of the car through the bug-splattered windshield.

'Who the fuck goes this far in for their English teacher?' she thought.

A short bubbly brat popped out from behind the wheel and a mousey-looking brunette followed on the opposite side.

"Oh my god! You're here!" the girl squealed as her whole body bounced. Then Lexa remembered: sad story.

For a sob story though, the kid looked like she lived off glitter and rainbows and all things of happiness. Lexa wondered if any minute her excitement would cause her to fart glitter everywhere.

Lexa pulled her attention from the glitter girl and fought her desire to laugh at the image of the kid's ass exploding into a rainbow that flashed in her mind.

Her eyes fell on the other girl still cowering behind the hood of the truck. She nodded to the kid whose hoodie had been pulled up to cover most of her face. When she turned her attention back to Glittertastic, the girl was still bouncing like her breakfast consisted of sugar and caffeine.

Lexa had to say something. She knew this yet she struggled to come up with something other than 'chill the fuck out.'

Finally, she asked, "So... where is this school?"

The girl's hand swung up and a sharp-tipped acrylic nail pointed toward the end of the longest road ever. "Just up there," she answered with too much energy. "You can follow us if you want?"

Lexa looked at the crappy truck, then her dusty Range Rover. She licked her lower lip and shook her head as she imagined a rock cracking her windshield.

"I better go first."

She moved to get back in the car but stopped when her body was slowed by the girl touching her. Lexa's neck cracked from how quickly she turned back around. Her arm raised ready to backhand the smile from the kid's face.

Glitter girl's arm came up over her face as her chin dropped to shield her nose, mouth, and eyes. Lexa knew the stance. She'd held the stance every time she'd done the dishes with not enough circles, or her edges refused to lay flat like a white girl's would.

She dropped her hand as quickly as it went up and reminded herself. 'You're not a monster. You were just caught off guard, but you didn't hit her so it will be okay.'

"Sorry," Lexa pathetically offered.

'She's okay. You're okay. You didn't hit her, so you didn't do nothing wrong,' the voice in her head told her again.

The kid nodded, recovering some as she scanned over everything but the ball player in front of her. "Uh... I just... I wanted to thank you, Ms. Jenson. I just know Marshall is going to be so happy. And I didn't think I would get to tell you later... so thank you."

"You're welcome," was all Lexa got out before she climbed back into the car.

She gripped the steering wheel. Her fingers turned the same shade as Sylvia's face when she wasn't livid. And Sylvia would have been livid if she had seen what just happened.

Lexa heard Sylvia's voice remind her, 'Fans matter. You are nothing without your fans so treat them better than you treat yourself.'

Flipping the visor down, Lexa checked for dust and that her curls weren't frizzing thanks to the dry air. She made sure the eyeliner was even and no black goop had accumulated in the corners of her eyes.

'I'm Lexa fucking Jenson. I'm not a monster. I'm a nice person. So nice I got up at the ass crack of dawn so this kid could wish her teacher a happy fucking birthday.'

She put the car back into drive and pulled forward. Immediately her ass vibrated as the coins in the change cup rattled. The rattling had every nerve in Lexa ready to fire, but she could finally see a small set of buildings break out in a cove of trees.

She parked the car in the gravel lot where a small sign marked one of three visitor's spots. Peering through the gate, it became apparent that Lexa had arrived way too early. The campus was practically empty and there were only two other cars parked outside the gate.

The truck pulled into an unmarked spot away from the visitor's spots, and the two girls jumped from the cab again. They pulled out the balloons, backpacks, and plastic bags of supplies.

Lexa tried to remember a single teacher she cared about enough to throw them a birthday party but came up with nothing. Maybe the government teacher, but even then, Lexa couldn't remember the woman's name. Just that she had long, curly red hair that didn't sit right like hers and three kids... or maybe two.

She studied the courtyard as she tried to remember the redhead's name. Lexa counted six two-story houses strung together. One had what looked like a carport attached to it and giant metal toolboxes lining the walls. Since she had time, Lexa decided to look up where she was.

Google told her about a woman named Dilynn Greyson who founded a school meant for troubled teens. The website featured pictures of students doing projects inside the windowed rooms. She read: 'Dr. Greyson hoped that by creating an environmental connection, she would improve student social understanding and improve their moral character.' The school worked only with youth unable to conform to acceptable societal expectations and provided a therapeutic alternative to the overwhelming public high school.

Her eyebrows rose as she read through the school's background, and a part of her wondered what type of creepy conversion practices this place was built for. She scrolled through photos of the tattooed teens in small circle groups to straight-faced young adults in business casual dress. The whole thing made her skin crawl, and she wondered how Phyllis, in all her homo glory, managed to send her to a place like this.

The faculty tab caught her attention. She clicked it hoping it had photos and she'd get a preview of the woman to determine if she was worth her time. Before the page could load, the phone went blank, and the computer panel lit up with Phyllis's face. Lexa rolled her eyes.

'Of course, she would be checking on me. She has no faith in me,' Lexa said to herself as her head fell back against the seat.

"Answer," she told the car.

Phyllis's children were laughing. Their voices were amplified in the surround sound. Lexa didn't say anything before the agent barked, "You there yet?"

Lexa sucked her teeth. 'No hello.'

She twisted her hands around the steering wheel. 'No good morning.'

Her molars ground. 'No thanks for getting up, Lexa.'

The decision was clear. 'I'm going to fire her.'

"I'm here," Lexa practically growled. But her teeth stopped aching when she remembered she paid Phyllis to be like this.

The children were still giggling, and Lexa knew that Phyllis was driving them to school. She was a good mom and started giving her a good mom lecture.

"Remember, this is for good press. Be nice and don't try to fuck her on the desk." Phyllis stated this so matter of factly it pissed Lexa off. Until the lightbulb flipped on in Lexa's brain. Phyllis wouldn't have said that unless Ms. Marshall was hot.

Lexa's lips curled into a smile. "So, you're saying she's fuckable?"

A crumbling Accord pulled in next to Lexa. The muffler popped as it shut down, and Lexa wondered what type of poor bastard can't get their shit together enough to have at least a decent ride.

"LEXA!"

Holding her fingers to her temples, Lexa yelled, "You're on fucking surround sound! I don't pay you to deafen me!"

A flash of honey blonde waves sped by the hood of her car, reminding Lexa of the girl from the bar. She'd missed her face, but the legs covered in black skintight material made her pray that the broke bitch was Ms. Marshall.

As the woman turned into the school's front gate, the cardigan sweater rose just enough for Lexa to see how the material of her pants clung to the thin thighs and toned ass. She checked the corners of her mouth for drool and decided whoever the woman was, Lexa was leaving with her phone number, so she could slap the pale ass hidden under those pants as she had her way with her.

Phyllis was growling still. "Lexa, if you fuck this up, I quit. I mean it. This woman and the kid are important—"

"I heard you," and Lexa hit the end button.

Grungy and tattooed teens began to flood the courtyard of the school as she waited in the safety of the car. She wasn't sure where they were coming from because she hadn't seen enough cars to carry this many kids, but it went from graveyard quiet to stadium loud in a matter of minutes.

Settling herself, she took a moment to get into character. This is for publicity. Flipping the mirror down again, Lexa took another look at herself. She checked that her makeup was still on point and her hair still wasn't frizzing out. Lastly, she checked her lips were glossy.

She smiled at her reflection and pepped herself up. "You are Lexa fucking Jenson. She's going to jump up and down, and she'll hug you and it will be okay. You'll take the pictures and then you'll find someplace quiet to spend some quality time with the blonde."

She must have missed the bell because the tattooed Stepford teens began moving quickly from where they were gathered into the tiny houses.

With the courtyard empty, Lexa figured it was time to leave the sanctity of the vehicle.

Once inside the small lobby, a teen in all black, twirled her nose ring as she stared at Lexa. She pointed to a three-ring binder. "Sign in there. Who are you here to see?"

Lexa's attention was diverted to a curvy Latina in a pair of pristine Retro Jordans walking by the door with a car battery pack in her hand. She watched the woman's ass cheeks lift and fall in the tight jeans. If the blonde wasn't interested, she'd try that one next.

As she scribbled her name on the paper, she remembered the question. "I'm here to see Ms. Marshall."

"Thompson," the nose ring girl yelled. "The basketball chick Marshall is obsessed with is here."

"Who was that?" Lexa asked the girl who had begun twisting the ring in her nose. The girl quirked an eyebrow at her in confusion, so Lexa pointed to the door where the caramel-skinned woman stood talking to a familiar redhead.

"Ms. Ramirez or Ms. Carter?" the girl asked. But Lexa didn't care either way. Both were hot and both were worthy of her time. She smiled at the thought of checking off the teacher from her fuck list with one thrust.

Her fantasy of fucking both women was interrupted by a potbellied man in a shirt too small grumbling under his breath as he made his way down the hallway. Lexa assumed he was the assistant principal, but she followed him past the office with the Asst. Principal Alex Trikru etched on the door to a closet with a desk covered in folders. She studied the tiny award on a filing cabinet that read: World's Best School Social Worker.

"Look Lexa, I can call you Lexa, right?" but he didn't wait for her to respond. "Charleigh Marshall is like a daughter to me."

Lexa tried the name out on her tongue. It was different, and she nodded to herself, because she liked the way it tasted. She felt the undeniable warmth of her confidence in the crotch of her pants.

'Fuckable Charleigh Marshall. Alongside Ms. Ramirez and Ms. Carter. The trifecta of a fucktastic fantasy.'

She was pulled back to the conversation with the tapping of the penguin man's pen on the desk. He waved his other hand in the air as though she wasn't even looking at him. She tilted her head and raised her eyebrows.

He cleared his throat and gathered a few folders on his desk. Once they were tapped into a unified formation, he set them off to the side. His hands folded atop the desk. "Look, after you were arrested last week, Charleigh and I agreed that she would stop..."

She watched his lips move, but her internal voice drowned them out. 'Of course, he knew about that. Everyone knew about the one time I almost fucked up. Got to paint me out to be a monster because they can't handle how good I really am.'

His hand ran over the bald center of his head. The tufts of gray hair surrounding his head reminded her of the creepers in the serial killer documentaries her wife used to fall asleep to.

"Lexa." Her name brought her back to the conversation. "I'm concerned that you will cause unwanted attention to be cast upon her."

Lexa narrowed her eyes on the man. Her tongue ran over her teeth. "Do you mean because I'm a lesbian or because I'm Black and a lesbian?"

Rolling her eyes, she added, "Look, I get you all are going for the Christian values and pray away the gay thing, but it's not like I'm here to hit on her."

She spread her legs wider as she leaned back, taking up more space. His bushy graying eyebrows were easier to stare at than actually looking at him, and Sylvia had once told her it was how to make the press back off.

"Charleigh's sexuality is no one's business." His hand came down on the table, and something in his voice told Lexa this wasn't the first time he'd had this type of conversation. The man dropped the poker professionalism. "My issue with you is the fact that you were just arrested for property damage and assault. She doesn't need to be a publicity ploy to fix your image. She has worked very hard to separate herself from people like you who enjoy trouble. She's a good person who has been dealt a rough hand in life, and she doesn't need someone like you threatening everything she'd worked so hard for."

Lexa's chin dropped slightly at his candor. She sucked her teeth, as she thought, 'Well, that didn't go as planned.'

The silver-filled molars ached as she chewed on potential retorts that couldn't hold up under the pressure of her bite. Irritated that she couldn't respond, and he was still talking, she reminded herself, 'This is why I don't do school shit anymore. There is always some uptight dickwad that was worried about what a photo with me could do to hurt them. Too homo. Too ghetto. Too much of everything.'

"Lexa, am I understood?" Thompson was looking at her, and she was looking back at him.

She shifted in the seat, crossing her feet and folding her arms over her chest. He shouldn't make her feel uncomfortable, but she was because she felt like a kid.

"I asked—" he started again.

"Got it," she snapped.

His phone rang, tearing his time-weathered gaze from her. He grumbled out a few yeses, before he pulled at the tie that wasn't even fixed around his throat. When his eyes were on her again, his exhale was loud and annoying because it was the same disappointed sound. She hated that sound and even more that everyone kept using it when she did what everyone wanted.

Well, until recently, but that was Kayla's fault. She was just there and got a little carried away. The woman understood that and forgave her, so that meant she didn't have to feel guilty anymore.

"Look, I know you don't want me here, so how about you show me to her classroom so I can wish her a happy birthday and give her the—"

Lexa looked at her hands, realizing she'd forgotten the ball at the arena and the photo in the car.

Phyllis would be pissed. Her mind ran through different scenarios landing on the only logical option. She would just leave Charleigh Marshall some tickets for the next game. Middle of nowhere teachers couldn't afford stuff like that, so Phyllis might even like the idea. They'd put her name on the big screen, and she'd take a real photo with real press.

Lexa cleared her throat. "And tell her about the tickets at the box office for the next game and then I'll leave you to this... place."

He nodded but Lexa didn't miss that he didn't smile at her. He just led her out a side door into the empty courtyard.

The blue door of schoolhouse number 6 was covered in a handmade sign, wishing Charleigh Marshall a happy birthday. It made Lexa wonder what this lady did for her kids to love her this much.

No time to wonder though, because they were at the door and there was cheering going on within. Thompson's phone rang, stopping him from leading her in. He held the door for Lexa, leaving her in the hallway to follow the voices of students for her meet and greet.

She could feel the birthday song pounding through her chest as she listened to the off-key singing. No one had ever sung the song to her the way these troubled teens were singing to the blonde in tight pants and mom sweater standing in the center of the room.

The blonde she saw earlier was indeed Charleigh Marshall. As the teacher turned, looking at her students all crammed in the tiny space, Lexa choked on the apple-scented air.

The pained stormy eyes met Lexa's, and she felt the blood rush from her face. Charleigh was more than fuckable; she was perfect. She'd been perfect at the bar and perfect courtside. And now she was perfect in a room full of kids bigger than her.

Lexa saw the exact moment Charleigh realized that Lexa was real. Her eyes didn't shine though. She stared at Lexa and swallowed.

"Hello, Ms. Jenson. Thank you so much for coming," she said, and Lexa looked at her lips because one was tucked between her teeth.

Charleigh Marshall was not Lexa's biggest fan. Not anymore at least. She stood there until the glitter girl hugged her and tugged her into Lexa's space.

"Happy birthday, Marshall!" the girl said. But those blue eyes were blank, even though she pulled her unpainted lips into a masked smile.

Lexa smiled back because she was here to get the job done though. Even if she's hot and not truly a fan, Lexa decided she needed to be the woman her agent sent. She fixed her $4000 smile and said, "Hello, Charleigh."

Charleigh's eyes smiled this time, but she didn't move closer to Lexa. Instead, she seemed to be trying to calculate the angles of Lexa's face, but she'd forgotten the formula. Lexa's smile faltered and the words she'd played faded in the thunderous storm of her mind. The storm was brought on by the blue and gray of her eyes. Like the sky had met the ocean on a cold dreary morning. Lexa was lost for a moment as waves began to rock within her until her stomach twisted.

She should have been relieved when Charleigh's eyes were no longer on her, but she needed them back. She needed to understand why those eyes were able to shake away every fleck of confidence within her.

"You guys are so sweet. Thank you so much," Charleigh told her students, not casting a glance back at Lexa.

Lexa's legs moved without her brain. She placed her hand on the woman's lower back but pulled it free when Charleigh jumped from her touch. The blonde's gaze returned to Lexa as students began to move around the room.

The kids raided the tables of cookies and treats, while others were grouping off. Charleigh turned away from Lexa again. "Guys, get your snacks and then get out your books. We are beginning with the dialogue that explains the phrase: 'Who is John Gault?'"

The honey blonde waves fell behind the woman's shoulder where the faded mark on Charleigh's throat caught Lexa's attention. It was poorly covered with probably cheap foundation. But was Lexa's reminder as to why Charleigh wasn't excited to see her, just like she hadn't been excited to get her number at the game.

Her fantasies vaporized when Charleigh looked at her again. The soft lip was tucked back between her teeth.

Lexa stepped forward to close the distance. She needed to remind the woman of her promise before making her exit. But Charleigh's hand came up as the woman created a forcefield to freeze Lexa in place.

"Ms. Jenson," she said, barely loud enough to be heard over the various conversations in the room.

"Lexa," she corrected the teacher. "Just Lexa."

Charleigh swallowed; her eyes more stormy than bright. Her hands hung by her side and the Jedi trick she'd used before was no longer in effect. Lexa reached forward and took one hand in her own. Rubbing her thumb over the creamy freckled flesh, Lexa said, "Charleigh, I went to find you after the game."

Lexa pulled the woman closer but the ugly, untied boots on the woman's tiny feet seemed practically glued to the floor and her body half flopped against Lexa as she wrapped the woman into the hug.

Her hand patted Lexa on the back without returning the embrace.

"Thank you for coming," Charleigh said. But each word had the same pitch.

The same tone Sylvia used to illustrate her disinterest when Lexa would talk about the latest fanfiction she'd read about them or when Lexa had suggested taking a year off so they could start a family.

Lexa held on as she remembered Sylvia shrugging out of her hug before getting in her car to drive to Chicago without her. She didn't let go of the woman in her arms squirming. She only left the memory when the cheap shampoo cleared away the fog in her head.

Charleigh pushed against Lexa's chest until she was free from the hug but not from the grip. She held on to the teacher's arms still hanging by her side. The blue eyes shifted back and forth, scanning around them. And Lexa felt the woman shaking so subtly at first, she didn't realize the waves within her had not returned.

"Please let go," Charleigh said so softly Lexa didn't hear her, just watched her lips move.

Lexa blinked a few times trying to figure out what she did wrong. She held on as the eye of the storm within her passed and the swells of the waves began beating against her. Beating like the bass of a drum with the students talking all around them. She leaned down to look at the woman again, but her chin was angled at the ground.

"Will you just look at me?" Lexa growled.

Charleigh didn't look up, but her arm stopped shaking. Her body stopped pulling away. She was just there, but she wasn't. And Lexa knew, like she'd known the retreat of the glitter girl.

Before Lexa could move, her body was pulled away from the woman, and the phone in Charleigh's hand crashed against the floor. She searched for whoever she was going to have to teach the hard way not to touch her and came face to face with a giant boy covered from the neck down in gang tattoos. Even when she stood at her full height the boy was at her eye level.

Lexa looked at the woman picking up the shattered phone, then back to see several teens with phones in their hands, held up at her face.

"You should just leave," a scrawny boy in a rainbow belt yelled at her from behind his phone.

The boy holding her, released his grip on her arm. "Look lady, I got six more months of probation and I'm not looking to go back to detention, but that's my girl's sister and if you try to talk to her again, then I'm going to do what I have to do and you're going to do what you have to do and both our black asses gonna be face down in handcuffs."

Lexa turned to Charleigh, who had stepped between the boy and her. She placed a hand on his shoulder. "It's okay, Bastian. Ms. Jenson was just apologizing for knocking me on my head at the game Ms. Ramirez took me to."

When Charleigh turned back to Lexa, she held out a pale hand. "It was nice to meet you, Ms. Jenson. I have been a fan of yours since you were drafted. I got to see you play in college. Thank you for coming to my birthday."

Lexa turned when a deep throat cleared in the doorway behind her. The grumpy pedophile penguin stared at her, and she shook her head.

She took Charleigh's clammy hand in her own and shook it. "Happy Birthday. I... uh... I left tickets to the next game at the box office for you. You just take your ID, and they have them. I... hope to see you there."

Charleigh smiled. "That is so sweet of you. You really didn't have to. We just appreciate you taking time out of your day to come all the way out here."

"I think it's time we get back to academics," Thompson grumbled. "Lexa, if you come with me, I'll show you out."

With a heavy sigh, she turned away from the woman and left the room with so many colors. The door slapped closed behind the man as his feet kicked up rocks along the path.

Thompson grumbled and growled gibberish under the heaving breaths. Only when the gate was latched from the inside, and Lexa was locked out did the mumbles turn into words.

With his arms crossed over his giant belly, he barked, "Think you're important. Putting your hands on women like they are something to own."

Lexa turned. Her head held high and her shoulders back. The same way she was taught to walk off the court after a loss.

"Take a look in the mirror. You're just a busted ball player, acting like anyone even cares about Women's Basketball. Get over yourself before you lose more than your biggest fan."

But she hadn't lost. No, Lexa fucking Jenson did not lose.

A delay in the game, that was all. And even though every single play Phyllis gave her, she'd failed, there was still time left.

Her car door hit the Accord as she leaned within to pull out a Sharpie. She yanked the glossy image out and looked at the smile shining back at her. That smug look of unstoppable pride. She hated it.

The phone rang and her fist hit the seat. She fished it out of her pocket, only to see Phyllis's face looking back at her.

'Fucking fuck. Fuck.'

Her finger hovered over the green button, wavering in the air as her mind played the list of recorded rants on repeat that she paused and replayed in a repeated rhythm until Phyllis's face disappeared.

A second later a text popped onto the screen still in her hand. The banner sitting on the screen with a video from the classroom that she didn't need to open to know it was the kid holding her back as she stared back at the door. She couldn't make out the words over the image, but it wouldn't be the type of publicity Phyllis requested.

A message popped up a moment later. She read it over and over again thinking that as long as she was reading it, Phyllis hadn't quit. The kid hadn't sent Phyllis a video of Lexa refusing to let go of the same blonde again. But even the $91,578 in her account wouldn't give her enough pennies to wish herself out of this corporeal nightmare.

She ripped the top of the marker off with her teeth and put the pen to the photo. Her hand shook as she took the first step toward making it right. Starting with the woman who hadn't forgiven her.

'Two VIP passes waiting for you for Saturday's game. Happy Birthday,' the voice in her head dictated.

When she tried to stuff the photo back into the envelope, it stopped before her slutty smirk disappeared within. It just kept laughing at her as she tried again and again. She tossed the photo to the seat and squeezed the envelope in her hand, but it fought back until she remembered. She dug the crumpled letter from the bottom and tossed it in a ball to the floor on the other side of the console. It rolled under the seat, no longer visible.

With the envelope empty, the photo slid easily within. The little metal tabs flipped over, securing the busted ballplayer. She held it, considering if it would be better to just drive away.

Leave this stupid school.

Leave this crushing city.

Leave this loser life.

Leave Lexa Fucking Jenson.

Leave

her behind, like Sylvia had.

But leaving had caused chaos.

Lexa didn't leave though. She'd never left before, and she wasn't going to leave now. Well, not in the grand escape sense. She would leave the school to find a Starbucks but only after shoving the orange envelope to the Honda's windshield and letting the tattered wiper blade secure it with a slap. She'd find the woman on Instagram and she'd fix it.

7

Charleigh's phone lay uselessly on the nightstand with the ancient iPad below it. The phone's screen shattered after it fell from her hands in her classroom. She was proud of herself for not breaking into tears over the new device's untimely death.

The birthday present from Marcus, which she'd just opened that morning, had replaced the ancient model no longer sustaining a charge. Too ashamed to ask Marcus for the old one back, she'd carefully applied a layer of clear packing tape to the surface and put it in her backpack until the end of the day.

The day-old packing tape was already peeling at the edges and when she'd tried to open the device it ended in glass slivers poking out through the tape. It wouldn't last the two weeks she'd needed. but she wasn't sure if pulling it off would make it impossible to answer any calls from her case manager.

She'd at least managed to back up all her photos of Joey and the videos of her students' stand-up poetry.

At least the iPad she'd been issued in high school still worked, sort of. She tried to reach for it, but the dog lying across the bottom of the bed pinned her foot to the mattress. She lifted her untethered leg over the lump of fur and stretched as far as she could. Her fingers scooted the device toward her when the fitted sheet snapped off the corner and smacked Charleigh in the face.

She ripped the material away as it tried to suffocate her. Rolling back to her initial position, she stared at the nipple on the titty-shaped light fixture, hanging above her.

'If I reach for the iPad to look at the Instagram request again, are you going to come apart and impale me?' she silently asked the boob lamb. It seemed implausible, but so did the house's continued assault on her whenever she considered accepting the follow request.

The toes of her trapped foot began to tingle. She pulled and twisted the tightly secured foot. No amount of wiggling bothered Rexa enough to move her. Her snoring grew heavier until she snorted like a horse in the Kentucky Derby.

The dog's legs kicked into a run as she heaved out a heavy whine. A paw caught the comforter, giving it purchase on just enough material to send the pit into momentum. The short-haired dog glided off the bed and landed with a thump on the ground. Jostled from her dream, Rexa sat up and looked at Charleigh with a twist of her head.

"Don't look at me like that. I didn't throw you off," she said. The dog tilted her head in the other direction and studied the woman getting up.

Charleigh fixed the sheet with a sharp tug, but the corner only made it halfway down the mattress as the chubby dog returned to the top. She knew the sheet would attack again, but at least this time it would hit Rexa and not her.

The iPad's bright glow ricocheted off the mirror. Shadow monsters danced along the walls as she stared at the follow request again.

With the next game of the play-off series tomorrow, she struggled with whether going was a good idea. She'd left before the last game ended to avoid having to talk to Lexa Jenson. To escape back to being a fan in a sea of others. But now Lexa Jenson knew her name and where she worked, and she was stalking her on social media.

A candid photo of the woman smiling lay in the small circle. Charleigh realized the request hadn't come from Lexa Jenson's account. It came from Lexa Winters. A private account with only 752 followers. She would be important enough to see Lexa's actual world if she accepted the request. Her social media status would elevate her to being an acquaintance of Lexa Jenson's.

Her free hand rubbed her fingers over the soft material of the sheets. The feeling of the dark cotton made Charleigh wonder if Lexa was lying in bed, staring at her phone waiting for her to accept. She tried to picture the large bed with high-quality sheets. Did she sleep with a comforter at night even though it was summer, or did someone like her have a different blanket for each season like Charleigh imagined rich people did?

She clung to the $30 comforter set from Walmart realizing how stupid she was to think that Lexa Jenson was lying in bed waiting for her. She would be out with a girl or in bed with two. It's what she'd wanted that night. She'd wanted Charleigh and the other woman to go home with her.

'But what if she's not?' a small voice asked, lighting a spark within her. 'What if she meant it when she said she'd make it up to you?'

Charleigh considered what had gone through the woman's mind when she had shown up in her classroom. The way Lexa's upturned eyes had grown when Charleigh looked at her said Lexa didn't know she was visiting her. She was just there to say happy birthday because a student had asked her. That wasn't something a monster would do.

So maybe she meant it.

She clicked accept, giving Lexa access to her pathetic digital world. The photos of her life pre-sobriety, along with the friends she'd had in high school and college were long since deleted or blocked, so she could wipe away any hint of who she'd once been.

Now she had a world of twenty-four friends. Twenty-four people, mostly former students, with whom she shared images of books she'd read. That was all Lexa would get to see.

Photos of Joey were things she kept private after she'd gotten the message from Kyle's wife that she wanted to get in touch. She didn't even want to think about opening that door, especially since it was probably another one of Kyle's sick games. She hadn't gotten the abortion like he demanded, but he probably knew Joey wasn't with her after having dinner with Marcus, Mona, and Kinsley. She couldn't put it past him to try to ruin any chance of her getting Joey back after he'd promised to kill her in high school if she didn't get an abortion.

The banner flashed across the screen almost immediately. Lexa had messaged her. A simple statement. 'You won't regret this.'

She read the message again and again. Too many times for any sane person to care about the vague compilation of words.

She sorted through the consequences of responding and not responding. The more she thought about it the more confused she was. It wasn't a question. Just a few words. A few words that made her wonder more ifs and their counterpart thens.

Charleigh left the message for the private profile now hers to peruse. She ran her finger down to posts from years prior. Lexa didn't use the account often as each group of images spanned months apart.

The woman posted pictures from trips around the world to more countries than Charleigh could name. Then there were intimate photos of Lexa's wedding. Charleigh clicked on a video of Lexa and Sylvia Winters in their white gowns. Then she scrolled to a picture of the dark-haired girl from the bar standing next to the brides in the white dress. 'My beautiful wife and the best sister-in-law a girl could ask for. Thanks for the introduction, Kayla,' was what the caption read.

Some pieces started to fall into place for Charleigh. The woman in the photos who'd ended Lexa's marriage wasn't just some girl. It had been Lexa's sister-in-law. Charleigh drafted a broken-hearted narrative for Lexa. The happy smile on the woman's face as she stood alongside Sylvia Winters. Their complimentary wedding dresses pulled up in their hands on the dance floor surrounded by their teammates. The sister-in-law watched the couple from the side with Sylvia's bouquet in hand. No smile, just staring at the happy couple, who were unaware of the plot being hatched by the dark-haired sibling in the forest green satin gown.

"I'm sorry she hurt you," Charleigh said to the image of Lexa smiling aboard a boat. The last picture of her smiling. More recent photos showed the glassy eyes of the woman Charleigh had met at the bar. The dark-haired villain by Lexa's side in every one of them, the scales of her snake-like form hidden from view as she held out a phone to immortalize their time together.

She wished Lexa could tell her that her twisted tale was right. That the monster everyone had come to expect from Lexa was a result of the poison fed to her by the true villain.

But Lexa could tell her. She was awake and had messaged her.

Charleigh tried to type a response, but it sounded dumb. She deleted it and tried again. Deleted. Typed. Four different messages before she settled on, 'Big game tomorrow, you should be sleeping.'

The little icon next to the message had a check mark that it sent, and then a second check mark appeared, showing Lexa had read the question.

Three dots told Charleigh the woman was writing her back. She felt the embarrassment creep through her as Lexa had probably seen her trying to type out her multiple messages also. Thoughts began to race toward a finish line of worst-case scenarios for responding.

Lexa's message came through faster than a winning scenario could be determined.

'It's only 9 pm. I think I stopped going to bed at 9 when I was like 7.'

Charleigh's thumb tapped three letters. A single-worded termite in her brain. A single question that had eaten away at her since she'd pushed her way through the door and slid down the wood to the floor. Her tears were licked away by the dog.

'Why?' she left out the 'me'. She doesn't know if she is ready for that part of the story. To know why Lexa fucking Jenson looked through a crowd of lesbians and chose her.

The answer appeared quickly. 'Because only children and people that work before dawn need to go to bed that early. Plus, practice is usually late morning and games are afternoons or nights. I never have to be up early.'

A logical answer to the question that she hadn't meant. She scratched Rexa's head behind the floppy ear. When she moved, the dog shifted closer and closer. Finally, she complied with the request and resumed scratching.

As she did, she received another message. 'I didn't mean to scare you yesterday. I got caught up in my head and I didn't realize I was holding on to you. I'm not a monster and I don't enjoy scaring people. In fact, I hate it when people jump out at me or like pranks.'

Charleigh held the tablet as the three dots appeared again and another message came through. 'I know you said you forgive me for what happened at the bar, but I think you lied. I'm not mad you lied, but I am sorry for what happened. You didn't do anything other than look stunning, and I told myself that you wanted me, which is stupid because I shouldn't have assumed you wanted me.'

The raindrops hit the roof and the gravel outside. Rexa's snores were louder and normally it helped with the emptiness of the space. In the moment of Lexa's apology, the emptiness seemed to swallow Charleigh. Her heart raced at having someone like Lexa hurt her and apologize for it.

Tears fell again for the basketball player. So many tears that the floorboards should be warped in the bungalow. She wiped at them uselessly because in less than a week Lexa had apologized more times than anyone in her life. Not either of her mothers for dumping her. Not Mona for choosing the bed in their shared room over their relationship. Not any of the others that had used her for their gratification.

The disappointment in Lexa rode the stream of tears until Charleigh's body felt lighter. Her fingers tapped out the truth: 'I want this to work.'

But she didn't know what 'this' was, so she deleted it.

'Can we start over?' came next, but Lexa wouldn't know where to start over from. Lexa didn't remember that they'd met before the bar. She couldn't remember Charleigh from a week before, she surely didn't remember the class they shared in college.

She settled with, 'Thank you for apologizing. I shouldn't have been at the bar, and I shouldn't have let things go as far as they did before trying to get you to slow down.'

Embracing the safe distance, she had to tell Lexa whatever she wanted, she typed out. 'I really want to go to the game tomorrow, but I think I need some boundaries so neither of us are put into a situation that makes us uncomfortable. Like rules.'

The sky and Charleigh seem to be linked in some fashion because as she waited, her heartbeat faster and the rain pounded against the roof harder. She waited for Lexa's response, wondering what the woman was doing as they were talking. She didn't have time to craft another narrative when the call request appeared.

She couldn't ignore the call. Not when they were just talking.

As the call connected, Lexa's face appeared on the screen. A sapphire satin bonnet was secured on her head and her face was pale.

"*Hey.*" Lexa's voice sounded like it had been dragged over a gravel road.

"Are you okay?" Charleigh asked. She scanned over the swelling under Lexa's eyes and rosy nose. "You sound sick."

Chapped lips lifted into a weak smile. "*Eh. I'll be fine. It's just a stuffy nose and a cough. I took some nasty shit that is supposed to help, and I'm starting to get tired.*"

Lexa's fingers pressed into her eyes and then pressed against her sinus. She sucked up her snot, then said, "*I didn't want to fall asleep before we went over the rules. Don't want you to think I left you on read or something and then you miss the game because of cough syrup.*"

Charleigh bit her lip. Typing and talking were two different things. Typing out the rules with being able to edit them felt easier than spitballing them.

Lexa squinted, and her face moved closer to the camera. "*You, okay? Your eyes look red.*"

The round puffy face with bloodshot eyes stared up at Charleigh from the bottom corner of the screen. "I'm just tired," she lied. "Sorry, I didn't respond sooner. I dropped my phone in my classroom and shattered the screen."

Lexa looked away from the screen and licked her chapped lips. Quietly she asked, "*Did you get it replaced?*"

The laughter rumbled in Charleigh's chest before breaking free. "No. I... uh... have to wait until payday. It'll cost a hundred dollars to get a refurbished replacement on the insurance. Totally sucks but I guess that will teach me to keep the case on it. I mean, I needed to get a case for it because it was like new. I got it from Marcus for my birthday. You met him. Sweaty guy, who kinda smells like parmesan cheese. He's like family, not like a creeper trying to buy my affection, just, like, my fill-in Dad, I guess."

"*I can Venmo you the money,*" Lexa offered immediately.

Charleigh shook her head. "I'm not taking your money. Actually, let's make that friend rule #1: no loaning money."

Lexa rolled her eyes. "*Fine, don't call it a loan. It's not that big of a deal. Just give me your phone number, and it will be in your account in like five minutes.*" She put a large water bottle to her lips and took a long drink.

"I know how Venmo works." Charleigh pinched the bridge of her nose. She looked back to the screen. "In your world, $100 is not a big deal. In my world, it is. So, no loaning money."

The brown eyes rolled. "*Okay. No loans, even though this wouldn't have to be a loan.*" The bite in Lexa's voice made Charleigh curl up into a ball under the covers.

Lexa squinted at her again. "*Is that a dreamcatcher above your bed?*"

Charleigh glanced at the map above the metal railing of her headboard. She wasn't sure how Lexa had gotten dream catcher from the carefully placed pins that connected a planned path across various states.

"No, it's a map. Do you need glasses? It would explain why you can't hit an outside three anymore."

With a tilted head and suck of her teeth, Lexa explained, "*I took my contacts out, so I didn't fall asleep in them. Last time I slept with them in, one got stuck on the side of my eye and they had to pull it out with tweezers.*"

Lexa wiped her eyes. "*Okay, no more eyeball talk. Back to the rules. What else is on the list?*"

Charleigh tapped her finger to her nose. Her lips scrunched up, as she considered where to start. "Hmm... let's go with an easy one. No talking about poop. I know that has nothing to do with me coming to the game but it's easy."

When Lexa's mouth dropped open and her upper lip curled in disgust, Charleigh knew she'd distracted the woman from her rude comment. "*What type of weird ass people do you know that poop talk?*"

Charleigh rolled her eyes. "You never lived with a boy."

"*Only child,*" Lexa said with a shrug.

"Yeah, I know." Charleigh grimaced, realizing how creepy she must've sounded.

"*Stalker,*" Lexa poked.

"Says the person that found me on Insta after showing up at my work." Charleigh cocked an eyebrow and dared the woman to say something else.

Lexa rubbed a hand over her face, trying to wipe away her smile. "*The girl you were with at the game. She's your sister?*"

"Yeah. We're foster sisters. Kind of. So, Mona was a foster kid, and my mom signed over guardianship of me to Mona's foster dad until my mom formally gave me up, and I had to go live at the school you visited today. My room was actually above my classroom."

Lexa tilted her head to the side.

"Just ask," Charleigh said.

Lexa twirled a stray curl in front of her ear. "*Did they like try to make you pray the gay away? Like is it one of those places that they like electrocute kids to make them not gay anymore?*"

"So... no. There is no praying and there is a lot of gay," Charleigh stated. She picked at her lip. "Basically, we have a lot of kids that should be in juvie, a lot of foster kids that were living in group homes, and then there are kids like me, where their parents think they sent them to a place like what you are talking about."

"*Wait really?*" Lexa asked. "*Like your mom sent you to get electroshock therapy?*"

"I mean, I wasn't present for the school pitch, but I think she would be down if it meant I would have married the first wife-beater I met right out of high school and became a housewife."

"*Damn. I mean, my parents were messed up, but I don't think they ever considered shipping me off like that.*" Lexa took another drink of water and popped a yellow coughdrop in her mouth. She sucked on it for a moment, then said, "*Okay, back to the rules. Do I get to make up rules to go on this list?*"

"Well, sure. They should be mutual."

"*Then, I want a rule about hair.*" Lexa tucked the stray hair she'd been playing with earlier. "*No touching my hair. No asking to touch it, or how long it takes to brush, or how many products I use, or anything that you couldn't google yourself.*"

Charleigh watched Lexa look everywhere but at the camera. She sucked in her lower lip. "I can respect the no hair questions, but I think that's kinda a strange rule to add to the list when I'm just trying to cheer on my team. I mean, I am thinking like no touching. Like you in your bubble and me in mine."

Lexa looked like she was calculating a geometric theorem. She sucked her teeth and squinted at the camera. "*What if you're choking? I'm supposed to let you die?*"

Charleigh laughed with just her eyes. "Extreme, Lexa Jenson. But for now, yes. If I am choking on a pretzel at tomorrow's game, then you have to let me die according to friend rule number 4. Unless you know, you could just ask the medic to keep me alive like they did last time."

"*That sounds like an anti-friend rule, and I don't think I would let you die.*"

Charleigh held up three fingers, "Girl Scout promise, I will do my best not to choke when I'm around you. I will not even get a pretzel tomorrow."

A yawn broke free from Lexa as her head lay back against the pillow. Quickly she popped back up. "*Sorry. I wasn't sleeping but the cough syrup made me floaty.*" She opened her exhausted eyes. "*What else do you need to feel safe around me?*"

"I mean it's just going to be, like, tomorrow, but if we were to ever see each other when you were, like, a normal human, then I say no alcohol."

"*Can you drink when you're with me?*" Lexa asked, her eyes only partially open.

Charleigh contemplated what Lexa had planned since she'd bypassed the reality that they were supposed to be talking about her attendance at the game.

Not sure what else to say, Charleigh stated, "I won't drink around you. I mean last time I wasn't even drinking, so it's not really an issue for me."

"*Okay.*" Lexa set the phone down and laid her head on one pillow. Then she pulled another into a tight embrace and looked at the screen. "*Anything else.*"

"I also don't want to be mentioned in any social media posts. I don't want to be tagged in pictures or memes. I won't do that to you either." Charleigh bit her lip. "I told the kids they couldn't post any of the videos yesterday either. They agreed, so don't worry about anything coming back to you."

"*Got it.*"

A wet cough started slow, then grew more violent. Lexa's firm breast peeked out from the corner of the sleeveless shirt. Her hand pressed against her chest.

"You shouldn't play tomorrow," Charleigh stated as Lexa's cough evened out.

Lexa sipped some water and popped another cough drop. She looked at the camera, "*That's for the team medic to decide. If they say play and I say no, I'm in breach of contract, and after everything at the bar they would love to cancel my contract. But I already know that I am limited to twenty nonconsecutive minutes.*" She took another drink. "*Any other rules?*"

"Those are the big ones that pertain to the game. I mean, I have others that are common sense rules like don't try to make me eat food that I don't like. Don't piss with the door open. Oh, and don't touch me with your feet. Feet are gross, and I bet yours smell like a teenager's gym bag."

"*Hey, I take very good care of my feet.*" Lexa pulled her giant leg up and tried to smell her toes. She sucked in her snot, then tried again but with no success. "*Okay, well I can't smell shit right now, but I washed them with actual soap and a washcloth.*"

"A washcloth?" Charleigh's eyebrows cinched in the middle. "Is that like a dish towel or the loofa?"

Lexa's mouth opened, and then it closed.

"I know what a washcloth is, Lexa."

Charleigh could almost feel the breath Lexa exhaled through the screen.

"*You had me scared.*" Lexa wiped her face. "*You won't believe how many white girls I've seen in the shower just rubbing the soap directly on their skin. No loofa, no cloth, just hands and soap. AND it wasn't even foamy.*"

Lexa grabbed another pillow and put it behind her before she laid back. She yawned again, triggering Charleigh's yawn.

"*Stop it,*" Lexa said with a smile.

"You started it," Charleigh whined.

"*So, just to be clear. The rules are: No social media. No touching. No drinking. No talking about poop.*"

"And no hair talk," Charleigh added then pointed at the screen. "AND no loans"

"*I was testing you,*" Lexa said with a smile. A real smile.

"Six rules."

Lexa looked directly into the camera. "*I will respect your rules, Ms. Marshall.*"

"Ugh," Charleigh said with a grimace. "My students don't even call me that. At least not since my first year teaching."

Lexa's brows scrunched. "*What happened in your first year?*"

Charleigh looked across the room. The dark shadow behind the sleeping lamp didn't move. The shadow was one of many that watched from the corners of the quiet house. No matter how many lights she'd invested in, they peaked out from behind the furniture. A constant reminder that she'd never be safe.

"Some people have these fantasies about fucking a teacher on their desk. I think it's about feeling powerful when as a kid they didn't have power and the desk is like the symbol of power. My AP students last year had to write an essay about the power of a chair, so I kinda think it's like that."

Charleigh realized she was rambling when Lexa's eyes began to droop.

She looked at her own face at the bottom of the screen. "So, there was this kid. He was new, just exited from juvie. He had that type of fixation, and I was the target of his harassment most of the year until he wanted to make his fantasy come to life. He was expelled though."

Lexa's eyes scanned up and down the screen like she was studying for a final exam. "*He didn't—*"

"No," Charleigh lied. She hoped the iPad's reflection wouldn't show the heat that crept up her neck and found rest in her cheeks.

She looked at the guilt on Lexa's face. Shaking her head, she asked. "You have the teacher fantasy too, huh?"

Lexa turned away. "*I... I never stopped to think about how... I don't know... like I forget the ugliness sometimes with stuff like that. Race stuff, of course, I'm hyper-aware of what people think of my color and I know that our photoshoots are done specifically to fetishize us, but... yeah. I definitely thought about a hot teacher and a desk.*"

Charleigh placed a thumb above her lips. She tried to keep the question in, but it burned like hot sauce, so she spit it out, "Lexa, can I ask you a real question?"

"*Yeah.*"

"What do you expect to get from this? I mean, I just... I wanted to go to the game and not feel, like, I was throwing you off or, like, you thought it was something more."

Charleigh held her breath as she waited for Lexa to organize her words. She seemed to try out several different answers before she said, "*I... uh... I want to... mhmm... show you I am not a bad person.*"

"I'm just a teacher at a school no one knows about," Charleigh reminded her. "Someone like you has nothing to prove to someone like me."

"*You fake dad told me no one cares about women's basketball,*" Lexa said after a moment. "*I know teachers are underpaid, but you just said that you're a teacher like you would say you're a garbage man.*"

"I am pretty sure Waste Management pays more than Greyson Academy," Charleigh said with a half-smile.

"*Maybe that's true, but you are something special.*"

"You don't even know me."

"*No one has ever sung happy birthday to me like those kids sang to you. And that is something. I don't remember any of my high school teachers. But they love you. That one kid, the one who should be a linebacker—*"

"Bastian"

"*Gang tattoos?*"

"He's my foster sister's boyfriend."

"*Yeah. I remember that now. Well, he was ready to go back to jail for you.*" Lexa licked her teeth. "*No one is willing to go to jail for me. Shit, Emma was the one that held me down for the cops to handcuff me.*"

Charleigh studied as different emotions flashed across Lexa's face. She seemed to be practicing lines for both herself and Charleigh to determine which would give her the best outcome.

"*I want to be around you,*" was what she settled on.

Another simple statement. Something that Charleigh didn't get because no one just wanted to be around her. Even Mona realized she wasn't interesting enough to hang out with anymore. Parker would learn soon enough as well.

"I lead a really boring life." Charleigh looked around the dark room. "The fact that we ran into each other at the Escape was a fluke. I don't drink. I don't go out. I just sit at home like an old woman. Like, I legit considered learning how to knit the other day, but... Do you have any idea how expensive yarn is?"

Lexa's chuckle turned into a cough. She popped another cough drop into her mouth, then said, "*You make me want to be a better person. And there is nothing wrong with knitting. I mean, I don't know what people knit really. But I bet you'd make like a kick-ass blanket and, like, sell that shit on Esty. I buy stuff from there all the time. You should knit a blanket and I could buy it. I could prepay for the yarn and everything and I would buy the blanket for a hundred dollars.*"

Her head tilted as she looked at a woman trying to cheat on her final exam.

"First, I'm not stupid enough to be like, 'Oh yeah,' Lexa Jenson wants to buy my first blanket for the $100 it would take me to get a new phone. Second, you have been around me twice for a total of, like, 20 minutes, and after 15 of those minutes you ended up in jail and the other 5 clearly made you sick."

She dared Lexa to disagree with her.

"*Okay, yes, but...*"

"Nothing good starts with a 'but'."

"*Look, yes, I went to jail. But I needed to go there.*" Lexa sucked in her lips, then popped them out. "*I'm sorry. It shouldn't have been at the expense of you, but I needed to hit bottom, and, trust me, that cell was the bottom. And I didn't get sick from seeing you at your work. I got sick from going playing ball in the rain in my driveway.*"

Charleigh tapped her chest. "I was the one that should have been home. I shouldn't have been at the bar at all so it wasn't your—"

"*Don't say you forgive me again. You can't. You still haven't. You can't forgive me. You just gotta let me show you I'm not who you think I am. That I am worth being the player you stalk online.*"

Her eyes traced over the animal shapes in the rough plaster covering the ceiling. She'd created a zoo, composing a hundred different stories of Joey seeing the various animals for the first time. Several of them were tales of Joey doing the thing she was told not to do, like climbing the rope with the chimps. The child she imagined was just like her, every don't do that as a new challenge.

"So, you're telling me what I can and can't do now. If I remember correctly that ended up with you in handcuffs last time."

"*I mean, yeah, I guess I am. But Emma said it was as bad as everyone thinks it is, and I didn't want to believe it, but you were scared of me yesterday. I saw it. And I think... I think I needed to see that you were scared to believe it was. So, you can't forgive me because what I did to you was unforgivable, and if you forgive me, then I can forgive myself, and I can't forgive myself and be a better person. Not really.*"

"So... I'm a reminder of your mistake. You need to be around me to punish you." A single blonde eyebrow rose.

"*I mean when you say it like that...*" Lexa looked back up at the screen. Her lips pulled into a flirty smirk.

"Are you, like, a sex addict?" Charleigh's hand slapped over her mouth. "I... sorry. I know you didn't mean—"

"*Addict, no.*" Lexa groaned. "*But I won't lie that going two weeks without it has been... frustrating.*"

Charleigh's thighs clenched. Her desire for that flirty smile she'd fantasized about so often was just a reminder of how long it had been. "Try almost two years."

Lexa's eyes bulged. "*You haven't had sex in two years?*"

"No." Charleigh chewed on her lip. "You were going to be the first. It was supposed to be like a dream come true. Celebrity crush wanted to have sex with me even though I'm a nobody."

She shook her head. "I made a promise to myself I wouldn't be the girl that other people get to have sex with for fun. I wish I could say that was why I wanted you to stop, but... it doesn't matter. Look, I need to know, what do you really expect from this? Is this just a more elaborate way to mark the teacher off your check list or are you looking for something else?"

"*I don't honestly know.*" The brown eyes that rose were red, and the bags under looked heavier. "*To get to know you. Maybe see a movie. Go to a Cardinal's game. Take a hike in Sedona. The food truck festival in Chandler is coming up next month. I guess, I just want to hang out with you.*"

"Those all sound like dates," Charleigh whispered.

"*I have never been on a date before,*" Lexa answered.

Charleigh shook her head at the lie. "Sylvia Winters never took you on a date? I find that hard to believe."

"*Long story or short?*" Lexa asked.

Charleigh looked at the alarm clock. They'd been talking for almost a half hour, and she felt guilty for keeping Lexa up so long. "Summary version."

Lexa sat up and she held the phone out. She inhaled deeply, and words slipped out with all the air in her lungs. "*Kayla, the woman I was with at the bar... Well, we met in college. She said she was Via's sister, and she could introduce me. I had followed Via's career in high school, and so I agreed. Kayla took me to my first Devils game, then afterward we went to Via's house for a pool party.*"

With a sigh, Lexa continued with a faster tempo. "*I thought we would go and maybe I would get an autograph, but Via.... She actually looked at me when I talked.*"

"I've met her."

Lexa's eyes shot back at the phone. "*How?*"

"She owns I think the land Greyson Academy is on. And I met her because I won the Winter's Student Grant for school. It's how I paid for college. There was, like, an award dinner and I have a photo of her and I in my classroom from when she gave me my scholarship."

"*Oh.*"

"Sorry, I... uh... I interrupted."

"Oh, yeah. Well, that Saturday Via asked me to say the night, and like you said... it was like getting to spend a night with my basketball crush. And after that, every day she had a plan, and every day I stayed until the summer was over. And even then, she still had a plan. We didn't go out to, like, dinners unless they were with her friends, and when she went away for business, she called each morning to check in with me. I went back to school, and she just called every day and came to get me when she was in town, and I stayed with her.

"It was, like, we were just together. She came to the games and then would drive me back to her house. She would cook and go over what she saw, and we would watch ESPN or some murder documentary. Then she would take me back to my dorm room, and we just kept the routine until I joined the draft after my third season."

Lexa glanced up at Charleigh. She licked her lips as she confessed, *"I quit school when we got engaged after the draft because I didn't need school with a career, and then we were married. We were only together during the season, and she would walk me to the plane at the end of the season, and I would be in another country, then a different one the season after that. Then she got traded, and, I mean, you know what happened with Kayla so... she sent me her ring and divorce papers, and that's... the story."*

Lexa's gaze was fixed somewhere else like she was watching her relationship on fast forward. Then her eyes snapped up.

"I have never told anyone that before."

"Thank you for trusting me with it."

Lexa looked at her lap. *"I know that I still have a lot of work to do on myself and, like, groveling and shit, but do you think... I mean... would you ever like... let me take you out?"*

The girl in the bottom corner of the screen looked down, ashamed and scared. She too had never been on a real date, never held a relationship. Never been anything to anyone, let alone someone like Lexa.

"Lexa." She held her breath for a moment. Gathered her words to make sure it was right. "Right now, I'm a new shiny thing for you to fixate on. I think you should know that being in my life means... there's something you should know before you—"

Charleigh didn't get to explain that it wasn't just her. That her world was barely over three feet tall and added an s to the end of every word because Lexa cut her off.

"No, I get it. I wouldn't want to go out with me either. That's why I have to show you that I'm better than what you see online... and that night."

Lexa wiped her face and then searched for something off-screen. The empty water bottle appeared. She tried to drink the last drizzle but choked when nothing else came out. Her choke turned into another fit, the wet cough more like a bark now.

"It's not that I don't want to go on a date with you. We just live in different worlds. You have your bars and you're traveling, and I.... I have never even been out of Arizona."

A smile crept up Lexa's plush lips. Her pink tongue soothed the chapped skin before, she started to sing, "*I can show you the world...Shiny... shimmering spleenahhhh—*" the serenade was cut off by a wide-mouthed yawn.

Lexa rubbed her face with the hand not holding the phone and leaned back against the tower of pillows. "*I think the drugs kicked in,*" she said.

"You should go to bed, goofball." Charleigh bit her lip as Lexa's lids started to shut. Her breathing was ragged, but at least she wasn't coughing.

She could get used to this. Watching the woman fall asleep with her. She'd never fallen asleep with someone before, well, besides Mona, but that didn't count because she slept in a twin bed across the room and snored like a Mac truck.

"*Will I see you tomorrow?*" Lexa mumbled.

She would love that. She knew, though, that after the Devils won Lexa would take to the streets, and she'd find someone else to ask on a date. Maybe that was a good thing though. Charleigh could be important for one more night. A night to remember before she came back to her house as the rest of the world continued to grow up without her.

"I'll see you tomorrow," she whispered.

"*Good.*" Lexa's eyes slid closed once more. "*Can I... your number?*"

"I don't have a phone," Charleigh reminded her.

Lexa's head slowly began to slide to the right side of the pillow. The opposite side of the bed that Charleigh slept on.

"*'Kay. Dinners after the game. Tomorrow. No... cough... medi....*" The final word's wavelength faded before it made it to the microphone.

Charleigh watched as the phone slid from Lexa's hand. The only sound was a mixture of Lexa's drug-induced breaths and Rexa's racehorse whinnies.

She ended the call and listened to the rain's lullaby. She closed her eyes and watched the new narrative she'd created. An afternoon at a lake in a place that didn't look like the desert. A little girl with a head full of curls laughed and tugged Charleigh by the hand. They are running from Lexa, hobbling after them with outstretched arms doing the zombie walk toward them. A new fairytale that didn't seem so twisted.

8

The twist came apart once more. No matter what angle she tried, Lexa couldn't position her hands to get it set for the start of the game. She had to get it right. Everything had to be in the right place, so her game wouldn't be off. They had one win and a loss. If they won tonight, she would have to get on another plane that her legs wouldn't fit in to play in New York, and she hated New York. Hated that it smelled like a sweaty human and gutter trash.

Her fingers pulled until the strands were unraveled, and then she twisted each individually in the same direction. That part was simple most of the time, except when she twisted them in opposite directions last time. That time it was hard, but this time, she got it to work. The real tricky part was when she had to twist the twists together.

She held the strands up from her head and tried to remember which way she'd twisted them to begin with. When she couldn't tell by the way they looked, she closed her eyes and tried to remember how her hands had moved. She had twisted and retwisted them so many times though, she couldn't remember.

With a, "fuck it," and a "counter-fucking-clockways," Lexa started the final step of the two-strand twist. As they wrapped together, it began to look like a snake instead of a rope, and as soon as she let go, it unraveled.

Her palms pressed against the counter, and she cinched her eyes shut. When she opened them, the orange container with a red top stared back at her from the hygiene bag. Her hand slammed against the counter, and she reached for the pill bottle.

"Can I just do it for you?" Lexa heard the music spilling through the doorway to the locker room.

She found Danaya's chestnut eyes in the mirror. The trade from Chicago who sent her ex-wife, Sylvia packing. A rookie fresh from a down south college who had only ever known Lexa as a cheating jerk. Her soon-to-be ex-wife since the papers were delivered again. Well, if she signed them, which she hadn't.

A part of her felt guilty for asking Charleigh out when she had torn the second set of divorce papers up. She blamed the cough syrup on the whole thing, but the part that didn't feel guilty wondered what dating someone who couldn't buy out a whole restaurant would be like. That was the thing about Charleigh. She was the opposite of Sylvia.

"Come on," Danaya said, pulling Lexa from her comparison of the two blondes she desperately wanted to spend time with.

Danaya's locs were set in place, but her nimble fingers routinely resecured them before a game. An act that made Lexa's jealousy thicker, since her white mother had never been in a state of mind to teach Lexa how to manage the hair that came with the pigment the woman couldn't understand.

Lexa's hand closed around the bag, hiding the pills.

"Come on," Danaya said again with a nod of her head back to the locker room of people who still barely spoke to her.

The music in the locker room beat into her chest. The playlist Sylvia had created before leaving the team after three games was still the pre-game soundtrack, so everyone could still feel like their leader was with them when they'd been left with Lexa to fill her shoes.

Danaya grabbed the seat cushion from Lexa's locker and dropped it on the floor. It was there specifically for this purpose, and over the years there had always been someone there to twist her hair for her while her wife would lay across from her, stretching her legs.

Fingers pulled apart her curls to create a rough part as her neck strained backward. Lexa stared at the purple and orange ceiling and tried not to squirm.

"You got the good hair, Lex," Danaya said, pulling the strands apart.

"Thanks," Lexa said, but she'd never been sure what the girls had meant when they said that.

Danaya used a comb to carve a part against Lexa's tender scalp before the woman's fingers dipped into a container of holding gel. Lexa couldn't see how she did it, but the practiced hands moved with ease, maneuvering the strands and roping the two into a full twist in a single motion.

"I got a girl that can do you up right, so you don't have to do this before every game," she offered.

Emma sat on the floor across from them. The center's legs stretched out as she leaned forward in Sylvia's spot. When she sat up, she said, "That bitch too bougie to ever go see your girl. She spends her time getting that good hair silk pressed to fit in with the white women she's always chasing. Speaking of white women, did Sylvia stop making your appointments for you, 'cause you lookin' busted?"

Making appointments had never been Lexa's responsibility. She was supposed to follow the schedule on her phone. But her calendar hadn't been updated since June, so her silk press hadn't happened all season. She didn't know the first thing about finding a stylist.

"How do I make an appointment?" Lexa asked. "With your girl? I've been thinking about trying something new... maybe some braids or twists."

Danaya hummed as she applied some Jam to her fingers. "I'll text her and see if she booked up. You send me a photo of what you want so she can slot you for the right time. She can silk press you if you want."

"What's the easiest to take care of?" Lexa asked.

With a sharp tug, Danaya said, "Probably some box braids."

Lexa wondered what Charleigh would think about her in braids. As she thought about the white girl coming to the game, she realized Emma would be pissed she hadn't said anything.

"So, remember when I went to that school thing on Wednesday?" Lexa asked Emma.

Emma leaned over her leg, reaching down to hold her foot. "Yeah."

Lexa leaned into Danaya's touch, fighting back the cough, threatening to overtake her.

"So, the girl from the bar... she was the teacher. I didn't know she was the one I was going to see until I was there and I... I gave her tickets to tonight's game," she explained.

Emma sat up and stared at Lexa. "Did you fuck it up? The birthday visit?"

With a deep sigh, Lexa leaned forward. Her head was pulled back by Danaya's grip on her hair. She felt around her duffle bag and pulled out the iPhone box.

"I startled her, and she dropped her phone. When we were talking on Instagram last night, she said it was a birthday present from her dad and she had to wait to afford to get it fixed."

Lexa felt like her scalp was on fire as Danaya twisted her hair even tighter. She winced but Danaya tisked, then said, "Stop being a crybaby. It's gotta be tight if it's gonna stay."

"So, you stalked her on Instagram, gave her tickets to the game so she would have to see you, and now you bought her a phone?" Emma asked.

Lexa licked her lips. "Yeah."

"So, is she a ball bunny or your rebound?" Emma asked.

"What?" Lexa's lip curled up over her teeth. "Neither. I broke her phone, and the tickets were because I forgot the damn ball Phyllis gave me to give to her for her birthday."

"So, you ruined her birthday and you're trying to make up for it. That doesn't sound like you," Emma stated, leaning to her other side. "It sounds like you met a girl that didn't give you sex, so now you tryin' to buy her attention. You're never going to change."

Lexa stared at the box. She hadn't expected Charleigh to sleep with her for it. Well, at some point, she'd like to sleep with her, but she wanted to take her out. Especially since her marriage was possibly over. She could take Charleigh out, then if it didn't go well, she could focus on making Sylvia love her again.

"Why can't you just let her be? Like you don't take care of yourself. You're bouncing off the damn walls all day and night, and you're going to put her through that. Just like you put Sylvia through that."

She'd put Sylvia through so much. And Sylvia had known what she was getting into. She'd known from the beginning. Lexa looked at her bag where the hygiene kit was poking out of the top. Her sanity within that bottle would swallow her wife's hurt from ricocheting through her skull with one pill.

Ex-wife. She sent the divorce papers again. UPS Overnight this time. Lexa swallowed the reality Sylvia wasn't coming back for her this time. Her season had ended, and she should have already been here.

"Okay, ladies. Circle up," their coach called.

Danaya twisted the remainder of Lexa's hair into a bun and fastened it tightly. "All done."

The silence surrounded Lexa when the women left her on the floor and joined their teammates. No one cared Lexa stood outside the circle, even though her place had always been in the center. She lost the right to lead the pre-game chant when the managers began begging other teams to take her off their hands.

An MVP trophy meant nothing when she embarrassed the organization the night she was celebrated. It's why Charleigh was even at the bar— to celebrate her.

The team walked out of the tunnel and passed the crowd of children lining their path. Lexa was at the end of the trail. Her eyes searched over the little girls and women screaming her name. She stopped a few times to sign the jerseys of the women who held out Sharpies to her.

The seats she'd reserved for the teacher were empty when she made it to the court. She searched the arena seats to see if the woman was making her way toward the floor, but Lexa couldn't find the honey-haired head in the crowd. Five minutes of warm-ups was just enough time for the disappointment to shift from simmering frustration into boiling anger.

'Biggest fan, my ass,' she told herself as the three-pointer bounced off the rim. 'Just a ball bunny after my money.'

The buzzer rang out over the crowd and the balls were tossed to the teens working at the game. She'd missed every single shot, but she'd still start. She'd start because she was Lexa fucking Jenson. And no ungrateful bitch was going to steal away her win tonight.

Winning was all she had left.

Winning had not happened. Not when Lexa spent the first fifteen minutes searching the stands for the blonde. She didn't hit a shot in the first five minutes and spent ten on the bench as her blood boiled over being stood up.

She was choking on her own mucus, and her lungs burned. It was halfway through the second quarter before Charleigh made it to the game. She'd missed most of Lexa's playing time in that quarter too, which was cut short after a coughing fit sent her back to the bench. The medic gave her a hit from an inhaler, which at least made it, so she didn't feel like she was going to pass out.

After the game, she just wanted to leave. But leaving wasn't on the agenda for Emma, who'd stopped to ask Charleigh to dinner on their way to the locker room, and Charleigh had looked at Lexa.

"Are you coming?" she asked Lexa.

Emma answered for Lexa though. Not giving her the chance to tell the blonde bitch, she'd be going to drink with normal people. Not stupid girls that put together rules like Lexa was supposed to let her choke to death to keep from being touched.

Lexa pushed the phone box to the bottom of her bag and slung it over her shoulder. Danaya had stayed behind to ensure Lexa didn't bail, but the scene they returned to solidified for Lexa that her chance with Charleigh had been stolen by the center leaning over the blonde against the locker room doorway.

Danaya's chin pressed against her chest, while Lexa's nails dug grooves in her palms. If she hadn't already been betrayed by the blonde, the gentle laugh between the two would have done it.

"Charleigh has never been to Coach's," Emma stated. "So, I figured we could just walk there and get dinner."

Locs hung around Danaya's face as she mumbled, "Sounds good."

The tired ball players led Charleigh through their private exit to the mostly empty parking garage. They paused only long enough to leave the duffle bags in their vehicles, and then Emma pulled Charleigh's backpack from the smaller woman's arm and slung it over her shoulder.

The woman with all the warnings to stay away from the teacher leaned into the conversation she led, asking how Charleigh first became interested in the game.

Lexa and Danaya trudged behind them; their heads hung in defeat. With Coach's Sports Bar and Grill across the street, Lexa figured at least she wasn't committed to watching Emma take Charleigh home with her. The rookie crushing on the center would get to listen to Emma clean the cobwebs from Charleigh's pussy though.

The table farthest from the bar wasn't big enough for the three Devils, but Charleigh had already sat down. As Emma hung Charleigh's pack on the back of the woman's chair, Lexa and Danaya fought for space under the table. Lexa ended up with most of the legroom as she plopped down as far away from the blonde as possible. When Charleigh didn't look up from the menu covering half her face, Lexa added it to her list of things she didn't like about the woman.

As the waitress in the tight black skirt approached, Lexa smiled smugly. Red-painted lips lifted in a sultry smile, while Lexa measured her bust and waist. At least there was something to occupy her attention while Emma tried to seal the deal with Charleigh Marshall.

"Hey ladies, can I get you something to drink?"

Lexa ran her tongue over her lips when the waitress stopped alongside her. Not that she would use it on someone so far below her, but it was part of the game. A new game where the teacher was subbed out for a waitress who paid attention to her.

"Just water for me," Emma ordered. When no one else spoke up, she asked, "DayDay, you want a water or a Sprite?"

"Sprite." Danaya rolled a loc between her thumb and index finger. She glanced over at the waitress, then at Lexa staring at the tits in her face. Then she mumbled, "And some fucking space."

The waitress took a step back from Danaya, only pressing herself further into Lexa's bubble. Reaching over and running a finger over the waitress' hand, Lexa said, "Can I get a beer, honey?"

She didn't look at Charleigh. She didn't look because she didn't care what the blonde thought. She was only there because Emma made her come out, and if she had to sit here, she was going to order what she wanted. Damn those stupid rules. Besides the rules were so the woman would come to the game. The game was done and after Charleigh went home with Emma, she'd never have to see her again.

"What kind?" the waitress asked, not moving from Lexa's caress.

The thin red lip disappeared between overlapping teeth that Lexa didn't notice because she was studying the heavy bust threatening to tear out of the work-issued shirt. Lexa glanced at the name tag pinned above the nipple poking through the material, and said, "Your favorite... Callie."

Charleigh cleared her throat. She waited for Callie to look at her, before she asked, "Can I please have an iced tea?"

Callie scanned over Charleigh like an uninteresting playbook before turning back to Lexa. She placed her hand on Lexa's shoulder, sending a hoard of roaches crawling under Lexa's skin. She fought the urge to knock it away when Charleigh's stare fixated on the contact.

"So, a water, sprite, iced tea, and my favorite beer for our hometown star."

The woman walked away with Lexa's eyes fixated on the skirt lifting with each step. She stared until her shin erupted into a fiery pain.

Lexa shot up in her seat. Her knee on the other leg smacked against the table. Danaya and Charleigh jumped when the table lifted the menus in their hands up and into their laps.

"What the fuck, Delango?" Lexa barked, rubbing the lump already forming on her shin.

"We came out to have dinner," Emma stated. She pushed the menu at Lexa. "Just don't be a jerk."

Lexa inhaled as much air as she could, then pushed it all out in a huff. She'd get this done faster if she just did what Emma told her to.

The menu finally dropped from Charleigh's face. She pushed the hair from her forehead. A polite smile looked to be painted on her lips. Her eyes had lost the sparkle from the Instagram call, and Lexa swallowed, running her tongue over the inside of her cheeks.

"I'm sorry you lost." The blue eyes searched Lexa's face. "But at least you get to play another home game, right?"

The fake smile and the carefully picked-over words were a version of Charleigh Lexa didn't want to know. She turned away from the blonde to Danaya, staring at the menu vacantly. Her eyes were not even moving around to pretend like she was present.

"Yeah," Lexa offered to avoid getting kicked again.

"Playing in front of a home crowd is always better. We are not out of it yet," Emma said, filling the space of the bubble around them. "Once we win this round, then we move into the semi-finals."

"Are all crowds the same?" Charleigh asked. "Like, do they root hard for the home team and ignore the visitors?"

Callie returned with the drinks before Emma could lie to make Charleigh feel like the home crowd was special. It didn't matter where they played; all the fans sounded the same. The voices of the crowd just bounced off the floor during a game, and it was impossible to hear who was being cheered on. That was why being on time mattered. The only time Lexa would have heard Charleigh cheering for her was during warm-ups, but Charleigh hadn't given a damn about her.

Lexa leaned back to give Callie room to set their drinks on the table, only to be rewarded with the woman's tits millimeters from Lexa's mouth. The bottle of beer on the tray did not get set on the table with the other drinks. It was placed in Lexa's hand, fingers grazing over the stumpy unpolished tips.

"Can you give us a minute?" Emma requested. Callie dropped her eyes to Lexa but abided by the request.

Lexa scanned the label of the IPA, instantly regretting letting the waitress choose. She raised the bottle to her lips, making a show of taking the first drink. The bubbly harshness tasted like shit; Callie's favorite beer being Lexa's least. But she swallowed it.

She glanced over at Charleigh to find the woman searching for something in the backpack she'd brought. When the blonde didn't find what she was looking for, she pushed back from the table. Her hand dug in her front pocket, then the other side until she pulled out a wad of cash and dropped it on the table.

She tugged the strap of the backpack on, and said, "Thanks for the invite but I forgot that I promised my sister I wouldn't take the last train. That should cover everyone's drink."

No one could say anything before her body zigzagged through the tables. She lost her balance when Callie pushed through the narrow space toward her. Charleigh grabbed the tray of drinks Callie had been carrying and pulled it into herself, saving the waitress from being covered in backwashed beer and watered-down liquor. The glasses tittered on the tray in Charleigh's hands as she set it on the table and held her hip, which had struck the metal surface.

She looked to whisper an apology for the collision that wasn't her fault. The purple jersey with Lexa's last name left droplets of alcohol on the floor as she set back on her path and left the bar.

"You're a fucking dick." Emma's spittle flew from her mouth as she pointed to the door. "What happened to you showing people you're not an asshole?"

Lexa rolled her eyes, then reminded Emma, "You're the one that said she needed to stay away from me. So, she's away from me. You should be happy."

Emma's chair shook the table as she shoved it in. She grabbed the cash Charleigh had left to cover their drinks. The bills crunched in her hand.

"I told you to leave her alone and you didn't. I told you she deserved to know the truth about what she was getting into with you," Emma growled. "At no point did I say be an asshole."

Without even a word to Danaya, Emma chased after Charleigh.

Lexa smiled into the mouth of the bottle. "She's going to go be princess charming and you'll be listening to them fuck tonight if she doesn't leave your scrub ass here."

When Danaya didn't react, Lexa prodded at the girl who'd been under the center just a week ago. "I give it two weeks and you'll be coming out for breakfast to find that blonde hair fisted in Emma's hands as she gets eaten out on the couch."

Lexa tilted her head, wondering how close her sharp words were to the bull's eyes. Danaya wasn't in tears, so Lexa tried a different tactic.

"Do you stay up listening to her fucking the girls she brings home, playing with yourself as her headboard bangs against the wall? Or does she let you play with the whores she fucks when she's done?"

Dark eyes rose slowly from the table to Lexa's smug face. Words slathered in venom were catapulted at Lexa's egotistical fortress. "You knew she came out tonight to spend time with you and you just didn't care. Just like last time."

Just like last time echoed in Lexa's mind, bouncing from one corner of the emptiness back to the other side. Just like last time, when Charleigh did everything right and Lexa just didn't care. Lexa just didn't care to listen to her.

Danaya was holding her glass so hard Lexa worried she may shatter it. Her other hand shot up the door, "You're sitting here talking about that woman like she's just a hole to fuck. But she's a fucking person that you hurt, Lexa. You tried to fucking rape her at the bar and we gave you a goddamn pass."

Lexa sucked her teeth. The tangled mess of words slid off the walls she'd built around herself. She could take the hits. Her parents had said worse in her entire life.

"Like you fucking cared about the bar. You sat there and watched. Is that your thing, to watch?" Lexa snapped back. She took another drink, watching Danaya's jaw grind back and forth. "Or were you jealous that I chose her over you? If that's the problem, then we can solve that shit right now. I'll take you back to my place and clean the cobwebs out of your cunt, so you can stop walking around like a bitch in heat."

She should have seen it coming but she was busy trying to come up with something shitty to say. Her body lurched away from the cold soda seeping through her sweatshirt and the crotch of her jeans. The chair moved with her, until it reached the tipping point.

There was nothing to grab onto as Lexa felt her body falling in slow motion. The metal crashed against the concrete floor. Lexa's head was only protected from a full concussion by the cushion of her hair.

Danaya stood over her. "You think I want to fuck you? Bitch, they brought me here to replace you."

Looking down at Lexa once more, she unleashed more of her truth. "You're a busted wanna-be that chooses to destroy everything good in your life."

Danaya ripped her jacket from the back of her chair as she kept up her lashing, "You not only want to ruin your life but everyone around you. You say you're not a monster but look the fuck around. You're the goddamn villain in this story, hell-bent on bringing everyone down around you."

She doesn't turn when she throws the last dagger, lodging a knife in Lexa's chest to drain the wickedness poisoning her soul. "I'm better than you, Lexa. I am fucking better than you will ever be, and next year when you're finally gone, that arena will be filled with fans who have forgotten you even existed."

Danaya walked through the semi-circle of angry lesbians and confused old white dudes. Eyes everywhere were watching as Lexa pushed herself up from the ground. Pushed and slipped in the spilled soda. She hit the ground once more. Her body knew it would have been better just to lay on the ground until it swallowed her. Die right there, especially when Lexa saw the phone cameras all angled at her. Muscles, already tired from the game, shook as she pushed herself up.

"Fuck," she muttered, but Callie was there after a moment to help her up. Lexa looked her over, and she could tell the waitress was trying to make something out of what she just heard.

The wallet was out of her pocket, and the cash was pushed into the woman's hand. "That should take care of it," Lexa said and started to leave. She started to leave but Callie's hand was on her again, and this time Lexa was pissed.

"Are you fucking deaf?" She snapped her arm out of the woman's grasp. "I don't give a shit about anyone. I'll forget you by tomorrow even if I fuck you tonight because you mean nothing to me. You're tops a 4 and that's only 'cause your tits are hanging out and you just tried to put them in my mouth."

The pale-skinned hand collapsed against Lexa's cheek. But it was the wrong hand. It was the wrong hand that hit her. Because it should have been Charleigh. Charleigh had every right to hit Lexa, and all she did was offer forgiveness. Forgave her, showed up for her, and cheered for her.

Lexa pressed her hand to her cheek and rubbed, feeling the pain deepen. Letting it fill the void within. The angry waitress opened her mouth, but Lexa cut her off with, "I deserved that."

The closest door led Lexa to the small fenced-in patio. She used her height to her advantage and hopped the spiked rail. The pocket of the faded Devil's sweatshirt hooked on the small protrusion from above the railing. She moved to leave another scene she'd caused but got pulled back.

She tugged the fabric sharply. It didn't come loose, though. She pulled harder, but it didn't give the way it should. Instead, the material screamed as it was pulled apart. The metal prong had torn a hole from the pocket to the elastic band around her waist. The bottom no longer clung, instead hung off her. She played with the tear and closed her eyes to fight back the tears.

'It's just a sweatshirt,' she thought.

'It's just a fucking sweatshirt,' she chastised.

"It's just a goddamn, fucking sweatshirt," she shouted.

Except it was Sylvia's sweatshirt. The only thing she'd left after the photos went viral along with the videos of Kayla's tongue down her throat. The moment she ruined her marriage. The moment she decided to hurt Sylvia. She decided to hurt her as close to home as possible by pulling her wife's little sister by the ass into another kiss that she led. She reviewed every detail as she walked down the dark street.

The tears started to fall as Lexa walked across the empty dark street toward the parking garage. They hit the concrete after rolling off her chin silently.

Her shoes scraped against the ramp, but the voices bouncing off the pillars drowned out the sound of her steps. The self-made bubble of isolation wasn't soundproof, and the voices grew louder the closer she got to the level where the team parked their cars.

She saw Danaya first, standing a few feet out from the Escalade. Emma leaned against the SUV. A blonde head tucked into her chest because of course she got her to come back with her. Rescued her from walking through the dark streets to the train stop a block away.

It should have been Lexa taking her home after the game. She was the one who asked her to come, Charleigh came like she said she would. The anger she'd felt now filled her lungs like helium gas, making her feel like a clown with a painted frown. Because Charleigh was letting Emma hug her. Of course, Emma could hug her.

'She's only scared of me, the fucking monster,' Lexa reminded herself.

"Look, she just drops when things don't go her way," Emma explained to Charleigh. "You didn't do anything wrong. She doesn't handle any loss well, and DayDay and I backed her into a corner going out. It's not your fault."

They were talking about her. About how she wasn't normal. She hated when people talked about her like she wasn't there. Even though they don't know she's there, she can't help but feel smaller than the woman who had shown up.

Danaya doesn't say anything. She said it all to Lexa in front of the crowd. But she was there to support Charleigh.

They were apologizing for her, shouldering the blame just like they did with the bar. Lexa had pulled them into her cyclical cone of destruction making her way through their lives and Charleigh's.

They were trying to be her friends. Something she had sworn off when Kayla told her she was a big star. But they had been there. Been there the whole time and were now doing what she had said she would do. They were being better, while she'd chosen to act monstrously.

More tears broke through the damn she built with pussy and booze. Guilt and sorrow spilled from a source that seemed never-ending. Her breath caught as she held the concrete post to support herself.

She choked for air. The flood on her face seemed to be blocking her throat, but then there were arms around her. Pale arms with six freckles on the back of one hand in the shape of the little dipper. Arms that were too small for a ball player, and were wrapped around her as Lexa's heart tried to break through another barricade. It fought like it wanted to be free from within her. Leave her like everyone did.

Lexa couldn't stop the tears from falling. She didn't want to. She didn't want to stop the pain from filling her to the brim and overflowing because at least then it was something. It was something besides the combustion of spider webs, freeing ghosts of the past in continuous reminders to echo through her empty soul that she was not important, and that she ruined things.

"I'm going to do better," was all she could say. Even then she was not sure if it came out.

Charleigh held Lexa's head and let Lexa touch her. She held Lexa, and said, "You have to because you're important. You matter and you have to do better so the world can see how amazing you are."

Emma's hand pulled Lexa to her feet and out of Charleigh's arms. She dug into Lexa's pocket until she found her keys. She didn't give Lexa time to fuck up again. She just guided her by her arm to the passenger's seat of Lexa's Range Rover.

Lexa could hear Emma's lecture about driving before she gave Danaya the keys to her Escalade. Charleigh had protested. Explained she was used to riding the train after games and had only come to the garage to make sure Emma got in her car safely, but Emma had been a good friend. The type of friend Charleigh deserved.

"I would never be able to live with myself if something happened to you tonight when I made you stay out so late. Just let Danaya take you home," Emma pleaded with the woman.

Lexa watched as Charleigh's shoulders slumped. She pulled out her broken phone from her pocket, but Emma shook her head and handed the girl her phone. "Just use mine," Emma told Charleigh.

The bile burned in Lexa's throat. The phone was broken because of her. She'd heard the glass shatter in the classroom when she'd shook the woman in front of her students. She closed her eyes and tried to think of a way to get Emma to give Charleigh the replacement she'd bought her. She'd destroyed so much of the woman's life, that the least she could do was replace the phone.

But Emma didn't get into the car until Danaya was already pulling away.

The lights of the Range Rover illuminated the cab and Emma crawled into Lexa's seat. Emma's hands twisted the steering wheel.

"The worst part of all of this, Lex, is that that woman thinks everything you do to her is her fault."

Lexa wiped her face, the headache returning as the meds she'd taken earlier that afternoon began to wear off.

Emma looked over at Lexa before putting the car in reverse. "You owe her an apology. A real apology. Not bullshit where you just say you're going to fix it. You're not fixing shit if you can't even say you're sorry and actually be sorry. She needs to know that what you did wasn't anything to do with her. She needs someone to tell her that so maybe she'll not fall into the hands of some abusive fuck that feeds off that shit. You want to fix something. Fix that by taking responsibility for the shit you do."

Lexa chewed at the skin inside her cheek. "She's never going to talk to me again."

"I doubt that." Emma sucked her teeth. "For some fucked up reason, that girl worships you. Which means she has terrible taste in women. But it also means that she'll probably let you say you're sorry."

9

Charleigh closed the work-issued laptop, then slipped out the back door of her classroom when the parking lot had mostly emptied. She skirted around the school through the brush until she was covered by the cornfields.

The walk to her ancient farmhand's home was four miles. With the car refusing to start again, Charleigh was left with her own feet to get her to work and back as the summer wound down. The shade of the fields made it almost bearable.

She stripped the cardigan off as sweat slid down her spine. The leaves of the stalks only moved with her steps as she listened carefully for the fearful rattle of a snake.

The chill of fall was still weeks away, but she started to plan for her new reality of walking every day until she had enough to replace the alternator. Tomorrow she'd trek to the outlet mall to get a new pair of shoes for the walk. Hopefully, Famous Footwear will have some sneakers on clearance. She needed to pick up some clothes for Joey anyway to show she was contributing to the child's needs. She could get more if she went to Goodwill. She'd map it out and see if she could get there instead. They would have sneakers for cheaper as well.

As she approached the house, she noticed the Escalade parked in the driveway. She swallowed the reality that Danaya Tanzon hadn't forgotten where she lived. She'd figured after she hadn't heard from Lexa in a week, her friends had finally talked some sense into the woman. Charleigh wasn't that lucky.

She stepped out of the field closest, walking past the dead Accord. She stopped before she got to the door when not one, but three basketball players ceased their hushed conversation.

Lexa's head hung as she toed the gravel under the toe of her giant Nike slides. With a smile forced on her face, Charleigh cinched her backpack on tighter.

"Hi," Charleigh said to the uninvited guests.

Emma held out the packing tape-wrapped phone to Charleigh. "I found this lodged between the seat and console. Figured you'd want it back."

Charleigh took the phone and nodded. "Thanks. I thought I lost it in my house."

"Can I see the puppy today?" Danaya asked.

Charleigh laughed and nodded. Danaya had wanted to play with Rexa last time but said Emma would be pissed if she brought the car back late and the seats were covered in dog hair.

She made her way up the rickety steps. The lock and her did the familiar dance. She pushed the key in at a slightly downward angle, then jiggled twice before she twisted.

"She's not a puppy though, so if you want your clothes unmarred, give her a minute to work out her wiggles," Charleigh said, still holding the door closed as Rexa pawed at the wood.

"No problem," Danaya said, practically bouncing in her shoes.

The door was barely open before Rexa was out. Her huge dog arms wrapped around Charleigh, who reciprocated the hug. She trapped the lumpy brown head to her chest as they danced a two-step.

"It's a dog!" Danaya squealed like she had never seen one before.

Rexa noticed the woman, and she dropped from Charleigh's arms. Approaching the stranger with more caution than she ever used with the blonde or her sister. She sniffed Emma's leg, then Lexa's crotch. Lexa's whole body tensed as she put her hands over herself and avoided looking at the dog.

Danaya held out her hand and Rexa moved forward. She sniffed it. Licked it. And jumped up to hug Danaya too. Danaya didn't shy away, taking the pup in her arms. Her lower lip jutted out, and she looked at Emma.

"Can we please get a dog?" she pleaded.

Emma's eyes grew wide. And Lexa laughed next to her mumbling under her breath, "I bet she'll forget the dog if you give her some chocolate dick."

Emma shoved Lexa out of the way and told Danaya, "No dogs. Against the lease, remember?"

Then everyone was staring at Charleigh. Her small frame blocked the equally small door. She pulled it back by the handle revealing the partially lit house. Holding out her hand, she said, "This place wasn't built for giants so watch your heads."

The pit lay down on a bed in the middle of the floor. A TV remote in her mouth. Danaya flopped down next to the dog, gathering all the shed on her black sweatshirt. Charleigh smiled as she realized Emma would make Danaya strip before getting back into the Escalade.

As the curtains were pulled back, Lexa's eyes grew, and Charleigh realized Lexa was probably overwhelmed with her life. She looked back at the orange plaid couch with frayed arms and her butt print in the left cushion resting against the only window in the room, then the dilapidated scarlet recliner she'd found at Goodwill.

Lexa walked along the wall of books previously blocked by the open door. Fingers ran over the titles with no recognizable organization strategy beyond the small stickers on the bottom of each spine. She stopped at the spine of a Harry Potter book. It was one of the few hardback covers on the shelf, worn on the edges, and possessed a small purple sticker fixed at the bottom edge. Lexa seemed to be looking for something, and she searched the shelves, stopping at each Harry Potter book and tapping the sticker along the bottom. Charleigh felt like a puzzle, and Lexa was searching for the pieces to put her together.

Her attention was diverted to Rexa and Danaya wrestling on the floor. Then turned back to Lexa as the wood under them shook and the bookcases rattled. A frame teetered from where it leaned against some books, then fell into Lexa's outstretched hand. Charleigh swallowed as she watched Lexa study the photo of the little button-nosed girl with wild blonde curls.

She smiled and set the photo back down. As she continued down the shelves, Lexa picked up a small unlabeled plastic trophy. A piece of a memory. Lexa held it up to her, but before the woman could ask whatever question she had, Emma interrupted.

"Can I use your bathroom?"

She pointed down the short dark hallway and told Emma, "Bathroom is down there."

Charleigh turned back to find Lexa's lips curled up at Danaya sprawled on the floor with the giant pit bull lying across her chest. A stream of drool dripped from the floppy lips onto Danaya's sweatshirt.

"Don't like dogs?" Charleigh asked cautiously. She held out her hand for the trophy her students had given her the year prior when she'd been left out of the thank-you to each faculty member at the graduation ceremony.

Lexa handed back the trophy, raising her eyes to Charleigh. Warm earthy eyes like fresh soil to be buried in. She felt like a jawbreaker was stuck in her throat, and no matter how many times she swallowed, it wouldn't get smaller.

Emma was back from the shortest piss ever. Her hands pressed into her pockets, eyes taking in the room where her head nearly touched the ceiling.

"I like your place," Emma said. "You read all those books?"

"Thank you," Charleigh said. Tucking a lock of hair behind her ear, she was grateful the mark the woman had left on her neck had finally faded. "Yeah. Many I read in high school and college, but a lot are proof copies from local authors. They do this, like, Christmas party that is, like, a teacher appreciation event and they give out copies. I usually end up with two or three copies of a book and since my classroom library is full, I keep the spares here."

Emma's stomach grumbled, just loud enough to be heard over Danaya's puppy talk. She smiled sheepishly at Charleigh. "I guess we should get going. Thank you for the bathroom."

"I have Egos... or I can make some Mac and Cheese," Charleigh offered. She looked at the bright doorway to the kitchen. "It's not like real mac and cheese. I'm talking Kraft, well not even Kraft. I think it's the Great Value kind, which is actually worse than Kraft."

Her hand came up and pushed her hair back again. "Sorry, summers are rough when you're a teacher, so I get it if you want to go and get real food. I just feel bad because you felt like you had to drive out here to return my phone."

Charleigh moved to a backpack on the floor by the bookcase. She dug through it and pulled out a wad of crinkled bills. "Here, it's only ten bucks but it's the least I can do. I mean, it will get you, like, two gallons of gas or a Big Mac, or whatever for, like, going out of your way to bring me my phone."

Emma cupped the outstretched offer in her hands and told the blonde, "It was no big deal, and I grew up on Great Value Mac and Cheese so that sounds amazing."

Charleigh's chin dropped. Then she confessed, "I ramble when I'm nervous."

"I do too." Emma pulled Charleigh in for a hug.

The blonde's face, barely at eye level with Emma's breasts, relaxed into the embrace. She wrapped her arms around Emma. Pressing her hands flat against the woman's back until she felt the tension relax from the woman's body.

With a smile, Emma offered, "You worked all day. How about you let me make us some food?"

Charleigh nodded against her. Her arms wrapped around Emma like a lifeline. Emma's cheek dropped to rest on the top of Charleigh's head, and she said, "You really give the best hugs."

"She will...," Lexa said quietly in the shoebox-sized room of Charleigh's tiny house.

"She will what?" Charleigh asked.

Lexa searched the room for an answer to the question. Her gaze fell to the woman still on the floor with her head nuzzled into the neck of the dog. She pointed to Danaya, "She'll never let that dog go."

Charleigh read the lie on the woman's flushed cheeks.

"Can I stay forever?" Danaya begged Charleigh, and the childish tone pulled a warm smile from Emma.

Emma stepped over Danaya and ducked her head as she went through the kitchen doorway. Without asking for instructions, Emma opened the cabinets and withdrew three boxes of macaroni and cheese.

Charleigh disappeared down the hallway with her stomach grumbling. Once in her bedroom, she took a moment to breathe. She didn't have long so she pulled off her work clothes and tossed them into the pile of laundry she'd have to wash in the bathtub since she couldn't make it to the laundromat. She put on her sweatpants and pulled the string tightly realizing she was probably down another size. She added 'go to the grocery store' to her list.

10

With Charleigh gone into a room at the back of the house, Lexa made her way into the kitchen. She opened the cabinet where Emma had found the boxes. The shelves were nearly bare. A few packets of ramen, four cans of green beans, and a single blue box left. She turned back to Emma and took two boxes from the counter, putting them back on the shelf.

Emma glared at her as she growled, "What are you doing?"

Lexa pointed to the cabinet and then opened the fridge. She gestured up and down the shelves with a mostly empty carton of eggs, a jug of coffee creamer, and the only required ingredients for macaroni and cheese.

"You can't eat her food," she hissed. "You just watched her come out of a goddamn field because she is walking to and from work. How's she supposed to get to a store to replace what you eat?"

Emma held up the single box Lexa had left. "I know you're right, but I am so fucking hungry right now."

"Just make them."

Emma and Lexa looked over to find Charleigh leaning against the door jam in her baggy T-shirt and sweatpants. She pushed Lexa's arm off the refrigerator and retrieved the remaining boxes of macaroni.

Setting them on the counter, she said, "Seriously. I just haven't gone to the grocery store with my car acting up, but I will get there tomorrow. It's not too far away, and I mean in Africa kids walk five miles a day just to get water."

Neither of the women with stocked pantries at their homes could argue with Charleigh as she added the half gallon of milk about to expire and the last stick of butter to the pile of boxes. Lexa's gut twisted at the knowledge they were consuming everything Charleigh would have for the rest of the week. She couldn't press the issue though without making Charleigh feel worse than she already did.

"What's wrong with your car?" Lexa asked, unsure what else to say as they waited for the water to boil.

Charleigh shrugged. "Dunno. It's a piece of shit. It was given to me by Marcus when I moved out on my own. He never had a problem with it, but I'm not a good car owner so she's rebelling against me right now."

Lexa looked out the kitchen window to the corn stalks surrounding the fenced-in yard. "So, you walked to work and back?" Lexa asked, wondering how far the school was from the house.

"It's only, like, four miles," Charleigh said. "And the fields make it cooler. My sister said she thinks I need a new alternator, so I'll get one in a few weeks. I have to replace my phone first, so I don't miss any calls, and walking doesn't bother me."

As the water came to a boil in the dented pot, Charleigh popped up on the counter. She leaned against the wall and tucked her knee up to her chest to rest her head.

"Where'd you grow up, Emma?" Charleigh asked.

"Portland." Emma smiled as she tore open the boxes. "My mom and nana and my nieces and nephews are all up there. I have one niece that is going to be bigger than me someday. She's already playing in these showcase tournaments. It's crazy how much things have changed from when I was in school."

The noodles rattled against the bottom of the pot as all the boxes were added.

"I bet it's pretty there. Actual trees, and real seasons," Charleigh said dreamily. "I've always wanted to live where there were trees. Like the big ones, not the bush trees we have here."

"It is green when you're not in the city, but it rains all the time."

"Is that where you live, like, full-time?" Charleigh asked. "I know you all only, like, stay here for the season."

"I don't live anywhere full-time." Emma pulled the pot up from the stove as the bubbles rose to the rim. "When playoffs end, I'll be here for a few weeks, then DayDay and I will head to Italy. After that, I go to China for their league that starts in February. When I'm overseas, they rent me a flat or apartment. I figure in a few years when I'm done, I'll buy a house and finally have a home."

"So, you've been all around the world." Charleigh looked out the window. "I just want to leave this fucking state someday."

Lexa busied herself with locating a measuring cup and fork in Charleigh's kitchen. Like the library, she found no system of organization. Not even a silverware sorter in a drawer. She made a mental note to look up those dream house renovation teams to nominate Charleigh. However, the idea even sounded dumb in her head, so she wiped the thought when she found the measuring cup with half the numbers missing from age. She decided to memorize the house number and Amazon a new kitchen to Charleigh in the morning.

Studying the lines, she found the 1/4 cup line. Then she calculated the number by four. Her head shook when she realized how stupid she was and emptied the remainder of the milk into the yellowed plastic. She added the packets of cheese powder into the cup one at a time and stirred them.

Emma looked over at Charleigh, "Where's the strainer?"

"Oh... uh... hold on." Charleigh slid down from the counter and rummaged through a cabinet. She withdrew a giant metal saucepan lid and held her hand out.

Emma looked at her, then Lexa, then back at Charleigh. "That's not a strainer," Emma stated when Charleigh continued to hold out her hand. "You sure your head is okay? You hit it a few weeks ago, but concussions can be a bitch."

Charleigh took the pot from Emma. "I... uh... I don't have one, so I just use this." Holding the noodles back with the lid, Charleigh drained the water from the pot into the sink.

Lexa added strainer to the growing list in her head.

The finished macaroni was dished unevenly into a bowl, a Tupperware that had once held lunch meat, and a plate. Emma ended up with the most still in the pot it was cooked in and a potholder.

As they ate in the living room, Lexa noticed the photo on the small end table. She picked it up and studied it. Charleigh, the sister, and a blonde boy with a big nose were scrunched on the tiny couch. The boy's arm was wrapped around Charleigh's middle as she leaned as far into the sister as possible. Lexa assumed this must be the brother Charleigh had mentioned. The penguin-shaped social worker was on the arm, and Lexa thought about him saying the woman was like a daughter to him. She wasn't like a daughter. She was his daughter. On the other side, the gassy glitter girl knelt on the floor next to the sister. A family photo. Charleigh's family. A mismatched family in a mismatched house.

Looking up, Lexa pointed to Kinsley and asked, "This is your sister, too?"

Charleigh took the photo from Lexa and set it back in its place. She answered as she moved into the kitchen with her empty bowl of the smallest portion of pasta. "In a sort. We are all... fosters except Kyle. He's my foster dad's bio son. A real douche canoe because he knew there was no sending him away like the rest of us. Kinsley is the newest, and only because I begged Marcus. He didn't want any more kids after Mona and I graduated and is regretting bringing Kinsley home since Kyle can't come to visit with her there. Also, she is testing his nerves by sneaking out of the house to spend the night with Bastian, but Mona and I were worse."

"Bastian?" Lexa asked, trying to place the familiar name.

Her lips twisted, as she looked at Lexa from the doorway. "The big guy with the tattoos. You met him in my classroom."

"So, you are like a legit foster kid?" Emma asked. She set the empty pan on the coffee table.

"Eh... yes. Technically, Marcus just had guardianship of me, which means my mom, like, signed papers that gave him rights to me." Charleigh turned around before anyone could ask her another question. "I became a foster kid when I was seventeen and my mom unadopted me. I had to move into a dorm room at the school after that because Marcus wasn't allowed to officially foster me without amending his license. And like I said, Mona and I were worse than Kinsley, so I just don't have parents. But Marcus didn't adopt Mona either like he said he was going to. So... yeah, I was a legit foster kid. Left high school with a state-issued check for six hundred bucks and my best friend.

"Rexi," she called. A metal bowl rattled with dry dog food. Charleigh talked louder so they could hear her from the kitchen. "We still see Marcus on holidays, and we are supposed to have these, like, weekly family dinners. I don't go often because it's just like a game of pretend. I have to pretend I tolerate Kyle and pretend Marcus didn't turn his back on Mona and me. Mainly Mona though. She thought he actually cared about her, while I knew... I just turned his life upside down."

Emma leaned into Lexa's space. "I brought you here to apologize so get to it before she kicks us out. I want her to be okay with us being here."

Lexa's glare was nothing less than a warning. She shoved the final scoop of chalky noodles into her mouth, chewing loudly in Emma's direction. When she swallowed, Lexa hissed, "Why? So, you can try to get her to fall in love with you?"

Emma's eyes fell to where Danaya was dusting off dirt and hair from her sweatshirt and jeans. Quietly she said, "Lexa, I'm not interested in getting involved with Charleigh. I have someone that I...."

Emma didn't need to finish the sentence. Lexa scoffed, "You need to pick a room in that rent-a-flat of yours and fuck her senseless."

Danaya's eyes flew up, staring at them on the couch. "I'm right here!" she said. "I can hear both of you."

"Who needs to get fucked senseless?" Charleigh asked, returning from the kitchen with a half-empty pack of generic Oreos. She threw them on the table and shrugged. "Sorry, no milk but that's the closest to dessert that I got."

"Emma and Danaya," Lexa said, putting her fake Tupperware in the pot. She set the pot on the table next to the cookies.

"Bedroom is on the right. Queen bed, just no squirting on the bed. I think I forgot to put the mattress pad down when I changed the sheets last," Charleigh stated. Her arms crossed her chest as she leaned against the Charleigh-sized doorway.

Danaya's mouth opened, then closed. Everything the girl seemed to want to say dissolved on the tip of her tongue. Emma wasn't fairing much better as she fisted her pants.

A laugh tore through Lexa, followed by Charleigh. Lexa watched as the blonde doubled over, waving her hand in the air. "I was joking. Please don't have sex on my bed. I don't even have sex in my bed."

Emma slugged Lexa in the shoulder, but she dodged most of the blow. She moved from the couch and ended up closer to Charleigh. More quietly, but still loud enough for the other two to hear, Lexa said, "They wouldn't do it. They just like to carry around hard-ons for each other. Though I think, given the chance, Danaya would top Em easily."

Charleigh looked back and forth between Emma and Danaya. Her hand disappeared into her pocket and pulled out the wrinkled ten-dollar bills she'd tried to give Emma.

"I'll put ten on it that one of them would climax just kissing. Have you seen the way they drool over each other?" Charleigh's eyes flitted to Danaya. "It's kinda cute in a gay Hallmark film sorta way. Nothing but please notice me stares when the other is not looking."

Lexa's teammates were doing everything possible not to look at each other. Lexa held her hand out to Emma. She gestured to herself. "Gimme ten bucks."

Emma pushed up from the couch. She brushed the dog hair from her clothes unsuccessfully and announced, "Well, it's getting late. Time to go."

Lexa held up her hands.

"But you just said you wanted to stay!" Lexa protested. Her hand flung toward the blonde. "She's offering to let you stay all night and take some DayDay dick in your dark chocolate twatwaffle."

Danaya's body twisted as she pushed herself up from the floor. She dug into her pocket and waved a twenty-dollar bill in her hand.

"I will see your ten, Charleigh," Danaya announced. "And I raise you another ten that Emmi will be the one to fall apart first." The woman glanced over at Emma before she added, "Because I'm that good."

She started to hand the money to Charleigh when she stopped and looked at Lexa. The bill crunched in her hand as she dug the digit into Lexa's shoulder. "But only if you give Peaches the present that we drove out here to give her."

Lexa's mouth dropped open. She stared at the traitor. The 'I'll be friends with Tomorrow Lexa.' Apparently, friendship came with a figurative bus for Lexa to be kicked in front of.

"Peaches?" Charleigh asked. She scanned Danaya's face, and then her eyebrows rose. "Oh, white girl. I get it."

Charleigh turned to Lexa, "What present?"

"Sorry, but I forgot it in my car," Lexa lied.

Danaya's feet thundered against the wooden floor. She ran out the front door as she screamed, "Liar, liar, pants on fire! Your bag is in the fucking car."

"Is this present why you were the equivalent of a bag of dicks last week?" Charleigh asked.

Lexa leaned forward just enough to enter the blonde's bubble. Blue eyes drop to Lexa's lips as she said, "You think of me and think of dick. Something on your mind?"

She paused, trying to read if she had gone too far in Charleigh's face. The woman was still staring at Lexa's mouth though. She took a chance when Charleigh sucked in a deep breath by adding, "I can make that dream happen sometime if you would like."

The dog pushed between Charleigh and Lexa, then through the door to reconnect with her best friend. Lexa almost lost her balance, but Emma was looking out. She pushed Lexa forward. Just a little too hard. Just a little too much force. Lexa barely caught herself before her body slammed Charleigh into the wall.

Charleigh's warm breath cascaded over Lexa's throat.

"I'm sorry," Lexa said.

She pulled back, but the small hand on her hip stopped her from moving completely out of the woman's space. Charleigh's voice had dropped an octave as she whispered, "If anyone would be taking the other's dick, it would be you and I wouldn't be gentle."

Lexa leaned back to stare into the blue eyes no longer looking at her lips. With a cocked eyebrow, Charleigh added. "I would even let you choose the color."

She couldn't breathe. The image of Charleigh above her... Charleigh thrust into her as she begged for more. Yeah, she would beg for her. Because then she would get to touch her.

Licking her lips, Lexa said, "Blue."

"I have blue." Charleigh's thumb rubbed a circle into Lexa's hip bone. "But you'd have to be very nice. Say please and thank you. Do you even know those words, Devil Dickhead?"

Lexa didn't get to tell her yes. Wasn't able to promise she knew those words. Unable to explain she would use them if it meant Charleigh would spread her open on the blue dick. She couldn't say any of it because Danaya was pulling Lexa, pulling her out of Charleigh's grasp.

Danaya shook her head. "No," she added with a wagging finger. "No means no, Lexa."

She pulled Lexa to the couch. When Lexa's calves hit the worn fabric, Danaya pushed her downward.

"Hands to yourself," she said.

The package hit her thigh with the corner of the box. The pain rushed to the area as though she'd been stabbed instead of humiliated. No matter, Lexa's face felt hot and her temper hotter.

Emma was still standing awkwardly in the room. Her hand rubbed the back of her neck. She turned in a circle, unsure what to do while Danaya was playing director for the live show, she was about to call action for.

The younger woman grabbed Charleigh's arm. Her hold was looser on Charleigh, not as pully. Without a word, she guided Charleigh to the armchair where Charleigh sat without having to be pushed.

Danaya cast a glance back at Emma. Lexa watched as Charleigh held up the money, meeting Emma's eye. The blonde issued nothing less than a challenge.

Lexa assessed the situation. If Emma backed out, then Charleigh would at least be able to buy some food. But if Emma backed out, there were also probably no second chances with the rookie. That didn't sit well with Lexa now that the possibility of Emma's attraction to Charleigh had been flushed out. But, if this blew up with Danaya, Lexa wouldn't put it past Emma to be petty and go after Charleigh just to ruin Lexa's chances at a date with the girl.

Danaya moved toward Emma, tugging on the hem of her t-shirt. A cocky smile spread over her face, crinkling her almond eyes. She made eye contact with the veteran ball player as she said, "I won't ever mention it again if you let me show you just how good I am. There's been so many almost... if you let me show you, I could prove to you this isn't a mistake."

Emma bit her lower lip. Her chest froze. Lexa couldn't blame her. If Charleigh was telling her those things, she'd be terrified too.

"I... I don't know if this is smart. Maybe we should just go home," Emma said. "We can talk about... I'm old-der. And the team rules...."

Danaya didn't give her any more time to think about it. She was moving closer within Emma's bubble. Lexa held her breath as she watched Danaya place a tentative hand on Emma's waist. She seemed to just be breathing the other girl in, urging her to relax under her touch. It was soft and slow, each moving in closer as though the magnetic pull could no longer be denied. Danaya patiently waited for Emma to close the remaining distance.

But she didn't.

Emma turned away. Hands rubbed her face, and she shook her head. "This is stupid. I'm not kissing you for some twenty-dollar bet."

With four steps and a head smacking into the door frame, Emma was out the door. Charleigh jumped to her feet, chasing after Emma, just like Emma chased after her.

Lexa's stomach flipped as Danaya's chin fell. She felt the familiar taste of guilt rise in her throat. Felt the shame of pushing the last two people in her life after just last week using her venom to spread doubt into the younger girl's circulatory system.

The twenty dollars didn't mean anything to Danaya and losing the money wouldn't alter any aspect of her life. But her pride and confidence had fled with the woman she'd pined over. Even if Lexa took her back to her place, at some point, Danaya would have to go back to the townhouse she shared with Emma. She'd have to play not only this season but the next in Italy, where they were already committed to the same team.

When the door flew open, it barely missed Charleigh's face. Her hand came up in time to catch it before it hit the bookcase.

Emma stomped back into the house, rattling the window with her giant footfalls. She pulled Danaya's shattered self against her chest. Her hand held the other girl's neck, then wiped away the tear that had broken free. She pressed her forehead to Danaya's.

"I'm an idiot for making you doubt for even one second that I don't want to kiss you," she told the younger woman. "I have wanted to kiss you since the first time I heard you laugh. Thought about kissing you every time you came to my room to tell me good night. This won't change that we need to talk, but I'm tired of trying to hold back anymore."

The kiss started slowly and softly. Danaya's hands found Emma's waist and pulled the other woman flush with her. They held their lips together, letting their electrons exchange. Bonds were created before lips parted and melded into each other even closer.

Lexa shouldn't be staring but she couldn't stop. She pulled at the neck of her sweatshirt as the temperature of the room rose.

Emma backed Danaya to the space on the wall where Lexa had been over Charleigh only moments before and Danaya allowed it. Allowed Emma to press so completely into her.

Charleigh held her hand out. Lexa moved to slap it in a low five, but she pulled it away. Shaking her head, she said, "I want my present. Friend rules are still in place so you don't get to touch me, Devil Dickhead."

Lexa looked at the gift on her lap. She tasted the blood from biting her lip, and her whole body felt heavy enough to sink into the couch. She picked it up and twisted it in her hands. Without looking at Charleigh, she said, "I don't want you to get the wrong idea."

"Did you buy me a strap?" she asked.

Lexa's gaze shot up. She quickly determined she would never want to play poker with that face. The way the teacher just stared at her without emotion.

The sound of a too-real moan came from the other side of the room, and Lexa remembered Danaya and Emma were ten feet away in a full-blown make-out session. The grip Danaya had on Emma's ass and the movement of her thigh between the older woman's legs told Lexa that she needed to add groceries to the Amazon list.

"You're going to lose your money," Lexa said.

Her attention was still locked on the women across from her. She turned only when the present was jerked from her hand. She started to reach over to take it back, but Charleigh was tearing the birthday paper from it.

Her smile was broad as she said, "Never bet money I'm not willing to lose. Plus, I got a brand new...."

The storm had returned to her eyes when she looked at Lexa. Her freckles stood out against the scarlet face.

"I told you no to the $100 for the replacement. Why the fuck did you take that as go spend $1000 on a phone?" Charleigh growled as she shook her head at the white box. "Jesus, you really won't stop until you get me to have sex with you, will you?

Lexa felt like she was suffocating. She pulled on the neck of her sweatshirt. Her mind raced over how she could explain she wasn't trying to buy Charleigh's pussy.

When no words came out, she got up. Her body moved, walking away from the women making out. She pulled at the neck of her sweatshirt again, then remembered if she wanted it off, she had to pull it over her head.

Her hair got stuck in the hole. She had to tug it. As the thick material came up, Lexa's T-shirt went with it. In nothing but a bra and baggy jeans, she tried to speak again but nothing came out.

Charleigh's voice stopped Lexa in her tracks, even though she had no idea what Charleigh said. Her blood was pulsing too fast in her ears.

The hollow path Lexa was quickly treading over the creaking wood floors was halted in the tiny house in the middle of nowhere. In the house that said so much, and yet the blonde said so little. She looked so serious though, and Lexa didn't know how to be serious with Charleigh and not have her laugh. But Lexa couldn't think about it because that tiny finger pointed to the dark hallway.

It was telling her to go to the bathroom because Lexa could hear Charleigh's finger but not her voice. Lexa stopped, not moving down the hallway. Her feet grew roots, but Charleigh's hands were pushing her.

Lexa closed her eyes when Charleigh's hand closed around her arm and pulled her away from the other two back in a lip lock.

"I'm sorry," Lexa said as she was pushed not into the bathroom but into a bedroom. The room on the right with a bed and... 'Why the fuck is she taking me to bed?'

The mattress springs dug into Lexa's sore muscles as she fell backward. Charleigh was pulling off Lexa's shoes, and then unbuttoning her pants. She started to tug them down when Lexa stopped her.

"I don't want it to be like this," she tried. "I don't want this."

"Of course, this is what you want," Charleigh snapped. She stood up between Lexa's legs. "You are just going to keep showing up until you get it. I'm not stupid, Lexa. You're not the first. You won't be the last, so let's just get it over with."

She tugged the jeans off Lexa's hips that had lifted for her. Dropping them to the floor, she stood between Lexa's legs.

The blonde hair shook around the flushed face. Charleigh closed her eyes. She breathed deeply before she laid into Lexa again.

"I know I'm just a fucking challenge for you so let's mark the teacher off your list."

She grabbed Lexa's legs and tried to push her farther up the bed. As she pushed, her body smacked against Lexa's barely covered crotch. Charleigh froze, looking down to where her hips were perfectly positioned to grind into the woman. "Don't even think about it. You didn't respect my boundaries. You didn't say please or thank you, so you are not getting my dick no matter how much I want to fuck the bitch out of you."

Lexa's eyes grew wide as Charleigh pulled the sweatpants down and crawled up Lexa's body. She ran her core over Lexa's abs and then rested her weight on Lexa. Sitting up, Charleigh looked down. "Well, tell me what you want. Ass up so you don't have to look at me? Want me to sit on your face? Or do you just want me to eat you out so you can cum and leave?"

Lexa licked her lips. She could do this, but the words echoed in her head. 'The girl people fucked for fun and left.'

Charleigh moved her hips over Lexa again. The moan that came from the woman wasn't real, but it didn't make the situation in Lexa's boxers any better. The baggy t-shirt still covered the woman's body, so she couldn't see the pussy pressed against her. It wasn't wet. It was hot though.

"Please fuck me, Lexa Jenson," Charleigh begged. Her body ran up and down the dark skin as she squeezed her breasts through the t-shirt she still hadn't taken off. "Make me cum like a proper slut."

Lexa scrunched her eyes shut, not wanting to hear the words she'd told the woman to say at the bar. Her breath caught in her throat when Charleigh replaced her hand with Lexa's on her breast. She squeezed Lexa's hand into the soft flesh.

Charleigh reached back and pushed her hand under the band of Lexa's boxers. As the fingertip grazed over Lexa's slit, shame washed over the ball player. Charleigh's body told Lexa she didn't want this, but her core was drenched.

Lexa whispered, "Please stop."

Charleigh didn't have to be asked twice. She pushed off the woman below her and pulled her pants back on. With a scoff, she cinched the pants until the waistband bunched around her hips which Lexa realized were too small. Too skinny from the lack of food in her house.

"Changed your mind, then?" Charleigh said. "Got a taste of reality and not interested in fucking the poor bitch anymore."

She turned away from Lexa. Her shoulders sunk and Lexa was certain the woman had stopped breathing.

That was until Charleigh's voice cracked. Her arms wrapped around herself. "Sorry, I don't live up to your standards."

Pushing up from the bed, Lexa stood behind the woman and wrapped her arms around the tiny body. She pressed her lips to the woman's hair and sucked back her own emotions.

"I replaced your phone because I was the reason it broke," she explained finally. "I came here.... I wanted to apologize. Apologize for the bar. For after the game. At no point in time did you ever do anything that justifies what I did to you. How I disrespected you. You did nothing wrong. It was all me. I'm the one to blame."

Lexa sighed when Charleigh didn't move in her arms. Didn't turn to hug her like she'd hugged Emma. And Lexa knew why.

She'd broken another one of Charleigh's rules; the don't touch her rule. Even if she was choking, Lexa wasn't supposed to touch her.

Lexa let her arms fall to her sides, wondering what a hug from Charleigh was like. Emma said it was the best hug in the world, but Charleigh didn't hug her because the woman didn't want her. She'd never hug her because she thought she wasn't good enough for Lexa. And Lexa hated that Emma was right about Charleigh thinking she was the problem and not the other way around.

Charleigh sniffed and ran her hands over her face. "I think they're done... so you should just go. Tell Danaya... I will get her the other ten bucks when I get paid."

She'd been asked to leave, and she would respect the woman's wishes. With everything she'd done to Charleigh, she'd show the woman she knew what it meant to leave when asked.

Grabbing her clothes from the ground, she pulled her jeans back on and the blue T-shirt that she'd accidentally picked up as well.

Lexa looked around the room, then up at the map above the bed. The world with tacks and string to pictures of book covers. 'She wants to see the world,' Lexa thought as she walked out of the room.

Danaya pressed a soft kiss to Emma's cheek as the woman standing over her heaved out a shaking breath. Lexa was grateful she'd missed the finale of the worst porno ever.

"She wants me to go," Lexa told them. She picked up the cash Charleigh had dropped on the table and held it out to Danaya. "She said she'll get you the other half of your money when she gets paid next week. I'm going to go wait in the car."

Danaya fished out the car keys from Emma's jeans and traded the money for the key. Without a word, Lexa left the home with decorative throw pillows on the cushions. She headed to the sleek leather seat in the car that reminded her of her colorless house.

She leaned her head against the back of the seat and closed her eyes. In her mind, she walked through Charleigh's house like she would replay a game in her head. Her mental list expanded from an Amazon order of new kitchen supplies to a trip to the mattress store, then Target for a frame to add of Charleigh and herself on the bookcase. More bookcases were needed, so the blonde could show off all her books. The grocery store so the cupboards would be filled, and the fridge would have something healthy in it. A new car that didn't break down when the woman was trying to get to work.

When Emma and Danaya came out of the house holding hands, Lexa tucked herself into a ball across the backseat.

"So, you fucked it up again, Lex Luther," Danaya stated from the front seat. "Did you try and fuck her, and she realized you have no skills, so she kicked you out."

Lexa ran her hands over her face. "She thought I... She said the phone was me trying to buy her. She tried to have sex with me so I would leave her alone. I told her to stop, and she told me to leave."

"Did you at least apologize for everything?" Emma asked.

Lexa licked her lips. "Yeah. I told her it wasn't her fault. That she didn't do anything wrong, but she's pissed at me. I have to find a way to make her realize that I'm not trying to buy her attention."

11

Charleigh hadn't slept well for two days because her pillow smelled like Lexa's rejection. The sheets smelled like honey when they should've smelled like sex. Sunday morning, she lay against the dog, still upset the woman hadn't just taken what she'd wanted before leaving. It was more embarrassing to have thrown herself at the ball player only to be rejected. Seeing where she lived had brought Lexa back to reality that they could never mix.

Rubbing her face, she wiped away the hint of tears. It was better Lexa left. It was going to happen anyway. At least this way she hadn't added to her list of mistakes.

In scaring the woman away, she'd done the right thing by Lexa and herself because Dilynn made her promise no dating, clubs, bars, or anything that didn't resemble community service. Staying home and single was supposed to help her focus on what was most important, preparing to be a mom. It felt a little like Dilynn Greyson was trying to ground her for six months though, and she felt even more conflicted about doing what the woman asked. She told herself it was so Dilynn would go with her to court. She'd promised to go and be a character witness if she played by the Dilynn Greyson Rule Book.

But now her bed smelled like Lexa. Her clit pulsed when she thought about sitting on Lexa's lap. She tried to hold her breast when she got herself off yesterday with the blue dildo, she should have just offered to the woman instead of being a bitch, but her hand was too small to squeeze the whole thing like Lexa was able to. The woman had touched her boob and ran away. Maybe Lexa didn't like her breasts.

'That was probably what changed her mind.'

They had grown with her pregnancy, but she'd not expected them to stay big. Dilynn had large breasts, though, so it was probably in their genes. Everyone always said they looked so much alike, and it finally stopped bugging her so much. Dilynn was pretty for being in her forties, which bode well for Charleigh's future.

If she had a future after January. 'After court' had been on her mind this weekend more than usual. The plan was obviously to get Joey back. To bring her home to stay, then Charleigh could move past preparing to be a mom to actually being a mom. No plans had ever gone her way though, and Lexa's rejection only added to the list of reasons she shouldn't get her hopes up anything would work out like it was supposed to.

She scrolled through the Devils' Reddit tag. There were rumors the team was going to be sold, which meant players would be traded. A lot of posts focused on Lexa getting traded and Emma getting dropped, that Sylvia Winters trade was probably just the start of a new roster to rebrand the team. The idea of her team being taken apart at the same time as her title of mother being stripped away made her think of the hidden bottle of rum in her couch.

"Grocery store," Charleigh said aloud to shift her thoughts from the bottle. Her body needed food, not booze. She needed to make a list and get to the store because it was a farther walk to the store than the school.

Still in her sweatpants from Friday, she made her way into the kitchen. The phone box, still wrapped in plastic, lay in wait on the table. It was larger than the shattered one. She'd never had the latest version of a phone let alone the largest. Marcus' credit score wasn't high enough to qualify for the fancy stuff, but at least he allowed Mona and her to stay on his family plan. She knew he kept it as a way to say he was sorry for dumping her and Mona, just like the car he'd sold her but never cashed one of her payments. He probably knew she was struggling to pay all her bills and her weekly fee to DCS to contribute to the subsidy her mother received for taking care of Joey.

She flipped the box over, considering if she should just keep the phone. The price tag told her absolutely not. Lexa's $1500 investment to fuck a pussy she didn't want was obscene. Had they had sex, then maybe Charleigh could have convinced herself she was an expensive prostitute. That hadn't happened though.

It would have to be returned. She dug in the junk drawer, searching for the paper with Emma's phone number. Sure, she was Lexa's friend, but she'd told Charleigh to call her if she needed anything. And calling her wasn't asking for something, just for the woman to give it back to Lexa. Emma would understand Charleigh couldn't keep the phone. She'd made it clear with just her looks she didn't approve of Lexa getting involved with someone like her. That's why she knew Emma would get the phone back to Lexa.

Charleigh pushed herself up on the counter and sat back against the cabinet. She studied the paper, struggling to make out if the last number was a five or an eight. Her head hit the wood when she realized it didn't matter what the number was. She couldn't call Emma without opening the phone, which meant she had to wait until Monday.

After a deep breath, she decided not being able to call Emma was a good thing. Emma would probably run over to get it, which meant Danaya would come too. They'd want to talk, and they'd ask questions. She'd have to kick them out to go to the store, and they would know she was walking so they would insist on driving her like she was a charity case. It was bad enough that Lexa already made sure Emma knew she was poor.

She didn't need them seeing her choosing between ramen and Rice a Roni. They didn't need to know that she only ate tuna because ground beef and eggs were too expensive now. And she didn't need them to watch her pocketing some of the free fruit from the kid's stand in the produce aisle.

A soft knock on the door made her stomach jump into her chest. She looked around the kitchen for something to defend herself with. Charleigh's hand dropped to the counter, picking up a fork from last night's late-night dinner of ramen and green beans.

"Charleigh," Lexa called from the front steps. "It's me."

She forced herself not to smile when she opened the door. Lexa held up a tray of Starbucks and a brown bag in her hand. If Lexa hadn't rejected her, this would have just solidified to Charleigh the woman who was looking for a sugar baby to slum it with. No, this was something else. Something sweet and thoughtful, which weren't things people did for her.

"I figured you liked to start your day off with coffee." Lexa ducked her chin. "I want to talk about Friday."

Holding open the door, Charleigh allowed Lexa back into her space. Lexa ducked her head, the top of her hair brushing against the door frame as she crossed the threshold.

Charleigh pointed the fork at the royal blue Greyson Academy t-shirt stretched over Lexa's muscular frame. "Is that my shirt?"

Lexa looked down at the shirt, then her lips scrunched as she looked at the fork. "Is that a dirty fork?"

Holding the tilted tined utensil up like a dagger, she shrugged. "It would do some damage. Probably hurt worse than getting shot."

Lexa smiled, dropping her eyes to her hands. She held out the tray to Charleigh. "I saw the creamer in the fridge on Friday. It's caramel with cream. I know it's probably not your Starbucks drink, but I figured it would be the closest I could get to being right without asking, since if I asked, you'd have said no."

Charleigh studied the labels of each drink to learn Lexa's preferences. Vanilla, four shots, a splash of heavy cream, shaken, caramel sauce drizzled on the cup. Then she processed Lexa's words.

"You knew I'd say no so you did it anyway?" Her eyebrows raised as she waited for Lexa to see the problem.

The cardboard holder was set atop the coffee table. The cup with a less complicated description was pushed into the smaller woman's hand. When Charleigh continued waiting for Lexa to acknowledge her question, Lexa coaxed Charleigh's cup upward toward her lips.

With a raise of her eyebrows, she said, "Caffeinated Charleigh, cheery Charleigh."

With a roll of her eyes, Charleigh took a sip and sat on the couch. There was no point in turning down a drink that would just go bad. Lexa tossed the white warm bag in her lap. Within it was a breakfast sandwich with bacon.

She hated how much she wanted to tear it open and swallow it quickly. Hunger was something she'd grown accustomed to over the past several months without Mona around. If she devoured it though, the ball player would remember the cabinets were empty.

It was another gift. Her stomach growled, but her head added the price of the coffee and the food. She had to be up to at least $1600 in debt with the woman if she counted the tax on the phone and the gas from whatever mansion Lexa had driven from. That was a whole lot of sex owed to the woman who didn't want her.

"I had coffee in the kitchen," she said, setting the cup down on the table. "You didn't have to come all this way."

"Kroger isn't coffee and it's nothing but chaos in there. Nothing is where it is supposed to be. If you want, I could totally put things where they belong and then you will be able to get to things when you're cooking easier," Lexa offered.

The bubbling of inadequacy from some hidden organ within Charleigh's being began to work in overdrive. It started in her gut, then gurgled in her throat.

"No. I like it this way," she said. She tucked her legs under her body and flipped the television on.

The dogs on the screen ran through a dense forest. Rexa parked herself in the way following the movement with her snout. Her head rested on the TV stand watching the dogs run through the trees with a whiny cat following.

"I used to love this movie," Lexa said. She sat in the armchair.

Since Lexa wasn't just going to spit out what she wanted to say and leave, Charleigh picked at the sandwich. Forced herself to break it into small pieces and nibble it like she did with the frozen waffles. She would save part of it to eat as she walked to the store.

After a few moments, Lexa pointed to Rexa and cast Charleigh a puzzled look. "Is your dog watching TV?"

"She just started watching a game with me one day. Now she turns it on whenever she feels like it." Charleigh gestured to the tray of busted remotes. "I went through a few controllers, but she seems to use her paws now and not her teeth."

"Okay, I officially love this dog more than Danaya does," Lexa announced.

The movie played, but Charleigh couldn't focus with Lexa shifting in the recliner constantly. First, stretched her legs out, which ended in her hitting her big toe on the table. Then she tried to squeeze into a ball, followed by hanging her legs off the edge of the arm.

Finally, Lexa sat up and strummed her fingers against the worn scarlet material. She huffed out a breath, and said, "You said no loaning money."

Words began to flow from Lexa like a flash flood, washing Charleigh's feet out from under her and sending her to the space Lexa wanted her.

"I sent the follow request, and I must have checked my phone every hour to see if you responded. After the game, I saw how Emma had to lend you her phone because I broke yours, and I had replaced it before, but then we lost, and I was angry. I was pissed because we lost, and I blamed you because blaming you was easier than owning that I sucked, and I have been sucking. I sucked on Wednesday, and I'll probably suck in New York next week."

Lexa shook her head, then looked at Charleigh. She took a deep breath, and said, "But last week, I wanted to talk to you. I wanted to apologize but I couldn't and then Emma found your phone in her car, and I begged her to let me come too. I wanted to give you the new phone so I could get your number. I wanted... I don't even know what I want other than to fix everything I have broken, and I broke your phone, so it's the first thing I could fix."

Realizing Lexa was waiting for her participation, she found only one way to explain why she was uncomfortable. "It's too much."

Lexa held a hand to her chest. "It's not too much for me, honestly."

"Would you buy Emma or Danaya a phone because they broke theirs?" Charleigh asked. She needed to get Lexa to understand so she didn't have to say it again.

"I don't give a fuck about Emma or Danaya having a phone," Lexa snapped. Her hands shot out from her body toward Charleigh. "I care about you. I care that you have a phone. I fucking care more now that I know you live in the middle of fucking nowhere with no fucking transportation. Like if you are in trouble, you need to at least have a phone. Just let me do this and stop making such a big deal out of it."

"I can't match gifts like that," Charleigh fired back, but Lexa was shaking her head. She seemed to be brushing away the words with her free curls.

"Gifts are not about matching a price. They are about intent. And my gift is selfish," Lexa explained. "And I'm not expecting anything in return. I never wanted you to think.... Look, I didn't give it to you so you would feel obligated to fuck me. So please just take it and give me your number already. I mean, I bought you breakfast."

Charleigh's eyebrows clinched in the middle as she listened to Lexa's hypocrisy flow from her lips. She tried to wait the woman out, but Lexa sat back in the chair. Her eyes were looking over the bookcases once again. Her life. Pictures of Joey. Stuff Lexa didn't need to know about.

"I didn't ask you to buy me breakfast, and I sure as hell told you not to replace my phone. And demanding my number is literally asking for something because you bought me breakfast that I don't even like and a fucking phone that I told you not to concern yourself with replacing."

Shoving the rest of the sandwich back in the bag, she tossed it on the table. It was a lie she didn't like it. A lie she wished could be true because throwing the bag away made her panic slightly. She didn't want the dog to snag it while they were fighting because the hunger in her was awake and angry.

Rexa padded across the floor. She placed her body between Lexa's legs like a traitor. Leaning back, Lexa's fingers locked on the arms of the chair. This was a side of Lexa, she'd yet to see. Scared Lexa.

"You never said if you were okay with dogs," Charleigh said softer.

Lexa glanced down at Rexa. The dog's lips were smiling back up at her. Her head wiggled as she waited for Lexa to scratch behind her ears. She held her fingers out toward the dog, earning her a nose boop.

"I was attacked by a dog when I was a kid," Lexa said. She bit her lip, before she added, "I'm kind of edgy around them, but I saw the sign that said she lives here and I'm a guest."

Charleigh swallowed and snapped her fingers, trying to get the dog's attention. Rexa was as attentive to her commands as the namesake though, and simply ignored her.

"I always wanted a dog." Lexa looked up at Charleigh, "Do you dress her up in sweaters and shit?"

"Only on Halloween and at Christmas. You know, normal dog-dressing times," Charleigh said, turning her attention back to the television.

Lexa mumbled something about white girls under her breath, but Charleigh couldn't make out what it was. Her mind was occupied in a NASCAR race of things she needed to say, roaring around a circular track in a race to determine which would be first.

When a Brawny paper towel commercial came on, the racetrack vaporized, leaving the rusty kitchen car alone in her head.

"So, the kitchen..." Charleigh whispered. "I know that we have other things we need to talk about, but I think if I explain the kitchen, maybe you will kinda understand me a little bit more."

"Okay."

"The kitchen is like me."

"You're a battlefield from World War I?" Lexa joked. The smile fell from her face when Charleigh's arms wrapped tighter around herself.

"I mean, metaphorically, I guess it fits." Charleigh looked over at Lexa. "Minus the old part, asshole."

She knew being wrapped in a ball wouldn't fix the energy of the room. She knew she had to open herself up, but when she sat up so her toes touched the ground, her head and shoulders became too heavy, pulling her down until she rested her weight on her knees.

"I wasn't trying to..." Lexa's words tapered off.

Charleigh sat up, tired or not, she had to get Lexa to understand. Tapping her chest, she said, "I am like my dented pot in there. I can do the things that the pot needs to do. But I'm not pretty."

Lexa raised an eyebrow at Charleigh. "I think you're very, very pretty."

"That's not...." The blood rushed to Charleigh's face. "When I say pretty, I mean like straight out of the box, all shiny. I have a lot of dents and scratches because I have been banged around, scorched over the fire, dropped in the donation bin, and picked up for a bargain price, but I'm still doing what I must do to be useful."

She wiped her face. "People like me, we get the dented pot because it does the job. We want the fancy one that is shiny, but we know that it's out of reach."

"Am I the shiny pot?" Lexa asked.

"Kinda, I guess. But no. Okay. So, if you were a pot, then yes you would be a shiny pot, and you would get purchased and put in a nice cabinet. But that wasn't where I was going."

"Okay, so you're a dented pot and I am a shiny pot. But you're also a dented pot owner, and I'm a shiny pot owner?"

"Yes."

Lexa looked at the ceiling, then back to Charleigh. "I still don't get it."

"Lexa, if you had a choice between the dented pot and the shiny pot, you would buy the shiny pot because it is new, and it is pretty and it fits your life. The dented pot doesn't have a place in your kitchen."

"So, you wouldn't say yes to a date because you don't think you fit in my life," the ball player summarized.

"I know, I don't fit in your life," Charleigh clarified. She took a deep breath. "When you asked me out, I didn't say yes because I knew that at some point you were going to realize that I can't be on your level. You're a celebrity crush because you are a celebrity. I'm just a teacher. I went to school to be a teacher, and it is all I will ever be."

"I think being a teacher is pretty fucking important," Lexa stated.

"Yeah," Charleigh sighed. "I mean what I do is important. Especially where I do it. Greyson is a stark raving bitch, but no one can deny what she built isn't important. And the kids I get to work with are amazing. But the thing is... I'm one of those kids."

Charleigh took a deep breath. "That's why I'm good at what I do. I know what they are going through. And I get to be there and show them that they can get out. I can help them get out and hopefully not come back like I had to."

The television moved on to another movie. Charleigh watched as the actors moved through the first scene without talking. She looked over at Lexa to find the other woman waiting for her.

"Look, I wouldn't have brought you here, to my home, probably ever. I'm not proud of where or how I live. And I know who your ex-wife is, so I know that you are used to more. More space, more comfort. Nice things that I don't have."

Charleigh looked around the room. She shook her head as she said, "I would go so far as to bet that my entire house fits in one room of yours."

She glanced over to find Lexa's eyes had dropped to her lap.

Lexa strummed her fingers against the arm of the couch. Then she said, "Did it hurt your feelings when I said your kitchen was wrong?"

Charleigh breathed. A real breath because Lexa was finally getting it.

"Yes, because it was like you're saying I'm wrong. Like my way of doing things was wrong, but I did them because I thought it was right. And when you have done the things, I have done, and someone is always there to tell you you're wrong, it sucks because... look, I know I'm not good enough already, and then it's like you're pointing out that I am not good enough. That you have to teach me where to put my things in my house."

"I didn't mean to hurt you."

"I know. I know you didn't mean to. Just like I knew you didn't want to hurt me Friday night by pointing out to Emma that I'm poor."

Lexa's eyes shot up. She opened her mouth, then closed it. Finally, she said, "I... I wasn't..."

Charleigh's head shook. She didn't want to hear Lexa's lies.

"Yes, you were," she countered. "And I get... I get why you did it. Just like you knew buying the phone was too much."

Arms wrapped around herself to hold the pieces together. She closed her eyes and told her the truth. "When people, like you, give things like a thousand-dollar phone to people like me, you want something in return. And the only thing I have to give you is sex. That's all I have that you want. But you didn't even want that. So, I have nothing for you. I'm nothing in comparison to you."

With closed eyes, Lexa breathed in and out. Pushing more air out each time, until she looked at Charleigh once more. "I get what you're saying, and I didn't think about you feeling like you would have to give me something in return."

Charleigh leaned back in her seat. "If I take that phone, and never talk to you again, what would you tell your friends?"

"Nothing." Lexa chewed on her lip. "Because if I did, they would laugh at me and tell me I got played by a ball bunny."

"See." Charleigh's head fell against the couch. "This is why I didn't even want the money to replace the phone I already had. I didn't want to feel obligated to be around you or talk to you. I didn't even want you to give me tickets to the second game because it's a debt, and you felt I was indebted to you, so when I was late, you were offended. You thought I didn't care about you."

"I hate that you're right," Lexa whispered. She leaned forward, putting her elbows on her knees. "So do you, like, want a rule about no presents?"

"I don't know what to do, Lexa." Charleigh rubbed her hands over her face. "I am not sure why you are even here."

Lexa licked her lips. "I want to spend time with you. That's why I'm here. I spent the last 36 hours trying to figure out how I could come here and apologize. I tried to think of a hundred different excuses to stop by, but the truth is I just wanted to see you. I wanted to spend time with you. Get to know you."

"I don't see how this ends well though. I'm a teacher and you're a professional basketball player. Everything about you and me... we are like putting oil and water in a pan together."

Lexa gestured to the books lining the wall. "You read all those books?"

"Yeah."

"How many of them were about two people from different worlds who met and made it work?"

"I see where you're going, but they are fiction." Charleigh waved her hands around the room. "This is reality. The bar was reality. The game was a reality. The parking garage... reality."

Lexa scoffed, and spit back, "Reality is just what you make it."

Charleigh narrowed her eyes at Lexa. "Okay Protagoras, let's hear your theory."

"Protogis? Pro... you know what, I'm going to pretend you are not making fun of me," Lexa snipped. She leaned back, chewing on her words before she said, "You have constructed a reality that I live in a world you don't fit in, but I have constructed one you do fit in. If you let me, I could show you—"

A throw pillow cut Lexa's sentence off. She sat there stunned, staring at Charleigh, who'd already armed herself with another.

"If you start singing, 'I'll Show You the World' again, I swear I will hit you again. Because you're not a prince in disguise and I'm not a fucking princess."

Lexa opened her mouth, and Charleigh threw the pillow. This time it was caught, and Lexa was up from the chair. With a swing, she whacked Charleigh, sending blonde hair in her face.

"I didn't sing it and you still threw it," she said. "And the song is 'A Whole New World' you uncultured heathen."

Laughing as Lexa attempted another strike, Charleigh grabbed the couch cushion and used it as a shield. The pillow caught around the top of the cushion and was yanked away from Lexa.

With Charleigh's weapon back in her possession, she whacked Lexa with the cushion and prepared to hit her again with the pillow. The ball player lost her balance, tumbling into the other side of the couch. But the arsenal was useless against the long arms that grabbed Charleigh's side, and then Lexa shoved her back. They wrestled until the cushion and the pillow were lost, and Charleigh was under the bigger woman.

There was not enough adrenaline in the smaller woman to harness the strength it would require getting herself unpinned from Lexa's body atop her. With her hands pinned above her head into the armrest by Lexa's hand and her hips locked open by Lexa's waist, Charleigh was defenseless.

Charleigh's legs were useless, kicking against Lexa's thighs. Expletives and giggles escaped while Charleigh thrashed from the playful fingers dancing against her sides.

Brown eyes smiled down at her. The powerful fingers attacked with precision. Her hand moved from Charleigh's side to her thigh, grabbing the kicking limb. It squeezed the outside, then the top, roaming down to her knee, then back up to her hip that wasn't ticklish.

A different sensation spread through Charleigh's body, and a different sound fell from her lips. She closed her eyes. The heat rose to her face and her hips pressed up into Lexa. Charleigh's legs wrapped around Lexa's waist, spreading herself open for the woman's body.

Lexa leaned over her, looking down at her lips. She didn't lean in for the kiss but also didn't release Charleigh from her grip. She stayed still while Charleigh's core continued to pulse in protest at being denied more friction.

"I'm sorry," Lexa whispered.

Her hand freed Charleigh, but her body didn't move. She cupped the flushed face, running the pad of her thumb over Charleigh's cheek and lips. "I want to kiss you, but I don't want you to think it's because I bought you a phone or breakfast."

She licked her lips before she said, "And I want you to want me because I'm Lexa, not because I'm a basketball player."

Her eyes fell to Charleigh's lips once more. "This is reality. You and me, crossing paths, at this moment... we're here for a reason. You're color and excitement and chaos. I have to organize chaos, but... I love the chaos of you, but I have to organize chaos, and I don't want to organize you because I can't even organize my head, but you are you and I am me and we are here, and I want to kiss you."

Charleigh didn't understand the need to organize chaos, and she truly had no idea how to organize the chaos in Lexa's head. But she did know how to temporarily distract the woman so Lexa could move forward.

"No more rules," she whispered. Her left hand moved down to Lexa's neck. She took the first step to freeing Lexa's need to be around her by pulling Lexa's lips toward her.

It was nothing like the last time they'd kissed. Not heavy with lust, stealing away their breath. It was soft and tentative. Sweet and careful. That was what Lexa needed, which was why she wouldn't go away.

Their tongues danced in the space shared between their lips. The hand on her hip slipped under the baggy shirt to her breast. Fingers kneaded her flushed flesh, pressing Charleigh into the couch.

Charleigh moaned into the kiss. Her perked nipple rolled between the pads of Lexa's fingers. Her self-maintained body broke into pressure-seeking mode.

Lexa's knee fell off the couch; her crotch grinding against the cushions as she applied the friction Charleigh's core sought. Her kisses trailed down Charleigh's chin to her throat; her lips careful this time to not leave a lingering mark. Fingers pushed at the shirt separating their bodies, but Charleigh couldn't do this here.

Not under the window where the sun shone through, and Lexa would see her. See all of her.

"Take me to bed," Charleigh said.

The room at the rear of the house didn't get the morning light. The curtains were still closed and would provide Charleigh the veil she needed to allow Lexa's eyes to see her naked.

Lexa kicked the door shut, locking Rexa from the room and shrouding them in near darkness. She carefully raised her hand to the back of Charleigh's neck, pulling her into the kiss. This one was just as gentle as the last, and the little voice in Charleigh begged to be happily ever after instead of a rebound.

Her body was set to the ground just before the bed. She turned away, allowing the woman to kiss her neck as she peeled away the shirt.

Hands found her breasts once more. Squeezing and pinching her nipples, Lexa nipped at her shoulders. Then her hands ghosted down Charleigh's chest until they hooked in the pants at her waist. Slowly they too were stripped from her body.

Lexa turned Charleigh to face her. The Greyson Academy shirt came off and Lexa's perky breasts sat in Charleigh's line of sight. She pressed her lips on the woman's skin, looking up at the powerful player gazing with hooded eyes down at her.

The brown eyes were hungry for the pale flesh in her hands. She bit at Charleigh's lip. Her hands picked up the toned cheeks, dropping the smaller woman onto the bed.

Depositing her jeans and boxers on the floor, Lexa crawled up the bed between Charleigh's legs. Her mouth bypassed Charleigh's core, settling her body between Charleigh's thighs. She smiled down at the breasts before her, her fingers rolling the nipples in opposite directions.

"I love your tits," Lexa said. Then she leaned down to take one between her lips. Her suckles were loud in the quiet space, but Charleigh's desire grew with the sound. She arched her back to give her more.

Lexa moved to the other side, slapping the nipple with her tongue. Her naked body pressed into Charleigh's pussy, becoming coated in the arousal. She lifted her hips, a finger slipping between Charleigh's folds. Desire coated the digit that moved quickly before another was added.

Charleigh's mouth fell open as the player stroked within her walls. She relaxed her cunt until it welcomed a third digit. Lexa's hand worked quickly but lacked the punch Charleigh needed. Canting her hips, Lexa seemed to understand. Her position changed to give the blonde pressure where she needed it.

Her toes curled every time Lexa's fingers pressed against the spot. She reveled in the feeling, moving herself up harder each time.

The stimulation from the attention on her breasts with the friction of Lexa's palm on her clit brought Charleigh to an embarrassingly quick finish. Two years had made her over eager and the fall off the edge didn't send her into a vacuum of bliss. She simply tumbled into Lexa's present reality.

Lexa sat back on her heels looking between her fingers coated in slick and the space around Charleigh. As the brown eyes squinted down at Charleigh's naked body, the blonde sat up. She took the fingers into her mouth and cleaned herself from them.

She sucked them dramatically, allowing Lexa to test how far she could push them in before she gagged. When she didn't, Lexa hummed in approval, popping them from Charleigh's lips free of any potential evidence.

Lexa fell against the mattress alongside Charleigh, a cocky smile plastered on her face. She was satisfied with step one of moving on. She just needed Charleigh to fill the next step.

Charleigh climbed atop the woman. Avoided Lexa's mouth after seeing the aversion the woman had to slick. She kissed her way down Lexa's body. Paid minimal attention to the perky breasts in pursuit of the source of need. Her lips pressed against the top of the shaved pussy, enjoying the way Lexa's body reacted to her presence. She ran her tongue over the soaked lips, a hand wrapping in her hair.

With legs spread wider, Lexa pulled Charleigh's face to where she needed her the most. Charleigh's tongue lay flat against the hooded clit, stroking up and gathering the tangy musk of Lexa's arousal. She circled the bud with her lips and sucked lewdly.

"Oh God," Lexa whispered, tightening her grip on Charleigh's hair. She pushed the woman against her hard, her hips grinding against the tongue that had come out to meet her thrusts, slipping within her. Lexa's canal pulled at the pink muscle, stroking shallowly within her.

Charleigh's nose was pressed into Lexa's clit as the stronger woman fucked her face. It wasn't what Charleigh had intended, but she let herself be used like a toy. Her tongue lapped at the dripping hole as her face was painted in a slick sheen.

Lexa came with a growl and a shudder. Her grip held Charleigh's face between her thighs while she rode out her orgasm. When the blonde's presence became overstimulating, Lexa released her hair and laid back against the bed. Her chest fell in heavy breaths as Charleigh reached for the discarded shirt. She used it to clean herself off and put it back on before Lexa saw her.

Lexa's hand reached out and pulled Charleigh to the bed alongside her. They lay in the dark room, only connected by their fingers wrapped together. It wasn't the experience she'd hoped for. There was no way the woman would want more of her when she'd done nothing that a dildo couldn't do. She had a drawer of toys that probably would have made the woman feel much more satisfied in fact.

'Not worth $1600."

But Lexa hadn't gotten up and left. That was something Charleigh had never experienced before. It was post-sex cradling. She'd only ever read about that, and she was beginning to believe that wasn't something people did. It would have been nice if people did things like that.

'Maybe someday,' she thought, not hearing the voice in her head saying she'd be worth it.

Charleigh stared at the boob-shaped ceiling light and squeezed Lexa's hand.

"Thanks for not leaving. Everyone else... they always just got up and left," Charleigh whispered.

Lexa's arm pressed over her face. She chewed on her lip as her chest shook.

"It shouldn't have been like this," Lexa said. "I didn't mean for it to happen like this. I shouldn't have done it like this."

"You didn't do anything, I didn't ask you to do," Charleigh said, tucking her head into Lexa's body. She knew it wasn't the same as cuddling, but she wanted to pretend for a moment she was worth an expensive phone and a real date.

"I know why you did it," Lexa whispered. "I'm not giving up though."

Charleigh licked her lips, savoring the woman's flavor for when she missed Lexa. For after the woman left and realized Charleigh wasn't the person people fought for, she was the one they gave up on. Everyone else knew, and Lexa would figure it out.

'Grocery store,' she reminded herself.

Patting Lexa's chest, Charleigh lied, "My sister is supposed to be coming over to drive me to the store. Probably better if you're not here when she comes over."

12

When the tears dried, clothes were put back on. But not the Greyson Academy shirt. Charleigh refused to let Lexa take that particular shirt, offering a State U basketball shirt in its place. Its fit was looser and more Lexa's style, but it didn't smell like Charleigh as the other had. It came from the back of the blonde's closet and wasn't something Charleigh wore often. That alone made Lexa want to slip the other shirt under it so she would have a piece of the woman who'd walked her to the door.

Whether Charleigh finally opened the phone or not, Lexa still didn't know since she hadn't heard from the woman. Apparently walking her out wasn't the same as Lexa just leaving. She'd been more than willing to face Mona. However, Lexa couldn't find any words to get the woman to let her stay after she'd promised she wasn't giving up.

More than twenty-four hours of silence had Lexa searching for a reason to go see the woman. The solution came when her phone buzzed. She'd never gotten an alert before about her car, let alone a message a payment was past due. Several payments apparently, which was new. Lexa had never had a bill to pay, just like she'd never had to make an appointment for a doctor or to get her hair done.

Her first instinct was to call Sylvia. There were people who paid the bills each month, and someone forgot to make the Range Rover payments. That was when she was hit by two trucks at the same time. The first was what she needed to do to see Charleigh once more. The second was Sylvia stopped her people from paying Lexa's bills just like she stopped putting her hair appointments into the calendar.

Lexa wasn't sure what other bills from the house were in her name. She hadn't even realized the SUV was in her name; however, it was something she could do. Paying a bill couldn't be hard when the finance company included a link in the alert.

There was a username and a password needed to make the past payments on her car. Because she'd never been trusted to be an adult and handle adult things, she wasn't given the information. She had to go through Sylvia's home office to find a file with her name where her social security card was kept because the finance company wouldn't let her pay the bill without verifying who she was with the last four digits of her social security number.

She flipped through the thick file she'd never seen before. Sylvia saved all of her medical records. Every discharge paper, prescription, and doctor's note. Things she hadn't been handed because Sylvia had always been there to pick her up after an injury, or that time the pills had a blue top, instead of a red one. Those had messed things up in her head, and Sylvia had scribbled notes in the margins as to how. Dizziness. Blank stares. Inattentiveness. Irritability. Dry mouth. Each was a side effect of the trial drug Sylvia had documented. As Lexa flipped through all of her papers, she found the same type of list where Sylvia tracked her reaction to the drugs Lexa never wanted to take.

It was too much. Too many pages of failure when she was fine without the pills. She shoved the file back into the drawer. It wouldn't close, but it didn't matter. She wasn't coming back in here now she had the card and was able to call the car people back to pay her past-due payments.

After the call was completed, Lexa sat back on the stiff couch. It wasn't made for sitting on unless she wanted her ass to go numb. Not like the worn upholstery with seats where butts had indented the cushions. That was what reminded Lexa Charleigh needed her tomorrow.

Her calendar still had the location of the school, and she'd remembered the address to Charleigh's house. She knew Charleigh's school started at 8 AM, so she googled the walking time from Greyson Academy to the color-filled brick house. With the app telling her it was about a 45-minute walk, Lexa set her alarm for 5:30 AM to make it from Scottsdale to the woman's home before Charleigh set out to work.

Even with all the preparations, Monday came too quickly for Lexa. Her body was yanked from sleep by the alarm screaming. She rolled off the bed and walked to the farthest corner of the master bathroom where the screech was coming from. She'd plugged the phone in that particular outlet the night before to ensure she'd have to physically get out of bed to shut it off.

She'd slept in her nicest sweatpants and laid out a shirt she'd hoped would appeal to the blonde. Her bed hair was a mess after using the clarifying shampoo Danaya recommended for her. Two hair elastics snapped in Lexa's attempt to create a messy bun. After digging through every drawer in the bathroom she'd located an ancient scrunchie from what looked like Sylvia's childhood. It was hideous but it didn't break.

Foregoing the twenty minutes it would take her to put the contact lenses in her eyes, she pushed her glasses up her nose. Maybe Charleigh would find the nerd side of her adorable.

By 6:30, Lexa pulled into the driveway. The house was already alive inside and Lexa could hear the dog barking in the backyard. She'd been scared to stop for coffee, worrying the drive-thru would make her miss Charleigh leaving.

As she got out of the car, Charleigh opened the front door still in her sweats and a holey Devil's t-shirt. She folded her arms over her chest. The smallest wrinkle creased in her brow, and she seemed to be waiting for Lexa to speak.

"I... uh... I came to drive you to work," Lexa said with a guilty smile on her face. "No rules about offering you a ride."

A pink tongue ran over Charleigh's teeth. The white fangs still showed as she said, "Commonsense boundaries of showing up unannounced should have been enough. I didn't realize it needed to be a rule."

Lexa toed the gravel with her slides. She shrugged and countered with, "You said no more rules."

"Hence the commonsense part," Charleigh snapped. She turned from Lexa, but the front door didn't slam behind her.

Lexa made her way into the house and stood alongside the couch like a new floor lamp. Charleigh ignored her existence as she moved back into her bedroom. When she returned, the sweats had been replaced with tight black pants and the baggy Devils shirt a soft blue cotton shirt.

"You want an Ego?" Charleigh called from the kitchen.

"No, I'm good," Lexa said, not wanting to diminish even more of the woman's meager supplies. "I'll take a coffee."

"Sorry, but apparently Kroger isn't coffee," the woman barked through the tiny doorway.

Charleigh whistled at the backdoor, then the dog thundered into the house. Kibble hit the metal bowl, and Charleigh reminded the dog, "Remember if you turn on a scary movie, you just have to turn the channel. No trying to crawl under the bed like last time. You're too big to get under there and the mattress is heavy."

When the woman returned to the living room, she'd already nibbled off two rows of the instant waffle. She grabbed her backpack and sweater from the dog hair-riddled floor and stood in the living room staring at Lexa.

The waffle moved across her face as she consumed another row carefully.

"What the fuck are you doing to that waffle?" Lexa asked.

Charleigh ignored the question, putting the waffle between her teeth before she pushed Lexa through the door. She locked it quickly, then grabbed Lexa by the arm.

Lexa's exhausted feet dragged along the rocks as Charleigh pulled her toward the car.

"My boss will have my ass if I'm late," she explained. She bounced next to the passenger's side door.

"Boss better not touch your fucking ass," Lexa grumbled under her breath as she unlocked the door and held it open for the woman.

Charleigh used the handle to pull herself up into the seat. Having spent her adult life surrounded by people with like height, the feat the woman had to go to was amusing.

When Lexa got to the other side, the woman within had done some form of gymnastics to pop open the driver's side door for Lexa before settling into her chair.

Lexa stared at the dashboard with a slight smile. No one had ever opened her door for her, and it made her feel oddly warm. She tried to pinpoint a name for the feeling, forgetting momentarily why she was sitting there.

"I swear to God if I am late because you move at a slug's pace, I'm going to make you regret it," Charleigh said.

Lexa turned and watched the woman chewing through another row of Ego squares, meticulously making sure she didn't corrupt the next line. Her eyes rolled, and she put the car into drive.

"I'll get you there, Princess," Lexa grumbled this time louder.

Charleigh's eyes shot up from her food. "Don't call me that. I fucking hate it."

Lexa gave the preposterous woman next to her a side-eyed glare. "I hate getting up before nine."

"Then don't volunteer to take me to work," Charleigh stated.

The steering wheel did not bend under her grip as she sucked her teeth. She'd expected at least a little appreciation for showing up.

"Do we at least have time for coffee?" Lexa asked through gritted teeth.

"What part of my boss will have my ass if I'm late, was unclear?" And with that, Lexa learned the blonde was less of a morning person than she was.

"I figured you'd be thrilled at not having to walk, Princess."

"That name comes out of your mouth again and I will jump out of this car while it is moving."

Charleigh checked her eyeliner in the mirror, then twisted her hair into a messy knot atop her head. Strands of gold fell from her fingers onto the floor, seat, and the cup holders. Lexa sucked in a deep breath and reminded herself she was trying to earn this woman's trust and yelling at her over her hair wasn't going to end well.

"I told you last week I have no issue with walking," Charleigh said as though a four-mile walk into the middle of nowhere was not a big fucking deal. "I'm beginning to think you need hearing aids."

Lexa looked at Charleigh, back to chewing her waffle like a raccoon.

"You have no issue walking eight miles a day," she said in disbelief.

"No, I don't," Charleigh stated. She checked the time on her phone and Lexa smiled at learning the woman had finally opened the device.

"I'm not going to let a shitty car stop me from being an adult. I only bought the car from Marcus because I was getting my own place," she explained. She looked over at Lexa quickly, "But I'm going to get a new one. Car, I mean. I thought I could just fix the Accord... but I'm getting a new one."

"Thought you said he gave it to you."

"I mean, it was basically a gift because he never cashed my checks." Charleigh looked out the window. "But I'm going to get a new one. Make the payments and everything all by myself."

"Lemme guess, on payday," Lexa quipped, and instantly regretted it. She tried to come up with some way to fix it, but nothing she could say would change the way Charleigh pressed her fingers against the compact squares of the waffle.

As they rolled through a stop sign, Lexa swallowed the shame. "I'm sorry. That was really shitty."

"You don't need to apologize," Charleigh whispered just barely audible over the radio. She stared out the window, chewing silently. "You know one of these days, you're going to get tired of slumming it. It's easier to be bitchy. That way when you don't show up, I can feel responsible and not rejected."

The change in the door rattled as they drove through the dirt road Lexa had cursed on her first trip to the school.

"Thanks for coming," Charleigh said. "I do appreciate you coming even though you didn't have to. I can Venmo you for gas since I was such an ass."

Lexa reached over and took the small hand in hers. She wrapped her fingers through Charleigh's. When she found no way to tell Charleigh she wouldn't just change her mind someday, she changed the subject.

"So, Wednesday is our next game," Lexa started. "If we win, I have to go to New York on Thursday for the final on Saturday. Then we start round two and that will be against Seattle."

"Yeah." Charleigh checked her phone again. "Do you think you're going to be traded at the end of the season?"

Lexa squeezed Charleigh's hand to reassure the woman she wasn't letting go. She pulled into the back of the parking lot to avoid any prying eyes and put the car in park. Turning to Charleigh, Lexa swallowed her pride.

"There's a chance they'll sell my contract. There is a chance they'll just buy me out. I heard the team is getting a new owner, so a lot will depend on who that is and how involved he or she wants to be. Honestly, how I didn't manage to get suspended for getting arrested is beyond me, but I had a pretty kick-ass agent then. Now... I don't know what is going to come, but I told you, I'm not giving up."

"So, there is a chance you're leaving," Charleigh said. "Like leaving leaving."

"If I get traded, it won't happen until next season after the draft, so how about we don't worry about that until April." She put her hand under Charleigh's chin and guided it toward her, waiting for the woman to look at her.

When Charleigh finally looked up, Lexa said, "If I get traded, we will talk about it then. Let's just deal with that when it comes. I'm not just leaving though. This is my home, and I want to be near you."

As the stormy eyes stared at Lexa, she felt like she was being measured and coming up short. Nothing in her past interactions with Charleigh gave the woman any reason to trust her. Even if Emma was right and Charleigh blamed herself for everything, she didn't trust anyone. So, she had to give her a reason to trust her.

Since she'd fucked up the sex and getting the date, the next play her insomnia devised was to get Charleigh to Wednesday's game. Wednesday would be the last opportunity for Lexa to show Charleigh she wouldn't be the brunt of Lexa's anger every time something didn't go well if they lost. She needed to prove to Charleigh that she was capable of controlling her emotions.

"Will you come to my game Wednesday?" Lexa asked. "I can leave you my car so you don't have to take the train and I can Uber."

The messy blonde bun bobbled as she shook her head. "I can't take your car, Lexa. I will figure out how to get there like I always do."

"You're right, you probably can't reach the pedals," Lexa said, earning a swat from Charleigh.

Lexa leaned out of Charleigh's reach, and an idea popped into her head.

"Hold on," Lexa said. "I think I have a solution to our problem."

"We don't have a problem," Charleigh stated. "We are not an us. You are you and I am me. Getting places is a me problem."

"When you refer to we then you refer to us, thus there is a we and an us. And because you and I are two individuals with a problem of you potentially not being able to get to the game due to lack of transportation, it makes it an us problem." Lexa raised her eyebrows at the woman. "Don't look surprised. I'm a girl. I had to get straight As to still get a basketball scholarship. And I got an A once in a Shakespeare class. Had to stand up and recite a sonnet and all."

Charleigh tilted her head, then rolled her eyes. "I know."

Lexa's finger hovered over the display screen. She asked, "What do you mean, you know?"

With a shake of her head, Charleigh said, "I was in that class with you. Only I was invisible and you were you."

Lexa turned to the school, trying to remember the woman. It was a class for a hundred people though and team rules forced her to sit in the first three rows. She'd never looked back through the crowd.

Through the gates, Lexa could only see a few kids beginning to gather in the courtyard. Kinsley's truck pulled into the lot a few cars down. The girl looked at Lexa through the window, then gave her a single finger wave.

Lexa glanced at Charleigh as she pressed Danaya's name on the car's computer screen. "We did have time for coffee," she snipped.

Charleigh smiled and shrugged. Her fingers pulled the waffle in half and offered it to Lexa, but Lexa shook her head. Processed carbs were not part of her morning routine.

"*What you want, wigga?*" Danaya groaned into the phone. "*Did the teacher get tired of your old ass? Give me her number so I can show her what it means to be with a real baller. I mean, if she's down with the whole threesome thing, but Emma's a beast so she'd enjoy herself.*"

They could hear her moving around. Then Emma whined in the background, "*No threesomes. I don't share.*"

"*Come on, Emi,*" Danaya said. "*She had to sleep with Lex Luther. At least let us show her what being with real Black women is like.*"

She felt her cheeks grow hot at being called fake Black. They burned worse at the knowledge she was not Black enough to even hide the embarrassment.

"*Okay. But just once. And we take our time with her because Lexa don't know shit about taking her time from what I've heard.*" Lexa heard Emma laughing at her. "*I bet she's a screamer. White girls are always screamers. Let's take her away for a weekend or something before we go. And I get to be the one to tell Lexa afterward.*"

"*We could rent an AirBnB in Sedona. They have these places to hike and waterfalls. We could do it there, and...*"

Lexa closed her eyes. She pictured taking them both out at once. A hard enough check at practice would send them both to the trainer with a busted something.

"Hey Danaya," Charleigh called out, leaning across the console.

"*Oh shit,*" Danaya grunted, then choked.

"*What's wrong?*" Emma asked, now farther away from the phone.

"*Oh hey, Charleigh.*"

Emma growled, "*Charleigh? I thought you were fucking with Lexa. Shit. Did she hear me?*"

The line went silent for a moment, but the call was still connected. When Danaya came back, she sounded out of breath.

"*How... uh... yeah... how you doin?*" Danaya asked.

"I'm good, just wondering if you wanted to set up some after-school tutoring, so I can show you how to work a clock." Lexa's mouth dropped open, but Charleigh wasn't done. "I was telling Lexa that you are always in such a rush, you tend to just go in head first, but your crossover is a little weak. So, I figured I would just offer some assistance with, you know, timing or some tricks to improve your technique."

"*Damnnnnnnnn, that's how you wanna play, Peaches?*" Danaya called from the other end of the phone. "*Emma's in the other room with heart palpitations and she needs you to know we just playing. You know, just getting under Lex Luther's skin.*"

Charleigh winked at Lexa. "Well, I don't play, honey. I educate. So, if I have to teach you both, then that's gonna cost you. I mean a weekend away sounds great, but Lexa spent $1600 to hump my face. A whole weekend being the cream in the middle of your Oreo fantasy should be at least—"

Lexa cleared her throat to stop Charleigh from putting a price on her pussy. When the blue eyes glared at her, Lexa said, "Uhhh... so, you're on speaker."

"*Thanks for the warning,*" Danaya groaned. "*What do you want? It's fucking 7 am! And why the fuck you with Charleigh? Oh, gurl, please don't tell me you let that sorry ass stay in your bed all weekend.*"

"Jesus, Tanzon. No, we didn't spend all weekend fucking like you two did." Lexa sighed. This was not what she'd expected when she dialed. She pinched the bridge of her nose and tried to redirect the play in her head. "I was calling because I wanted to know if you would be willing to lend Charleigh your Charger."

Charleigh's finger hit the mute button on the screen. "I am not taking her car. Boundaries, Lexa. Fucking boundaries."

"*Sure, it's not like I need it since Emma never lets me drive anywhere,*" Danaya said.

Lexa hit the mute button. "That's because you are a terrible driver and you hit the median at the Lightrail a month ago."

"*Stop telling my business,*" Danaya hissed.

"We've all done it," Charleigh stated. She shrugged when Lexa turned slowly to stare at her.

Caressing the steering wheel, Lexa whispered to the car, "Don't worry. I'll never let her drive you."

"*So, Peaches, your clunker's, like, dead dead?*" Danaya asked.

Charleigh glared at Lexa and let out a heavy breath of air. "My sister looked at it yesterday. The cables for the battery apparently are shorting and the manifold is not, like, folding. I don't think that's actually a thing. I honestly don't know. It's just more than just the alternator, but don't worry about it. I will figure it out."

Danaya hummed. "*Well, I'm only here for like three to five more weeks, so why don't you just keep it while I'm in Italy?*"

"That would be—" Lexa stated.

"I can't take her car," Charleigh said again, this time landing the slap across Lexa's arm. She turned back to the computer screen like she was on a video call. "I can't take your car, Danaya. Thank you very much, but I didn't know that was what Lexa was planning on asking you."

"*Peaches, it's really no big deal. I have to pay for it to sit in storage when I'm gone anyways. It was stupid to even buy it because I never drive it.*"

Lexa set her gaze forward, and said, "You borrow her car so you don't have to walk to work or I will be at your house every day to drive you myself. I bet your boss would love to see me dropping you off each morning."

Charleigh chewed on her lip. "D, are you sure?" she asked.

"*Yeah, on one condition,*" Danaya said.

"What do you want?" Lexa asked.

"*For Charleigh to come to the end-of-season party at your house,*" she said. "*Peaches, this shit is legendary in the basketball world. You gotta come.*"

Charleigh's head cocked to one side as she looked Lexa over. "End of year party?"

Lexa shook her head. "I didn't say I was throwing a party. I don't throw parties."

"*Your ass is throwing that party,*" Danaya barked. "*I have heard about this party all damn season, and I will be pissed if you fuck up one more thing for me. It's my rookie fucking year. I already got traded in the first month and all anyone from Chicago could say was 'at least you get to go to the Devil's end-of-season party.'*"

Lexa felt her stomach drop. She'd never been the one to plan the annual party. She didn't know how to even throw a party.

"She'll do it," Charleigh committed. She squeezed Lexa's hand and whispered, "It's clearly a suitable revenge for you making me borrow someone else's car."

"*Okay, awesome. Emma and I will come by tonight to drop off the car and maybe we can all go out for dinner. There's this crawfish boil place at Westgate that I want to try,*" Danaya offered. "*Also, if you can tease the shit out of Emma for the whole threesome thing, I'll be forever in your debt.*"

Charleigh covered her smile. Her chest quaked under her silent giggles before she said, "You want me to give her shit when you're the one asking Lexa for my number. Gurl, I know who wants the threesome and it's not your girl."

"I am not a speakerphone type of bitch," Danaya yelled into the phone. *"Fuck you, Jensen."*

"See you tonight," Charleigh said still laughing. "I'll be sure to wear something that makes you regret Lexa getting to me first."

"Bye," Lexa said before ending the call. She turned to Charleigh. "I don't even know what to say."

"I'm sorry for blindsiding you with a car you didn't ask for," Charleigh offered. "Or I recognize that 'boundaries' is a word I need to google since Shakespeare didn't use that term, and I don't know its meaning."

Lexa said none of these things. She instead watched students flooding the courtyard of the school. A basketball bounced against the wall of the building in front of them as a girl taller than Lexa trudged over the gravel, dribbling sideways.

Lexa's eyes grew wide, and she pointed at the girl. "Who's that?"

"Neveah. I wrote a grant application to your ex's foundation to try and get a gym because all we have is a cracked pavement court in the back of the school. She's already six feet and only 15," Charleigh said. "Only thing she loves is basketball."

The kid transferred the ball from the wall to the ground in a single motion. Then she realized with the other hand, the kid was dribbling a tennis ball at the same time.

"Do you have other girls who want to play?" Lexa asked.

Charleigh laughed. "Yeah." She rolled her head against her seat. "Don't laugh but I'm their coach."

"You?" Lexa choked. "You, coach basketball? But, you can't even reach the top shelf of your pantry."

"Lexa Jenson, I study basketball like I study books."

When Lexa just blinked at her, Charleigh waved her hand in the air. "Here is an example. I can tell you the reason you haven't landed a corner three all season."

"Because my wife left me and that was the first shot she worked with me to perfect," Lexa said. "It's in my head."

Charleigh rolled her eyes. "No. It's because your momentum is stunted. You're shooting from your heels. Toes literally pull up at the last minute every time. Watch the tape. I promise you will see your whole body sit back. Must be all the beer going straight to your ass."

Lexa looked at the computer screen, then back at Charleigh. "I'll watch the tape and if you're right, I will charter a bus for your whole team to Wednesday's game."

A hand extended across the center console. "You got a deal."

Lexa's eyes narrowed at Charleigh. She took the woman's hand and shook it. "This isn't an elaborate way to get out of having to come is it?"

"No, this is a bet I know I am going to win," Charleigh stated. "And I don't want seats in the fucking 200s. My girls have never seen a game where you all don't look like little white bugs scurrying around the court, fighting over an acorn."

"You got it, Princess." Lexa leaned in for a kiss but jumped away from Charleigh when Mona's hand slapped against the hood.

The broody brunette stared at them through the windshield. Two fingers pointed at her eyes, then she jabbed them toward Lexa. Her lips said, "Liquify you."

"Why is she the way she is?" Lexa asked.

Charleigh was already halfway out of the car, when she said, "I can't be late. See you at my house, like, around five. And stop calling me a fucking princess."

"What time does school get out?" Lexa called once she got the window to roll down. But Charleigh hadn't heard her. Or she'd chosen to ignore her.

Lexa sucked her teeth and committed another level of stalker behavior. She called out to a kid dragging his feet to the gate. "Hey, what time does school get out?"

"Three," the kid called back without looking up.

Lexa let her head fall back against the headrest. She had two hours before Danaya's stylist made her scalp burn and a Starbucks trip would only take up about twenty minutes. Shaking her head, she put the car into reverse as an Audi pulled up in front of the office. A small blonde with a flashy bag exited the vehicle.

She had never hated someone from just the back of their head before, but she knew this must be the bitch Charleigh was terrified of having her ass.

"Better leave my girl alone," Lexa growled through the tinted windows.

The school owner turned toward the Range Rover. Lexa knew she couldn't see through the window, but she reversed quickly to avoid being stopped by the woman. As she drove away, she hoped the 'MSWNTRS' license plate would go unnoticed.

13

Ten teenage girls in blue Greyson Academy jerseys screamed for the Purple Devil throwing t-shirts at the start of the fourth Quarter. Charleigh mouthed a thank you to a sweat-sheened woman looking back at her from across the court where she sat waiting for the game to restart.

A shirt was thrown over the girls' heads. The giant 15-year-old, sitting beside Charleigh hopped up and caught a shirt heading a few rows back from her. Neveah turned to Charleigh with a giant smile and waved the prize. The excitement in the girl only grew as she handed the shirt over to Jayla, the scrawny freshman with bulky soundproof headphones over her ears and sunglasses covering her eyes. Jayla stared at the gift and leaned her head against Neveah's shoulder, then flapped her hands at her side, soothing away the overstimulation of the arena. The girl wasn't officially on the team yet, but Nevaeh requested she come with them.

When the players returned to the court, Danaya jogged in front of them. She waved her hands in the air and looked at the girls.

"Whose house is this!" Danaya cried out.

Charleigh joined in the callback, "The Devil's house!"

The girls cheered loudly for Danaya's attention, but the woman returned to a wide zone defense as the Stars's point guard brought the ball down.

Neveah sat in the chair next to Charleigh. "How'd you pull this off, Coach?"

Charleigh watched as Danaya bounced off the screen. The Devils were down by three, and the guard was moving toward the hoop. She faked a shot, then passed, not seeing Danaya coming up the back on the recovery. Charleigh held onto Nevaeh's arm as she leaned forward with the pass to Lexa.

The voices of the crowd faded from Charleigh's ears to just the sound of the ball against the court and Lexa's sneakers screaming. Lexa dribbled to the bottom corner of the court and planted her toes. She breathed out and pushed the ball through the air.

The grip on the kid's arm was too tight, but Charleigh watched the ball spin through the net with a swish before half the Stars made it back to defense.

Jumping to her feet, Charleigh cheered for Lexa as the woman pointed across the court at her.

"Coach, she pointing at you?" Neveah asked, rubbing the feeling back into her arm.

"That's how I made this happen," Charleigh explained. "I told her she was pulling up her toes and that's why she couldn't get her shot to fall. She bet me I was wrong, but this is what winning looks like."

"No cap, you familiar with *the* Lexa Jenson? The GOAT?" Nevaeh asked. Her eyes weighed Charleigh for her worth.

Charleigh tucked the hair behind her ear, then nodded. "Yeah, I know her."

"Bruh, why you just now telling me this?"

With a chuckle, Charleigh said, "I prefer you think I'm cool without being associated with famous people."

"Yeah, I guess you're right. I mean I heard she was at the school and all, but I didn't know you know, know her," Nevaeh said, spreading out as far as she could in the cramped space. "When they makin' kicks with my name on them, I'm going to come back to Greyson's and make sure everyone knows you got famous people in your pocket so they act right for you."

"When you become a Devil, I'll be at every home game," Charleigh promised.

With the game closing after Lexa landed a buzzer-beating three for the win, Charleigh counted heads while the team waited for the stands to empty. The bus was on the opposite side of the arena, so waiting for the bulk of the crowd would provide them with an easier path.

The kids gathered their trash from the snacks that had been delivered to them courtesy of a woman still paying attention. Charleigh ducked under a seat in search of a lost phone when cries from her girls jolted her back on her ass. She searched for the source of their excitement over the chairs only to find half the Devils returning to the court still in their uniforms.

"Hey, Coach Charleigh," Lexa called. "We came to teach your team a thing or two."

A security guard smiled at Emma and nodded her head, stepping out of the pathway to the court.

The girls looked to their leader, whose lips set in a straight line.

"Pretty sure they could show you up," Charleigh called back, having pushed up from the ground. "They definitely wouldn't have let the Stars lead the whole damn game. Were you trying to give us a heart attack?"

Emma covered her mouth to hide her smile, but Danaya wasn't backing down from the challenge.

"Bet!" Danaya called out. "Ten bucks and my jersey, no one scores on me!"

Nevaeh looked down at Charleigh, "Can we?"

"Go make me look good," Charleigh said.

The seats twelve rows up from the floor emptied. Bleachers shook from their thunderous feet. The girls weren't dressed to play, but Danaya wasn't playing to lose until the tiny freshman took off her sunglasses and bounced the ball in front of the woman.

Danaya glanced up at Charleigh, and it was her downfall. The smaller girl dribbled left, then crossed back. Danaya couldn't stop the momentum of her longer body. With headphones still in place, Jayla ducked under Danaya's arm and went straight to the basket.

Emma's laughter was louder than the trash talk from the girls, but Danaya took her loss well. She pulled the jersey from her body and handed it to the child.

"I don't have any cash on me, but I'll get it to your coach," Danaya told Jayla.

With a crooked grin, Jayla ran over to where Nevaeh was getting a one-on-one lesson from Lexa. Nevaeh stopped dribbling for the younger girl, who held the jersey out to her.

"No way, bruh," Nevaeh told her. "You won that."

The freshmen didn't take no for an answer though. She pushed it into Nevaeh's hands and picked up the ball from the ground, passing it to Lexa. Lexa passed the ball back to Jayla who faked a shot before sending the ball to Nevaeh for a quick lay-up. Lexa stared at the tiny competitor, then looked to Charleigh.

"What are you teaching these girls?" Lexa cried out.

"Passing. You should try it sometime."

Lexa gripped the imaginary dagger in her chest and fell to her knees.

As the girls got autographs and pictures, Emma leaned her sweat-soaked arm on Charleigh's shoulder.

"DayDay, put a shirt on before you pose for any of those photos. They can't be going back to school showing off you in a bra," Charleigh called out.

Looking down at her abs, Danaya shrugged. She spotted when Jayla returned to her with the wrapped-up T-shirt in her hand. The smaller girl held out the shirt, and then pulled it back.

"You score, you win," Jayla stated, looking toward the ceiling. She set the shirt on the three-point line and stood with her back to the basket.

"How are you?" Emma asked while Charleigh watched Jayla keep pace with Danaya's dribble.

Charleigh tucked the hair back behind her ear again. She only turned her attention from the kid who would be trying out for her team when Danaya had to try to get past her.

She smiled up at the older woman who'd thankfully removed the stinky pit near her face.

"I'm good." She breathed out the fear she'd been holding in. "Really glad you all won tonight. I was worried there for a minute. You know, with the kids here and all."

"I was surprised when Lexa said you were coming. After we left your house Friday, she didn't have much to say. Then...." Emma sucked in her lips, before letting them pop out. "I'm sorry about what I said about the whole Sedona thing. I was too embarrassed to say anything Monday. It was all jokes. We talk like that too much, but it should stop."

"I get it. What's the label? Ball bunny right?" Charleigh sucked her teeth. "She confuses the shit out of me. Friday she rejected me, then showed up on Sunday morning. I'm sure she told you we slept together, and I figured she got what she wanted so she would be done. But then she showed up on Monday again. So, thanks for telling her where I live because until she meets someone new, she's going to keep showing up. Especially since I opened the phone. I am pretty sure now I owe her at least a hundred orgasms if I'm worth street value."

Emma rubbed the back of her neck. Charleigh followed her gaze to Lexa running a pick and roll with Nevaeh. If nothing else came out of this, maybe Nevaeh got a personal trainer.

Balls bounced all around them as the kids had dreams come true. Charleigh sucked in a breath. "I don't really know what to think about any of it, because it's like I know this isn't reality. I mean, not the reality I live in."

Lexa let her braids fall from the bun atop her head as she took her turn for the photos. Her smile was infectious, and Charleigh caught a glimpse of the girl who'd been drafted number one so many years before.

"I've known Lexa since she was a baby baller," Emma stated. "I can't say I am happy about this whole thing between you two, but I can say that in all those years, I have never seen Lexa take initiative for anything or anyone. But I am worried. I'm worried about her, and I'm also worried about you."

"Is she going to hurt me?" Charleigh asked.

"More than she already did?" Emma asked with a side-eye glance. "Physically, I don't think so. She's not violent, but she's aggressive and possessive. And you..."

"Are weak," Charleigh admitted.

Emma sucked her teeth. "I don't think you're weak. Look, I don't know you, but I don't think a lot of people have been there for you, and I am betting you've seen some rough stuff. You should know I'm friends with Sylvia, Lexa's ex. She said she met you before she was traded."

Charleigh felt her entire body set like cement. She could only move her eyes sideways to look at the woman.

"Yeah, I know about your kid. I haven't said anything to Lexa, and I don't plan on saying anything." Emma slowly exhaled, before she continued, "Just don't let the honeymoon phase trick you into thinking she's changed. This version of her is real, but so are those others."

"She said that," Charleigh whispered. "That I couldn't forgive her because then she could forgive herself."

"Good," Emma stated. "Maybe she's finally starting to grow up. I... I'm sorry. I know we don't know each other, I just..."

"Just tell me, because I probably already told myself the same thing."

"You're young, Charleigh. Just think about what it means to be involved with someone like us. Because trades happen and we have to go overseas if we want to live the ball player's dream. That kinda distance with this kind of attention, it's a lot to manage for both parties."

"Basically, you're sayin' she'll never be faithful," Charleigh stated. "Like with her ex. It was more than just the sister-in-law. Like before this summer."

"I can't tell you what she will or won't be." Emma pulled her jersey up and wiped her face. "Look, it's public knowledge that cheating ruined her marriage, but maybe she's learned from that. You just gotta think about what you really want in this life, because no matter what afterlife you believe in, this is the only time you will ever be you. So, live it for you. Not for someone else."

Chest shaking in humiliated laughter, she said, "You make it sound so simple."

"Maybe because it is that simple," Emma offered.

Charleigh scanned over the girls enjoying their moment on the court. The simplicity of being who they were with people they wished they could be. She bit her lip, wondering who she was. The person she'd been at the bar felt like a different person altogether, but when put in the position to be someone different with Lexa, both times she'd gone back to stripping down so Lexa could take what little she had to give and move forward.

"You look like someone stole your lunch money," Danaya stated as she catapulted her body into Emma's arms. When Emma dropped her to her feet, Danaya narrowed her eyes on the older woman. "Wha'd you say to her?"

Charleigh smiled as best she could, then spoke for Emma. "Nothing. I was just thinking about how much you made these kids' year. Thank you for coming out here. You really didn't have to."

"Gurl, this was the best," Danaya said. "I wish we were here when you all play so we could come to a game."

"Maybe someday," Charleigh said. She cupped her hands around her mouth and used her teacher voice. "Girls, we have to go. We have a curfew."

Groans and moans echoed in the empty arena, but farewells were bade and belongings were gathered. As they filed up the steps toward the bus, Charleigh counted heads once more. She scrunched her nose and counted again when she didn't get ten the first time. She searched the court to find Nevaeh and Lexa sitting in the home team seats.

Nevaeh's eyes were staring at the court as Lexa moved her arms around. It was clear they were talking shop. Charleigh walked over to them. The team waited at the tunnel to exit for them, going through the videos and filming TikToks.

"So, you keep your grades up. It's the first question they ask. And when you're on the court it doesn't matter how angry you are, you make the game look fun. Coaches want a team player, not a star. Stars break teams, they don't make them. So, when you make that three, you celebrate the person that handed you the ball. They got you there, and you don't forget it. No matter how good you are, you can't beat five against one. And don't let anyone tell you you're the reason they win. You always shout out your teammates and you hold them above you."

Nevaeh nodded her head.

"And you listen to your coach. I know, she's the size of a garden gnome, but she knows what she is talking about, so don't ever underestimate her ability to see things you can't."

Lexa's gaze drifted from the bubble they'd created for themselves. She smiled as Charleigh licked her teeth and tried not to smile at the insult.

"Nevaeh, we have to go," Charleigh told the girl.

"Thanks, Ms. Jenson." The teen offered Lexa her hand. "This was all really, really great, and Coach said you made it happen, so you know... it just means a lot to us."

Lexa smiled as she stood up. Bags had already formed under the woman's eyes. Her time off the court was minimal but she'd still brought everyone out for her team.

With Nevaeh a safe distance away, Lexa asked, "Can I come see you when I get back?"

"Was that a question?" Charleigh asked. She reached up and put the back of her hand against the woman's head, then dropped it. "You don't seem to have a fever, but I have never known you to ask permission for anything before."

Lexa pushed the braids from her face. "I looked up the definition of the word boundaries. Apparently, I am not supposed to just show up at your house unannounced."

"Well, I guess I should reward you for listening," Charleigh said. She tilted her head back and bit her lip to look up as Lexa stepped into her space.

"I'm not allowed to kiss you, am I?" Lexa asked.

"Two questions and you waited for an answer," Charleigh said. "I'm impressed."

Lexa shook her head, cupping Charleigh's cheek. "Two requests and no answers. I think you like ghosting me."

"You can come over when you get back." Her eyes closed as Charleigh tried not to choke on the smell of post-thirty-two minutes of game time. "But you stink and the girls are watching and my boss would have—"

"Your ass," Lexa finished for her. She tucked a lock of hair behind the woman's ear. "You know, I think this boss and I are going to have to have words about her thinking she has rights to your ass."

Emma's words echoed in Charleigh's head. Possessive. Aggressive. She glanced back at Emma and Danaya. Danaya's words must have been pointed because Emma flinched.

"I have to go," Charleigh said, stepping back. "The kids are waiting."

Lexa walked with her. Their arms grazed with each step. The concrete walls threw the girls' conversations back at them, keeping away the silence.

Charleigh left Lexa at the glass doors, moving out from Lexa's world into her own. Shadows danced around the walkway and a passing car's music paused her girls in a quick dance show.

"Call me," Lexa called out as the doors slid shut behind her. Her hand was held up like a phone to Charleigh.

"Damn, Coach," Nevaeh said. "She got a fever for you."

Charleigh rolled her eyes and pushed the girl toward the bus.

She chewed on the conversation with Emma, contemplating how to be herself when not being herself was what made all of this possible.

Too many questions filled her mind as she stared at the phone with the little girl's face smiling back at her. She'd brought a bus full of girls to meet the woman her child was willing to give her tooth fairy money for.

Emma had to be wrong. She couldn't live for herself. She wasn't one person, she was two. She was the slut Emma didn't know well, and the mother the woman didn't know at all. Just like Lexa. Lexa had no idea who Charleigh was, but she didn't know how long she could keep it that way.

14

Lexa revved her feet against the floor. Seattle had been the start of her rally, and Coach was talking to her instead of at her for the first time all season. It felt right again like maybe she wasn't the next to leave to earn back a draft ticket sold for Danaya.

The win in Seattle brought the Devils back home for Game 2 of the second round of playoffs. They'd had a five-day break, enough time for Lexa to visit Charleigh once and beg her to come to another game.

A part of her appreciated the way Charleigh fought her over every gift. The stubbornness of the woman made her want to give more, but she was working on the boundaries.

Every moment Lexa wasn't on the court her mind sorted through her Charleigh playbook to ensure she'd cataloged all the little things that made the woman smile. Smiles were all she had to peel back the layers of the woman who shared so little. And Lexa had several pages dedicated to the different types of smiles the woman possessed. Like the one she'd had when she said she was thinking about crocheting, which spurred another gift purchase of a Harry Potter crochet kit sitting in her duffle bag.

She wondered what type of smile Charleigh would be wearing when she came out of the tunnel. As quickly as she flipped through the mental snapshots, she remembered the empty chair.

'If she's not in her seat, it doesn't mean she's not coming. And even if she doesn't come, you gotta keep your cool,' Lexa told herself.

The excitement of her teammates was contagious. Lexa's heart beat with the bass. She smiled even though her braids were being yanked and twisted by Emma's fumbling fingers. She had tried to gather the mass of box braids twice before Emma had pushed her into a chair and took over.

"Your teacher coming tonight?" she asked.

The label made Lexa remember. Remember Charleigh's lying face when she said nothing had happened with the fuck boy with teacher fantasies. "Don't call her the teacher," she told Emma.

Emma's hands paused. "Why?"

It wasn't Lexa's story to tell, so she shrugged. "She just don't like it."

With Lexa's hair secured into a tight French braid finally finished and her face thrust forward roughly, the center flopped into a chair across from Lexa. Her hands played with a ball. "So, you maybe won't suck tonight since she's coming, right?"

Danaya sat down in Emma's lap, sending the ball away. The younger girl squeezed Emma's cheeks together and looked at the older woman. "Emmi, don't tease Lex. Blondes have always been her good luck charm."

Lexa picked up her Jordan Retro and threw it at them both. Emma karate chopped the projectile away, sending it into the back of the giant from Norway.

When the woman stooped down to pick up the shoe, Danaya pointed at Lexa. "She did it," she lied.

Lexa rolled her eyes. "Sorry, I was aiming for them."

"You throw like you shoot," the woman said. She shot the shoe at Lexa, knocking her phone off its resting place atop her bag. "That's how you do it. You push and you flick. Push and flick."

"Yeah, Lex. Push and flick," Emma chortled.

Lexa grabbed the phone from the bag and checked Instagram. There was nothing new from Charleigh, and it sucked. She'd hoped the blonde would send her something to tell her she left or even good luck, and without having the woman's number Instagram was still her lifeline.

She fumbled through the bag and pulled out the wrapped box. It flipped easily in her hands before it was pulled away just out of Danaya's reach as the girl grabbed for it. Lexa stared at the box and Danaya tried to grab it again, but Emma was holding the forward in her lap with one hand and the other hand held them both to the chair.

Danaya kicked as Emma's fingers found the danger zone on her side. The rookie arched her back, squirmed, and begged for a cease-fire. Lexa couldn't help but laugh at them.

"Keep your paws off Lexa's newest attempt to buy the white girl's attention," Emma said directly into Danaya's ear.

"Okay!" she cried, twisting away from the breath at her neck. "I will be good!" Emma gave the girl's side a few more pinches before she released her. Danaya fell from the center's lap onto her ass and glared up at her like a child. "You're cruel."

Emma's cocky smirk didn't hide the adoration in her eyes. She leaned back in the chair. "You like it."

Shaking her head, Lexa pushed up from her seat and grabbed her duffle. Tossing it into the bottom of the locker, she turned back to the sorta friends. At least she thought they might be her friends after she'd brought Charleigh's team to the last game.

Her lower lip was already mangled from chewing on it every time Charleigh seemed to be second-guessing talking to her, but she went at it with her teeth again. Unable to squelch the uneasiness, she said, "Hey guys?"

Both heads turned to look at her in unison. The words she'd chewed on when her lip wasn't sedating her nerves had dissolved in her mouth. She searched for them again while Emma tapped her fingers against the ball she'd retrieved.

Danaya lacked some of that control and snapped, "Say what's on your mind, half & half."

Lexa's brow furrowed. "Why you always gotta be calling me stupid shit? I'm not fucking creamer... and I swear if the word wigga exits your mouth, I'm gonna tear those locs out of your head."

"Well, you're not chocolate but you're not buttercream either," Danaya stated from her spot on the floor. "And half & half is fucking white. White white like all the girls you date. So, really I'm just calling you like you are. Half us. Half them."

"Why do people always compare skin to food? It's weird." Emma looked at Danaya. "And why you always gotta go there with the white girls? Nothing wrong with dating a white girl."

Danaya shrugged. "It's better than the other shit people say, and people talk. You know people have been talking about her chasing another white girl like a trophy. I don't know what your fascination with blondes is, but I love me some dark chocolate."

Lexa watched Emma to see if her dark chocolate ass had anything to say about Danaya's not-so-subtle hint. If she did, she didn't say it.

Danaya had lots to say apparently. "Plus, Lex Luther knows that she hot shit with her good hair, even if she is high yellow."

Emma's lips twisted in a smirk. "You do have good hair."

"Thanks, chocolate stud," Lexa poked.

Emma's eyes rolled so far back that they almost disappeared.

Hoping to move away from being not Black enough, Lexa spit it out. "So, I want to ask her out but every time I bring it up she says there is all this stuff that I don't know about her, but then she doesn't say anything else."

"Probably doesn't feel like you're listening," Emma stated.

Lexa looked up from the box she'd become fixated on to find Emma staring at her.

"I listen to everything she says, but I do most of the talking," Lexa admitted, hoping no one else was listening. She didn't want everyone to know. "It's like she is constantly running through a pro and con list of even talking to me."

Danaya nodded, her smug smile dropping into a more serious silence. She found her own chair close by and pulled it up.

Lexa twisted the box, and tried again, "I just don't really know how to do any of this. You know... uh... yeah, I'm sure she told you. Via did everything for me, and Charleigh... she's so different from Via."

Emma looked up with just her eyes, and said, "Look, maybe you should just give her some space. Give yourself a chance to settle into your new life. You haven't even signed the divorce papers yet. You're still living in Sylvia's house. Are you even looking for your own house because at some point Via is coming back home? Maybe that's where your head needs to be. Getting your own life. Maybe take a minute and get yourself in a place where you are stable."

She'd considered it. Especially when Charleigh had avoided any date conversation. She hadn't considered Charleigh knew she was still married. It would make sense because Charleigh seemed to know everything about her. Lexa glanced at her bag where the bottle of pills was still buried in her hygiene kit. Maybe not everything.

"Honestly, that is what should happen." Lexa shook her head. "But we seem to be in each other's lives for a reason."

Emma's eyebrow quirked. "You can't claim destiny if you keep setting up times for her to be around you."

Lexa thought of all she'd accomplished with the woman in her life. She hadn't touched a beer since that night at Coach's. She hadn't fucked some random chick. She hadn't even contacted Kayla, who had reached out on every messenger app possible after her number was blocked.

"She makes me better," Lexa said.

"I'm calling bullshit." Emma leaned forward, her voice lower as the room became quieter. "You haven't been better but this last time. You've been at your damn worst every other time you've been around her. Maybe you should just stop while you're ahead."

"Why you so against them?" Danaya asked. "Jesus, you are so focused on this girl, it's like you're trying to water the seeds of doubt already there."

Danaya's body moved into her own space. Lexa looked the woman over, wondering if the green tint to her teammate's skin was just her imagination.

"I don't wanna see Charleigh get hurt again. She has a whole life that doesn't need this basketball bullshit fucking with it. And if she finds out you're asking her out and still waiting for Sylvia to come home... that's going to hurt her, and she still ain't healed from all the other shit you put her through."

"I'm not waiting for Via to come back," Lexa stated, but the words tasted funny in her mouth. "I promised to be better for Charleigh and to make it up to her. So, that's what I'm going to do."

"So, what's the problem with just getting to know her without the pressure being something more?" Danaya asked. Her hand came to rest on Emma's thigh, and she gave it a little squeeze. "You're kinda trying to put a puzzle together by smashing the pieces together because you're in a hurry to get it done, but if this is destiny, then you know, like, it's not going to come together in one month. The fun comes from finding the ones that fit and celebrating those little moments. I mean if it was me, I would be taking my time with every single one because I don't want that puzzle to ever really be done. Even when it's hard because someone is obsessed with the same damn blonde."

The rookie's dark eyes turned to Emma.

"I'm not obsessed with Charleigh." Emma ran her hand over her curls. "It's just the therapist in me. The girl's been through a lot of trauma. It's in her eyes, just buried there. But you can see it when she's looking around. I bet she doesn't even have to turn her head to know when someone is coming close."

"You analyze everyone you meet?" Danaya asked, sitting back in her chair.

"Can't shut it off," Emma admitted. She licked her lips. "I see that girl and... and... I just want to hug her. I just want to hug her and tell her that she matters. It's not what you or she thought. Just like she's my little sister, and I wasn't there to protect her. And I just keep thinking about that story she told us about being unadopted after being sent away. I just feel like no one in her life has told her she matters. I mean, who lives in the middle of a cornfield? And she always comes to the games alone. She has that sister that she talks about, but I've only seen her once."

"She works with her sister," Lexa provided. "But that's her only friend, I think."

"Well, then maybe you should just be her friend," Emma said, tapping the ball. "Be her friend while you take care of you. You ain't ever been on your own, and she isn't capable of taking care of you like Via did."

Lexa held out the box to them, and explained, "I just... I've never felt like this before. And I'm scared of fucking it up and I know she's going to be pissed I bought her something else because she's like keeping it all tallied up like a debt she owes me, but I just want to see her smile, you know?"

She sighed and tossed the box toward her bag. It hit the back of the locker and fell within the duffle. "Damn it. I just don't want it to be so fucking complicated."

Emma stood up. She placed her hand under Lexa's arm and pulled her to her feet. "It's the playoffs and we need you here. Not chasing after a girl that wants you to back off. Just be here. Work on you and your game. That's all you need right now. No one else. You don't need no one else but yourself."

Lexa nodded. She understood what Emma was saying.

Leaning down, Emma reached into Lexa's bag and pulled out the hygiene kit. She handed it to Lexa.

"You've been sober for three weeks now. You should start taking care of yourself again."

Coach Quitin came in, calling them to the board where he explained the game plan. Lexa wasn't listening. She couldn't listen with Emma's words playing over and over again in her head. She pushed the hygiene kit back into her duffle without opening it.

She needed to be who she was right now, not in a numbed haze from the pills in the bottle. Just play the game and complete the puzzle with a clear head. She could do that. She had to do that.

Her rally was short-lived. Another loss in front of the woman who studied Lexa's face as she dragged her feet toward her. Charleigh held her arms across her chest tightly and bit her lip.

Lexa took a deep breath as she slouched before the blonde. "I hate losing. I hate it more that I made the foul that lost us the lead," she told Charleigh. "I don't want you to think that I am mad at you, so don't worry I won't ask you out tonight when I know I'm going to be whiny."

"Thank you for communicating that with me." Charleigh licked her lips. "I can let you go do whatever you need to, and you can message me tomorrow or not. I mean if you, like, want to go out and, like, meet someone else. Or I can listen as you talk about whatever you want, even if it's whining. I mean, those refs had to be paid off because you touched nothing but the ball."

Lexa pulled the jersey up and wiped the sweat from her face. She looked over at the tunnel to see Danaya and Emma babysitting her from a distance.

"Do you think..." Lexa looked up at the stands emptying. She took in as much air as possible and looked at the woman. "Could I maybe hug you?"

Charleigh tucked her lip between her teeth. She glanced around them, and then slowly she stepped into Lexa's very public bubble. As Lexa's sweaty arms encased Charleigh's body, the smaller woman held her tightly. Small, thin fingers were splayed, pressing against Lexa's back and applying tight pressure.

The footsteps of disappointed fans ceased vibrating through her chest as her sense of self stabilized in the woman's arms. Lexa let the smell of sweat be taken over by the fruit scent of Charleigh's new conditioner.

"Emma wasn't lying," Lexa whispered as she rested her head on Charleigh's hair. "You really do give the best hugs."

They stayed that way until the fans still waiting for her autograph began calling her name. She leaned back and looked down at Charleigh.

"I have to go sign some shit." Lexa nodded to the people waiting on her. "Can you wait for me? The pass will get you to the locker room door. I won't even shower. I will just grab my stuff and.... I'll be fast, and maybe we can go somewhere. Just us."

Charleigh leaned back and smiled. She pressed her hand over her mouth and nose, and said, "I drove here, so it would be strange to wait and then walk in different directions. You go shower because you smell like the girls' bathroom at my work. Then you can come over to my place and watch a movie or something. I even have popcorn because I went to the store."

"I can come over?" Lexa repeated, needing to hear Charleigh say it again.

"It's a school night, but.... Yeah. You can come over for a while." She tucked her hair behind her ear. "I can sleep on the couch, and you can take my bed since it'll be late."

Lexa licked her lips. "I'm not taking your bed, but maybe we can try out this crocheting kit I picked up. I want to make that little creature with the big ears."

15

All that was missing from the room was a bed. Just a twin bed frame and a mattress. There was one at Walmart that would work. Charleigh just had to get off the floor to go get it, then put it in the car Danaya loaned her. It was the last thing on Dilynn's list of demands.

She had the money in her account. A vehicle to get her to the store. There was no reason for the room to still be incomplete, yet Charleigh continued to lay atop the wooden floor staring up at the star stickers.

With a bed in the room, Joey could come home. She could do all the things she'd always wanted to do. Read the books she'd put on the shelves. Play with the toys she'd found at Goodwill over the years. Count the stars she'd hung on the ceiling for each day her baby was someplace else.

The fear of failure immobilized her. She knew if she didn't get the bed before January's hearing they would change Joey's case plan to severance. Her mother's lawyer had requested it at the last hearing, but the judge had given her another six months. Six months to get a place to stay where Joey would have a bed of her own. Just a bed, which should have been the first thing she bought for the house. Instead, she waited. Spent money on the red chair in the living room, then the television. Bought Joey books and toys here and there.

The phone rang, pulling Charleigh's attention from the ceiling.

"Are you dressed for Princess Greyson's engagement party?" Mona asked before Charleigh even said hello.

"I'm not going," Charleigh whispered.

The last thing she needed after seeing her daughter's tear-streaked face at the end of their visit was to watch her biological mother swoon over a woman she'd adopted. A woman only a few years older than Charleigh was. She'd adopted Evie Greyson at the same age Charleigh had been sent to Greyson Academy. Thrown Charleigh away, only to choose another girl.

Charleigh had spent every moment Evie Greyson and her paths crossed wondering what it was Dilynn loved so much about the woman. Tried to figure out what she could do like Evie to make Dilynn see her.

"Get dressed. You're going with me."

She knew the answer to the question about why Dilynn would celebrate the other woman while shunning her. It was the same question Charleigh had been asking herself as she lay on the floor.

'Will I ever be able to look at Joey and not see her dad?'

It was the logical answer to why Dilynn hated her. She'd decided a while ago Dilynn must have been raped. That her being alive made the woman relive that moment over and over again.

She hadn't been raped by Joey's dad, but she still hated him. She hated that Joey's ears looked like his. That she had his lisp. And it was those little things that stopped her from telling Mona to fuck off. Tell her sister that she had more important things to do, like drive to Walmart to get the bed for Joey to come to a house in the middle of nowhere.

If she did that though, she'd do the last thing she needed to do. The judge might tell her she did a good job after five years of being a shitty mom. He'd let Joey come home, and she would be an actual mom. And that was scary enough to not go to Walmart.

With a puffy face and hormones crashing through her body, she felt like the room was spinning even though she was sober. Charleigh had no interest in going to celebrate Dilynn Greyson's bitchy replacement daughter; however, the ancient house had taunted her enough. Getting into the loaned car to go to an AA meeting could end up with her at a bar instead, so going with Mona was the next best thing. There would be no chance in hell she'd drink while at Dilynn Greyson's house.

"Bring me something to wear."

The strands of lights hung elegantly over the fairytale backyard. Lights twinkled over every shrub. Tulle and candles decorated the tables whimsically. The happy couple and their parents were making rounds to greet everyone. Mona's entire body had gone rigid when the narrowed eyes stare of Evie Greyson fell on them arm in arm.

In a frustratingly attractive suit, Mona held her hand against the bend of her arm. Charleigh tucked in closer to Mona, as her sister veered them away from the couple. She turned to find Evie starting to approach her, but the muscular male pressed his hand to Evie's stomach and said something to her that made her eyes drop to their connection.

Charleigh tugged the stripper dress Mona had brought for her to wear. Then she asked, "Why does she look like she is trying to cut me open with just her eyes?"

Mona didn't respond. Instead, her fingers covered her mouth. Never had Charleigh seen Mona move so quickly before, but she vanished into the miniature mansion.

Charleigh's fingers played with the hem of the ice blue dress too short to be proper, before wrapping the bulky cardigan tighter around herself. Mona had left her in front of the occupied high-top tables. She searched the space for something more concealed to wait for the free food while she watched Evie Greyson stomp into the house after Mona.

She considered following briefly, then reconsidered as the glass door shut. Whatever Mona did to the real Greyson girl was her mess to clean up. There was no way in hell she was going to be accused of breaking into Dilynn Greyson's house. She felt sorry for Mona because the daughter may be the only person meaner and scarier than Dilynn.

She scanned the space, ducking her head when Dilynn's eyes narrowed at her. In her attempt to escape, she hadn't realized how close she'd ended up to the bar. Turning away from the booze she wanted, she made her way toward a table in the farthest corner where the culinary teacher sat perched. Their fling had been short-lived, but she could handle the smell of chicken nuggets if it meant Dilynn wouldn't be able to see her.

"Hey, I know you," a woman said, pulling Charleigh's attention from trying to make eye contact with the coworker who'd fed her in exchange for orgasms for a few weeks.

Charleigh's eyes widened as she layered the image of the suited-up brunette in the backward NWBA hat with the tattooed bartender. Without warning, the woman's arms wrapped around her.

"I was so worried about you after you left the bar, but Parker said she saw you at work the next day. She said you've been avoiding her, so we figured you didn't want anyone to know."

Charleigh glanced over her shoulder to make sure none of the Greysons were around to hear she'd been at a bar.

"I'm Echo by the way," the woman said, gesturing to herself.

Charleigh swallowed. "Parker's sister. You own the bar?"

Echo's shoulders raised and a smile spread up her face, crinkling the corners of her eyes. She gestured to the woman by her side, "This is my wife, Simone. Simone, this is Charleigh. The girl from the bar."

Simone silently looked Charleigh up and down, then nodded curtly. She didn't seem interested in any sort of conversation, but her wife made up for it.

Echo filled the space between them like they were old friends as she guided Charleigh to the table. She asked a thousand questions not related to the event leading up to Lexa's arrest, and gradually Charleigh began to appreciate her presence. Especially since Mona had apparently bailed, and Charleigh would be left searching for a ride home if Mona didn't show up after the free food came out.

She swept the crowd again in search of Mona. The soft masc in the suit was still MIA, but she found Parker in a tiny black dress making her way toward the eldest Greyson daughter. Parker smiled kindly at her, so Charleigh waved even though she prayed the woman would fall through a sudden sinkhole and never make it to another Greyson girl who was good enough not to be thrown away.

"Parker is amazing. And she is starting to like working at the school," Echo rambled. "She said you gave her the biggest clue to helping Olivia."

A flip switched in Charleigh's head, and she turned back to Echo. "You're Olivia's foster parents, aren't you?"

"Yeah. We adopted her baby, and now we have her," Echo looked at her wife, who held up her hand to Alex and left them without comment.

"Olivia is lucky to have you," Charleigh said. She tucked her hair behind her ear. "Like, you can always tell when a kid is feeling safe even in a new placement. I know I did when I moved in with Marcus after my mom tried to send me to conversion camp. I felt like I could be myself. He made being gay not the end of the world."

"Wow. This Marcus guy sounds pretty awesome. Was he a family friend?" Echo asked. Then added, "If you don't mind sharing."

Charleigh scanned the crowd again. Marcus and Dilynn were too close for him not to be there. She found him on the dance floor. He twisted and turned, shaking his rear without any concern for anyone else around him.

If she could gather up the courage to get the bed, she would let him meet Joey because Joey loved to dance too. They had similar rhythms or lack thereof.

She pointed to the bald head freshly shined. "The guy that legit looks like the Can't-find-my-puppy-kidnapper. That's Marcus."

Echo's mouth dropped open, then she quickly sucked in her lips and shut her eyes. Her lips popped as she breathed out heavily.

"That is the best description of a human I have ever fucking heard! Jesus, he really does look like he should be driving a white van."

"Oh, they picked me up in a white van." With a chuckle, Charleigh said, "I keep telling him he needs to shave the rest of his head, but he's worried he will look like a thumb."

Echo hit the table as beer spilled from her lips.

"Anyways, I needed you to see him to understand how they all played it off. So, you know how the camps.... They like to send people to your house, and they talk about all their effective therapies and stuff?"

"Yeah." Echo took another drink. "I see testimonials and stuff on TikTok sometimes. There was one that was a list of all these kids who had died while there."

Greyson Academy was horrible. The place needed some serious renovations, however, Charleigh knew no one had ever died there. There was a lot of drugs. There were as many assaults as pretty much any coed boarding school had, but the faculty did care about the students. Alex and Dilynn did care about the kids, and Charleigh couldn't take that away from them.

"Well, he did that, but he pitched Greyson Academy." Charleigh looked back at the crowd dancing to the music. Marcus's balding head was covered in sweat. "Trikru has this like outreach, and they make connections with social workers and counselors at schools. So, I told my counselor that my mom was trying to send me away, and she got in touch with Trikru, and they made my mom think that I was going to a conversion camp."

"So, she doesn't know that Greyson's like the complete opposite of hell?" Echo asked.

Charleigh laughed at the idea of Greyson's being anything less than hell. She swallowed the laughter as she saw the closeness of Alex and Simone, realizing her boss's friend's wife was probably not someone to bash the school with.

She fixed her face, then explained, "Honestly, everyone has done a really good job of keeping it a secret from her. I mean, the website isn't all religious, but all the language is very focused on rehabilitation and strong societal values."

Echo studied Charleigh. "Do you have any sort of relationship with your mom now?"

"Monthly. She... uh... she has custody of my daughter," Charleigh offered. "We... uh.... have a scheduled visit, and I just don't talk about the gay. I keep my life very private. She thinks that I went back to work at Greyson's so that I could keep myself safe from polluting thoughts. But if you could maybe not tell Greyson or Trikru I was at the bar. I wasn't supposed to be there because I'm an alcoholic. And I really came to just dance, but they won't believe me. So, if you... could just not say anything. I mean, you know I didn't order a drink and I wasn't—"

"I need to get out of here," Mona interrupted. Her eyes shot up at Echo. "Oh, hey."

Echo looked at Mona, then at Evie and Landon. Her gaze shifted back to Mona again. She took a drink of her beer and set it down.

"I named it Echo's Escape because I felt like that's what people needed. They needed an escape from any expectations."

Charleigh watched Mona nod, and she wasn't sure if Echo was talking to Mona or her. She found Evie wiping the corners of her lips and holding her pregnant stomach once more. The woman was staring at them.

Mona's arm wrapped around her waist, then she leaned in closer. "Let's go."

"Thanks for the company," Charleigh said, not having time to say a proper goodbye.

Echo waved and called after her, "Any time. And hey, if you ever are looking to make some extra cash, I could use another hot cocktail waitress. Between Parker and you, we could really bring in the business."

Charleigh felt the heat rise in her cheeks. She nodded to the woman as she was dragged away from the table.

Her stomach grumbled, but it didn't stop Mona's hand dragging her down the pathway to the street. Charleigh's heel caught between the pavers, sending her body into Mona's. Mona barely paused to let her get her balance before she was pulling Charleigh again.

"What's your deal?" Charleigh growled. "You made me dress like Skipper the Stripper doll. Then you didn't even let me stay long enough to eat something. That's the only reason we ever come to these things. Good food. Remember?"

"Evie followed me to the bathroom. She wanted to know why I hadn't called her, and I just couldn't. I couldn't lie to her, but luckily I puked, which then made her puke, so I was able to escape."

"Why would you call Princess Perfect Bitch?" Charleigh ran on her toes to try to keep up with the pull on her arm. "And why the fuck were you puking? And why was she puking?"

"She's pregnant. She's been puking for months."

When they hit the street, Charleigh planted her feet. Mona tugged on her arm again, but Charleigh leaned her weight back and resisted.

"I'm not taking another step until you tell me why you are running away from Evie Greyson."

Mona's head fell backward. She sighed, then filled her lungs with as much air as possible. As she exhaled, she said, "I have kinda been sleeping with her and her fiancé."

Charleigh looked back at the walkway when she heard the gravelly voice bounce off the steps in pursuit of them. She placed it now in the background every time she'd called Mona since moving out. They weren't just sleeping together. Mona had been living with them.

"No, Landon. I have to talk to her," Evie snapped as her shadow made its way down the walk.

When Charleigh looked back at Mona, she found her sister's eyes pleading with her to move. She swallowed her questions and ran down the street with Mona's hand in hers.

Lexa was sitting on Charleigh's steps when Mona's truck pulled into the driveway. She leaned against the door, staring up at the stars with a smile on her face. A smile that fell when Mona hopped from the car and glared at her.

"Hey," Lexa said. Charleigh wrapped the sweater around her tightly as Lexa's eyes ran up and down her body.

"You brought her home already," Mona grumbled. Her hands shoved in the pockets of her pants.

"Yes. I brought her home and I fucked her," Charleigh snarled. "And you fucked Evie Greyson and her boyfriend, so you don't get to talk shit about me bringing people home."

"Can we just go inside?" Mona asked. "I'll tell you everything, I swear."

Lexa stood up, picking up two large canvas bags from Whole Foods. She held them up in the air and said, "I brought food."

Charleigh's stomach rumbled loudly. She tightened her core to silence it, but it protested only more. Shaking her head, she tossed her keys to Lexa.

"We'll be in, in a minute."

Lexa let herself into the house. Charleigh could hear Rexa dancing around the woman. She almost smiled when she heard Lexa talking to Rexa like a person.

"Will you look at me?" Mona begged.

Charleigh turned to her sister and asked, "How long?"

Mona toed at the gravel. "Three years. On and off. Well, the first year was like twice, then it was more like a weekly thing until you got your place. I was staying with them all summer... until Evie found out she was pregnant."

Charleigh's head swiveled like a bobblehead as she tried to put the words together. She couldn't understand how Mona had never mentioned she was not only fucking one Greyson but the happy straight couple.

She narrowed her eyes at Mona, spit flying out as she said, "You have been in a relationship with Princess Bitch Face and the Hulk for three fucking years."

"Yes."

She pressed her hands to her face, then held the top of her head on so it didn't explode. "How did you...?" she started.

Then, "Why did you...?"

Finally, "She's fucking pregnant, and they're engaged!"

"So am I," Mona whispered.

Charleigh's eyes shot open. Her chin jutted out as more questions spilled from her. "You're engaged? To whom? How can you be engaged to someone when you were with the two of them?"

"No," Mona said. Her eyes fell to the ground, "I'm not...."

The hungry tummy twisted into a knot as Charleigh yelled, "You're pregnant?! And it's his...? They're getting married and you're about to have his kid and she's having his kid... and you wanted me to pretend to be with you to make them... jealous!"

Mona's arms wrapped around her middle. "They don't know I'm pregnant. I used Plan B, but apparently, it doesn't work if you're over 175 pounds. And I didn't know so I can't just you know go and take care of it now."

"Okay." Charleigh licked her lips. "Well, is that what you want to do? You want me to make you an appointment in, like, California? We can leave tomorrow if you want."

Mona's shoulders drooped. She kicked a rock. "I mean yes, but no. I don't know."

"Are you going to tell them?" Charleigh asked.

"I wasn't, but I just... they're going to know if I don't go get an abortion," Mona explained.

Charleigh looked at the two-bedroom house. A bed from Walmart. They sold cribs there too. They would have to get new jobs, but they could do that. There was a national teacher shortage after all. They could just move schools and start over.

"You don't have to get an abortion," she said. "We can do this together. You know, we can make it work."

"You literally have your dream girl inside right now making you dinner, which is weird because I thought she was in another state for a game." Mona placed a hand on her stomach. "This is my mess, and I have to clean it up myself. I'm going to tell them, but I need you to go with me."

"Of course," Charleigh promised. She wrapped her arms around Mona, letting the woman use her for support as she took several deep breaths. "We can go when you're ready."

"I need some time to plan what I am going to say and shit."

Charleigh held Mona against her until Lexa stuck her head out of the door and announced the food was ready. She wrapped Mona's arm in hers and took her inside. The house smelled of actual food, not something from a box or a can.

Mona looked Lexa over and nodded to the woman. "Thanks for letting me crash your dinner," she said.

Lexa held out her hand to Mona. "Maybe we could start over. I mean you're her sister, and I want to be her girlfriend. It would be nice if we could be friends."

As Charleigh tried to process Lexa's declaration, Mona said, "If you hurt her, I'll liquify your ass."

"You guys won. I thought that meant you stayed in Seattle until your next game," Charleigh interjected.

"You said I could come see you when I got back... and I didn't want to wait. We won, and I went to the airport right after. I caught the first flight back, which ended up being this morning," Lexa explained as she handed Charleigh the actual plate and Mona the old Tupperware container.

A little Doby head lay on the coffee table alongside the halfway finished body Charleigh was still trying to create from the complicated kit gifted to her. Lexa held it up. "This is the elf with the sock, right?"

Charleigh hummed in response and looked at the meal Lexa had created for her. A whole meal with vegetables, carbs, and protein. The last time she'd had a meal like this was the night her mother had told her she was getting picked up in the morning.

"What's it like being on an airplane?" Mona asked as she took a seat in the middle of the couch, forcing the other women to sit separately.

Lexa fell into the chair and stretched out her legs. "Cramped and rocky. And there's always somebody's snot-nosed duplicate screaming. Kids are so annoying."

Mona cast Charleigh a look that said enough. Charleigh's stomach twisted into a knot, and her appetite disappeared.

16

With three wins against the Seattle Sharks, the Devils moved on to the final round of playoffs. Danaya, high on life at being a rookie heading into the Championship, begged Charleigh to go out to celebrate Friday night. Lexa assumed the girl wanted to head to a bar and get trashed, but the address she'd been sent was a small cafe tucked off the street in the center of Mill Ave.

She felt strange walking past the chain restaurants, which had popped up in place of the poster shop and Indy bookstore she'd gone through when she'd gone to school here. She walked to the train station to wait for Charleigh, who had refused to allow anyone to pick her up. Why she wouldn't just drive across town when she had Danaya's car was beyond Lexa's understanding, but it had been a challenge just to get the woman to come out.

Charleigh stepped out of the last train compartment, wrapping the only sweater she owned tighter around her body. She was still dressed in her work clothes, and Lexa wondered if her closet was as empty as her pantry.

With a wave of her hand, Lexa caught Charleigh's attention. A smile pulled up the woman's lips only to fall when a group of fumbling frat boys stopped in her path.

"Hey baby, you look lonely," one said, putting his arm over Charleigh's shoulders and pulling her against him. "How about you let me walk you back to your dorm?"

"Yeah, we'll keep you company," another jeered.

The third grabbed the crotch of his pants. "We'll make sure you don't get bored."

Lexa pushed through a couple of girls trying to avoid getting noticed by the boys harassing Charleigh. "Hey," she called out, drawing attention from the dick holder.

The hold on his pants dropped as he hit the second guy. "Bruh," he said. But the other didn't have time to react before Lexa used his shirt to clothesline him and send him to the concrete on his ass. He scrambled backward and ran with his heavier friend a few steps behind him

Charleigh ducked her head when Lexa reached the one daring to put his hands on what she considered hers. She pulled him up on his toes, her face just inches from his. His body slammed against the support beam of the metal awning. The structure shuttered when she pulled him back and hit him against it again.

"You think it's fun to harass women." Spit flew from her mouth as she bared her teeth at him. She looked back to watch the two accomplices turning the corner at a sprint. "Who's lonely now?"

"I... uh... I'm sorry," he said. His eyes squinted as she shoved him against the beam again.

"You are a sorry piece of shit," Lexa growled.

She pulled back one hand as the man's face scrunched up preparing for her punch. A punch that didn't come because of the two hands wrapped around her bicep. She turned to Charleigh, holding her back.

The blue eyes filled with unshed tears begged her to stop, so she dropped her fist, then the man's shirt. Lexa took a step back so he could run too.

His eyes shot open, and he breathed. Just enough air entered his lungs for it to burn as Charleigh's knee slammed into his groin. His elbow made a sickening crack when it hit the concrete. He choked on the air as he rolled to his side clutching his busted manhood.

"Fuck you," Charleigh spit.

When Charleigh looked like she was about to kick him, Lexa pulled her away. She tucked the woman under her arm and walked toward the cafe where Emma and Danaya should be waiting for them.

Lexa swallowed around the jawbreaker in her throat, failing to make it smaller. Her heart beat too fast as she understood Emma's anger toward her to the fullest extent. She'd been just like those men. Her arm dropped off Charleigh's shoulder as she decided she had no right to touch her since she'd done what they'd done.

Silently they walked into the cafe. Lexa couldn't bring her eyes up from the ground, but Charleigh's fingers intertwined with hers and led her through the tables. When she didn't sit right away, Charleigh pulled out her chair and gave Lexa a slight push.

Danaya's smile dropped to the floor as she looked between the two of them. With an audible sigh, she rolled her eyes. "What the fuck happened now?"

Lexa chewed the inside of her lower lip until she tasted blood, while Charleigh started to explain part of the truth.

"Umm... Lexa was meeting me at the train and--"

"What's wrong with my car?" Danaya cut her off.

Charleigh waved away the question. "Nothing, just driving out here would have used up a lot of gas, so I just parked at the stop and took the train because a train ticket is only $3 round trip, and I don't get paid until next Friday." Charleigh dug through her backpack and pulled out $10. "By the way, here is the other half of what I owe you for winning the bet about getting the beast here to cum from kissing you."

With narrowed eyes, Danaya reached out and took her winnings. "You coulda used this for gas instead of taking the damn train that has you lookin' more like a ghost than usual."

"So, what happened," Emma asked.

"Some drunk guys stopped me at the station. They were saying the things that drunk guys say to girls that look like me and one of them put his arm around me, but Lexa scared the shit out of them, and they ran away," Charleigh spit out quickly.

Emma reached over and grabbed Lexa's hand, flipping it to examine her knuckles.

"I didn't hit him," Lexa stated. "I wanted to, but she stopped me. Then she kneed him in the dick."

Leaning back in her chair, Emma licked her lips and looked out the window toward the street. Her fingers tapped against the table until the clammer of the cafe around them broke through the bubble surrounding the table.

Charleigh jumped toward Lexa when blocks fell against the metal table alongside them. Her fingers gripped the jeans covering Lexa's thigh, but the larger woman leaned further away from the blonde.

A group of hipsters cried out, "Jenga!" The blocks were gathered up roughly, as Charleigh pulled back her touch.

"Thank you," she said quietly.

"I'm sorry," Lexa whispered, and she shut her eyes.

A fluffy-haired man arrived at the table to take their order. He pushed a metal headband back and smiled a childish grin. "Hey, humans! I'm Sergio. Have any of you been to Snakes and Lattes before?"

"Hey," Danaya said, changing the vibe of the evening. "We have not been here before but a friend of mine recommended this place. Can you explain how the games work?"

Sergio pointed to the walls of shelves filled with every board game imaginable. "So basically, it's $6 a person, and it gets added to your bill at the end. You go up and choose any game you want, bring it back, and play it. If you need someone to explain how to play, you just let me know, and we will find someone working that is familiar with your game and send them over for a tutorial. I'll just take your drink order, and then you can head over and start picking."

"That's a really cool concept," Charleigh offered. She patted Lexa's arm, which pulled out of the reach. Charleigh bit her lip while turning back to the waiter. "Uh, can I get a Dr. Pepper? Lexa, what do you want?"

Lexa didn't want anything. She wanted to leave so she could find a hole and die where no one would find her body until she was a pile of bones scattered around the desert from coyotes or snakes. She wasn't sure if a snake would try to eat her carcass, but she felt like she'd read somewhere that snakes did consume their own, so it would make sense if they wanted to eat her.

"She'll take water for now," Charleigh said before her eyes fell back to the table.

Emma and Danaya's orders were collected so Sergio could leave. Danaya pulled her girlfriend away from the window to the shelves. Lexa could hear Danaya laying into Emma about not ruining her celebratory night by being broody, and she knew she needed to get it together too.

"I know what you're thinking," Charleigh said. "I know that's why you don't want to touch me or vice versa."

"I have no right," Lexa stated.

"You didn't then." Charleigh sucked in a deep breath. "I mean, you're right. You don't have a right to touch me, but I give you permission to touch me. I'm here with you, and I know I haven't made it easy, like, being around me, but if you hadn't been there tonight something bad probably would have happened, so thank you."

"If I'd never put my hands on you, you never would have been on that train."

Charleigh nodded. "Yes, and I would still be walking to work. I wouldn't have been to any of the playoff games but the first one. There would be a lot of things I hadn't done or will do because of that night."

Lexa's head fell back, and she twisted it in a circle. Her neck popped and some of the tension in her shoulders relaxed. It was enough release to loosen her tongue.

"I was so angry when I saw him put his hands on you, and I just... I did that. I was him, and I sat here for weeks and made fucking excuses for myself, and you just forgave me." She searched Charleigh's face for the answer before asking the question. She watched the way her lips parted, then pressed back together.

"Why did you forgive me?"

Charleigh blinked a few times. She looked around the café, probably searching for something else to talk about. Then Lexa realized she was searching the tables around them. Looking at people to see if they were listening.

"It happens all the time," Charleigh finally said. "Like, since I was in high school. It's part of why I don't really go out. And for a while, I thought it was, like, a problem with me. Like, I just have this thing about me that is, like, a homing device for people that want a one-night stand. And I know this is going to sound ridiculous, but you have kinda been helping me change the way I think about myself."

"Me?" Lexa looked at the menu still closed on the table in front of her. "How?"

"So, don't get me wrong. The rejection when I was half-naked on top of you suuuckked," Charleigh's eyes widened as she held the last word. "But you came back, and I know... look, I know it was terrible... but you didn't leave even though you got what you wanted. I had to literally show you the door, and I thought I was giving you an easy way out, but then you just didn't give up on me. And I think I had given up on myself, which is why I have been so bitchy to you. I figured you couldn't actually care. Not really. And now here we are on, basically, a double date."

Lexa looked at Charleigh, then to the shelves where Danaya had found something that made her bounce on her toes. Emma covered her mouth with one hand and took the box with the other.

"Like a real date?" Lexa asked, the thought not having crossed her mind before.

Charleigh shrugged. "Well, that's why I did my make-up and didn't wear my sweatpants."

Lexa tapped the menu in front of her. "So, you're here with me because you want to be here and not because Danaya guilted you into it?"

Charleigh nodded.

The box slapped against the table. It barely survived the landing as the end opened up and tiny metal tools fell out.

"DayDay lookin' to start a war," Emma said as she lifted the lid of Clue. "I tried to warn her that this game ends friendships with the accusations, but she wasn't hearing it."

"You're just salty because I'mma show your ass up," Danaya said, flopping down into her seat.

Lexa studied the cover. She'd never heard of this game before, but the others all fell into a routine of setting it up. Having no siblings to play games with as a child and parents with no interest in being parents, she was unprepared for the meanness that came with board games.

They'd eaten and ordered dessert while Lexa was still staring at the board unable to understand how she could know the murder weapon but still have no idea who the murderer was. Charleigh's turn was almost up, and she was headed back to the library. Lexa had the library checked off. She searched the woman's face for a clue as to why she'd be heading to the library, missing the brunette's approach.

"Lexxi," Kayla said too loud for the cafe. A chair scratched across the floor as the woman pulled it to the end of the table and took a seat. "I haven't seen you in forever."

Lexa's throat locked shut, but her mouth opened and closed like a fish trying to breathe on land. The woman's hand reached out and twirled a lock of Charleigh's hair.

"Oh, I see you're with your second favorite blonde." The scarlet-painted lips spread in a pained smile. "Or is she now the first favorite since my sister cut you off like she did me?"

Charleigh's eyes fell to the table with her shoulders. Her body was shrinking in the chair, when Emma warned the woman, "Take your hand off of her, Kayla."

The hair fell from Kayla's fingers. "Oh, Emmie, I'm surprised you're here. Or did Lexi get you in the divorce too?"

"Leave us alone," Danaya said, gripping her glass. Lexa wondered briefly if the woman was getting ready to launch another soda.

"Oh, is that the way we treat our old friends?" Kayla asked. "I mean, we were all friends when we spent our nights out running up bar tabs on my sister's cards, weren't we? You all liked me when I was paying for your booze and the Ubers for the bitches you took home to bang. Like this little slut."

Sergio the server made his way over to the table. He leaned between Kayla and Charleigh, gathering half-empty cups. "We all good here?" he asked, placing the glasses on his tray. His body acted as a wall between the women, and Lexa never liked a man more.

"Oh, we're just fine. I just figured I would come over and catch up with some old friends," Kayla said.

Sergio nodded his head. He looked down at Charleigh. "You want another soda?"

"No, I'm good. Can we just get the bill, please?"

"Yeah, no problem. We splittin' the check?" he asked.

Emma shook her head and held out her card. "No, just put it all on here."

Sergio leaned across the table to take the card. Lexa couldn't be positive, but she felt there was no way the tray accidentally tilted in his grasp, sending the watered-down sodas over Kayla's head. He managed to save the glass from knocking her in the skull as he scooped the tray up and away without anyone else getting wet besides the minimal backsplash Charleigh took in her lap.

The woman screamed and the chair echoed as she thrust herself away from the table. Standing up as the soda dripped from her hair, she snarled at the man. "You fucking dickhead."

"I am so sorry," Sergio said. He grabbed Charleigh's napkin from her plate of Macaroni and Cheese and started to wipe the woman's hair. Cheese sauce was added to the soda, making Kayla look like she'd just crawled out of a dumpster.

"What the fuck is wrong with you?" she snapped at him.

Charleigh covered her mouth to keep the laughter within her, but the quaking of her chest gave her away. Danaya joined in but did nothing to hide her laughter.

Kayla's shaky finger raised at the woman. "Don't you fucking laugh at me. You think you get to just steal my girlfriend and get away with it. You and this stupid cunt that stole my sister away. All of you will fucking pay."

Lexa jumped from her chair. Her elbow knocked Charleigh on her ascent, but she didn't notice as she tried to push her way past the man blocking her path. His body fell forward sending the rest of the tray's contents into Kayla's body.

Glasses shattered against the floor. The other tables surrounding them already silent were now staring at the woman sending liquid droplets toward them as she shook like a drenched dog.

"You were never my girlfriend. I never wanted you. I only fucked you because if I was drunk enough you almost looked like my wife," Lexa cried out from behind the man holding up his arms to keep the fight from happening. "I blocked you from everything and you still didn't get the picture. I don't want anything to do with you because you ruined my fucking life. I was fine until you showed up. I was just sitting at home waiting for my wife, and you convinced me she wanted me to go out with you, and you fucking kissed me. You kissed me, and she asked for a fucking divorce, so no I don't want anything to do with you because if you hadn't manipulated me, then Sylvia would be home, and we would be happy. We would still be together."

Danaya got up from the table. She pushed the man out of the way and grabbed Charleigh by the arm.

"Let's go."

Lexa stopped trying to crawl up Sergio's back as she processed what she'd said. Her eyes followed the hunched body of the woman.

"I told you, you'd fucking hurt her," Emma growled. She got up and pulled her wallet from her pocket. She thumbed through the bills and pulled out two one-hundred-dollar bills. Trading the bills for the card, she told the man, "What's left keep as a tip," and she followed her girlfriend out the door.

Kayla licked her teeth before the smile rose up her face. "Guess you went and ruined that for yourself. Don't worry that little whore will still fuck you and then you'll get to see what it feels like for your life to be ruined."

Sergio kept Lexa pinned behind the table until Kayla made her exit. He turned before stepping out of her way.

"I didn't mean for all of that to happen," he explained. "I just figured you all needed some backup."

Lexa pulled her wallet out and handed him another fifty. "For the glasses and whatever," she said. "Thanks for stepping between them. I have to go... but thank you."

She walked out of the cafe, turning toward the parking garage where she'd left her SUV. The trudge toward her vehicle felt like déjà vu.

The tears fell to different slabs of concrete, but the turmoil felt the same. Someone had left a restaurant covered in soda and her friends had run off with Charleigh, only for her to walk into their conversation once more.

She didn't fall against a pillar this time though. She walked up to the three of them. The two sets of dark eyes narrowed at her, but they didn't matter to Lexa. They were Charleigh's protectors, never hers.

"I'm not waiting for Sylvia to come home to me," Lexa stated to the back of Charleigh's head. "I just meant that I have to apologize to her. I have to tell her that I'm sorry. I didn't mean for it to come out like I was still in love with her. I'm not."

Lexa sucked in a deep breath. Then she told her truth.

"I love you."

Charleigh didn't turn around. Her arms wrapped tightly around herself as blonde waves shook from side to side.

"You don't even know me," she said.

When she turned, Lexa saw the extent of the damage she'd done to the blonde in her attempt to get to Kayla. The side of her cheek was an angry red where she'd taken Lexa's elbow to her face.

"Look Lexa," Charleigh started. But Lexa didn't want to watch her walk away, so she dropped her eyes to the yellow-painted letters. She traced the E, then the X, followed by the I and T.

"We've played princess and the peasant for a few weeks now, but I think it's obvious there's no happy ever after for us at the end of the fairytale." Charleigh tapped her chest. "I'm not the girl you fall in love with. I'm the one you distract yourself with as you get over your ex-wife."

17

Lexa kept insisting she could drive herself, but Emma told her no. Charleigh didn't blame her. Looking at Lexa's slumped shoulders and shifting weight, Charleigh knew the tell-tale signs of someone itching for an escape route. A bottle that could tickle away the reality that she and Lexa had no business in each other's lives.

Reality was never rainbows. Neither she nor Lexa could reach a rainbow. They couldn't touch it. Charleigh knew they could only chase it through a storm until the clouds overhead cleared, which is why the bottle was such a threat. It had made her think rainbows were tangible and the intangible was possible to hold onto. But Lexa was a tangible rainbow in the storm of her life. She could hold her through the worst of it, but at what cost?

She stared at the pillar holding the weight of all of the floors above it. She felt like the stupid pillar with no feelings so really that didn't even make sense, but her reactions to Lexa had yet to make sense.

"Get in the back seat," Charleigh commanded, knowing she had to save Lexa from falling from the bridge she'd finally managed to start crossing.

Lexa looked up from the ground just enough to meet Charleigh's eyes. She opened her mouth, but Charleigh shook her head and stared directly between Lexa's eyebrows.

"Nooowwww," she took her time with the word. Forcing it through her lips. One hand found her hip, and the other pointed to the car.

Lexa ducked her head. Running the sleeve of her sweatshirt under her nose, she sniffed. "I won't—"

Her grumble was cut off when Charleigh barked, "I said now."

Lexa's shoulders dropped further to the ground. Her shoes dragged the seven steps to Emma's SUV. She opened the door and crawled into the back seat like a child.

Charleigh breathed out a breath she hadn't realized she'd been holding. Emma's hand came to rest on Charleigh's shoulder. She felt the soft squeeze and reached up to return the contact.

"Thanks for taking care of her," she said.

When the contact was broken, Charleigh turned from the car to the garage exit. "I'm going to head home."

Emma shook her head and pointed at the Escalade. "You too."

Charleigh's chest rumbled. "You don't have to. I know the whole thing earlier has you freaked out, but it wasn't that big of a deal. I'm used to... taking the train."

The most condescending part of Emma's reaction was the eye roll. Charleigh could have lived without another person rolling their eyes at her.

Emma held out her hand to Charleigh. "You've had a long day, just take a few minutes to rest."

Charleigh reached out and gave Emma a low five. Emma's smiling face dropped and a hand came up to cover the chuckle coming from her lips. A smile that fell when Charleigh said, "While I appreciate the offer, I'm a grown-ass woman, and I don't need you feeling like you have to take care of me."

Danaya moved directly in Charleigh's path to the exit. With a hand on her hip, she stomped her foot dramatically before pointing to the car.

"Get in," she demanded.

Charleigh's chin rose and she raised a single eyebrow at the woman probably a year younger than herself. "Sorry, honey, but you are clearly not a teacher or a mom, and have yet to master the voice."

The almond-shaped eyes hardened, and she shifted her weight to point harder. "NOW!"

Her tone wasn't scary, however, the sheer volume caused Charleigh to jump. The word bounced off the concrete, hitting her like stones from every direction.

She searched for an exit strategy as Emma closed off any retreat Charleigh could make from the rear. She'd have to go left or right. She could run, but she doubted she could outrun either of the women, and if she ran what would happen if they caught her? She'd tried to run before, and it hadn't worked.

Her breathing became heavier as she sorted through past and present. She reminded herself now wasn't then. Emma and Danaya weren't the monsters. At least not that she could tell, but she remembered them there. She remembered them watching, and her pulse quickened at the reality that some monsters had really pretty faces. Like Lexa with her fake, 'I love you's and her bullshit promises.

A hand was on her shoulder again. Her fingers curled up into a fist to stop them from shaking but the trembling only spread to her shoulders as the hairs on the back of her neck rose. She clenched her eyes shut and held her breath so it would stop her body from quaking.

"Charleigh," Emma's careful voice whispered. "I can see you're very scared right now, and I don't doubt you have a hundred reasons to be. We are not going to hurt you or let anyone else hurt you."

"If something happened to you because we let you walk out of here alone, we could never forgive ourselves," Danaya added.

Charleigh traced the crack in the concrete past Danaya to the street where the three men could still be lurking, now angry at having been embarrassed. They were right to be worried about her, and the fact they were worried made her feel less helpless. Like maybe she didn't have to fight every fight alone.

Danaya pushed the smallest of the trio toward the SUV and opened the front passenger's side door. Looking at her, Charleigh gave the woman her best what-the-hell-is-wrong-with-you face, and stated, "I am like a hobbit. There is no reason for you to sit in the back."

The woman sighed, her lips twisted in an unamused grimace. "Trust me, I know you probably should still require a carseat, but Lexa is in the backseat."

Danaya was setting up a screen for Charleigh. A safe way out of Lexa's reach. But Lexa had crawled into the bench seat because there was no way for her to fully fit behind the seats already pushed to the farthest distance.

"You take the front. It's not like she'll hurt me again." Charleigh paused for a minute, looking at the heap of ballplayer in the backseat. Moving toward the car, she pushed the heavy head of braids from her side of the bench. "Move over."

She didn't wait for Lexa to move as she hopped up into the lifted vehicle. Lexa pulled her head up only enough for Charleigh's ass to hit the seat before she lost her balance, falling downward. Her chiseled chin impaled Charleigh's thigh.

"Damn it!" Charleigh cried out. "I literally just said you won't hurt me."

Lexa groaned, rubbing her face. Then she said, "Well your thighs of steel weren't exactly gentle on my face."

Charleigh considered how Lexa's face would look with a black eye. She justified no one would blame her. It would be simple. Just a slight slip of her elbow. Emma would take a sharp turn, and *bam!* Lexa could walk around with her mark for a week and learn what it was like to be a walking display of weakness.

Emma was backing up before Charleigh would be able to land the strike and Lexa was already halfway off her lap. Until they hit the first speed bump in the garage. Lexa's chin hit Charleigh again. She gripped Lexa's face downward and held her in place as they went over another bump. Hissing in pain, Charleigh said, "Just don't fucking move."

As they ascended the circular ramp, Charleigh leaned back into her seat and hummed to fight away the nausea. Backseats and Charleigh had never gotten along, and Emma's need for speed on the ramp that a car shouldn't fit did not help her twisting tummy.

The music in the car was low, but the upgraded bass rumbled Charleigh's chest. Charleigh decided Emma and Mona would get along well by the spotless interior of the car.

Lexa's head rested in Charleigh's lap as they traveled down the mostly quiet back streets toward the I-10 freeway. She looked serene with her face partially buried in Charleigh's damp sweater. The grip holding the side of the woman's head had turned into a caress. The pads of her fingers massaged gentle circles into Lexa's scalp.

"Do you have any weird teacher stories?" Emma asked, her gaze focused on Charleigh in the rearview mirror.

Charleigh's hand pulled away from Lexa's head, realizing she'd crossed the only boundary Lexa requested. With Lexa so far in her bubble, she searched for where to put her hand. She couldn't hold it atop the seat without looking like a child. The center console was stuck behind Lexa's body, which left Charleigh only one option. She had to put her hand on the woman again.

She sighed, trying to just hover it over the woman's shoulder. Lexa grabbed her hand though, then put it back on her head.

"I like it when you do the scratchy thing. No one said braids would make my scalp burn or itch, but they do," she said, not looking up at Charleigh.

"Lexa, get off her," Emma called back.

With a heavy sigh, Lexa pressed her face into Charleigh and shook her head. "I don't want to. I don't want to quit."

Charleigh was sure no one could hear Lexa's words but her. But Emma shouted from the front, "I swear if you don't get off her, Danaya is going to come back there an' beat your ass."

Lexa started to move, but her legs were tucked up against the back of the seat. Wiggling around, she got to her knees and rolled her face down, her nose pressed into the crotch of Charleigh's jeans. Lexa's hot air traveled through the material straight to Charleigh's core. The blonde's abdomen contracted, and her breath shuttered. Lexa's hand pushed her body up, but the turn onto the freeway ramp sent her face careening into Charleigh's breasts, then back into the woman's lap with her ass up awkwardly.

"Jesus Christ," Charleigh groaned as her crotch was washed over with another wave of hot air. Then another.

She hated that she liked it. Hated how her self-serviced nethers became immediately slick with want at having a do-over with Lexa where the other woman was not in charge. And she hated it more the way her hips followed Lexa as she pushed herself up onto all fours.

"God, I could get drunk off your scent alone," Lexa whispered, which sent another wave of want through Charleigh.

Lexa groaned and turned back to her task. She looked down at the six inches of space between Emma's partially reclined seat and the front of the bench. Danaya had scooted her seat forward to give Charleigh more room when she'd gotten in the car, room Charleigh didn't need.

"I don't think I can fit," Lexa said. "Can you scoot up?"

"Figure it out," Emma barked. "Driver doesn't move, especially for dicks."

Lexa twisted, but nothing she did allowed her legs the space she needed. She turned, one leg in the air, and held herself up as she put the other foot on the floor behind Emma.

Charleigh sat watching the fumbled mission that ended with Lexa's legs in the air and head on the seat staring up at Charleigh. Charleigh sighed and pulled herself up on Danaya's seat. She looked down at Lexa.

"Scoot over."

Lexa pressed her feet against the door and spread her body over the bench as Charleigh side-stepped her way across the car. Charleigh transferred her weight to Emma's chair and waited for Lexa to pull her leg over.

The ball player got one leg down and her body up. Her other leg came down from the door as a car blazed past them and cut into the lane they were traveling in. Emma hit the brakes, sending Charleigh's already sore face into the headrest, then her body into Lexa's lap.

Lexa's arms came around Charleigh's body. Her hand held Charleigh in place as the blonde cupped her nose. Her face hurt so bad, that Charleigh didn't notice Lexa's hand holding her breast immediately.

She smacked away the protective grip around her, and spit, "Get your fucking hands off my tit."

Lexa's hands flew backward, spread against the windows.

Charleigh huffed and pulled herself up again. This time Lexa pulled her other leg out and moved to the other side of the car. As she stretched, the seat in front of her slid backward and the chair reclined into her bubble.

Danaya turned her head and winked at Charleigh. It settled an unasked question. The rookie was her new favorite Devil.

In turn, Emma pressed a button on her seat moving forward several inches and sitting up straighter. Maybe they had been right about her choosing the wrong baller. She considered if she should've taken them up on the weekend getaway. At least she would have known there'd be no games, and she wouldn't be left frustrated.

But she looked over at the woman still mumbling to herself in her bubble now.

"Funny teacher story now," Danaya requested.

Charleigh shrugged, then remembered to fasten her seatbelt. "Eh... I doubt anything that happens in my classroom is as exciting as traveling around playing ball."

"What area do y'all live in?" she asked, realizing in all the time they had come to her, she'd never considered where they resided.

Emma's fingers strummed against the steering wheel. "DayDay and I share a house in North Phoenix. Lexa lives not very far away in her Scottsdale estate in the land of old rich white people."

Charleigh bit her lip, realizing they were going to spend the evening driving from one side of the metro area to the other.

She pointed to the driver's side of the car, "Uh... you want to get on the 51 and turn that way on Camelback, so you can drop me off at Danaya's car."

Danaya snorted, and Emma said, "You realize that I can't see when you point, right?"

Charleigh was a horrible navigator. She held up her hands and made an L with both, but they looked the same. She dropped them back in her lap. "Uh... I struggle with telling left from right. So... can we go your way or her way?"

Emma's mouth twitched into a smile, and she nodded.

"Okay, so your side. Turn that way."

"Okay," she answers. "But I know which way to go to get to the last stop of the train."

Charleigh looked at her hands playing with the fabric of her sweater. "So, teaching stories... um...."

She searched through the faces of her students trying to find one to make them all laugh. She landed on the scrawny sophomore with a double nose ring.

"Oh, I got one," she said. "I teach this one class, it's called Academic Journalism. We put out the school newspaper and yearbook, and last year, I had a kid that wanted to write this story on stupid laws."

Charleigh laughed at the memory she'd yet to share.

"What happened?" Emma asked with her eyes not on the road but on Danaya.

"We were in class, and she was looking up all these laws throughout the US, and one confused her... so she asks me, 'What's a dildus?'" Charleigh's chest quaked as she tried to relay the story. "The problem was I wasn't really awake yet, and I hadn't finished my coffee, so I was just like 'what?'"

Danaya was already giggling, pulling Charleigh out of her seat of inferiority. Her hands moved even though the only person capable of seeing her was Lexa. "So, she repeats her question and then spells it for me. D-i-l-d-o-s."

Emma snorted.

"I slapped my hands over my mouth because I didn't want to laugh, but I was, like, dying inside. I can barely get out, 'Ask an adult.' But Rylee doesn't, and she was like 'Marshall you're a grown-up,' but I couldn't answer her question, or my boss would have my ass. She is, like, 'I'll just Google it.'"

The tension in the car faded as Charleigh continued, "I see when she figures it out. Like, her face was so red and all of a sudden she yells out, 'It's a fake dick! They outlawed fake dicks!' And she is, like, so proud yet so embarrassed."

Danaya was still laughing, when she hit Emma's arm.

"Remember that time Lexa got stopped at the security check because she had that—"

Her mouth was covered by Lexa's hand. The woman seriously lunged forward and managed to cover Danaya's mouth before she could finish. But she didn't need to.

Emma wiped the tears from her eyes as Lexa cried out and pulled her hand back to her chest protectively. She pouted as she said, "You fucking bit me."

Danaya didn't acknowledge Lexa. Instead, she picked up where she left off. "Emma told me she had a giant fucking dick and strap in her bag. Like HUGE! Like porn star status." The woman's hands were up in the shape of an o about the size of a baseball

Charleigh looked over at Lexa with one eyebrow raised, because if Danaya was telling the truth that was one huge slong, and Charleigh wasn't sure where Lexa would put it.

The color faded from Lexa's face, and she stuttered, "It... I didn't... don't... Sylvia's joke... not mine."

Emma pressed a few buttons on the phone, then cranked up the volume. Her voice scream-sang, "LEXA LIKES BIG DICKS AND SHE CANNOT LIE."

Danaya joined her. They changed the words and fumbled around for rhyming words while staying on beat.

"You other brothers can't deny when a white girl walks in with blonde hair in her face, Lexa hopes they get strapped. She wants them to fuck her. With her big old dick!"

The two in the front don't stop singing, but the words return to the actual lyrics, and they work in unison. Charleigh watched the way Emma looked over at Danaya who was moving in her seat with the beat.

Danaya's hips rolled and thrust the air to punctuate, "Baby. Got. Cock."

They sang the remainder of the song, while Lexa held herself. The song changed, and it was no less jarring as a woman calls out for someone to fuck her. Charleigh laughed when Lexa's head was thrown back against the seat. Her embarrassment was too much to not enjoy, but Charleigh tried to behave some.

Emma and Danaya were punishing her enough, so the blonde reached over and rested her hand on Lexa's arm.

"It's funny," Charleigh said, only loud enough for Lexa to hear. "But I think the TSA sees dicks all the time and makes it a point to embarrass people."

"I don't own a giant dick." After a pause and a subtle smile. "They are all average sizes and girths," and her eyebrows raised twice when she added, "And in multiple colors."

"Good to know," Charleigh said, withdrawing the contact. "I mean, you must not need one too big since you seem to manage to embody one quite often."

Lexa's face flushed almost immediately.

Charleigh pulled the replacement phone from her pocket. She searched through the collection of memes. She was stuck between, 'It's a joke not a dick, don't take it too hard,' and 'Shut up. I wear heels bigger than your dick.' She wasn't sure how Lexa would respond to the second, so she chose the first one.

Handing the phone to Lexa, Charleigh watched her swallow. Lexa's face flushed when she read the image. Her lips opened and closed like she was trying out comebacks.

"I actually like it hard," Lexa whispered.

Charleigh sucked in her lips to hide her smile. She should still be mad at Lexa about the love you bomb, but it was so hard. Because Lexa just confessed to wanting it hard. Charleigh felt like she might die of amusement.

Emma's eyes watched them in the rearview mirror as Charleigh scrolled through more images. She laughed at the next meme she found, then handed it back to Lexa.

"A big dick doesn't mean anything if it's attached to a bigger dick," Lexa read quietly aloud.

Charleigh laughed again, unable to control her amusement at the fact that she could do this all night.

Nodding, Lexa said, "Yeah, I deserve that."

"What are you two doing back there?" Emma asked.

Charleigh dropped her head to cover her red cheeks, unsure how to explain.

"She told me I am a dick, making my actual dick small because my personality absorbs most of my length." Hearing the explanation from Lexa's lips made it much more amusing for Charleigh.

She doesn't laugh alone this time. Danaya and Emma join in.

"Yep, laugh it up you three," Lexa said, waving at them. "You all can suck my dick."

Lost in thought, Charleigh almost missed Danaya's reply. Her voice was so subtle, but the way Emma suddenly swerved into the wrong lane, Charleigh knew she had heard the statement correctly. Unless they all heard wrong, but

Charleigh swore the girl just said, "There's only one dick for me and it ain't yours, Lex."

A car next to them was honking so Charleigh shut her eyes. She shut them and grabbed for something to hold on to as they died. They were going to die because Danaya wanted to ride Emma's dick. Like what sort of fractured fairy tale was this?

"Damn it. Damn you, Lexa. This is all your fault. You couldn't just leave me alone, and I am going to die because you had to chase after me like I actually mattered."

Emma managed to correct the car without hitting anything. Just swerving a little back and forth. She may have been playing around, but Charleigh didn't notice as she cursed Lexa out under her breath.

"Tell me how you really feel," Lexa said. Charleigh could hear her smile when she asked, "Are you always this rough?"

Charleigh's eyes snapped open to see her fingers digging into Lexa's thigh.

The music played quietly for the remainder of the trip. Danaya's fingers lay entwined with Emma's over the center console, and Charleigh wished for things to be different. Wished the night had ended with her and Lexa's hands holding like she'd planned on the way over. To take the woman home and show her the blue dick she'd promised for good behavior.

But Lexa didn't love her. She couldn't when she knew nothing about her.

Charleigh provided directions to the car parked alone in the Light Rail station lot. Lexa followed her out of the car.

"Please just let me—" Lexa started.

Charleigh turned to her. Her arms wrapped over her chest. "Let you, what? Say the words I waited my whole life to hear only for them to be another fucking lie."

Lexa swallowed, and she opened her mouth to say something, but Charleigh held up her hand.

"The only person that ever told me he loved me was my dad and he's gone. Ten years of no one loving me and you just drop it after telling your fucking sister-in-law that you would still be married if it wasn't for her."

"But that's the truth," Lexa stated. "I would still be married, and I would be happy, but that changed, and I've changed. You changed me."

"You changed yourself because you are trying to fit me into your world. The world I don't belong in."

"My world? What world have I put you in?" Lexa held up her hands. "You've never seen my house. We don't do anything I like to do. We have spent every minute living in your world, doing what you want to do, and I don't know that much about you because you tell me nothing."

Charleigh hated the truth she'd refused to acknowledge. Lexa had lept over every wall she put up and didn't stop trying.

"Do you really want me to give up?" Lexa asked. Her lip trembled as she whispered, "If you really want me to stop, then just say it. I will leave you alone, and I'll move on with my life like you thought would happen when you fucked me. The teacher is crossed off my list, so I coulda left then."

She threw her hands back to the car where Danaya and Emma stood ready to step in. "You wanna go away with them and get fucked senseless, I will get out of the way. You want me to ask for a trade, so you never have to see me again, then just tell me that. But it will not change when I said I want to be with you that I was telling the fucking truth."

Charleigh wiped the tear rolling down her cheek.

"But if you tell me to leave, then you have to know that it's you rejecting me. You rejected me because I was too much for you. So, you can go find less. Go find someone to treat you like shit because it's normal for you. Someone who leaves after they fuck you because then you can feel sorry for yourself."

"That's enough," Danaya said, stepping between them. She looked at Lexa. "You're going to ruin everything if you turn nasty now, so stop."

"She's right," Charleigh said to the ground. "You've been good to me, and I haven't really given you a chance, because I'm used to being treated like shit."

With a deep breath, Charleigh looked at Lexa. "Can we try this whole first date thing over? Next week, I will take you out and answer any question about me you ask."

She prayed Lexa wouldn't make a comment about her having to wait until payday. But the woman's lips curled up into a smile.

Lexa closed the distance between them. She cupped the unbruised side of Charleigh's face. Her thumb traced over her lower lip.

"Yes," she said before she placed a careful kiss on Charleigh's lips.

Charleigh wrapped her arms around Lexa's neck as the woman lifted her from the ground and kissed her deeper.

They lived off the air shared between each other, tongues soothing the sharp edges of words unspoken. Silent promises to be better for one another.

"Is this what it was like watching us go at it in the living room?" Danaya asked, pulling at the neck of her shirt.

Emma wrapped her arm around Danaya's shoulder and pulled her back toward the car. "Don't be getting any more ideas about Oreo cookies."

Danaya's elbow dug into Emma's side. "Clearly, it's more like a two-layer devil's food cake with chocolate mousse in the middle and vanilla frosting."

Charleigh's feet touched the ground as Lexa set her down. She smiled and whispered, "Your friends have some weird ass fantasies."

Lexa smiled, "They can fantasize all they want. There's no one for me but you."

With the door to the car open, Lexa stood guard as Charleigh ducked into the driver's seat. "I'll call you tomorrow, and we can talk about where you want to go for dinner."

Lexa nodded. Then she asked, "Can I come see you tomorrow?"

Charleigh bit her lip. "I... uh have plans tomorrow. I'm going with Mona."

"Sunday, before I leave for Dallas?" Lexa asked.

Charleigh thought about the upcoming visit with Joey. She'd have to find a way to tell Lexa the truth soon. Especially after she learned how Lexa felt about other people's kids.

"I have to go to my mom's," Charleigh explained. "I'm sorry."

18

Trees lined the gravel road of Greyson Drive. After they ran away last week, it felt wrong to be sitting down the street when their bosses' cars could be seen in their driveway. The engagement party was the first time they'd been to one of Dilynn and Alex's parties, but not the first time they'd been to their house. Last time was just like this, only it was Charleigh telling a Greyson she was pregnant.

They'd been in the car for almost a half hour, sitting in familiar fear. Charleigh felt ants crawling under her skin. She'd put a baseball cap on to not be noticed in the passenger's seat, but Mona's truck wasn't exactly discreet. Luckily, the occupants of the house seemed to all be sleeping in on Saturday morning.

"We look like we're casing the joint," Charleigh whispered, wondering how many houses Dilynn had to own to get the private road named after herself.

They continued to sit in the truck though. Charleigh guessed this is what Lexa's neighborhood looked like, and she tried to prepare herself for having to go there at some point.

"So, are we going to talk about you settling down with Lexa fucking Jenson?" Mona said. "Or about the fact that she doesn't like kids?"

Charleigh pressed the cap back on her head. There was no ignoring Lexa's rant about other people's kids. It was the first time they'd ever talked about children, but seeing Lexa at the game with her team felt like maybe it could be different.

"Honestly, I don't think she doesn't like kids. I mean, you should have seen her with the girls at the game. Especially Nevaeh. She was really invested in helping her make it. And it could have just been an airport thing. She hates airports apparently. She hates that they don't charter flights for the team, so she doesn't have enough leg room."

Mona's eyes rolled along with her head against the back of her seat. "God, rich people's problems are so weird. Like, could you imagine complaining about getting to fly to a different state?"

The trees shading the street shuddered in the breeze. Charleigh thought about the possibility of one day them sitting on a street where the leaves would actually fall. Her mind wandered to the possibility of Lexa getting traded to some place like that. She wouldn't be able to go with her unless she finally got custody of Joey, even then whatever Lexa saw in her might be gone when she realized Charleigh and Joey were a package deal.

"Are you scared?" she asked Mona when she saw the woman's grip on the steering wheel trying to twist it into pieces.

There was a slight nod, then Mona jerked the keys from the ignition and hopped out of the truck. "Let's just get this over with," she said with a sigh.

Having never known Mona to be scared, Charleigh's stomach dropped at what was about to come. She dragged her feet over the concrete walk to the shaded house across from Dilynn's mansion. Charleigh made it a point not to look across the street, in case Dilynn caught sight of them. Direct eye contact never failed to pull the fuming woman toward her.

The porch didn't creek like a haunted house, which Charleigh felt would make this just feel more real. She looked over the stucco walls, wondering what a house like this would cost and if she would even make it to a point in her life where something like it wasn't just a dream.

Mona knocked on the door, and they heard Landon's deep baritone call from within, "Coming."

When the door opened, Landon's dark frame filled the threshold. The smile he'd carried to greet the guests fell when his eyes landed on Mona.

"Uh, hey," he said quietly, glancing at Charleigh, then back over his shoulder. He stepped outside, letting the door almost close behind him. "Uh... now's not a good time. We are—"

"I'm pregnant," Mona spat out. She closed her eyes and said again, "I'm pregnant and it's yours and I need you and your fiancée to know because I have to keep it but I...." Her words fell off when the door of the house slowly opened behind the man.

Landon turned in time to catch Alex's fist flying at his face. The flesh of his cheek and jaw melded into the punch. The wall refused to move, and his body bounced against it, sending him back toward Alex. A thick forearm went up to block the second punch aimed at the side of his head, but the third came from the other side; a jab to the ribs. He slouched against the stucco entryway with his hands up to protect himself.

Alex stood over him. Their face was scarlet, and their eyes were set on murder. "You cheated on my daughter," they growled. Their hand came up and tried to punch through the massive forearms. "And you did it with someone you knew we care about."

The door flew open again, smacking against the wall. A very pregnant Evie Greyson held the bottom of the baby bump she'd carried with her to the fight.

She had her finger on the trigger of a gun, but it stayed pointed at the ground at least.

The pregnant woman looked at Mona, Alex, and then Landon's hunched body. Charleigh held her breath, staring at the gun. Evie clicked the safety back in place. Her face flushed with annoyance as she moved forward.

"What the fuck, Obi?!" she yelled. But when she tried to get to her fiancé, Alex's arm shot up and blocked the way.

"I trusted you. I trusted you with her heart, and you knocked-up one of my employees," they hissed.

Dilynn slipped past Evie and under Alex's arm. Her head twisted between Landon and Charleigh. Blue eyes turned to ice as they centered in on the younger version of herself.

"You," she snarled. She stepped toward Charleigh whose hands raised as Landon's had.

"Why is it always you?" Spittle splattered against Charleigh's freckles. "Is this your sick way of getting revenge on my family after everything we've done for you?"

Charleigh tried waving away the accusation. Fragmented sentences of denial and innocent pleas poured from her mouth. "I didn't. I... I'm not... it wasn't—"

"I'm pregnant," Mona yelled.

Before Dilynn could look away from Charleigh, Mona stepped between them. With her hand over her mouth, her body heaved. Charleigh had just enough time to turn Mona's frame before she vomited on their boss's chest. The bile splashed against the porch and Dilynn's shoes.

No one could tear their eyes away from the puke. It created a mote between the foster sisters and the Greyson family. One that almost grew with Evie's heaving. She at least managed to hold it back, while Dilynn continued to stare at her now-ruined shoes.

"He didn't cheat on me," Evie said, once she'd recovered. She slapped Alex's weakened arm out of her way, then pulled at her fiancé until he was standing up with one eye already beginning to swell shut.

"I would never cheat on Evie," he said, then spat out blood. "I think you broke my tooth."

Alex's anger fled their now green face. They turned from the vomit but continued to stare at the ground. They were trying to process while Dilynn's gaze had risen to Charleigh once more. She looked like she might apologize for a minute, but that would have meant Charleigh was dreaming. No, whatever Dilynn was going to say to Charleigh was swallowed before she focused on Mona's hunched frame.

"Mona, let's get you off your feet and away from the smell." Dilynn's hand reached out as though she was about to save Mona from some disaster area.

When Mona stepped over the vomit, Dilynn asked, "So, you and them are...?"

She didn't finish the question because her daughter answered for Mona. "Yes, Mom. We were a throuple." The angry turquoise eyes glared at the woman who chose her over all the other girls who could've been adopted. "Would you like me to go over the details with you? Like, that we typically meet up on Tuesdays at Echo's or do you want the juicy details like our favorite position to fuck is—"

"STOP!" Alex shouted.

A wicked smile spread over Evie's face as she glanced back at Alex. "Mona does this thing with her—"

"I DON'T WANT TO KNOW!" Alex cried out. Their fingers pushed into their ears. "LA LA LA LA LA LA LA LA LA!"

Dilynn pulled Mona into a tight embrace once the younger woman was on the other side of the mote. Her hug was quick, then she was holding Mona's face so Mona couldn't help but look at her.

When Mona's eyes raised, wet with tears she'd refused to let fall, she closed them again. Her lip trembled as the words fell from her mouth, "You weren't supposed to know. I didn't want anyone to know, and if I had known anyone was here—"

Dilynn pulled Mona's head down to her shoulder. She cradled the black hair, and told her, "It's going to be okay. No one is mad at you."

With Alex no longer in the way, Evie led the babies' daddy into the house, followed by Dilynn with Mona wrapped under her arm. Charleigh remained on the other side of the pike, unsure if she was supposed to follow.

She looked within to see Parker wrapped in the arms of the eldest daughter. The friendship Parker said was possible now felt like another person who would hate her in a few weeks. The third and fourth Greyson girls in family photos she'd studied for so long stood alongside them. They all stared at her, and she at them.

Parker stepped out of her girlfriend's arms. She held out her hand like Dilynn had for Mona. The woman wasn't a Greyson though. She didn't have the power to give her safe passage within a Greyson house. She must have known it too, because she quietly begged, "Please don't leave me alone with them."

She watched Mona being led into the living room, knowing she may only see her sister at work from this point forward. Quietly, she explained, "I don't think it's a good idea. You saw what happened when she thought it was me."

"Isn't she your sister?" Parker asked, her outstretched hand wavering slightly.

"Yeah."

"Then staying outside and having her do this alone, seems like a worse idea," Parker said. She took Charleigh's hand. "Trust me, I have been on Dilynn's fix-it list since we met. You can't leave Mona alone here with something like this."

Charleigh couldn't fight the therapist's logic, so she followed the redhead within the perfectly decorated home. Her sister hadn't run away while Alex and Dilynn lectured her the last time there was a pregnancy announcement made. The Greyson girls and Parker took up positions alongside the kitchen island. There weren't any walls between the rooms, so the spot provided them space to watch the live soap opera being played out. Charleigh decided to join them, rather than move to where Mona was being hovered over by Dilynn.

The room was filled with gifts from the engagement party. A worn farmhouse table in the great room was covered in thank-you notes and wedding invitations. Their arrival had interrupted what looked like an assembly line of wedding preparations.

Mona sat on the couch in the center of the room. She was joined by Evie after the woman had holstered her gun and tossed a bag of frozen chicken nuggets at the viral man still bleeding in the chair off to the side.

"I can't believe you hit me," he groaned. His one good eye looked at Alex hovering in front of the TV as big as Charleigh's bed. "This hurts worse than that time you and Uncle Ryder shot me with paintballs for Evie kissing me in the driveway. And one of those hit me in the balls."

"You had your hand on her butt," Alex grumbled. "You're lucky we didn't cut them off."

"Well, I guess you know you better not cheat on me," Evie snarked. "And obviously your balls still work fine, so stop being a pussy."

She leaned into Mona's space, her hand hovering over Mona's stomach. She asked, "May I?"

Mona nodded, moving Evie's hand to where a specific place on her belly. Evie's lips rose in a soft smile.

"Have you felt any movement yet?" she asked.

Mona shook her head. "Just nauseous, like, all day."

Dilynn lifted the chicken nugget bag from Landon's head. Then she took her partner's hand, uncurling the blood-coated fingers. They winced and pulled their hand back.

With a roll of her eyes, Dilynn demanded, "Text my mom. He's going to need stitches, and you need an x-ray."

Alex sighed and pulled out their phone from their pocket with their good hand. As they typed out a text message, Dilynn turned to her kids and Mona. "So, start from the top. How did this happen?"

"Leave out the details," Alex pleaded with wide eyes at Evie.

Evie didn't look up from where she'd placed Mona's hand on her own stomach, so they could feel the growing fetuses together. She licked her lips, then began, "I met Mona a few years ago. And before you go there, perv, no it was not while she was a student. That wasn't why I said no to her coming home. It was that stupid Family Fun Day you forced us to go to. We met in the fall that first time and hooked up after the second one."

Parker's girlfriend leaned against the counter and whispered to her sister, "I think this means we have officially been removed from all future family events."

The younger sister held out her fist and the two exchanged a celebratory bump. Parker rolled her eyes and elbowed her girlfriend in the side.

"If I have to suffer through one of those things, then you will suffer with me. But you won't be leaving with one of my co-workers for a threesome. Never going to happen."

The eldest daughter groaned, earning her another elbow in the gut.

Evie didn't notice the side commentary, giving Charleigh more of the story than Mona had provided her. "Mona and I had some angry chemistry and ended up fucking on Obi's desk," she held up her finger, "with Landon's full knowledge. There are no secrets between us. "

Alex's face paled. Their good hand pulled at the back of their neck, and they choked as they said, "You two had sex on... *my* desk?"

"You had to tell them now?" Mona grimaced.

Evie leaned against Mona's shoulder, her body shaking with laughter. "I have waited three years to see the look on their face when I got that revenge. Best deal I ever struck."

Mona looked up at Alex and mouthed 'sorry' to them.

It took several attempts for Evie to regain her self-control. Each time she seemed to be done laughing, Alex would open their mouth and Evie would lose her straight face again.

"Fix your face," Dilynn commanded Alex. She waved at Evie. "She is just going to keep laughing at you if you look like a catfish stuck on land."

Alex shut their mouth, letting their breath rush through their nose like a bull. As they continued to quietly fume, Evie got control of herself.

"Anyways, things were going well, and they took me to Disneyland for my birthday and what was separate became... not so separate. We had a very long dinner and talked about everything as the three of us and what was casual sex between me and Mona turned into the three of us seeing each other. That was until I found out I was pregnant."

Evie turned to Mona. As much as Charleigh hated her replacement, she could see the hurt in the woman's eyes. There was enough pain there to tell Charleigh the woman cared about Mona deeply, which made Charleigh relieved and scared at the same time. There was no way Evie was going to let Mona walk away again, which meant Charleigh would spend Christmases alone moving forward.

"You straight up ghosted me again, asshole. I came home, and you had moved out all your stuff. Didn't even leave a note, and I couldn't just show up at the school because last time I did that you had a shit fit."

"Wait!" Dilynn's glare turned from Evie to the audience in the kitchen. Her gaze centered on Parker's girlfriend, Lyra. "She was living with you all, and you didn't say anything?"

Lyra's lip curled, but she didn't acknowledge Dilynn. Instead, she growled at Evie, "I fucking told you I didn't want to be in the middle of this. That she would be pissed when she found out you were playing dive the digits into one of her employees."

Evie rolled her eyes, not seeming to care Lyra was the one in trouble for her secret. It made sense to Charleigh though. She'd always known Evie was Dilynn's favorite princess.

"Mona didn't want anyone to know," Evie said, before turning back to Mona. "I fucking missed you so much and you stopped answering my calls and you came to the party, but you ran away. You came with Charleigh, and I thought you dumped me for her. Shit, you even dressed her in one of my dresses. And... And... you just left without telling me what I did wrong. What did I do wrong?"

Mona wiped the escaped tear from her face. She shook her head slowly, then took a deep breath before she began to explain. "I ran into Alex at school. They said... they said you were moving into the house across from theirs. You didn't tell me you were moving and it was like I should just leave because I couldn't come here with you, and I had just taken the test and found out. I couldn't just come here with you. They would see my truck and they would have known that something was up... and I didn't want to make a scene."

"So much for not making a scene." Evie turned to her mother. "So, that's it. It really isn't that big of a deal."

"Not that big of a deal?" Dilynn's small hand shot toward Mona. "You kept her a secret for three years. Three years you loved someone enough to make a baby with her, but not bring her to Christmas or Thanksgiving. After what happened to your sister, you should know better. She should have been with us on holidays. She shouldn't have been alone."

"She has a family, Mom," Evie snapped. Her hand flung out to where Charleigh stood. "What was she supposed to do? She had Charleigh to take care of, and she couldn't bring her to the house. So, no, we didn't tell you."

"She's pregnant," Dilynn growled. "She's having yours and Landon's baby. And Landon is bleeding all over the place. And Alex probably has a broken hand. You thought it was a big enough deal to keep it a fucking secret. She shouldn't feel like she has to apologize for your relationship with her if it wasn't a big deal."

Charleigh studied her hands as the mother and daughter fought. There must have been a conversation about Christmas at some point. Mona must have chosen to take care of her instead of spending it with Evie, something the woman seemed to resent. Something Evie wouldn't have to worry about anymore though. Mona was here with them, and they weren't a secret anymore. They were a family with kids and everything. The thing Charleigh and Mona talked about being before Alex and Dilynn forced Mona to choose between Charleigh as her girlfriend or Marcus as her father.

"I don't even understand what would drive you to start a relationship with someone else. You and Landon are happy. This just seems like excessive attention-seeking behavior, E."

Evie scoffed. "From the person that likes to be tied up and whipped and who begs while she's getting fucked all over the goddamn house, it seems pretty judgmental, Mom. If anyone is seeking some attention, it's always been you."

Parker and Charleigh turned to each other. Their pale cheeks flushed as they shared a knowing look. They would never be able to look at their bosses the same with the information they now had to hold.

Evie turned her attention to Mona. "How far along are you?"

"About four months."

"FOUR MONTHS!" Evie cried out. "You are still tiny. I swear if yours comes out all cute and tiny when I have a push out a fucking watermelon-sized head because of Mr. Soccer Ball Skull, I am going to be pissed."

Dilynn sat on the coffee table across from Mona. She took Mona's hand in her own. "Honey, I want you to know that no matter what you decide to do, we will support you."

"I kinda don't have a choice anymore," Mona said. She looked at Evie, then Landon. "I took the morning-after pill when," she sucked in her lips before she finished, "you know, that night that we all got carried away."

A wicked smile spread over Evie's face. She looked at Alex, and said, "Oh you mean the night that I had your face—"

Alex reached down and grabbed the toddler who'd made her way to her parent. They dangled the child in the air like a shield. "Don't pollute your sister's mind," they cried out, hiding their face behind the miniature version of themself.

"Yeah, because she hasn't already walked in on you screwing mom on the kitchen table. I bet she needs therapy before she's ten." Evie shook her head, then turned back to Mona. "Yeah. I remember."

"Well, I followed the instructions, and I assumed it worked. Except it hadn't and with Arizona's new heartbeat law, I can't get an abortion now."

"Do you want an abortion?" Landon asked sincerely. "I am not in any way suggesting you get one. Your body, your choice. I just don't want you to think that I or Evie want you to get one."

Charleigh appreciated the concern buried in the crevice of the one good eye. She'd always considered him a good man, especially with the way he put up with the barking brunette he'd proposed to.

"Well, I did," Mona said. "Originally, I was going to come here and tell you that I needed to get one. That I couldn't do it alone because they want someone there with you and both Charleigh and I can't miss that much work. It's hard enough when one of us is gone for a day let alone both for a week."

Evie took Mona's hand in her own. "Baby, if you don't want an abortion. You shouldn't get an abortion."

The tears Mona had held back broke through the damn. Her face fell into Evie's body as she said, "I never wanted this. I told you. I told you I didn't want to be a mom. But now.... I just feel like I tried to get one and this kid said no. So, I came here to tell you that I can't. I can't get an abortion."

Mona sat up and raised her chin. She took a deep breath and Charleigh watched the mask fall back over her face.

"I am going to have it." She looked at each of her partners for a moment. "Your life is here, and you are getting married. I have always wanted that for you two. I don't want this to complicate the dreams you have. So, you two can have whatever type of relationship or non-relationship with it. I won't give it up, and I damn well won't leave it, so I needed you to know that."

Charleigh felt the knife slice between her second and third rib as she replayed Alex taking Joey from her arms. She'd given up her daughter to the couple and left a few months later for college. Mona's blade sunk just enough to poke a hole in the vacuum of Charleigh's chest. Whether her sister knew it or not, she'd created a hole big enough for the air to slowly leak from her lungs.

"I came here because I needed you two to know, so you could talk about what you guys want people to know or not know. I won't ask you for money, and you don't have to be involved." She glanced back at Charleigh. "Charleigh and I talked about it already. We're going to leave Greyson Academy at the end of the year, then you won't have to hear from me. Then no one will know."

Dilynn moved from the coffee table to the couch. Her arm wrapped around Mona's shoulders again. "No matter what these two say, you are not raising this baby alone. Alex and I will make sure that you don't have to worry about anything. Whatever you need, we are here for you."

The knife pressed deeper, opening Charleigh's lung. This was the same woman who'd told Charleigh to abort her granddaughter. There was no promise to help her. Dilynn had told her she wouldn't be able to finish school at Greyson's with a kid. That it would be too hard, and she needed to get an abortion. She'd had to beg them to foster Joey. Dropped to her knees and begged Dilynn to keep her own flesh and blood long enough for her to get out of high school. She hadn't known then Joey was her granddaughter though. Dilynn did though. Dilynn had to know what she was asking.

She took a deep breath. Told herself it was different then. It was different because she was a kid and Mona is an adult. Mona was having a baby that didn't need Dilynn or Alex to help.

After a moment, she looked back to the scene. With her feelings put into a bottle and capped, she watched Evie and Landon silently having a conversation. It ended with Landon sliding off the chair to the floor.

He walked on his knees to the women carrying his children, blood still dripping from his eyebrow. The giant frame of his body was at eye level with Mona, and he took the hands of his fiancé and girlfriend in his. He looked at Evie, and said, "I know we need to talk through this, but we need to do it together. The three of us. It was the three of us. This baby is ours, just like the one in you is ours. We did this together. Made these lives together."

Evie sniffed, tears running down her face. "What is there to talk about? We will raise them together." Then she looked at Mona. "If that's what you want. If you still want us, because we never wanted you to leave. You left before we could propose. That was the plan. We were going to propose to you, and we were going to tell mom she could fuck off if she had a problem with it. We were going to celebrate Christmas here with Charleigh invited so you wouldn't feel like you had to hide anymore. But... that was when you wanted us. If you don't want us, then we want to co-parent with you. You're not a single mom. You will never have to do it alone. We want to be there for everything because we love you and we love them."

"I don't know what to do," Mona whispered. "It was supposed to be casual and you two are getting married. I never wanted this. I... I don't fit into family stuff. I don't know how to do family. I told you... I told you from the start that I was good with our relationship because when you wanted that family, you could have it. And now I'm here and I'm going to be a mom and I just... this can't work. How is it supposed to work?"

Evie tucked the hair behind Mona's ear. "It's already working. And now it doesn't have to be a secret. I never wanted this to be secret, I wanted you to let me tell the world. And since you don't have to worry about my mom being pissed anymore, just try. Please, baby. Let's try. Landon's mom will be on board too. She is so excited to be a grandma."

"What will the neighbors think?" Mona asked as she cried and laughed.

"We're the neighbors," Dilynn said. "And since that's my grandchild, I don't think we will mind."

Parker turned to the other daughter. "Does this mean she'll stop dropping hints about us having a kid? I mean seriously, we got back together a week ago, and she came in to talk about that empty house at the end of the damn street. And don't you lie to me and tell me it's not yours. I know you are planning on moving in there because you can't stay by yourself."

Lyra's lips tugged in a smile. "Are you kidding me? Now the pressure will be even worse. They didn't just have one baby, they made two. They will be so far up our asses to get married and start having babies it will be insufferable."

"At least no one expects me to have any kids," the third Greyson said. Then she raised her brows at Parker. "You picked the wrong Greyson-Trikru."

Lyra scoffed. "That's because you still live in Mom's guest house. And the only human you ever brought home would be murdered if she stepped in the house—fuck the house, the street. Evie would be out there playing bad cop as she shot Casey with the whole magazine."

The third girl turned her head to Charleigh. "Hi, I'm Sadie and since your sister and my sister are moving in together we should get acquainted."

"Sadie," Lyra hissed. "This is Charleigh. You know, Charleigh. About Charleigh and...."

But Charleigh didn't care Sadie didn't remember meeting her, because if Dilynn Greyson found out the princess even looked at her, she too would be murdered in the street.

"This is bullshit," Charleigh muttered under her breath. She turned away from the siblings' waiting area and made her way out of the house.

The door shut quietly behind her as she went to the truck to wait. With her phone in her hand, she considered calling Lexa to come get her. As much as she wanted Lexa to play knight in a shining SUV, she knew the woman would have too many questions.

She leaned against the truck, looking at the neighborhood Mona would be moving to. The trip over was like reliving a nightmare. The nightmare had been real the first time, and it was just as real this time.

"Charleigh," she heard from the front door.

Alex stepped off the porch and into the sun. Their boots screeched against the pavement as they jogged to where she'd stopped.

"You okay?" they asked, placing a hand on her shoulder.

She wiped the tears from her face and stared at the mini-mansion across the street. The mailbox with her bosses' last names was painted to look like a prop in a Disney movie.

"Yeah, I'm fine," she said. She turned to Alex, causing their hand to fall away from her. "I'm glad that everything is... worked out."

"I know you love her," they said.

Charleigh sniffed. "She's my sister. Of course, I love her."

"She's going to be okay," they promised. Just like they'd promised last time. But last time it was a lie.

"Yeah, I know." She wiped her nose across the sweater she'd bought to look like Dilynn like she ever needed clothes for that. "She's going to be better than okay. She's going to be inducted into the royal family and she'll forget all about the peasants."

Alex looked back at the house, then returned their studious stare to Charleigh. "You're worried she's going to leave you."

"Of course she's leaving me," Charleigh choked. She waved her hand at the house. "Which is fine and great. She always wanted to be your daughter, and she gets that now. She gets the family she never thought she would. And I'm happy for her. She's going to have a great life and her kid will grow up without ever wanting for anything with two moms and a dad because you all have great kids, and they have great lives, and they love you all so much that they all live in your own little cult. And I know a lot about cults because I was raised in one. At least if Mona's kid kisses a girl no one will come pick her up in a white van."

Alex's lips straightened into a line. "That's a little harsh."

Charleigh's chin dropped to her chest just as it had every single time she'd come to them. But this time she hadn't come to them or their wife. She hadn't fucked up so she shouldn't have to cower to them.

"I know it's harsh, but you know what? I'm not sorry because what is the point anymore?" Her gaze rose. "I mean, seriously I don't owe you or your wife anymore fucking apologies. I did my part. I did what you asked of me. And all I get from you is looks of pity. And she just... she just screams at me constantly for every little goddamn thing. I will never be good enough for her."

She looked up at them with their straight back and steady gaze.

"I was the one she didn't want. The one she never wanted and threw away, but I thought maybe, just maybe, she'd keep a promise to me. I got pregnant just like she did. I had a baby with a man that I can't stand to be in the same room with because I knew if I didn't then I was going to die in there. I was a fucking kid." Her hand shot up to the house. "But Mona gets knocked up having a threesome and because it's with your goddamn perfect princess, she gets a happily ever after and I get left behind as she joins this, which is what you always wanted. You and Dilynn even made her break up with me because you wanted her, and she hated me."

With hands up, Alex held her words away from them. "Charleigh, we never hated you. It was different then. We were trying to protect you and her. We tried to help you, and it didn't go the way any of us planned but—"

"I was sixteen. My dad just fucking died of a heart attack. My mom tried to send me to fucking conversion camp because I kissed a girl. You picked me up in a white van and brought me to fucking hell. You told me I could be myself. That being gay isn't the end of the world and then you made my girlfriend dump me. You and Marcus gave her an ultimatum to break up with me or lose her fucking bed in the first safe place she'd ever been. He'd even promised to adopt her!"

"Charleigh, Marcus couldn't have you and Mona sleeping together under his roof. Mona was in foster care, but you were there under guardianship. You couldn't move so we were trying to protect both of you."

"Well, she broke up with me. I was stupid and I was hurt. And I was sad, so you sent me to that fucking shrink that asked me two questions and gave Marcus a script to make me not feel sad anymore. And it worked. I didn't feel sad. Made me feel like I wasn't even there. So, I took more pills to feel something and then I drank because that was what everyone else was doing. And I had sex with boys because they asked me to. Sometimes they didn't even fucking asked. Joey's dad never asked. Not once did he ask. He just told me he knew how to make me straight and shoved it in. But you didn't know that because there was no way in hell I could tell you or your fucking wife that. So, I just let it happen and I closed my eyes and I told myself that this is what straight girls do, like he said, and if I could be just straight enough for my mom, then maybe someone would fucking love me again. Maybe I could just go home."

"Charleigh—"

"And then I got pregnant." Charleigh's hands ran up and down her face. "I was so fucking scared, and Marcus couldn't help me and I couldn't keep the baby and live at the school, and my mother fucking unadopted me. I didn't even know that I was adopted but I found out in court when she signed away being my mom. Because no mother ever wanted me. They both hate me. They both look at me like me being alive is ruining their lives."

She turned her back to them. Every inch of Charleigh's body shook. She wrapped her arms around herself, trying to hug herself like Mona hugged her.

Tried to make things okay again even if it was just for a moment. She'd have to learn how to do it alone since Mona was a Greyson now.

"I was scared so I begged you and your wife to help me. There wasn't a hug. There weren't promises that I wouldn't have to do it alone. No, she told me to get an abortion. And I couldn't. I couldn't do that. I wouldn't have been able to live with myself. So, I begged you and her for help. I had to get on my knees and beg you like a dog for table scraps. And I still got nothing but ultimatums. I just wanted one of you to help me find a fucking answer because I just wanted to finish school. You said it was important, and you all just expected me to grow up overnight, and I fucking tried."

Her body snapped around. Spit flew from her mouth as she yelled, "You even told me I was doing the right thing when you... you fucking took my daughter out of my arms and took her home to your wife. She didn't even show up. No one came. Marcus didn't come. Mona didn't come. I had to give birth all alone and you came to just walk in. You walked in and you took her away and you left me in the room with machines beeping and nurses looking at me like I was nothing. And I was nothing. I was nothing but in pain and I was wheeled out of the hospital a few hours later to figure out what the fuck was going on with my body that didn't look like my body anymore. And I didn't even get to go to Marcus's. No one told me I didn't get to go back to Marcus's. You had an intern drive me to the school and drop me off because no one had the courage to tell me that Marcus didn't want me anymore either. That I was all alone. And so I took more pills. I took so many pills because I just wanted to die. But I didn't die."

Tears streamed down her face. The tears she'd tried to hide from them every time she took the blame for their choices.

"I didn't even get to see her after you whisked her away to your mansion and your wife took a fucking maternity leave. So yes, I drank. I drank every fucking night in the shitty dorm room you stuck me in. Three months of drowning the pain as everyone looked at me like I was the biggest piece of trash there. Even though... Even though I was the first kid to graduate early.

"I was the first kid to earn a scholarship to college not paid for by your family. In fact, I am pretty sure, I am the only kid that wasn't offered a scholarship ever. But I went to college on our agreement that I would get my degree and come back to work for you, and I would take my kid home with me. But you fucking lied to me."

She stared into their eyes. "You said you would take care of Joey, and then she could come home with me if I just did what you two said." She held up her hands and turned in a circle. "But look around, she's not fucking here."

Charleigh stepped into their space, as she screamed, "Because your wife GAVE HER TO THE HOMOPHOBE THAT TRIED TO BREAK ME!"

She licked the venom from her teeth. Sucked in as much air as possible, then attacked again.

"And I still came back. I came back to that fucking school finally knowing why Dilynn looked at me like being alive was a crime. I got a degree in what she loved. I bought clothes to dress like her. I learned to talk like her. I tried to act like her. Because I thought maybe she would see me. And I kept telling myself that if I did what she said, and I pretended to be straight for Grace Marshall, then I would finally get to bring Joey home. That I wasn't going to abandon my kid like my bio mom dumped me. And all the AA meetings and all the parenting classes, what the fuck did they get me? Do you even know?"

Alex's eyes rose from the ground. They took a deep breath. "I don't."

"I get to see my kid two days a fucking month. Two. Days. A month!" Charleigh held up two fingers. "Two. I never got to tuck her in. Never told her a bedtime story. Never sang her a fucking lullaby. Imagine getting to see your baby two days a month for a few hours. Think about knowing you missed every single milestone. Every first."

"Charleigh, you have to understand—" Alex started.

"Oh, I understand. I think I understood a long time ago, but I wanted to believe that she didn't just throw me away because she hated me. I wanted to believe that someone fucking saw me. But she'll never see me as anything more than nothing."

"I don't think you're nothing, Charleigh," Dilynn stated. She walked down the walkway. "I think you're still the same little girl screaming for attention. I couldn't stop your mother from taking Joey from us because the court favored her grandmother over us, and you were too far in a bottle to even show up to court and make your wishes known."

"Dilynn," Alex tried, but Dilynn silenced them with just her eyes.

"No," Dilynn said. The index finger shook in the air as she pointed at Charleigh. "She doesn't get to throw herself a pity party on my property while screaming at you because she's mad at me."

When Dilynn stepped into Charleigh's bubble, the anger boiling within her seemed to break down the ligaments and tendons holding her bones together. The scab that had sealed her lung dissolved and she couldn't breathe with the woman who threw her away so close. Charleigh's shoulders fell, cowering to the woman with her same eyes.

Dilynn's nose rose and she looked down at Charleigh's tear-stained face. She sucked her teeth, then said. "You know why people call me the queen, it's because I earned my crown by putting my people first. Mona and Marcus call you Princess because after all these years everyone is still cleaning up after you."

Charleigh swallowed the hate for the name and the woman who didn't know. Didn't know it was Marcus's stupid son, Kyle who'd first started calling her that to make her feel like the victim of some horrific fairytale. He hadn't known she was the princess given away by the queen of rescued kids.

"Not everyone," Charleigh whispered. "You put everyone else first. I was the one you threw away."

"I gave you everything," Dilynn countered. "Just like I will give Mona everything. A job for life. That baby will have the same college fund that I gave yours, which is why you didn't get a scholarship from me to go to school. The only thing I didn't just give you was a fucking car. That might be the only thing I didn't do for you because you never asked, but everything else you asked of me and of Alex we did."

Dilynn's hot breath rushed over Charleigh's face. "The only one who has stopped you from being a mother to your daughter is you. Because you did what your mom did. You gave her away and you didn't come back when she needed you."

"But I came back," Charleigh protested as she stepped back. Her hands pressed against her chest. "I went to college like *you* told me to, and I came back."

"You came back a drunk with a degree," Dilynn spat.

"She's no more of a drunk than you are and not more likely to walk out on her family than Alex," Mona growled. She stepped in front of Charleigh, shielding the shaking blonde from any more strikes Dilynn tried to land. "You sit on a self-created throne throwing back shots of vodka and reminding Alex of all the times they walked out on you, but you are going to judge her? If anyone standing here is a drunk, it's you."

Mona looked down at the future grandmother to her child. She took Charleigh's hand in her own. "Charleigh goes to an AA meeting every fucking week. She went to the parenting classes that you required of her. She moved out on her own and she pays all the bills, so she could prove to you that she could make it. That's the only reason we don't live together anymore. She wanted to show you she was an adult and could do it on her own."

"Stop trying to protect her, Mona," Dilynn demanded.

"Then stop trying to shoot her down." Mona looked at Alex, then back to Dilynn. "She did everything you told her to, and you just kept coming up with more. She just got a new car. I could go out and buy the bed on our way home, but we both know you still won't go to court with her like you promised. You never were going to."

Mona licked her lips.

"I didn't fucking understand because to everyone else you act like a goddamn white savior. So, what is it that Queen Dilynn Greyson can't stand?"

After a deep inhale, Mona launched her final attack.

"She gave you a baby that you wanted so badly, and then didn't show up to make it possible for you to keep her, so your heart broke all over again." Mona's shoulders rose and her eyes narrowed. "Lost another baby in less than two years. I get it you were hurt but stop lying to her."

Dilynn took a step back. Her eyes looked over Mona, toward the woman who was coming down the porch with the rest of the Greysons. They stopped several yards away, creating a semi-circle behind Mona and Charleigh.

"What did you tell her?" Dilynn hissed.

"The truth." Evie kept her distance, choosing to stand with her sisters. "You told me I didn't have to keep secrets that hurt people, and she was hurting. So, I told her the truth about why Charleigh could never come to Christmas. Why you'd never forgive her. The truth is you loved that baby more than you loved any of us because she finally gave you a perfect baby girl that looked just like you. Like the one you gave up when you were a teen mom. That you hated Charleigh because she reminded her of you."

Dilynn's lower lip quivered for just a moment. Something Charleigh would have missed had she looked away. But hearing that Evie knew about her made her feel just for a second brave.

"Because I am you," Charleigh whispered, pulling Dilynn's gaze back to her. "Just a generational curse that you got to see come to fruition."

Dilynn's eyes narrowed, but for the first time in Charleigh's life, she felt like Dilynn was looking at her. The older blue eyes studied each of Charleigh's eyes. Scanned over her nose to her lips, and then up her jaw to her ears.

"Do you see me now?" Charleigh asked, realizing all these years Dilynn didn't know. She might still not know by the way she was still searching her face. "They didn't change my name. My dad liked that I had a piece of my past."

Parker cleared her throat and reminded Dilynn they weren't alone. "Dilynn, do you feel like you maybe—"

"You're going to counsel me, Parker?" Dilynn snapped, but her eyes didn't move from Charleigh.

"First rule of therapy: you can't help someone who doesn't think they need it." Parker's shoulders straightened. She took another step forward. Standing alongside Mona. "So no to the therapy, but I'm not going to stand by and let you talk to my friend like that."

Dilynn glared at her daughters' partners. She opened her mouth, then closed it.

"Don't worry," Charleigh said, stepping close enough that Dilynn and she were sharing air. "No one knows. I thought you did all this time, but no one will have to know the real reason you hate me so much."

Dilynn's eyes closed, and her lips trembled once more. She exhaled slowly, then asked, "When did you—"

"It doesn't matter," Charleigh interjected. She brushed her hair back from her face. With a nod, she told the woman who gave up on her long ago, "Once you told me when someone shows you who they are to believe them. You said it because you saw me as nothing but a problem. I didn't want to believe what I saw. I didn't want to believe you hated me. But you've shown me again and again and again. So, I'll keep your secret. I'll leave at the end of the year and you won't have to see me ever again. And until then, just pretend I don't exist. You've done that my whole life anyway."

She stepped to the side to walk away but froze when Dilynn caught her by the wrist. It wasn't a firm hold, but having never felt her mother's touch sent a shock wave through her.

"Charleigh," Dilynn whispered.

"You know, I changed how I spelled my name to be like you," Charleigh whispered. "I just... I was so stupid."

Mona took Charleigh's hand from Dilynn's grasp. "Come on. Let's go start applying for new jobs."

Charleigh stopped as she was about to pass Alex. "I shouldn't have yelled at you. You said we should all sit down and talk, and I let it all boil up. Today was supposed to be about Mona, not me."

They reached out to put their hand on Charleigh's shoulder but stopped. It fell helpless to their side because they never had it in them to care about her like they had Mona.

"You were the first kid we brought to Greyson's to protect you from a conversion camp. We didn't know what we were doing, and we put you in an impossible situation with limited support," they said. "I failed. I failed you in every single way I could have. I'm sorry."

Charleigh shook her head. "I learned a long time ago that all of this is my fault for ever being born."

She didn't look back at Dilynn to see if her words hit the woman. A part of her wanted to see if Dilynn cared now she knew. Mona shut the door though, and she kept her eyes facing forward.

The truck moved slowly down the street. It wasn't a grand getaway like last time. There wasn't a need to run when the war was finally fought. No side had won, but both were wounded. That was the whole point though. This wasn't a war to win, it was to cause the most amount of pain as possible.

"What doesn't anyone know?" Mona asked carefully.

The promise she'd made to Dilynn moments ago now felt like a burden she didn't know how to carry, the truth swirling in the hot, sun-drenched space between them. The woman never kept her promises. She didn't plan on keeping the last one either.

"She's my birth mom," Charleigh whispered.

The sun hung high in the sky, casting sharp rays that cut through the car's windshield, making the air inside feel warmer than it should. The engine hummed steadily beneath Mona's feet, but her fingers gripped the steering wheel as though she was bracing for impact. Mona glanced over at Charleigh for just a second, her gaze nothing less than murderous.

Charleigh sat quietly in the passenger seat; her face turned toward the sunlit world outside. Her reflection in the side window was hazy, her shoulders tense despite the warmth in the air. Her breath came slowly, almost inaudibly, as if she were still processing what she had just said.

"How long have you known?" Mona asked when Greyson Dr. could no longer be seen in the mirrors.

"Right before that first court date." Charleigh took a deep breath. "I went to the courthouse and got my adoption records. I was going to find my birth mom. I was going to find her and ask her if she regretted giving me away. I was going to ask her because I was going to ask Dilynn and Alex to adopt Joey. But her name was on my birth certificate, and I took a handful of pills."

Her tongue scraped against her top teeth. She could never forget the taste of charcoal or the sound of Mona's voice calling out to her not to give up.

"I thought it was that you were going to have to see your mom in court," Mona whispered.

"It was." Charleigh stared out the window. "I was going to have to stand in court and watch two women that didn't want me to fight over my kid."

They drove in thick silence for a while. Charleigh could feel the steam coming off of Mona. It was too hot, and she felt like the car might explode.

"Tomorrow, I have my visit with Joey," Charleigh reminded Mona. "You coming over afterward?"

Mona hummed. "Yeah, I was thinking I would invite Parker too. You good with that?"

Charleigh thought about the woman who'd come to her aide twice, even though she barely knew her. Even though she also hooked up with a Greyson Princess, maybe she wasn't that bad. Evie the Replacement maybe wasn't that bad either.

"That's fine," she said. She licked her lips and closed her eyes. "I'm going to hire a lawyer. A real lawyer, and I am going to fight for full custody at my next hearing. I can't keep waiting for Dilynn to help me. I got to do this on my own."

"I can ask Landon to do it," Mona offered. "He's a criminal attorney, but he kinda owes me big time since he put this creature in me that has me eating pickles wrapped in turkey and cream cheese. It's so gross and so good at the same time."

Charleigh scooted to the center seat. She leaned her head against Mona's shoulder.

"She's never going to forgive you for putting her on blast in front of everyone," she whispered. "And I don't want her pissed at you and him. I'll figure it out and I'll get a lawyer myself. Or I will put my nose to the computer. I mean, I can read, and I can usually talk my way out of anything."

Mona shook her head. "When have I ever cared what the evil ice queen has thought about me?"

With a grimace, Charleigh said, "I still can't believe you slept with both of them. Was it like weird at first or are they kinky freaks like Dilynn and Alex are?"

"It wasn't weird, just different. It took a long time to get to the point where we were all together. For the first couple of years, it was just Evie and me and Evie and him, but we went on a few weekend getaways together, and he is so kind and nothing like the boys we grew up with. Always super considerate, and I guess he just grew on me."

They sat at a left turn light for two cycles before Mona got annoyed with the arrow not turning green. She pulled a U-turn and took them down a different path.

"I'm happy, you're happy. Sad that you will be, like, there. I definitely won't be allowed to drive down that street without Dilynn calling the cops on me, but you deserve to be happy." Charleigh looked up at Mona. "You have to go back to your girlfriend and boyfriend to have make-up sex tonight. Four months is when you start to get super horny again."

"Oh, I'm aware," Mona said with a smile. "I showed up at your house yesterday, but you were out, no doubt, with your dream girl. I had come to clean the cobwebs out of your coochie with some stupid thought that we could start over, and I could steal you away from her. Crazy how all of this played out."

As they drove down the street, Charleigh sighed. "Think she's going to fire me?"

"No," Mona said quickly. "But make sure you behave with Lexa, and remind that bitch the next time you see her that if she hurts you, I'm going to—"

"How does someone liquify someone?" Charleigh asked. "Is it like putting them in a bathtub of Mountain Dew? I heard that some guy tried to sue them for a rat in a can, but Mountain Dew won because they said a rat would have dissolved in the can."

"Better you don't know the details." A smile spread over Mona's smug face. She tapped the steering wheel. "Does Lexa know about Joey?"

"I have been trying to figure out how to tell her. It didn't seem like there was a point because she said there was a chance she was getting traded. But yesterday.... It looks like we are going to try to date date, so she should know," Charleigh explained. "Kinda like you and them; she needs to know, so she can make her own decision about what she wants."

"Just be careful with the whole waiting thing. You don't want her to find out by accident and it seems like you were intentionally hiding it from her." Mona pressed a kiss to her hair. "So, you are going on a date date?"

"Yeah. When she gets back from Dallas. If they win, then she has to stay in Dallas, and she texted me this morning her coach told her she wasn't allowed to fly back between games this time."

Mona deviated from the path to her house, heading north on the 101 freeway.

"Where are we going?" Charleigh asked.

"To buy you some new clothes," Mona stated. "I always knew you were trying to make Dilynn like you by dressing like her, but it's time to ditch the old threads. You need to be you because you are better than she will ever be."

Charleigh glanced down at her sweater, then back at Mona. "How do you always have so much more money than me?"

A blush blossomed on Mona's cheeks. She licked her lips before the smile rose with her blush. "Don't laugh."

"Not promising that."

"Evie and Landon liked to spoil me. Landon had the lift put on my truck last year for my birthday. And E. goes shopping every time she has a bad day. She figured out I like shoes, and well, you get it. Plus, one of them always fights to pay for dinner. Actual fights have taken place, and we almost got banned from Echo's bar after Evie body-checked Landon so hard that he fell through the guys' bathroom door. Luckily, Echo was the one trying to cash us out, and even though he ran into her, she didn't get hurt."

"Echo seems really nice."

"Yeah, she's good people." Mona tapped the steering wheel. "Anyways. I don't make more than you. I just haven't had to spend money like I used to. And I was living with them until a few weeks ago so I didn't have any bills." With a soft chuckle, she said, "When I moved out, I actually bought a duplex.

I was going to offer you the other unit, but you were so excited about living in that house. You kept talking about writing a book about being gay on the frontier, and I didn't want to get in the way. So, the other unit was rented out this month, and the rent covers the mortgage. Basically, I don't have a lot of bills anymore and I think I'm starting to grow up. Which is probably a good thing because It is going to need me to grow up."

"You're going to fit in as a Greyson," Charleigh said, pulling the sweater off. "Alex was always meant to be your parent. Pretty sure they are the only person you ever listened to, so it's going to be good for you."

"You're my family, Chuckie." Mona took Charleigh's hand, placing it on her stomach. "Meet your It."

"Stop calling your baby It."

Mona intertwined their fingers. Quietly, she said, "I know I wasn't there when Joey was born. I swear, I tried to get there, but Marcus was so drunk after you went into labor because he and Kyle got into a huge fight. He called Kyle's mom and told her to come get him and then he just left. He didn't come back for two whole days, and he told me after he came back that DCS moved you. I was so angry, and I told him to move me too. I told him to call Alex and have me moved, but he was crying. He just couldn't stop crying, and I couldn't leave him like that."

"It was really scary," Charleigh confessed.

"Will you be there when it comes out?" Mona asked. Her dark eyes didn't move from the car in front of them.

"Of course," Charleigh promised. "I will be at the hospital, and I will take a picture of your pussy being torn apart for a keepsake."

"You always loved looking at my pussy," Mona said. The fear fell away, making space for the smug grin. "I bet you still have the photos I took of you licking through it."

"How do you think I managed to be celibate for a year straight? Just a drawer full of Mona pussy pics and my trusty vibrator."

Mona's angry steam finally left the truck's cabin. They were able to talk like they had before anyone was pregnant.

"I think you need something that accents the girls because they are your best features," Mona stated, reaching over to poke one of Charleigh's breasts. "But no Devils shirts and no more Dilynn sweaters. Something that says I am Charleigh. I am smart and sexy and not gonna take any of your bullshit."

"Okay, but you better not be picturing me while you get spit-roasted between your lovers tonight."

19

Dallas swept the Devils in three tight games over the course of a week and a half. Lexa had nothing to be ashamed of in regard to her performance, but she'd missed her date with Charleigh. At least the blonde had come to her last two home games, but losing both didn't put her in the mood to go out. After the second loss, Danaya reminded Lexa of her deal to throw the end-of-year party.

With the rest of the team preparing to head overseas in a few weeks, the promised party was scheduled for the Saturday following their last game. She didn't know the first thing about planning a party. Before her arrest, Lexa had every intention of throwing the Play-Off party with as much pussy as she could pack in her house. The type of party she'd seen in teen movies growing up but never attended. An event Sylvia would call trashy or ghetto, because Sylvia would fill the yard with activities befitting children's birthdays and hire two to three food trucks who offered options most of the team was not supposed to eat during the season.

She'd tried to do it Sylvia's way, but her credit cards had been cut off as Kayla had said was going to happen. It hit her as she checked her account balance. She was going to have to make it on her own moving forward because Sylvia wasn't coming back. She should have known that when Chicago didn't make it to the playoffs and Sylvia hadn't come home. The woman had at least a dozen homes, some Lexa had never even seen. But the divorce papers were delivered practically weekly by Sylvia's stupid lawyer's daughter. She'd never opened them though. Just let them pile up on the entry table until she trashed them all earlier that morning and pushed Sylvia out of her mind to get ready to host the party.

Her teammates loved Sylvia's parties, so they arrived even with short notice on Saturday evening. Smiles turned to sideways glances as the players and their small troupes of significant others and friends in their shorts and tank tops covering bathing suits stopped to greet Lexa. Several passed by her, making their way through the house to find nothing more than some pool floats in the back and a DJ in the living room. Half of the team was grumbling about Lexa's failure before Charleigh even arrived.

There were a few hoots and a couple of whistles when the blonde stepped into the house dressed for a cocktail party. Black satin covered only the essentials, and Charleigh sparkled. The dress made Lexa's mouth water before she panicked over not having told the woman the event was always casual.

"Didn't know I was the entertainment," Charleigh grumbled as eyes around the room locked on her.

None of the players said a word to Charleigh, who'd taken up position behind Lexa as the other guests gathered in small cliques. The DJ turned the music up, causing Lexa to tuck her girlfriend behind her more as people turned their eyes to who they assumed was going to start taking off her clothes.

Lexa smiled brighter when Emma and Danaya burst through the door. Emma shouted out her arrival, and Lexa counted on the center to help her fix this. She didn't get a chance to ask before she saw both women's eyes turn to her in frustration.

With a tisk of her tongue, Danaya growled at Lexa, "Where's your fucking bedroom?"

After a few simple directions, Charleigh followed Danaya's lead down the hallway. Charleigh's dramatically high heel twisted, causing her to stumble. She only managed to remain standing by grabbing hold of Danaya's arm.

The rest of the guests arrived while Lexa leaned against the kitchen island with Emma, watching as beer bottles popped open. The evening was thus far a bust, and Lexa hoped it meant people would get bored of meandering through her and Sylvia's house. She'd had the common sense to take down the photos from the walls before Charleigh had arrived and hide them in the hall closet.

The wall of trophies and awards still held their shared accomplishments, but at least Charleigh wouldn't have to look at her in a white dress. She hated that dress, so at least taking them down was a reminder she didn't have to play dress up for Sylvia anymore. Not if she signed the divorce papers that would arrive again tomorrow.

"You weren't a part of the planning committee before, huh?" Emma asked. When Lexa didn't respond, she gestured to the doorway. "Well at least DayDay was able to sort out your girl, so she doesn't look like you hired the team a stripper."

Lexa's eyes rose from her water to find Danaya in her bathing suit top, pushing a different Charleigh toward her. The heavy breasts peeked out of a tank top Danaya had worn into the house. A pair of Lexa's boxers layered under a pair of Lexa's shorts sagged just under Charleigh's hip bones.

"Fuck, she's beautiful," Lexa whispered.

"Go tell her that," Emma said with a nudge.

Lexa left her position at the counter only to be intercepted by the hunk of muscle that even she had to look up to. "Where are games?" the Norwegian asked. "They say party there will be games, and I get to hit you with big airbags on fist. I would like this very much."

Danaya bounced next to the woman. "Yeah, Lexa, where's the games?"

"Uh... no bounce houses this year. The... the neighbors complained last year, so we had to keep it more chill this time. The pool is ready though and there's food in the back."

Charleigh took up position along Lexa's side as the Norwegian walked away grumbling.

They made their way back to the kitchen. Lexa sighed and looked at Charleigh's wandering gaze. "There's usually games, but I don't usually plan the parties, so I guess we can add this to the list of shit I'm not good at."

"What kind of games?" Charleigh asked.

Lexa handed Charleigh a bottle of water. "Last year, Sylvia rented a bunch of bounce houses and we all beat the shit out of each other in bouncy boxing." She smiled, remembering how she'd knocked Emma on her ass after the center had called her a coconut.

"That sounds expensive." Charleigh picked up the bottle of water she'd been sipping from. She flipped it, landing it upright again. With a subtle smirk, she cast Lexa a side-eye. "You want games?"

Lexa looked at her, then around the room.

"Don't worry. I got games," Charleigh promised.

At first, Lexa watched without much hope as Charleigh began to dig through the drawers in the kitchen. The woman moved drawer to drawer until Lexa's stomach twisted. Quickly she slid her ass in front of the utensil drawer where she remembered the first set of divorce papers had gotten dropped in, hoping Charleigh didn't ask what she was hiding.

After three unsuccessful searches, Charleigh looked up at Lexa, "Which one is your junk drawer?"

Scratching between her braids, Lexa said, "Uh... there isn't one. Everything has a place."

Charleigh looked at her like she'd grown three heads. With hands on her hips, she said, "I need tape. And a pack of cards. And shot glasses."

Lexa pointed to the bar at the other end of the living room. She'd avoided going over there so she wouldn't feel the need to grab a beer. Even though they'd thrown out the rules, she planned to stay sober for Charleigh tonight. Show the woman she could have fun without alcohol since the woman didn't keep any in her house.

Charleigh went to the bar and dug through the drawers. She shot up a hand with blue tape and then smiled when she found a pack of playing cards.

The strips of tape began to form a smaller version of a checkerboard on the glass coffee table. Charleigh beckoned her over, but Lexa declined with a shake of her head from her position in the kitchen.

"You need at least two," Charleigh said.

Lexa wasn't about to look like a fool at her own party while trying to play a game just been created on a whim. Even for the pitiful pout of the plump pink lip.

"Oh, I see you, Charleigh!" Danaya whooped as she returned from the bathroom. She skipped toward the table and set up three shots on each side of the board. Then, they made their way to the bar scanning the bottles of liquor.

"Some whipped cream vodka for Peaches," Danaya proclaimed, holding the bottle out to the blonde.

Charleigh laughed, then ran her fingers over each label. "And for number twenty-seven, coming in at five foot eleven, we have popping cherry vodka. Should we get Em to pour it for you?"

They laughed and hugged, and Lexa stopped regretting the events of the bar. She couldn't wish it away and still be here.

"What are they doing?" Emma asked. She sidled up alongside Lexa as the other two slouched over the table flipping cards and moving shot glasses one space at a time.

"I think they are about to get very, very drunk," Lexa said.

Emma hummed. "I thought your girl didn't drink?"

"Me too," but Lexa stood back as the party came to life around her as it always had when a different blonde was running the show.

The made-up game, Shot Wars had gotten Charleigh and Danaya lubricated. When others called next, Charleigh moved to the next table with a trail of Lexa's teammates following her like lost puppies. A solo cup of tequila and a stack of cards atop had the groups testing their lung capacity and control as they carefully tried to not be the one to blow the last card from the cup. Charleigh participated in the first round of this game as well, barely managing to leave two cards for Danaya to blow away on her turn. The next round, Charleigh wasn't as lucky, this time having to mix the tequila with the vodka she'd already been consuming.

Lexa wasn't sure at what point Charleigh ended up with a beer in her hand. But it was there, and Lexa had found herself popping open a bottle for herself. She coddled it, letting the bitter hops bubble away the anxiety of failing at something else.

Each time a new game took off, Charleigh would move to another space in the grand room and set up a new drinking game. With a pack of playing cards, a roll of painter's tape, a couple of red solo cups, and a few shot glasses, Charleigh created a station rotation of activities fitting one of the old frat houses on Alpha Lane. Beer pong was set up on the dining room table. And three more games popped up as her teammates began to create their entertainment.

The group of players who'd ignored her upon arrival looked to her as the hostess, and the world Charleigh was afraid of welcomed her with open arms.

Tension eased from Lexa's shoulders. She knew it could work if Charleigh gave it a chance. And there was no way the blonde would be able to deny her place in Lexa's life anymore. They could get a place like this of their own. She'd sign the divorce papers tomorrow, knowing now she had a future.

"Sexy, Lexi," Danaya said, humping the air as she hopped over. Her chest was dripping wet.

"Did you know white people make up the craziest shit? Look at that." Danaya pointed to where a group of women were lying on the floor as big-breasted ones stood over them with shots tucked into their cleavage. "She called it Waterfalls, and I had to catch the shot she poured from her breasts. Her breasts, Lexi. I mean, I thought your girl's titties were nice and all because what breasts are not. But damn. They just bounced and I'm covered in my shot because I couldn't stop laughing."

Lexa's face grew hot. She scanned the room in search of the tiny human among the semi-giants. She wasn't still pouring shots into the mouths of her teammates with her breasts, so Lexa continued to search until she finally caught sight of Charleigh sitting on Emma's knee.

The two clinked shot glasses together and downed the clear liquid. Even though she knew her teammate was committed to the woman twerking in the living room, Lexa didn't like the way her hand rested on Charleigh's hip or how Charleigh's head fell back in easy laughter.

Charleigh looked over at Lexa. She smiled and Lexa smiled back at her. The blue eyes were pulled away from hers when Danaya tugged Charleigh off Emma's lap and onto the dance floor.

She could feel the booze in her veins, but it wasn't anger. She'd had enough of sharing her biggest fan and was ready for everyone to leave.

Lexa's eyes scanned over the bottle of vodka gripped in the pale fingers. Watched as it dribbled out of the corners of Charleigh's lips. Danaya laughed, leaned forward, and licked the alcohol from the woman's chest. Then Danaya's hands were on Charleigh's hips, and they were dancing and laughing.

Danaya was laughing too loud, and when Lexa looked at Emma, she realized Emma wasn't even close to as drunk as the two younger women were. Emma leaned back against the stiff couch with her legs spread. Her eyes ran over the women on the dance floor.

Lexa's mind replayed her friends' discussion on taking her girl away to Sedona. The pair of them had wanted her girl. Joke or not it was enough to make them a threat to her relationship.

"You guys staying here tonight?" Lexa asked, putting herself between the women and the center.

Emma shook her head. "I ordered an Uber, so I can tuck that drunk ass into bed." She looked around the room that had begun to empty for the night. "I was just considering if I need to take blondie with us tonight, so you don't do something stupid."

"No," Lexa quickly answered. She waved the warm, mostly empty bottle at her side. "I'll ask her where she wants to sleep when everyone's gone."

"Do you want us to stay?" Emma asked, her eyes scanning past Lexa.

No way in hell was she letting Emma and Danaya sleep in the same building as Charleigh when the woman had demonstrated too many times her need to please people who asked anything of her.

"Naw. We'll be fine."

Charleigh slapped Danaya's ass twerking practically in her face. And the jealousy was back. Lexa moved in behind Charleigh. She placed her hands on Charleigh's hips. The drunk blonde leaned back and smiled up at Lexa. Her arm wrapped around the woman, and she swayed with her.

The song switched, and Charleigh was still turned, so her back pressed against Lexa's front. Lexa remembered the boasting about the tiny woman being a top, but with every verse, the woman wrapped herself tighter in Lexa's grasp. They only stopped dancing when Emma told Danaya, "Our Uber's here."

Lexa tightened her grip around Charleigh's middle as Danaya came in for a hug. The woman's arms wrapped around both of them, pressing Charleigh's face into her bust.

"Time to go make my woman moan," Danaya bragged. Her long arms looked lanky as they hung around the masc's solid frame.

"If anyone is moaning tonight, it's you," Emma said. She picked Danaya's sloppy drunk ass up and tossed her over her shoulder.

Charleigh laughed and turned to face Lexa. Her little lower lip stuck out, and she looked up with a lowered chin to Lexa, "Is she the only one that's going to moan tonight?"

Emma turned back to Lexa and stared at her. "She's drunk."

Lexa could taste the alcohol from Charleigh's breath. She wasn't sure how drunk the blonde was, but there was no doubt she was more open to physical contact than she'd ever been before. But Lexa also didn't want her to regret anything in the morning.

As Emma carried Danaya away, Lexa swallowed the hungry glint in Charleigh's eyes. She licked her lips, and asked, "Do you want something?"

"You, Lek-sa," Charleigh said. "In me."

Lexa's crushed ego was put back together with the way Charleigh's tongue stroked her name. The confidence previously quaking was solid once more. This was what was meant to happen. She and Charleigh were always meant to do this, and she gave up all her apologies because she knew Charleigh was right. The bar had happened to get them here. They weren't alone again, but they were together the way Lexa had wanted.

There were people still in the yard, but she didn't care about playing hostess anymore. They'd leave when they were ready like they'd done every year before.

She took Charleigh by the hand, leading her to the master bedroom at the back of the house. As they stepped into the room two lights illuminated the floor dimly, making the path to the bed unencumbered by shadow monsters.

A sloppy kiss that started slowly began to build. The alcohol on Charleigh's tongue eased the unsteadiness in Lexa's mind if she was doing the right thing by Charleigh at this moment.

This wasn't the bar where the woman had pushed her away or the bedroom where Charleigh's moans were fake. They were both consenting and Charleigh's hand on the back of Lexa's neck was pulling her closer. She stood on her tippy toes until Lexa lifted her and felt the woman's legs secure around her waist.

Lexa's fingers kneaded the soft flesh of Charleigh's ass, ignoring the dings on her phone alerting her that the front door had opened and then closed, or the way people were cheering in the living room.

Only when she needed Charleigh's naked flesh in her hands did she lower the woman to the floor and turn her away. She stripped away the borrowed clothes from the woman's narrow frame, replacing the material with kisses. Charleigh's hands locked over her abdomen and her shoulders tensed.

"I don't look like you," she said.

Lexa wrapped her arm around the woman and pulled the freckled flesh against her still-clothed body. "You're beautiful," she assured her.

The remaining teammates cheered loudly, but whatever was happening out there didn't matter. They could be stealing the TV for all she cared.

She swayed with Charleigh to the music, feeling her body relax back into her touch. Her fingers ghosted over the skin of Charleigh's stomach until the woman's hands fell back to her sides. Her fingers explored further up, taking a heavy breast in her hand. The fullness she felt when she squeezed made her slick with need.

"Do you want to be fucked like a princess or a dirty whore?" she asked with her lips just past Charleigh's ear.

"Like I'm Lexa Jenson's dirty whore," Charleigh whispered in the dim room.

Lexa's hands squeezed the supple flesh. She knew how to fuck a whore, and she loved she would get to show Charleigh how powerful she was. Give her everything she'd been holding back.

"Get on the bed," she commanded as she started to pull her shirt up and over her head. She reached into the nightstand's drawers and fondled the various dildos she'd kept on standby. Selecting what she believed to be an average size, she withdrew it and the harness. She dropped her pants next and slipped the harness on. When she looked up, Charleigh's ass was perfectly presented to her.

She followed the woman onto the bed and knelt behind her. Her hand kneaded the milky surface and then slapped it hard enough to send the woman face down into the mattress. She loved the way the flesh burned red from her touch, so she added another handprint on the other side to match.

With a muffled cry, Charleigh's back arched. Lexa reached over the woman, twisted the silky curls between her fingers, then pulled Charleigh back up by her hair until Lexa's perked nipples pressed against the woman's back.

The fingers of her dominant hand explored the terrain of flesh Charleigh still hadn't shown her.

Charleigh's hand came back up, and she gripped Lexa's neck as the ghost touches ran down the front of the woman to her soaked core. They parted the trim landing strip and dipped within, until her digits met the small bud she'd make present with pulsing need soon enough.

The first touch melted the woman into Lexa. She complied with each following touch, vocally urging Lexa on. Lexa's other arm wrapped around the woman, holding, then kneading her breast as she hooked a single finger within the woman.

Her pace increased with each whimper that fell from Charleigh's lips.

"More," Charleigh pled.

And Lexa didn't hesitate to give her more. Another finger and a palm pressed flat against the woman's clit had Charleigh gasping. Lexa scissored her fingers to ease the dick's entrance.

"Lek-sa," Charleigh cried out in reward as Lexa found the sweetest spot within the trembling woman. She started to chant Lexa's name as the long digits hit the spot again and again.

She rolled the thick nipple between her fingers and suckled on the small ear lobe. Her desire dripped down her thighs. She kept up a steady pace until Charleigh broke the last ounce of self-control she had.

"Fuck me like you own me," Charleigh demanded.

Lexa pinched the nipple tighter until she felt Charleigh's walls pulsing around her digits. Feeling the flutters made her want more. She wanted all of her.

"Mine," she growled against the skin of her throat before she bit down around the mark that had faded with time. Then she sucked it back into place.

Her palm pressed harder against the blooming bud as she added a third finger and thrust within the pulsing pussy.

"Yes. Fuck me, Lexa," Charleigh begged. "Don't ever stop fucking me like your dirty slut."

But Lexa had to stop because the blonde asked to be fucked like a whore. She pulled her fingers out. Pushing Charleigh's face back into the mattress that had seen this scene too many times before, she grabbed the bottle of lube. It shook in her over-excited hands. The pump shot the clear faux slick on the sheets. She had to aim more carefully before she managed to hit the silicone head.

After a few strokes, her gaze shifted to admire the soaked entrance spread for her, and she aligned the tip with the opening. She stalled for a moment, remembering the woman she was about to fuck wasn't a whore but a woman. Her woman, so she didn't slam her hips against her like she'd done to all the others. She moved slowly, watching as the caramel-colored cock spread the rosy ring.

Charleigh moaned into the mattress, but Lexa needed to hear the blonde say her name. She pulled her up by her hair until the small pale arms held her body on all fours and the silicone was fully sheathed within.

Her fingers tighten their grip on the soft waves. She pulled out halfway, only to thrust back with a quick snap.

"I want to hear you beg," Lexa commanded. She thrust again.

And Charleigh obeyed. She pleaded, "Please, Lek-sa. Please, fuck me."

Lexa watched the dick disappear within the woman. Her fingers released the golden reins to grip Charleigh's hips, rocking her back and forth shallowly, then stronger. Her eyes never tore away from their connection until her resolve to be gentle crumbled with the woman's gratitude.

"Thank you," Charleigh choked out between thrusts.

The woman beneath her said all the things she always wanted to hear from those pink lips. Her chest filled with pride and her mind with power.

"Pussy fucking waited years to be filled properly," Lexa snarled. "Don't you dare touch yourself until I tell you to."

She pulled out to the tip and then snapped her hips forward until the pale cheeks jiggled. Faster wasn't what would turn a whore into a mewling mess, so she focused on making each thrust harder than the last. Her arms worked as hard as her thighs to drive into the woman. Pushing her forward until her tits and face hit the mattress. Charleigh's moans once more were muffled by the mattress Lexa had pressed her back into.

"You fucking like being fucked like a bitch in heat, don't you?" she jeered. "Ass up to be rutted like a goddamn animal." She took the delicate fingers gripping into the sheets as a yes and drove into the drenched channel again.

Lexa's pace only increased when the base of the cock had ignited her own need. She pistoned her hips against the flushed backside.

"Who owns this cunt?" Lexa demanded, her hand holding back the blonde hair so Charleigh's face had to lift once more.

"You do," Charleigh cried out. "I'm yours. Your whore."

A guttural growl escaped her gritted teeth as Lexa's core was fully stimulated with the proper pressure.

"That's right. Mine."

Her arms began doing more work as she chased her release with less coordinated thrusts until the white heat spread through her body. Her abs contracting sent the silicone appendage deeper into the moaning mess below her.

Lexa's orgasm slowed her movements momentarily as she caught her breath and her eyes refocused on the ass gliding off the glistening dick. Charleigh rocked herself back and forth, her fingers still holding onto the sheets. She'd been a good girl and not reached down to finish herself, which meant she needed a reward.

A prize for being obedient while Lexa took what she wanted. That was what Sylvia taught her with the women they shared. Rewards were for whores who obeyed.

Lexa reached the honey hair once more, pulling the woman up like a sex toy still bouncing on her dick. Lexa loved the way it felt to be in control of the blonde who had driven her crazy. She wrapped her arm around the woman's front, playing with the breasts Charleigh had dangled in Danaya's face. Lexa's breasts. Everything that was Charleigh was Lexa's now and she was going to have it all.

Leaning back on her heels, Lexa rocked her hips as she tweaked the nipples between the fingers of her left hand and rubbed the raised nub with her right. She pinched the perked flesh, then padded against her clit as Charleigh begged her not to stop. From the moaning, Lexa felt like Charleigh was getting close to her edge. But she didn't want it to end like this.

She'd had enough of dirty whores. She'd fucked her way through several metro areas' whores for three months in just this way. And it wasn't enough of a reward for Charleigh's obedience.

She wanted to see her come apart. Her hands let go, and Charleigh's position was unsustainable as Lexa rocked her hips upward. The thin body was sent sprawling back to the bed, while the silicone appendage flopped in the air.

Lexa trailed her fingers down each vertebra as Charleigh's body curled toward the mattress. She grazed over the dimples above the woman's tailbone. Tomorrow, she needed to get Charleigh on a normal eating schedule. Needed to make sure she consumed enough calories each day so every bone in her body wasn't visible. That was a tomorrow problem, and she filed it away as something she would do for the woman along with all the ways she was going to make Charleigh's life better by being in it.

With little effort, she flipped Charleigh onto her back. Before Charleigh could finish the squeal, her lips were met with Lexa's hungry kiss. Her tongue licked the roof of Charleigh's mouth while she turned on the lowest setting of the rabbit cock ring, then lined herself back up with the woman's abused vulva and pushed within her again.

She held nothing back as she swallowed each gasp from Charleigh. Lexa's tongue stroked Charleigh's until she lowered herself to the heaving bust. She traced circles around the areolas and watched as the already perked nipples grew larger. She wrapped her lips around one and sucked. Her teeth grazed the pert flesh, earning her a hiss of pain.

The milky thighs shook as Charleigh's pussy was filled and the silicone trendles danced against the fully presented clit. She breathed heavier and her legs pulled Lexa in closer.

"I don't think I can hold it back." With clenched eyes, Charleigh cried out, "May I cum? Please Lexa. I was a good girl."

Lexa's tongue froze on the abused nipple. Never having been asked permission before, she knew she should say yes. But she wasn't ready to be done.

After weeks of waiting for Charleigh to give her what she wanted, she needed more. Needed Charleigh to break apart so she could put her back together. Once she was repaired, she would see how much Lexa cared about her.

"Not yet," Lexa whispered.

When the vibrator and dick pulled away from the slick core, Charleigh cried out. Her fingers pulled at her hair as her chest rose and fell. Seeing how close the woman was to coming undone brought a smile to Lexa's face. She loved seeing the woman who always had something to say unable to make words.

Lexa made her way down pale body barely visible in the light from the backyard. The vibration trapped between the mattress and Lexa's core worked magic on edging Lexa toward her second orgasm.

She fixed her attention to memorizing the details of the woman's spiced scent she'd breathed in weeks before. Lexa had to taste the woman whose name had filled her mouth so pleasantly. Her tongue traced around the hot bulb, licked a strong stroke up and down, then circled it, gathering all the richness of want. She barely began when the small fingers gripped her hair and pressed her deeper.

"Fucking fuck," Charleigh's kiss-swollen lips swore. "Please, don't stop."

But Lexa had to stop again. She had to stop just for a moment to tell the woman to do the one thing she'd never wanted before. "Cum in my mouth."

Her mouth returned to the engorged clit. She lavished the woman's core with her tongue, licking laps around and over it. She sucked, then flicked. Pressed down, then flicked again. Her fingers pressed into the pulsing hot walls and hooked upward to touch the place that earned her a gasp and a pull of her hair.

She didn't stop when her second orgasm hit, and the vibration became torturous. She didn't stop, when Charleigh's walls clamped around her fingers, locking her digits within. She didn't stop when the woman's gasps turned to a scream and the spasms shook her body.

She didn't stop until the first wave rolled through and the second began to build. She didn't stop until the sheets were soaked from the gush flooding her face when the second orgasm crashed into Charleigh.

Charleigh's exhausted body lay quaking. Her chest rose and fell so quickly as her muscles continued to contract.

Lexa moved from between her thighs and up the bed. The small frame curled up in a ball. Her sweat-soaked skin glistened in the dim light of the room. Lexa pulled a pillow from the top of the bed and eased it under Charleigh's head. She covered the still-shaking frame with the satin sheet and the comforter, wanting her to get used to this type of pampering.

With Charleigh tucked in, Lexa went to the bathroom to relieve herself. Her mind replayed every second over again. Each moment they'd shared. Each conversation until she remembered the last time they were together.

Her heart was pounding too fast, she didn't even flush the toilet. She ran back to bed where the woman lay quivering so subtly, Lexa knew she was silently crying. She held her close, pulling her so Charleigh's head could rest against her chest.

"I'm right here," Lexa told her.

"I thought you left to... sleep somewhere else," the smaller woman whispered. Her chest quaked, and Lexa felt Charleigh's arm move up to wipe her face.

Lexa pressed soft kisses to the hair she'd pulled. Her fingers held the woman's ribs to keep her flush against her. Softly, she said, "I didn't mean to make you think I was leaving."

"Thank you for coming back."

Tangled in a mass of limbs and sex-scented sheets, Charleigh's breathing became deeper. Lexa closed her eyes, but she was still replaying the way the game was finally going in her favor. Her teammates had fallen in love with Charleigh, just as she had. There was no way Charleigh could argue she didn't have a place in Lexa's world any longer. Not when she'd turned the party around, or how their sexual desires complement each other.

The last of the voices from the party had finally faded. Her phone beeped as the door opened and closed once more, and she patted herself on the back for paying the DJ earlier. There was still someone in the house, but she couldn't leave Charleigh again. Whoever was out there would find one of the five other beds to sleep off the booze.

20

A steady tightening of a vice grip around her head pulled Charleigh from sleep to squinting at the sliver of sun slicing through the dark shades. She clenched her eyes shut, but the red glow taunted her. As a plus one for a party where she didn't belong, she'd given up a year of sobriety.

She turned away from the judgmental light. Her body was wrapped into a ball as the chilled air from the fan bit at her naked form. The lump of bedding created a cocoon around Lexa, leaving only a few braids poking out.

Her gut twisted as the vice gripped her head a little tighter. She'd take nothing to ease the pain so she wouldn't forget the price of fitting into Lexa's world. The woman who'd promised her possibilities had finally gotten what she truly wanted, and the morning would tell where she stood.

It was a shitty test her brain devised upon pulling up to the house. A test she'd most definitely failed. Lexa was the one who was supposed to be tested though. A challenge concocted not unlike all the ways Dilynn had set her up for failure. She hated she hadn't thought of it yesterday. Didn't stop to consider the game she'd devised would hurt her more than the woman who'd stolen all the covers.

A part of her crumbled when Lexa left. But she'd been stupid to think Lexa would leave when she knew she was in Lexa's bedroom. The room Danaya had brought her in to strip her down and learn her secret when she'd tried to dress her in a bikini top alone.

Charleigh swallowed the shame, realizing she'd spent her whole life preparing for this. And when given the choice, she'd used the words Lexa told her to say the first time. Played the role she'd been cast in Lexa's life. Just another whore Lexa had taken to her wedding bed. She couldn't be the princess. Lexa already had a real-life princess with power and wealth with her presence painted into the walls of the house.

A single tear slid down her face before she put away all the pain and committed to doing what Mona did to become a Greyson. She could be whatever the woman wanted, however, the woman wanted.

She held her legs and listened until Lexa's breathing settled into a snore. Only when she'd heard three snores did she get up from the bed.

The faded Devil's sweatshirt lay in a pile on a chaise lounge. She picked it up and looked back at the heap of blankets. Every time she'd seen Lexa, the woman was wearing or carrying it. She'd wear it so Lexa would have to take it off her.

Silently, she pulled the hoodie over her body and made her way to the hall bathroom. The reflection staring back at her looked tired. Charleigh wiped away last night's eyeliner and mascara from under her eyes. She searched the drawers until she located a faded scrunchie to twist her hair into a messy knot atop her head. She pulled a few trendles down in her face to give Lexa a reason to touch her.

Cabinets in the kitchen slapped closed like a movie clapperboard calling her to enter the scene. She practiced a smile that went all the way up her face. She should be smiling after all. Her pussy felt empty, so she'd get Lexa to fill it again. Fucked and fed would keep Lexa entertained for a while. Hopefully, it would be enough time for her to find a way to tell Lexa about Joey. She'd need to make Lexa want the child as much as she did, or at least convince the woman Joey wouldn't cramp her lifestyle. Maybe her daughter would have a second parent, and she could give her a life-like Mona would give the baby growing within her.

If she could show the Greyson-Trikrus she wasn't poor trash anymore, maybe Joey would get to spend time with her cousins. Dilynn would possibly invite Joey to the birthday parties they would throw for Mona's kid, and they wouldn't have to have a separate party. She could be part of a family bigger than just the two of them. She just had to get Lexa to be okay with one more.

"You can do this," she told her reflection. "Joey's her number one fan, and she loves being important. Just make her feel important. That's what she wants. To be important."

The refrigerator was open when Charleigh entered the large space. She stared at the ground as she made her way into the kitchen. Sitting in a chair at the counter was not sexy, so she pushed herself up on the counter. The cool stone eased the ache in her backside.

"Charleigh, you don't have to make breakfast," Lexa called from the bedroom. "We can go to Snooze. They have great brunch options. I just gotta get dressed."

All the air fled Charleigh's lungs. Her eyes ran up the fitted jeans to the loose gray cotton top. A blonde ponytail swished to the side as the woman turned with a carton of eggs in her hand.

"Have you seen my sweatshirt?" Lexa asked, moving around the room. "It's the black one with the old Devil's logo on it."

Familiar azure eyes ran up Charleigh's naked legs still spread open to the sweatshirt Lexa was searching for. It barely covered her core, but none of that mattered as she sat atop the countertop before the woman who owned the house.

"Good morning," Sylvia said cooly.

The two words struck Charleigh in the chest, causing her shoulders to shrink inward. She tried to pull the sweatshirt lower to cover herself, but the room started to tilt on its axis. She prayed for Spidey's grip as she held onto the counter, hoping it would keep her from sliding off the raised surface to the floor.

Sylvia stepped into her bubble, unaffected by the room's loss of gravity. Her body pressed against the counter between Charleigh's legs, trapping the smaller woman in place. She set the eggs on the counter, then leaned against her hand.

Gently, Sylvia tucked a stray hair behind Charleigh's ear. Her eyes ran over Charleigh's face, then down her body once more.

"I heard you've been a very good girl since I last saw you, Charleigh Marshall," Sylvia stated. "I hope little Joey is doing well. She was so excited about kindergarten."

Charleigh's chin fell to her chest, but Sylvia raised it back up with a single finger. "Say good morning," she commanded.

The finger kept her head in place, but her eyes dropped to the woman's straight lips. She tried to swallow, but her mouth was too dry. The words scratched against her tongue as she whispered, "Good morning, Ms. Winters."

"See, good girl." Sylvia's finger didn't leave her chin. "You look just like your boss. Same blue eyes. Same blonde hair. She used to sit on my counter every morning for my breakfast."

Charleigh's eyes grew, but she couldn't make words. Dilynn hadn't ever looked at her long enough to know, but Sylvia seemed to know. And that caused questions to race around Charleigh's mental track once more. They moved too fast for her to grab even one of them to try and answer herself.

She tilted Charleigh's face from side to side, then tisked when she saw the hickey. "I always told Lexa to take care of her belongings, but she has a thing for playing rough with her toys."

"What are you doing here?" Lexa growled from the hallway. Her breasts disappeared under a sports bra as she froze in the middle of the great room.

Sylvia turned to Lexa as she turned Charleigh's face to her former wife as well.

"Just looking over the newest toy you brought home to play with. She's pretty, obedient, and very, very smart. Too smart not to see through your bullshit."

Charleigh couldn't breathe, let alone move. With Lexa's wife keeping her legs spread open, she felt the shame rise in her. Asking Lexa to make her a whore wasn't a wish on a star, but she should have known better than to say it at night since it was officially coming true.

"I am thinking about keeping her as my own since you don't know how to treat things well." She turned Charleigh back to her, searching Charleigh's face once more. Her eyes were calculating her value, which would fall far short of the woman's expectation. "I bet she'd look so pretty on my arm at the gala next week. She looks made to stand beside me on a red carpet."

Sylvia placed a hand on Charleigh's thigh, kneading the flesh. "So, tempting when she's already dressed in my clothes. I was just thinking about how she'd look on my counter with nothing on. Like that one girl you brought back to my beach house in Los Angeles. Remember how we took turns with that one? You fucked her until your legs were shaking from trying to be a stupid werewolf, then I soothed away the ache with my tongue. This little doll smells richer though. So soft, I bet she's sweet."

Sylvia stared at Charleigh.

"That's how it usually goes, Charlotte Leigh Marshall. Lexa gets off on turning those naughty, rough fantasies of hers into reality, and if they are good, then I take my time giving out rewards. Orgasms. Maybe a new car. Whatever she wanted if she was good. At least that's how it used to be. Maybe one or two a year. But never here. Never in the house that my father purchased for our wedding. You see we had rules."

"Get your hands off her," Lexa growled.

Sylvia's head fell back, a rich laugh filling the space. Slowly she turned her gaze back to Lexa. "Or what? You'll hit me like you hit Echo?"

When Lexa did nothing but shake in the spot she stood, Sylvia turned her attention back to Charleigh.

"If you wanted, you could be mine. Just say the words, 'Yes, ma'am,' and she'll be gone. I'll make all the bad go away." Sylvia ran her finger down Charleigh's cheek to her lower lip. "Lexa doesn't follow rules, so I asked her for a divorce. But I hear you're very good at following rules now. And I could give you what you truly want with a phone call. Then we could make rules. You and me."

"Please," Charleigh whispered, her head aching with the volume of their words. "Let me go."

Sylvia released Charleigh's leg immediately, then she offered Charleigh a hand. Unable to get down without potentially falling on her face, Charleigh took the offer and slid off the counter.

She kept hold of the granite in case the room decided to tilt again when she couldn't move due to Sylvia's proximity.

Lexa took a step forward then stopped when Sylvia reached over Charleigh. "Via, please don't," Lexa whispered.

Her hands went up as Charleigh saw the silver glint of the chef knife held over her. Her feet still didn't move, so she prayed Sylvia would end her time quickly. She held her breath, sending out all her thoughts to the little girl. Prayed Dilynn would take Grace to court now she knew she was Joey's grandmother.

"Give her a home," she whispered to herself. "Love her."

"I may be pissed, Lexa, but I'm not a psycho."

Sylvia left Charleigh at the side counter. Moved to the wooden cutting board where a variety of greens, an onion, and a bell pepper awaited her. She carefully began to chop each one as she explained, "I would never hurt Ms. Charleigh Marshall. After all, like you, I made all her dreams come true. Well, not all of them, but I was working on that. I already told Dilynn there were consequences for breaking our deal."

The blade sliced through the pepper with a hard hit, and then Sylvia cut it into thin strips. She paused and looked over at the true intruder of the home.

"Her picture from the bar looked familiar. I knew." She shook her head. "I knew I'd seen her before, but the name.... I almost couldn't believe it when Emma told me. The woman you stopped fucking my sister for was someone else I knew. Someone I cared about. Someone I tried to give a better life. Lexa, you know I never forget the scholarship winners. It's one of the things I was always truly proud of... besides you. Everything you could have done. The person you could have been if you just took care of yourself."

Shaking her head, Sylvia looked over the counter at Charleigh. "She was a cute teen, but the woman she grew up to be.... I understand why you wanted her. When I saw her all grown up at a game wearing the wrong last name, well, if I didn't play by the rules we made, I probably wouldn't have passed up the chance with her either. I know, you wouldn't have been mad, but she was too good for you to do what you do, and I didn't want her to get hurt."

Sylvia smiled to herself as she slid the knife through the greens. "Only Charleigh, you'd be smiling the next morning if it was me, instead of her."

"Why are you here?" Lexa interrupted.

Sylvia paused momentarily. She studied Lexa before swirling the knife in a circle around the room. "Last I checked this is still my home, and I always considered it rude to not cook for someone who was fucked in my bed. She must be hungry after playing the role of... which did you choose, dear, whore or princess?"

Charleigh whispered, "I'm not like you. I'm not a princess." She didn't say she was a whore. Standing in the kitchen half-naked already proved it without her having to say it.

Sylvia's slicing paused momentarily as she looked at Charleigh's downward gaze.

"How did you...?" Lexa started but stopped. "You watched the footage of us having sex?"

"Oh, don't act surprised. We both know you frequently log into the security footage to watch yourself fucking your toys." Sylvia hummed to herself once more. "But I didn't just log in. I sat here waiting for you to kick out whoever was screaming your name in my bed. When I heard you finish and she still didn't come out, I may have logged in to watch the last little bit. I was shocked at first. I mean, I don't think I have ever seen you get a girl off, let alone twice. But then I've never seen you go down on anyone besides me. I used to think I was special. Did it feel special, Charleigh? How brutal she was and only when she was satisfied did she remember you were even there, doing everything she told you to do?"

"Please stop," Charleigh pleaded. Her eyes cinched shut at the knowledge Lexa had recorded them having sex and Sylvia had watched it. Sylvia had seen her pretending to enjoy what Lexa gave her.

Sylvia looked up at Lexa. "I came back to the room. Figured I would at least pay for the girl's Uber to send her home, but you'd fallen asleep with her in my bed."

She set down the knife and looked over at Charleigh. "You don't deserve this. You never deserved any of it. Emma has told me nothing but good things about you. That story about the dildos was quite funny," Sylvia explained. "And I wish we would have seen each other again once the divorce was finalized. I had planned to email you about your grant application—to meet with you to go over your proposal. That would have been better, but now you're here for me to play the villain. But I'm not a villain, Charleigh. You'll see in time."

The burner clicked on, and they all stood still as the pan heated up. Sylvia added a slice of butter, staring as it melted away. Then she dropped the onions and peppers into the pan, letting them scream as the butter bubbled around them.

"Charleigh, be a good girl and go put on some clothes. Breakfast should be ready in a few minutes."

Charleigh straightened her shoulders, refusing to give Sylvia another reason to comment on her obedience. She may not be a princess, but she wasn't a dog.

"Not such a good girl after all," Sylvia said with a smile. "I had a blonde brat before I met Lexa. Quite the temper and a dirty mouth. It was a challenge to get her to comply, but the fun me and her partner had when she did. A compliant pet. Small and delicate like you. You'd make a pretty pet, you know."

"Stop talking to her like that. She's a person," Lexa growled.

Sylvia flipped the vegetables in the pan and set them back on the flame.

"I'm aware she's a person. You're the one who treats her like a toy. Bending her over to fulfill those fucked up fantasies you have from the trashy fanfictions you read about yourself without having to look at her. So, you don't have to see what you're doing. You fucked her just like the other fifty; or was it a hundred other women in our bed?"

"You left me," Lexa stated. "You sent me divorce papers."

"I was traded, Lexa, and you waited three weeks to make out with my sister, who you knew was off limits. But I still came back. I came back to fix things and found you using her the same way you used Ms. Marshall." Sylvia's hand extended to Charleigh. "I could have had a hundred girls in the time I was gone as well, Lexa. But do you know how many I fucked?"

"No," Lexa whispered.

Charleigh watched as Lexa's shoulders fell inward at the thought of Sylvia being with someone else. She associated the sadness in the dark eyes with how she'd felt every time she'd heard Evie's voice in the background when she called Mona.

Sylvia's teeth bared as she spits out, "Zero. Because I didn't try to punish you with every cunt in Phoenix, Dallas, Seattle, New York, or Los Angeles."

"You asked to be traded," Lexa said, shaking her head. "You asked to be traded because I asked you for a family. I told you I wanted to stay home with you this year, and I wanted us to have a baby."

"Always pretending to know things when you pay attention to nothing but the next ass you want to tap." Sylvia licked her teeth. With a shake of her head, she explained, "I was part of a package in a grander plan you wouldn't understand. So let me break it down for you in simple words. My contract was up at the end of this season. I'm not going to be signed again. Danaya needed to be a Devil. She needed to replace me or we would have to pay twice as much for her. I was never playing for the Devils after this year, not when they could have two number-one picks side by side. I'm a veteran of basketball, not a star. You and her draw in more fans. And the price was me and two draft picks over the next two years. Honestly, the deal was complete trash because Danaya was worth more."

Sylvia's hands slapped against the granite. "I guess the plan backfired though. I mean, we have Lexa the Lesbian Lasso. No one thought in three months you would become Lexa the Liability. Destroying Echo's bar, Lexa? She was a friend, and you cheated on me repeatedly in front of her."

The vegetables in the pan were quickly turning brown. Charleigh didn't have a reason to, but she moved into Sylvia's space and pulled the pan from the burner. She searched the stove to shut off the flame, but the computer panel had more options than her phone had apps.

"Charleigh Marshall, do you know what this comes with? Has she even told you?" Sylvia asked, waving the knife at Lexa. "She's never going to choose you. Not just you. You're just the new me. The new girl at home waiting for her. Because there's always some fan putting her panties in Lexa's pocket. Some ass pressed to her crotch on a dance floor she has to go to after a big win. Next week or next month she'll shut down; that's what Lexa does. She shuts down and she says she's sorry for not being able to control herself and you'll forgive her because you'll tell yourself she can't help it. You'll agree to participate sometimes because it will make it feel like she isn't cheating on you."

"That's not true," Lexa protested weakly. But her cheeks were pink, and Charleigh knew. She knew what she'd already assumed would be her life if she committed to Lexa.

She'd never be enough, but that wasn't a new reality for her. Lexa wouldn't change for her, and who was she to ask for fidelity when she had nothing to give the woman. Well, besides the family Lexa admitted to wanting. That was something she could offer after this.

"Really. Look at us." Sylvia waved the knife between herself and Charleigh. "If she was a foot taller, she'd practically be me because you only chase women who look like the mommy who never loved you."

Charleigh watched the way Lexa's brown eyes fell to the ground. She knew the loss; the feeling of not being good enough for the woman who gave birth to her. But Lexa asked Sylvia for a family, and Sylvia refused. Charleigh could give her everything she wanted, so she moved to Lexa. She'd give Lexa a daughter and more if it meant the woman would choose her.

"My mom hates me too," she said. Her arms wrapped around Lexa's waist, and she hugged her tightly.

"It's not..." Lexa tried. Her arms wrapped around Charleigh. "I have issues, but I am going to be better."

"It's okay," Charleigh whispered. She locked her hands around Lexa's back, using her body as a shield for anything else Sylvia threw at her.

"Don't play her game, Charleigh," Sylvia growled. "You saw the real Lexa the first night in the bar. You saw her again in your classroom. You don't want to come home and find her in bed with your sister."

Charleigh snapped around, holding Lexa behind her.

"My sister loves me enough not to fuck my partner," she spat. "And so what if she hurts me? You have no reason to give a shit if she does because I'm nobody remember. I am just another toy she brought home to fuck in your bed, right? I mean, you've made it crystal clear that I am just a fuck doll, so why worry?"

Sylvia's jaw ground. Her eyes weren't locked on Charleigh though. They were on Lexa, trying to shoot daggers through the woman who'd hurt her.

"Because it's not about me. I'm just a nobody so she shouldn't want me," Charleigh said without the bite. "It's about you. You're only worried that if she actually cares about me, then it means she didn't care enough about you. Just like your sister didn't care about you when she kissed her."

"Charleigh, you are not a nobody," Sylvia stated like she knew it to be a fact. "I'm going to fucking kill Dilynn and the goddamn action figure for what they did to you."

Her neck rolled, and Charleigh could hear the pop.

"Charleigh, you are special. You might not know where you come from, but I do. I know that you are someone special and more should have been done by all of us to protect you from all the hard things in your life." Her hand shot up. "You shouldn't have to feel like a whore because she wants you to be. You shouldn't be groped in a room full of people or embarrassed in front of your students. You deserve better than what she is going to give you. I only wish I would have had someone tell me that in the beginning. I could have saved a lot of women a lot of heartache."

"What do you want from me?" Lexa choked. "You want me to go back to the shrink? I will do whatever you want, just stop talking about me like I'm not even here."

"I want out," Sylvia snapped. She picked up a pile of folded papers on the counter and slapped them against the surface. "Give me a fucking divorce, so I can move on with my life. I am tired of being the one to put you back together. If I have to, I will take that sex tape of you and every bitch you fucked in my bed to court. I will fight you and it will be loud and embarrassing, and your career cannot take another scandal."

Charleigh studied the floor. She'd thought Lexa's divorce was already completed or at least in process. Every narrative she'd drafted to excuse Lexa's behavior had been fiction, not even creative non-fiction. She'd not blurred some details. No, the truth was because of Lexa, she was now a peasant in a new land of battling royalty who would sacrifice her to punish each other rather than let her just walk away.

"Stop stalling, Lexa. You are moving on. Everything you ever wanted is standing right there. A blonde mommy replacement. A constant cheerleader. A baby maker. She'll worship the ground you walk on. And she has a kid already, so you get your instant family."

Charleigh's eyes shot up from the ground. "I—"

Sylvia silenced Charleigh with a single finger. "I invested too much into making sure you had a fresh start to just stand by and let her hurt you. Because you are more than what you think of yourself. You have a whole life and a kid to look out for. You aren't just the girl in the stands with the glittery signs. You're the girl who wrote an essay for a scholarship. An essay about you being someone your daughter would be proud of. Becoming a teacher so you can build a better life for little Joey."

"You have a daughter," Lexa said. Her eyes widened as she scanned Charleigh's face.

"I was going to tell you. I just—" but Charleigh's confession was cut off.

"Sign the papers, and I bet she'll let you put another baby in her this year so you can pretend to be the mommy of the year," Sylvia barked.

Sylvia waved the papers as Charleigh's eyes begged Lexa not to run away.

21

Lexa swallowed the apology stuck in her throat. The one she'd been saving for months, waiting for Sylvia to finally come home. The one she'd practiced daily before there was a Charleigh... and a daughter.

She tried to figure out how Charleigh had kept a whole human a secret. Her mind scanned through the mental pictures she'd taken of Charleigh's house. The rainbow of books, tiny television, and raggedy couch. Disorganized cabinets of mismatched dining ware. The empty refrigerator.

"You have no food," Lexa growled at Charleigh. "How do you have a kid and no food?"

The smaller blonde backed away from Lexa as the chapped lip curled, exposing her teeth. Two shades of blue eyes shifted between Lexa's face and her fists. Sylvia glanced at Charleigh as she ran out of space when her back hit the opposite end of the counter from her.

Lexa's hand flew up toward the front of the house where Danaya's car sat in the driveway. "No car seat. Not a single toy. I've been to your house multiple times, and I have never seen any indication that you have a daughter."

The vein in Lexa's neck protruded as she rose to her full height. Blood boiled at the possibility that the blonde bitch had lied to Sylvia. Took advantage of her wife's kindness. She seethed, "Did you just lie to her to get her to give you money?"

New questions catapulted from her mouth at the woman shrinking before her eyes. "You never gave a damn about me. You were just going to tell me you had a kid so you could get me to give you money? Emma told you she left me because I wanted a kid and you knew it had already worked on my wife, so you figured why the fuck not try again."

Trendles of blonde hair fell in front of Charleigh's face. Lexa watched Charleigh's chest quake under each of the verbal blows.

"You're just a fucking prostitute, aren't you?"

She imagined each blow slicing through the sweatshirt. Sylvia's sweatshirt Charleigh had put on to seduce her. She was just pretending to be Sylvia because Charleigh knew she loved her wife. She said as much at the game night with Danaya and Emma.

"Didn't you know you're supposed to get paid before you give up the pussy?"

Charleigh shook her head.

"Don't fucking lie. This poor little white girl act. You were just trying to trap my Black ass. Did you really think I wouldn't realize that you were just using me?" She raised her hands to the house. "Did you think I would give up all this for you? Or were you planning on fucking your way into my mansion just to rob me blind? It's not like you're even good at the fucking. Just lay there as I did all the work. At least shoulda rode my dick like a proper slut."

The teacher's hands came up trying to hold back anything else Lexa could throw at her. But she was just as weak as she was thin. She was just a ball bunny after her cash.

"I... I thought..." Charleigh tried. Her hand started to wipe her face but stopped as she looked at the material covering her flesh.

"You thought what?" Spit flew out of Lexa's mouth with each word. "Thought you would fuck me, and I would just take care of you after I found out you already robbed my wife?"

With a heavy breath and a loud sniff, Charleigh stood up straight. Her chin raised, and she breathed shallowly through her mouth.

Tapping her chest with a single finger, Charleigh said evenly, "I was the one that told you one day you'd get tired of slumming it. You'd realize I had nothing to give you besides my body to use."

The storm in her eyes raged against the red rims with the tears gathering like a tsunami. They fell down her cheeks, destroying what was left of her makeup from the night before. Leaving her bare and broken, just how Sylvia had predicted she would feel when Lexa was done with her.

"I went with Mona and watched her tell her perfect boyfriend and perfect girlfriend that she was going to be having their baby, and everyone was so happy for them. I never got that when I had my kid. I was scared and I lost custody of her because I trusted people I shouldn't have. And Mona... she told me I had to tell you because you said you wanted to be my girlfriend. And I thought... if you really meant it, then yes of course you needed to know. But then I pulled up here and it was probably what you felt when you realized that if you laid on the floor of my living room you could practically touch both walls." Charleigh's hands gestured around herself. "You live in a mansion in a city that people associate with not just rich people but rich rich people. And I realized that I ... I realized a dented pot like me could never belong in a kitchen like this. So, I... I got super drunk to make everything else easier."

Lexa glanced over at Sylvia. Her thumbs were hitting the phone screen in a specific rhythm. It was a subtle, yet dignified type of war drum she played against the device every time she was calling in her legal team to sue someone. However, her face said she was bored of Charleigh's confession.

"Make what easier?" Lexa asked, wondering what Sylvia would hope to get from suing Charleigh. The woman didn't even have money for food, and Sylvia had to know that just by looking at her.

"Being the whore you wanted at the bar," Charleigh admitted. She wet her lips, then continued. "I knew once you got what you wanted, you would move on. You kept saying it wasn't true, but last night I knew. I knew I finally fulfilled your fantasy, and you would walk away."

She gestured to Sylvia. "Like she said, I'm really fucking smart. I may be poor, and I am unimportant, but I was never naïve about who you are and what you wanted. I've known people like you my entire life."

Charleigh tapped her chest again. "I'm the girl you picked to share with your wife's sister. I wasn't your happily ever after because this isn't a fucking fairytale. And I knew that when you tried to convince me that we were just like the people in stories. I told you it wasn't reality, and I told you this is where we would end up. But you wouldn't listen. So last night, I said the words you told me to say because I knew you needed to finish what you started. You'd finish and you'd be done."

A tear fell down her face and dropped to the floor. "And I woke up this morning and you were still there... I thought maybe I could be part of your life, but I was.... No, I'm so fucking stupid because, of course, you didn't leave. I'm in your house. I was the one that was supposed to leave so you could make up with your wife. But I tried to believe you. Believe in what you told me when it was all just bullshit."

Charleigh looked at the room her entire house would fit in. "This is the type of place people like me dream about. A house that I imagine winning the lottery to buy so I could bring my daughter home to it, and she would be proud of me. But this is reality. I am in this fucking house and I got fucked like I was supposed to get fucked weeks ago only I fucking thought I mattered. Where before... before I just wanted to be near you because I had a crush on a celebrity... and the worst part was I would have done anything you told me to do because you were Lexa fucking Jenson and I was your biggest fan."

She ran her hands up and down her face before she let them drop. She didn't look at Lexa when she explained, "I would have done everything I did last night with your fucking sister-in-law if you hadn't tried to do it where people would videotape us. You could have put me in a fucking Uber right afterward and sent me home and I would have cried a little, but it would have been just fucking a celebrity."

She choked as she looked up at the camera in the corner of the room. "But stupid me didn't realize that you weren't going to do that anyway. I mean, seriously Lexa, I fucking gave you everything you asked for even after I told you. I fucking told you this is what you would decide, and you still made me fucking love you. I mean it didn't take much since no one in my entire life has ever loved me, so when you chose me in a room full of women, I didn't care that you never even asked my name. I knew I was nothing. I fucking told you I was nothing. And now you made a goddamn documentary for my mother to finally beat me in court. To cut the last fucking thread of my rights. My entire world shattered because I came here believing that I was the main character of a story when you cast me as the side piece."

The heart in Lexa's chest pounded against its cage. The love she'd decided she had for the woman flooded her system as she tried to deny Charleigh's truth. She would have never remembered Charleigh's name if she'd been allowed to bring the woman home like she'd wanted if she hadn't had to go to the school.

Charleigh's face was red like when she had told Emma to cook all the macaroni, ashamed of who she was. Everything Lexa had told the woman; she'd taken back in a fit of anger.

Lexa toed the floorboard, squishing an imaginary bug. "So... you're not after my money?" Lexa asked again, needing Charleigh to say it.

Charleigh choked on a pained laugh. "I told you I never wanted your money. I never wanted the phone, the tickets, or Danaya's car. I tried to give you the phone back and I told you and Danaya no to the car. But you insisted and you swore that this wasn't what it is. The only thing you can say I used you for was the fucking tickets to take my team to the game, and even then, I earned that shit by fixing your shot."

Lexa watched Charleigh swallow thickly. "And I let you inside me because I found out my best friend was pregnant and getting a happily ever after that I will never get to be a part of, and I just didn't want to be alone in this world. And you kept showing up and sending me messages on Instagram and pretending to be someone you're not. And when you were around, I didn't sit on the floor of my kid's room and cry because she is never even going to get to see it. She's never going to see it because you fucking lied to me and she's going to fucking ruin me to hurt you."

Sylvia set the phone on the counter and tapped the granite with her fingers. She popped her lips, then said, "I expected her to at least wait until I left to prove my prior statements that she would in fact hurt you."

Charleigh shook her head as she forced a smile to her lips. Lexa watched the mask fall over Charleigh's face. The mascara and eyeliner only made the defeat more obvious as she turned to Sylvia.

"It's not an excuse, but I thought you two were already divorced," Charleigh said apologetically. "And I didn't realize that this was yours this morning or I would have never put it on."

The older woman looked down coldly as Charleigh tugged at the sweatshirt, pulling it off her body. She covered her breasts and slid it across the counter to its owner.

Stripped of all dignity, Charleigh held the last pieces of herself together. "I'm not a gold digger and I'm not a side chick. That's not who I am or who I want to be. I hope one day you will be able to forgive me or forget me. The latter is probably more realistic."

Charleigh's arm cradled her breasts, and the other covered her cunt as she turned from Sylvia. Lexa's eyes traced down to the space she'd always hidden from Lexa unless they were shrouded in darkness.

Rosy lightning bolts streaked down Charleigh's abdomen. Lexa's needed proof of motherhood was etched permanently into the pale skin. The evidence passed by her as Charleigh made her way to the bedroom where her dress had been discarded in Danaya's effort to make her fit into another one of Lexa's broken promises.

She had a daughter. A real daughter. A buttoned-nosed blonde baby girl who looked exactly like her mother. So much so Lexa realized she'd thought she was looking at baby pictures of Charleigh in the Dollar Store frames decorating the shelves of the quiet house.

"Emma said that girl has done nothing but try and keep her distance from you," Sylvia stated, tapping the papers on the counter. "She's your only chance right now. But you need to tell her the truth. She can't be there to pick you up when you fall if she doesn't know."

"I fucked up," Lexa whispered. She'd said the same thing so many times before, and Sylvia had always made it better.

"You really did this time. And she didn't have a chance to fall in love with you before you drop. But it's coming. You know you're going to drop soon. And you don't have any more chances with her. Don't let her walk out of here believing you're just like every other person who used her and dropped her." She tapped the papers to the counter again. "Finalize our divorce. It's the only way you are going to be able to commit to her and give her that happy ending you promised. Because we both know she has what you want. The life you're never going to get with me."

The seal of Arizona was stamped into the first page. The words bled together as Lexa flipped each one. She couldn't process anything more than this was it. This had to be it because Sylvia had given her all the chances and Lexa didn't want another one. She held the feeling, so it didn't run away again. She didn't want another chance because it was a chance at really nothing she wanted. Charleigh had what she wanted.

She held out her hand. "Give me a pen."

Lexa moved through each page. Signed the lines where the little tabs indicated. Every one. She double-checked the forms to make sure she'd signed them all. Then she handed them back to Sylvia.

Sylvia stopped in Charleigh's path to the door with the papers in her purse. She ran a finger down Charleigh's cheek, then lifted her chin once more. Smiling down at the woman, Sylvia said, "You are intelligent, talented, and courageous. Out of the hundreds of applicants, I loved the fire in your essay. I loved the way your teachers spoke of your drive and ambition. Your commitment to getting up. Stop telling people you are nothing, Charleigh Marshall. I see you."

Then it happened so fast. Sylvia leaned down and pressed her lips to Charleigh's, swallowing Charleigh's gasp and taking advantage of her surprise to stroke her tongue within the mouth Lexa had used for her pleasure. Sylvia's arm was wrapped around the black satin, pulling Charleigh into the kiss.

The long pink tongue withdrew from Charleigh's mouth hanging open as she leaned back. She stared at Lexa's soon-to-be ex-wife in utter disbelief.

Sylvia turned to Lexa still holding Charleigh's rigid body in her embrace. "Don't be angry, Lexa. After all, it was just a kiss. It's not that big of a deal. It's not like I fucked her."

Then she looked into the bewildered eyes below her. "I am sorry I stole a kiss from you. Normally I take my time getting to know a woman before I kiss her, but I had to." She ran her thumb over the plump bottom lip. "You see, when I saw the photo of Lexa kissing my sister and I called her, that's what she told me. By the look on her face right now though, kissing someone important to a person is apparently a big deal."

Lexa stared at the counter, trying to settle the guilt and rage both boiling within her. Remembering Sylvia's tears. Four years of marriage and she'd never witnessed Sylvia shed a tear unrelated to injury, but Lexa could feel the tears traveling through the line when she finally answered the phone the next morning. She'd held the phone over her head as the tears and screams of betrayal showered over her. Lexa had just kissed Kayla, and she had told her wife, 'Wasn't like I had fucked her. It's not that big of a deal.'

Her eyes scrunched shut, replaying all the pain she'd caused. To Sylvia. To Kayla. To Charleigh.

The memories were interrupted by Sylvia's cold tone. "I expect your stuff out of my house by the end of tomorrow."

Lexa's eyes snapped up from the counter. "What?"

Sylvia rolled her eyes. "You didn't expect me to let you keep my house, did you? Well, it doesn't matter really because it's mine. Originally, I was going to eat the cost of your debt to Echo for the damages to the bar in exchange for her dropping the charges against you and Kayla. However, hurting this girl has consequences, so I went ahead and transferred that from your account. Oh, and I paid off your car since you didn't do that when I asked you to months ago."

She turned to leave but stopped. "You get to start over, Lex. Don't fight it. And don't hurt this girl again or I'll marry her and give her the life you always wanted."

She ran a finger down Charleigh's cheek once more. "Do you hear me, Charleigh Marshall? She hurts you and I will marry you and drown your mother in legal fees, so she has to give your kid back. I will even adopt her. And I'll show you all the rewards good girls get. Because you are a good girl, Charleigh. You are good and smart, and you deserve a good life after all the pain people put you through."

Lexa didn't know what to say. She didn't know what to say because Sylvia was gone, and Charleigh was staring at the path Sylvia took out of the door.

"Don't worry. I'll never call her, just like I'll never call Emma," Charleigh whispered. "Please delete the recording. Whatever you want I'll do, just please delete it."

The room was too big and Charleigh too far away. Her voice sounded like it was traveling down a tunnel toward Lexa promising her servitude.

"I'm sorry. I know I should just go, but Lexa, please just delete the video. Please, don't let her hurt me," Charleigh pleaded. Her arms wrapped around the dress that should have made her feel special.

Charleigh hadn't turned to Lexa. Her body was still ready to walk toward the door. The front door was left open and the light showed Charleigh the exit.

Sylvia had shown her the way out, and Lexa needed to stop her. But her legs felt so heavy. Her emotional baggage was too much to lift as the woman refused to look at her. Unwilling to help because she'd forgotten about the security cameras.

The system in place to protect her was the threat, and she had to fix it first. Fix the footage, so she could describe the distrust and clarify the chaos. Help the woman process the cognitive plague in her head. Then Charleigh would accept her apology.

She would...

She could...

Tell the woman everything so Charleigh was prepared to catch her when she fell off the edge, she'd pretended wasn't coming. The high she'd been on was too bright this time, blinding her from the monstrous doubts slithering through the crevices of her brain. The seductive serpentine speech struck the stronghold she'd sheltered her soul; a siren's song shattering her sanity.

The lullaby was interrupted by Emma's SUV screeching to a stop as Sylvia's engine roared to life and sped from the house.

"What the fuck is going on? I just saw Sylvia's Porsche leave." Emma said, running through the open door with Danaya on her heels.

"What happened, Peaches?" Danaya asked, stopping at Charleigh's side.

When Charleigh didn't answer her, Danaya cupped Charleigh's face in her hands and wiped away the tear stains and makeup with her thumbs. She turned Charleigh's face and looked at the angry bruise on her throat.

"What did she do to you?" Danaya growled, putting her body between Charleigh and Lexa.

"She didn't force me to do anything against my will." Charleigh closed her eyes. "I just don't belong here."

Charleigh pulled back from the hands. She placed the Charger key fob in Danaya's hand and curled her fingers over it. "I can't keep your car, and I know it's too much to ask, but will you please drive me home?"

Danaya tucked Charleigh under her arm as Emma nodded to the door. The rookie leaned against the woman as they walked out, just as Sylvia warned the blonde would.

Lexa heard Danaya say, "You gotta drive. I think I'm still buzzed. We're getting some burritos on our way to your place because, gurl, I don't know what the fuck we drank last night but my whole body hates me today."

Then the door to the house shut, and Charleigh was gone. Gone without Lexa being able to apologize. Without her showing Charleigh she deleted the security footage. Her new beginning was swept away in a protective hold of someone else.

Lexa ran from the room to get her phone. She'd show Charleigh before they drove away. She started to log into the security system as she made her way to the door, but the app to the bank was right next to it.

'Consequences of hurting Charleigh,' Lexa reminded herself.

The bank account took forever to log in, and the Charger had started. She heard the tires squeal as the account loaded. The six-digit number from the day before was now five. Five digits to live off for the entire year. Sylvia left her fifteen fucking thousand dollars and took her house. Took her house and everything she would need to start over.

Lexa threw the phone across the room, shattering it against the wall. Her fingers pulled at the roots of her hair until it hurt so badly, she screamed. She screamed, the pain only registering after she'd already hit the hard floor on both her knees.

The front door slammed closed, but a heavy set of footsteps came into the bedroom.

Choking, Lexa cried as she looked at Emma. "She took all my money. Everything I worked for. She just walked away with it."

Emma sat down on the bed and folded her hands together. She sucked her teeth. "Where's your meds, Lexa? You can't fix this if you don't get your shit together so tell me where you hid your pills."

Lexa closed her eyes. The air caught in her throat. She choked and gasped. Fingers dug into the floorboards. The room pressed against her. Walls were too close. Charleigh gone. Sylvia divorced her.

The drawer to the nightstand opened and then slammed closed.

"Pills, Lexa," Emma said again.

Lexa banged her fist to the ground. Then put her face against the wood. Her breath hit the floor. The heat suffocated her. She fell to the side. Her legs came up to her chest.

Bathroom cabinets opened and closed. The mirror cracked as the medicine cabinet smashed against the metal casing. Bags were emptied. Contents crashed against the counter.

Emma picked her up. She pushed the bitter pill into Lexa's mouth. She tried to spit it out, but Emma held her hand over her mouth. She choked again. But she swallowed her shame with the capsule. Tears fell as Emma held her and waited for the fog to cloak the chaos in her head.

22

Student voices blended into a constant rumble as they debated their place in a world where adults were failing them. Charleigh silently charted who spoke and how often, keeping the same learning objective posted to avoid having to participate. There was no teaching taking place in the room. She was just running a glorified book club at this point, but it was all she could do with her mind someplace else.

The basic responsibilities of classroom management kept her moving as her stomach twisted in knots. Her thoughts ran in a continuous loop. Three weeks of going over and over again each potential outcome that could arise with the sex tape. Each came back to the question: what did Lexa do with the video since she'd finally gotten what she wanted and stopped showing up?

At the end of Friday, the overnight staff arrived to supervise the dorms above the classrooms. The social work intern waved to Charleigh as she returned from her classes at the university and made her way to the bedrooms on the floor above. Charleigh shut the door to her classroom and sat back on the well-worn couch.

She stared at the email from Sylvia. It arrived in the middle of second period roll call. Initially, she hadn't even looked at the name of the sender. Her mind was caught in a whirlwind of fear whether or not the footage of her still existed. Now, she annotated each sentence. Her eyes drew imaginary lines under the words she heard from the woman's lips.

Ms. Marshall,

Your application for the Winters Educational Resource Grant has been received. I have personally reviewed your request for funding the construction of a youth sports facility at Greyson Academy. Your proposal is very passionate, and your assessment of need demonstrates the type of fire I look for in project partners. That being said, I would like to schedule a date to go over the finer details of your vision for development, maintenance, and long-term operating costs. These details cannot be overlooked to ensure both our needs are met. Additionally, I wish to go over the rewards for both parties this potential partnership would provide. I will be in the area for the remainder of the month. Please contact me on my personal cell, so we can arrange this meeting.

Sylvia Winters

Charleigh looked at the classroom phone, and then the cell phone number. If she was going to make the call, she'd have to do it from here since she'd sent Danaya back with the cell phone. Told her friend to remind Lexa that she never wanted the woman to see her as a grifter.

Calling Sylvia for the grant wouldn't be breaking her word to Lexa. Sylvia had reached out to her about the grant, but her stomach twisted. The words were right for the context. If Dilynn or Alex read it, they would see a business deal. But they hadn't had Sylvia's tongue in their mouths or watched the same words form on the mauve-painted lips.

Sylvia could delete the video though. Charleigh licked her lips, considering if whatever fee Sylvia asked for would be worth knowing for sure the recording was gone forever. The cost of deletion could be her bare atop the counter once more for Sylvia's breakfast, like apparently, she'd had Dilynn. That was a whole other level of crazy that had Charleigh vomiting in the trash can when Danaya had them stop for burritos that morning. Whatever twisted tale she was living was some form of a Greek tragedy, because Sylvia's tongue had been in her mouth after being in her biological mother's cunt.

Shaking her head, she knew being Sylvia's breakfast would only lead to another sex tape. Another debt to the woman who'd turned her life into a casualty of war. A part of her had questions for Sylvia though. She'd known Dilynn was her mother when Dilynn hadn't, and Sylvia didn't want kids. A new question joined the race she was already carsick from. One thought spiraling around and around: did Dilynn throw her away to be Sylvia's sex slave?

She closed the laptop. Monday she would forward the email to Alex. They could handle the negotiations, and she would just see herself out of the conversation. After all, it wasn't like she would be around next year to even see the project to fruition. Not after she'd promised to leave. Had she known telling Dilynn who she was would stop the woman's laser gaze trying to blow her up, she would have done it years ago.

Slipping through the backdoor she'd used before there was a dependable vehicle waiting for her, she started her walk home. The corn stalks had been cut, but she didn't need to hide her poverty any longer. Throughout her years at Greyson Academy, she'd feared being invisible. Now she considered it a gift. With Mona under the protective arm of the Greyson-Trikru name, no one seemed to remember she existed. Well, except Danaya. That would be done in a week when the woman left for Italy though.

The trek through the chopped fields was more bearable now the weather had shifted into fall. Clouds were rolling over her, and a breeze reminded her the day would be getting shorter. She wrapped the hoodie tighter around herself and decided tomorrow she'd walk to Goodwill. The sun wasn't up when she'd had to leave that morning, so she needed to get a thicker jacket before they didn't have any more.

She stepped out of the field closest to her house four miles later and walked past the Charger with the basketball player leaning against the hood.

Danaya looked up from her phone with a smile. "I came to see my best friend," she said for the fourth time this week. A plastic bag dangled in the air from her fingers. "And I brought tacos for you."

Charleigh took one of the Styrofoam cups from Danaya and tasted its contents. The horchata was waterier than she liked, but it wasn't just water, so it was a nice change.

"Where's Emma?" Charleigh asked as she unlocked the door. "I haven't seen her in a while."

Rexa pushed out the front door and passed Charleigh to her best friend. Danaya wrapped an arm around the dog standing on two legs to hug her.

"Packing," Danaya said. Her face nuzzled Rexa's lump of a head. In a baby voice, she explained, "She kicked me out, didn't she? Yes, that big meanie said I didn't label the boxes on all four sides. And she kicked me out, Rexi. Isn't she rude? At least you still love me. Don't you, best friend?"

Charleigh snorted, dropping her backpack and her work hoodie by the bookcase. The other two followed her into the house.

"So, are you excited to leave?" Charleigh asked. She slid a new novel a student had brought her onto the bookcase closest to the door.

"Yeah, and nervous," Danaya admitted. The bag rustled as she pulled out the food. She scooped up the little plastic containers of guacamole and hot sauces, then sat back in the armchair. Rexa brought Danaya the remote to the TV, and the girl searched for something to watch.

Charleigh tapped the unopened door to Joey's room, grateful for Danaya's visit. As she turned into her bedroom to change, she called to Danaya, "What are you worried about?"

Danaya didn't answer until Charleigh returned bra-free and swimming in State University basketball swag.

"Okay.... I know this is stupid, but I straight up feel like I am U-hauling with Emma." Danaya held out the unopened box of tacos to Charleigh as she passed.

"Well, you two already lived together. What were you supposed to do? Move out to date?" Charleigh asked. Then she smiled at the television. "Really, you two had that whole friends-to-lovers thing. The real gay Hallmark movie, so maybe don't think about it."

"It definitely hasn't been a Hallmark movie. First, I'm way too Black to be a Hallmark star. Second, what type of Hallmark bitch listens to her dream girl fucking other people all summer and then only gets her chance because of a bet?" Danaya's head hung over the plate.

"So, Netflix movie then," Charleigh offered. "Or some Amazon Prime shit."

"I don't care if she was with other people. That's not what makes it weird. It's more like she just packed all our stuff up together and it's like we are going together together."

"Okay... but all of that was already planned. Like, you had the place secured before you two started making out on my wall." Charleigh watched the woman's eyes running over her bookcases. "So, what's really freaking you out?"

Danaya opened her mouth, then closed it. She sucked her teeth and tried but failed again to get the words out. The episode was almost over before Danaya found her words.

"She already leased us a condo for next year when we get back. It's a one-bedroom instead of two and, I know, she's super conservative with her money... but it's like she is asking me to move in without ever saying anything, and then I was like, what if she isn't asking me to move in but instead preparing for me to move out because I didn't have to sign shit for the place. And it's just like fast and I haven't really ever done this whole life shit. You know, life has been basketball and now basketball is my job, and my life is with Em and.... What if she doesn't want me in six months?"

"I wish I could tell you it's all in your head, but honestly, I think you just go with it. Talk to her about it. Not like 'Hey, crazy bitch, you're moving too fast for me.' But 'What are you looking for in this? Where do you see us next year?' Lesbians love that shit anyways. They want to know you are thinking about the future." Charleigh opened the Styrofoam box to find more tacos than she'd be able to eat in two sittings. She looked at Danaya and gestured to the plate. "How many tacos do you think I eat?"

Danaya shrugged. "I figured what you didn't eat, you could save for tomorrow. Speaking of tomorrow, what are you doing, and can it be interesting enough for me to get out of packing again?"

Charleigh chuckled and pulled her feet up under her butt on the couch.

"I'm going to Goodwill. I need to pick up a jacket so walking to work isn't so fucking cold and some clothes for Joey."

She looked down at her cracked phone. The new screen protector she'd picked up was holding the glass together and she didn't get any more glass splinters in her fingers at least. Checking her account, she saw the money she'd managed to save. She checked her credit score app next.

"I am thinking about going to a dealership too. I found one that does the cash-for-clunkers thing, so if I can get the Honda to run long enough to get it there, then I can use it as a trade-in. I need to get a car of my own by January. You're welcome to join me at least for the shopping part. I know the dealership will be boring as hell. Shopping will probably be too. It's just searching through racks to find something without flowers or pink for my punk rock star. 'Purple and sparkles, Mommy.' That's what she said last time I saw her. Oh, and no dresses. She's only allowed to wear dresses most of the time because my mom is basically in a cult that is the whole women are lesser bullshit."

"When do you get to see her?" Danaya asked. She squished the taco into a tiny burrito and bit into it.

"Next Sunday," Charleigh said. "I spoke to my case manager yesterday and she set up a cab to come get me. We will walk to a park by my mom's house like we always do. She likes to play basketball. Don't have it in my heart to tell her she will probably be a midget like me."

"My mom had me in prison," Danaya shared. "Crazy that she did time for weed and now we can just walk into a store and buy it. I lived with G-Mama until I was seven."

Charleigh picked up a piece of carne asada and studied it. "Were you angry with her when you went back to her?"

Danaya shrugged, then took a sip from the Styrofoam cup she'd brought in with her. "I mean, I wasn't angry. But it was an adjustment. She was young like you when she had me. But once she was out, she was my mama, and I loved her. We got used to each other."

"So... there's hope," Charleigh said.

"More than hope, Peaches. You got this." Danaya smacked her lips as she finished off a second taco. "Sooo, it's been weeks. It's time to tell me what happened that you gave back my car."

"Doesn't matter," Charleigh said for what felt like the twelfth time. "I gotta get my own car. I've been living off favors for too long. It's time to grow up."

Danaya set her tacos aside. She moved her hands as she said, "But you see... I canceled the storage place when I lent it to you to begin with."

"So un-cancel it," Charleigh stated. "And before you say you can't then find a different place. It's not like there ain't hundreds of storage facilities in Phoenix. I bet you can even keep it air-conditioned."

"That's dumb." Danaya sat back in the armchair, spreading her legs out. "You're being dumb. Hiking through the fucking fields. Don't you all have snakes and shit that will kill you out here?"

Charleigh set the taco down. She stared at the food. "She was being dumb; a one-sentence summary of my life."

The show Danaya had chosen to watch moved on to the next episode, filling the silence just enough for Charleigh to wonder if Lexa decided to delete the recording. Her thought was interrupted by Danaya's sigh.

The taller woman slapped her hands against her legs and stared at Charleigh. "Look," she started, even though there was nothing to look at. "I know Lexa hurt you, but she ain't shit. Just forget that bitch and whatever she said to you to make you feel like you had to back out on our deal. I'm your friend and friends help each other. So, be my friend and help me out by keeping my car running. It's bad for her to just sit in storage. Does fucked up shit to the engine."

She was tired of having this conversation with Danaya. If she had the car, then she'd have more time to put more into saving so her payment would be lower in the long run. "If I say yes, will you stop asking what happened that day?"

Danaya smiled and rubbed Rexa's head. The television filled the silence as Charleigh finished off two tacos.

"So, Sylvia was at the house yesterday," Danaya said.

Charleigh rolled her eyes. "Fucking crazy, that one. She kissed me... at the house. Said it was to get back at Lexa for kissing her sister. Then she emailed me today."

Danaya laughed. "Well, that makes sense why she asked about you."

"What did she want to know?" Charleigh asked. Thinking about the cryptic email.

"How you are. What you've been up to. She didn't ask about you in a petty way. She, like, actually gave a damn about you." Danaya twisted a loc between her fingers. "She's a trip. I only met her, like, twice, but I get why Emma is friends with her. Anyways, she said Lexa said some shitty things to you and asked if we had heard from you. She seemed kinda worried and shit that you were hurt. Like, she said someone needs to come over here and check on you. I didn't know you two went back, back."

Danaya took a long sip of her drink as Charleigh said, "She told me she was going to marry me."

The yellow beverage sprayed from Danaya's lips, contaminating Charleigh's food. The liquid speckled her arm as Danaya gasped for air. Her eyes were watering as she gasped out, "Lexa said she was going to marry you when she was still married to Sylvia. What the fuck?"

"No," Charleigh shook her head. She got up from the couch and retrieved a towel. Tossing it to the other woman, she explained, "Sylvia said if Lexa hurt me that she was going to marry me and adopt Joey. It was fucking weird, and it was like she had made this promise to Lexa, and I didn't have a say in it. But even then, she told Lexa this and I was already leaving because Lexa basically called me poor white trash only after her money. Oh, and all this happened after she told Lexa she was thinking about eating me out on their fucking kitchen counter like I'm some food to be shared between them. And we don't go way back. I won a scholarship in high school and this one time at the beginning of summer I took Joey to a game, and she recognized me when we went to get autographs. We spoke for like five minutes. Well, Joey talked the whole time, but Sylvia said she remembered me and was proud of me. Like, normal shit I would expect when you found out you sent someone to college."

Charleigh tucked her hair behind her ear. "I didn't answer the email because it's like cryptic as fuck and she used a lot of the same language she used when she was talking about marriage and shit."

Danaya gawked at her. She licked her lips and asked, "Do you know who Sylvia is?"

"Yes." Charleigh rolled her eyes. "I mean, I'm a lowkey stalker. I know who every Devil or former Devil is, but she married Lexa, who I've had a crush on since college."

"No." Danaya's chin jutted out. "Like do you know how fucking rich that woman is?"

"Why does that matter?" Charleigh asked, sitting back down.

"Because Sylvia offering to marry you is a big fucking deal," Danaya stated. She leaned forward. "Emma said a big rift between Sylvia and Lexa was that Sylvia never wanted to have kids. But she is also like old, old, old money. Like 1% type money. So that money has to go somewhere, and Sylvia doesn't just say shit, at least not according to Emma. She says what she means. No cap. So, she straight up is offering to give that all to your kid. Dude, fucking call her and take that offer. She is not asking for your love, and honestly, she's fucking hot as shit for being in her thirties. You could do way worse, and I've heard she's like a goddess in bed. Plus, you have terrible taste in women so if your gut is telling you no, then she's probably good for you. And... your kid will be set for life. Your kid's kids would be set for life since the girl is actually a heiress. Like, basketball is something she does for fun because she can."

Charleigh rolled her eyes. "You know if I did what you just said, I would literally be exactly who Lexa accused me of being. Only worse because I would literally be marrying someone for just the money. Not a ball bunny. A sugar baby."

"Fuck Lexa and her broke ass," Danaya spat out. "You take Sylvia up on her offer and you would never have to think of Lexa again. You'd be sitting on a beach somewhere with seven million layers of sunblock to keep you a fucking ghost but still. Bitch, I don't know how you're sitting here pretending like this isn't the fucking chance of a lifetime."

Charleigh's brow furrowed as she tried to make sense of the parts of Danaya's rant she cared about.

"Lexa's broke?"

Danaya rolled her eyes. "That's what you heard? Like you bypass the beach and being some perfectly kept house hoe to the woman who treated you like trash."

"Why is Lexa broke?" Charleigh repeated.

Danaya's head fell back against the chair. She groaned. "Sylvia drained her bank account. Left Lexa like fifteen grand."

"Where's Lexa?" Charleigh asked. "Did Emma take her home with you guys?"

Danaya licked her lips and shook her head. Then said, "I mean, yes, she brought Lexa back to our place because she couldn't leave her at the house. But she isn't there anymore."

"Where'd she go?" Charleigh asked. She narrowed her eyes at the woman looking everywhere but at her. "What aren't you telling me?"

The woman's hands ran over her pant legs. She chewed on the inside of her cheek, then pulled out her phone. She didn't send any messages before she shoved it back into her pocket.

"Emma's going to kill me."

"What doesn't Emma want me to know? Where's Lexa?"

Danaya's tongue prodded her cheek next before she finally looked over at Charleigh. After a huff of breath, she growled, "I fucking hate secrets."

"Secrets don't make friends," Charleigh pressed.

"Lexa is in an in-treatment facility."

Charleigh searched Danaya's face for the lie. But the golden-flecked eyes finally met her gaze.

"Why is she in a treatment facility?"

"She said she wanted to hurt herself, so Emma took her."

Charleigh put the plate of tacos on the side table. "She what?"

"Charleigh." Danaya tapped her fingers against the armrests. "Lexa is bipolar. She... she went off her meds at the start of the season. Emma said that is why she was drinking and all the girls... Sylvia made sure that Lexa took her meds every morning and that she ate right and when she left Lexa's whole routine was fucked. Summers I guess make the mania bad and when you left, and Sylvia left... she just dropped hard. That's why we didn't leave right after the party. Emma was trying to get Lexa stable before we left, but Lexa said she didn't want to do it anymore. She chopped all her braids off and when she saw what she'd done she said she shoulda just ended it a long ass time ago. Her mom apparently always told her she was a demon and that she never shoulda been born and so she grabbed a knife and she said she was done trying to fit in a world she never belonged in. Emma talked her down and like took her to the hospital where she self-committed."

"How long ago did she go in?" Charleigh asked.

"Sunday."

"That's why you've been here all week, huh? In case the news dropped." Charleigh's fingers gripped the roots of her hair and she reminded herself to breathe. She inhaled deeply, then counted as she breathed out. "When does she get out?"

"Tonight."

"This is my fault," Charleigh whispered. She got up and went into her bedroom. Her neck turned on a swivel until she found her home hoodie lying in the corner of the room. She shook the dog hair into the air.

Danaya leaned against the bedroom door as Charleigh stripped off the oversized t-shirt and sweatpants.

"It's not your fault," Danaya told her.

Charleigh pushed her head through a Greyson Academy t-shirt that clung to her frame. She pointed at the floor next to Danaya's feet. "Give me my pants."

Danaya picked up the jeans Charleigh had worn to work. She righted the legs but left the woman standing in her bedroom in her thong.

"You can't blame yourself," she said. "Lexa's got issues. She's been manic for months and the drop was coming. Emma tried to get her to take her meds, but she refused, so we all knew this was coming. She is getting the help she needs, but there is nothing you can—"

Charleigh walked over to Danaya and ripped the pants from her hands.

"If I don't do something, then who will?" Charleigh spat, pushing one leg through the material, then the next. "She has no one. Sylvia took everything she would need to get on her feet, so when they release her, where is she supposed to go?"

"Charleigh...."

Charleigh snapped around. "Have you ever been in a mental hospital?"

"No," Danaya said.

Tapping her chest, Charleigh said, "Well, I was. I was escorted after they pumped the pills out of my stomach. They get you on meds and stable and then they kick you out the door. And when you got no one, they just put the script in your hands and send you on your way."

Charleigh rubbed her hands over her face. "She is going to get out and you and Emma are leaving. Sylvia fucking robbed her. So how is she supposed to get up?"

"Charleigh, I know where you are going with this but it's a bad idea."

"It's the only idea," Charleigh stated. She turned back to Danaya and jabbed a finger in the air at her. "You're supposed to be her friend."

Danaya held her hands out to Charleigh. "I'm your friend first."

"Okay well then be her friend second, but still be her friend," Charleigh pleaded. "Be her friend and help me figure out what we need to do to keep her stable."

Charleigh grabbed the taco container and put it in the fridge. As she pulled the hoodie on, she said, "Get your keys. We need to talk to Emma. Emma knows more and she can tell me what to do so that Lexa's life doesn't get flushed down the toilet when she walks out, and no one is there."

The room felt smaller as Danaya stared at her instead of following instructions. There was nothing Charleigh could do but wait for Danaya to help her. Something the woman had no reason to do because she didn't understand.

"Charleigh, who was there when you got out?" Danaya asked rather than moved.

Charleigh tightened the straps of her backpack as she stared at the ground. Remembering the glass doors of the hospital. The people walked in and out, but no one saw her.

"No one," she whispered. She looked up and begged Danaya to understand. "No one was there, and this is where I ended up. My kid is in foster care, and I survived on favors. I am holding my head above water because I am finally learning to doggy paddle. But Lexa is drowning because she needs some fucking floaties and a lifeguard on duty. And she's got no money to buy floaties and all the lifeguards found jobs at other fucking pools." Charleigh shook her head. "No. No. Lexa deserves better. She's not trash. She's not a nobody."

"But how are you supposed to hold her up when you are barely treading water?" Danaya asked because she was leaving.

No one would be there to save Charleigh if Lexa used her as a floatie. She knew she wasn't strong enough to fight Lexa off. She'd never been strong enough to fight anyone, which was why she couldn't swim well. She could hold her breath though. That was something she'd learned to do along the way, and it would be what she could offer. She could be a floatie until Lexa could doggy paddle.

And if she couldn't, then the world would keep turning without her. Dilynn would go to court to fight for Joey since she was probably already doing that. Mona wouldn't have to worry about having two Christmases. Life would go on, but Danaya wouldn't leave if she shared that sentiment. So, Charleigh stood up straighter.

"I'll figure it out." She gave Danaya a confident nod. "I always figure it out. It's what I do."

They stared at each other. Charleigh prayed the woman's superpower wasn't mind reading or lie detection.

"Emma's going to kill me," Danaya whispered and pulled out her phone. She sent a text, then put the Charger key fob in Charleigh's hand. "You're driving. And you're fucking ass is keeping my car because Emma is never going to let me leave the house again. I had one goddamn job. Not tell you about Lexa being in the hospital."

As Charleigh locked the front door, she heard Danaya growl. When she turned around, Danaya's phone was inches from her face.

"See. 'You had one job!'" Danaya gripped the phone. Her eyes glared at Charleigh as she said, "Now she's going to make me help her pack. Gonna make me label all the sides of the boxes as she lectures me about HIPPA laws. Do you have any idea how many HIPPA laws there are?"

23

The automatic doors slid open, then closed. No timing to it beyond the people moving through the space. The hospital greeter handed out scratchy masks to anyone not already hidden. A level of anonymity Lexa could hide behind as the metal rails of the thinly padded seat dug into her forearms. The new dose of Lithium and an antidepressant rattled against the plastic containers in the paper bag she clutched.

She'd sat down in the lobby. The safety plan crumbled in her hand as she weighed her options. A hotel was the only sensible move for the next couple of days unless Sylvia changed her mind about kicking her out. Maybe Sylvia would let her stay in the guest house if she said she was sorry now the pills had muted the colors.

Her wife couldn't really make her live on the street.

'Ex-wife,' she remembered. She'd signed the papers canceling her medical insurance. Made the cost of her hospital stay impossible to afford, so they released her with no place to go. No family to pick her up. No friends left, not that they were ever her friends.

Lexa closed her eyes. Her tongue scratched over her teeth, and she tried to swallow but there was nothing to swallow besides bland emotions, and those just caught in her throat.

She stared at her fingers. The nails were bit down to the quick; the tips were scabbed over. They'd changed her dose when her fingers were bleeding and the shaking increased.

"Lexa."

She dropped her head, the hoodie of Sylvia's sweatshirt covering as much of her face as her hair would allow.

The chair next to her creaked as someone sat down. She looked at the tattered boots on only touching the ground with the tips of the rubber soles. The pale hand reached over and rested on her arm. Little freckles stood out against the ivory skin in the shape of the little dipper.

"Why are you here?" Lexa asked. She licked over the peeling skin on her lips, but her dry tongue offered no relief.

"You're coming home with me," Charleigh told her.

Lexa glanced over, realizing Charleigh had updated her wardrobe. The grey hoodie, covered in dog hair, was new. One Lexa wouldn't mind stealing the first chance she got.

"I said some really mean things that I didn't mean," Lexa confessed.

"You meant every word." Charleigh squeezed her arm. "But I understand why you were angry. I was angry too."

Lexa felt the weight of Charleigh's head resting against her shoulder. The hand on her arm moved down to wrap around Lexa's fingers and the safety plan.

"I should have told you about Joey when we first started talking. I wasn't ashamed of her, but I am ashamed she's not with me."

"I don't have anything left to help you," Lexa said. "She took everything."

"I know," Charleigh whispered. "I know about everything. I know about the money. I know about the medication and the episodes. I know the paper in your hand is the safety plan you made with your doctor."

Lexa's fingers tightened around the photocopies. She'd lied so the woman in the white coat with lipstick on her teeth would release her. The desire to live was fueled by a middle-aged woman bashing her oily head into the metal grates covering the windows.

"May I see the plan?" Charleigh asked.

Lexa scrunched the papers tighter as she shut her eyes. "You shouldn't be here. I hurt you and I don't want to do it again."

Charleigh licked her lips. "Ten. I was 18 years old when I sat in a place like this waiting for someone to come get me. Nine. I swallowed a handful of pills because I found out my mother had won custody of Joey from the people I had signed over guardianship to. Eight. I used booze and pills to mask my depression until Mona checked me into rehab the summer before my last year of college. Seven. I did just enough work on my case plan to keep my rights, but never enough to actually get custody back. Six. I have never admitted to anyone that I am terrified to be a mother. Five. I have been attending AA meetings for over a year. Four. I don't have food in my house because when I do, I binge eat until I'm sick so that I can throw up and it will hurt like it did when I drank too much. Three. I gave up one year's sobriety when I went to your party. Two. I never wanted you to believe I was using you. One. I love you even though we may be star-crossed lovers. Ten things you should have known about me before we slept together, so you don't have to find out from someone else."

Lexa squeezed Charleigh's fingers tightly. Her head rested against the blonde hair. The floral aroma coated over the antiseptic stench of the hospital.

"I can't do this alone," Lexa admitted. Her face felt numb, the lithium stopping her eyes from welling up. "But it shouldn't be your problem. I shouldn't be your problem."

"You're not a problem, Lex. Your brain works differently and that's okay. Because the truth is everyone is different." Charleigh's breath rushed from her. "Do the meds help you feel less impulsive?"

"Kinda." Lexa stared at the single tile set in the wrong direction. The pattern flowed left to right instead of up and down. "They make me feel human. Like things can break me, but then stop me from breaking at the same time."

"Why did you stop taking them?" Charleigh asked.

Lexa scraped her tongue over her teeth again. "Sometimes they make me sick. I have to eat before I take them. If I don't eat, then I can't take them because I get sick. I wasn't eating because I didn't want to get up when she wasn't there."

"Is part of your plan a schedule?" Charleigh asked.

"Yeah." She shook the bag. "And to take the pills."

Baby-faced success stories in their white coats chugging coffee from to-go cups rambled in a language of anatomy and instruments. Their sneakers squeaked against the gray tiles as they passed by.

"Can you tell me what's on your schedule?" Charleigh probed. Her thumb traced over Lexa's in a gentle circle.

"Eat protein and a carb. Take pills with water. Walk or run around the block. Drink a glass of water. Do something productive with an outcome. Drink water. Write about the outcome in a journal. Eat lunch. Drink water. Practice. Drink water. Shower. Dinner. Take pills. Drink water. Listen to meditation. Lay in bed. Don't drink water," Lexa listed.

"That's a lot of water," Charleigh said with a chuckle. "You may need to tow a porta-potty behind your car."

"I hate water," Lexa admitted. "But the doctor wouldn't let me put Starbucks on my schedule."

"If I pencil in Starbucks, can you do the rest of those things at my house?"

The tiny house flashed in Lexa's head. Scramble the eggs in the scratched pan. Frozen waffles in the toaster. Chase the dog. Maybe teach the dog to race. She momentarily tried to decide if she could beat the dog in a race.

Read books with purple tags. Put books in order by tag. Organize kitchen cabinets. Duck under Charleigh's midget-sized shower head. Pretend she's Rapunzel and brush her hair. Learn to twist correctly.

Charleigh's spiteful bed. A new bed that her feet didn't hang off. And a pillow with actual cotton in it that doesn't smell like a dog and 2003's most popular conditioner.

"Everything but practice. Could I put up a hoop in the driveway?" Lexa smiled softly. "Work on keeping my toes down."

Lexa watched the doors open and close. Even with their masks on, Lexa knew it was Emma and Danaya taking the seats across from her. Emma's legs reached across the floor; her giant shoe blocked the wrong-facing tile.

"How ya feeling?" Emma asked. Her finger slipped under the team-issued mask and scratched her nose. Emma must have forgotten the point of the mask.

Lexa tried to feel the blood running through her veins. Then if her heart was pounding. Everything was muted like someone had turned her body's volume all the way down.

"Like a lump of rock," she said. "That's good, right, Doc?"

Emma's eyes crinkled in the corners. "Well, you know that is going to change as your body normalizes again, but a lump of rock is good for now. Plus, you're a cool rock like obsidian."

Danaya snorted. "Obsidian is black. She's a diorite."

Emma's brows cinched together in the middle. She gave the preposterous woman a side-eyed glance.

Danaya shrugged. "What? I like rocks. That's why I begged you all summer to go hiking with me in Sedona. There's limestone and sandstone, and peridot can be found there."

"I thought you studied broadcasting in college," Emma said.

"Well, I couldn't tell people I got a degree in geology. They'd think I was a nerd."

Lexa's head shook as Charleigh's body wiggled with giggles. Charleigh told her, "You are a nerd, but it's okay Rock Star. Your secret is safe with us."

Lexa's stomach gurgled but her mouth still felt like it was stuffed with cotton. "I need some water," Lexa said. "And something that is not lime jello or Charleigh-looking chicken."

Charleigh's thumb slapped against Lexa's hand. "Don't you start with your white people don't know how to cook, bullshit."

Emma cleared her throat. "Uhh, I saw your kitchen. You don't even own white people seasoning."

"What is white people seasoning?" Charleigh asked.

"Salt and pepper. You don't even own salt and pepper," Emma said. Her eyebrows raised to her edges.

Danaya pulled a water bottle from the plastic bag she was carrying. She held it out to Lexa but moving meant losing her contact with Charleigh. Lexa closed her eyes and inhaled the scent of the blonde's cheap shampoo again.

"Can I really come home with you?" Lexa whispered.

"Yes, Lexa. I'm here to take you home." Charleigh sucked her teeth. "But you better keep your unseasoned chicken and ghost jokes to yourself."

Danaya waved the bottle at Lexa. "This shit gets heavier the longer I hold it."

Charleigh groaned and sat up. She took the bag of pills and papers from Lexa's hands, and pushed them into her hoodie's pocket, then grabbed the bottle from Danaya as the woman slowly sunk to the floor with it.

When the lid of the water bottle didn't open, Charleigh pulled down her mask and used her teeth to break the little plastic tab. She pressed her finger to the pop top, sending the lid to the floor.

Lexa watched as Charleigh's eyes grew bigger, following the cap's path.

"Well, I guess I don't know my own strength," Charleigh said. She held the bottle out to Lexa.

When Lexa extended her hand, Emma got up and tugged her to her feet. She wrapped her arms around Lexa and hugged her.

Slowly Lexa's arms came up and around Emma. Her face pressed into Emma's shirt. "Thank you," she whispered. "Thank you for not giving up on me."

Emma leaned back and looked down at Lexa. "I'll never give up on you, but it's your girl who came to get you. So, you are going to stick with the plan. No cheating."

Lexa nodded. Her body was pulled into another hug, forcing her to look at Charleigh's tiny body under Danaya's arm. The little fingers curled into a heart on her chest. A simple flutter pleasantly warmed her insides.

An ambulance siren echoed off the buildings heading in their direction. Cars rumbled on the street. A woman, large with child, screamed at a scrawny man with a scraggly beard as he wheeled her into the lobby.

Tucked under Emma's arm, Lexa walked through the sliding glass doors with Charleigh at her side. The water eased the pain in her throat. Lexa's fingers intertwined with Charleigh's as they headed through the parking lot into Lexa's new reality.

24

Walking into the house, Charleigh was already emotionally drained. Too many students showed up to class without having read the pages they needed for any of her objectives to be accomplished. She would have to spend part of the night redrafting the remainder of her unit to adjust their pace. But teaching on the fly wouldn't have been such a big deal if Dilynn hadn't walked in to conduct a teaching observation when discussion protocols had been thrown out the window by three students who'd decided their opinions needed to be everyone's opinions, but those opinions sat on different sides of the issue.

Normally, Charleigh would have handled the situation calmly. It would have been a time to show Dilynn she was worth fighting for as a teacher. However, she and Lexa had spent a good portion of the night dealing with the nausea from the woman's body rejecting the nightly antidepressant.

Emma had warned Charleigh it could take up to six weeks for Lexa's meds to fully take effect, and even then they would probably have to be adjusted because the doctors were trying to find the correct portions for the cocktail to help Lexa stay balanced. So as the voices raised her temper went with it.

Dilynn left as silently as she'd come. When Charleigh went for the post-evaluation meeting, Dilynn and her sat on opposite sides of the woman's desk in silence until Charleigh repeated her promise to leave at the end of the year. She walked out after Dilynn couldn't look at her. Whatever was written on her evaluation didn't matter anyway. She wasn't getting a letter of recommendation from the woman who'd never had a good thing to say about her. Maybe she could get one from Alex, but she'd have to face them. Something she'd been avoiding because Alex wouldn't give her the silent treatment like Dilynn.

The only thing Charleigh had left was to look forward to whatever Lexa managed to construct from the limited ingredients since she'd been banned from the kitchen. She didn't find dinner though. No, what she found was Lexa seated in the middle of piles, upon piles of books. Every text was pulled from the shelves.

Looking at the stacks, Charleigh felt her sense of self stripped like wax off her entire body. Lexa messing with her kitchen was frustrating, but her books were her timeline. The path of reading since her father's death and her mother's betrayal was cataloged by each book. Each novel had been placed in order of when she had read it. And it was destroyed. Destroyed by the flustered brunette, who was repeating the alphabet.

"G, H, I, J... K... there you go," she said, and she placed *Never Let Me Go* on top of *Narnia,* which wasn't even the correct title.

"What do you think you are doing?" Charleigh said, dropping the stack of short stories in her arms to the floor. The papers slid over the dented and dinged hardwood.

Lexa gestured to the various piles, smiling broadly. "I sorted them by your little tag, and now I am alphabetizing them by the title so it's easier for you to find them."

Her smile fell when the first tear slid off Charleigh's chin.

Dropping her backpack and stepping through the books, Charleigh tripped on the stack closest to the hallway. The books fell across the floor, but she didn't stop. She didn't stop until she was in her room. The only place that hadn't been rearranged in the week since Lexa moved in.

Charleigh threw herself onto the bed. Her muscles shook as she choked, trying to breathe. She heard the soft rap and the door opening quietly.

"Go away," she cried out.

Lexa's footsteps approach though. She walked over to the bed and Charleigh felt the mattress shift. Charleigh's face buried into the pillow Lexa had said needed to go that morning.

"Charleigh," Lexa whispered. "Please talk to me."

"I can't," Charleigh said into the pillow. Unable to face the woman who needed her to be stable and strong. "Just go away for a minute."

"I didn't mean to." Lexa's feet caused the floor to creak. "I'll put them back."

Charleigh's body snapped up. She narrowed her eyes at Lexa's indifference to her destruction. "You can't just put it back."

She gestured to the door. "That was my life, and you just destroyed it. Destroyed my system because it wasn't good enough for you."

Her tears were falling again, and her voice was only getting louder as it fought its way out of her chest.

"I'm never going to be good enough for you. And if I can't be enough for you, I will never be enough for her. And I tried. I tried so hard to be everything that everyone wants of me."

Lexa stood and moved to the doorway. Her shoulders slumped as her feet dragged away from the boiling blonde.

Charleigh threw herself back on the bed. She lay there until Rexa's wet nose nudged her face. She rolled over and heard a huff from the living room. Rexa laid her body down alongside Charleigh, and her heavy head on the woman's chest. Scrunching down, Charleigh tried to kiss her head, but she was too far away.

She heard a groan and a crash in the living room. Rexa was up faster than Charleigh. Moving through the doorway, toward a tear-stained Lexa knelt in front of a shattered frame.

"You are so fucking stupid," she muttered to herself as she picked up the pieces of glass.

Charleigh gripped Rexa's collar to keep her walking through the glass.

"Lex," she called, but Lexa was still shaking her head and talking to herself. "Lexa!"

When the dark eyes looked up, Lexa held up her hand. A thin trail of blood ran down the edge where the glass was still clutched tightly.

Charleigh traced the scarlet path. "Did you...?"

"My hand," Lexa said, watching the blood drop from her elbow to the cover of *It*.

Charleigh pushed the hunk of dog into the bedroom and closed the door. She heard Rexa scratching the wood. She shoved her feet into Lexa's running shoes and picked up Lexa's slides. The glass crunched under her steps when she tried to navigate the extra length of Lexa's shoe over a stack of books.

She held up the shoes. "I'm going to take the glass from you, and you are going to put on your shoes before you get up," she instructed.

The blood seemed to put Lexa into a trance. No matter how many times Charleigh called to her, the woman didn't seem to notice. She just watched the blood fall like she wasn't still holding the glass.

Charleigh snapped her fingers to get the woman's attention, only for the brown eyes to search over the piles of books surrounding her.

"I can't fix it," she said, and fresh tears began to fall even though her face didn't crunch up. "I tried, but I can't remember where I took them from."

Charleigh could not pull or push Lexa from the trench she'd created herself. She gave up on trying to coax the woman from the floor and instead brought the trash can to Lexa. She turned the woman's hands over and dumped the glass into the trash.

Looking over the small slices in Lexa's palms, Charleigh shook her head. "They're just books, Lex. You can't hurt yourself over books. Your hands are more important than that."

Charleigh held their hands up to Lexa. "We need to run water over them and check for any more glass shards. I need you to get up and put your slides on."

Lexa licked her lips and studied the cuts. "I can tell it hurts but my body says it's okay."

She got up and she put her feet into the shoes. They negotiated their way to the kitchen. The red water circled the drain as Lexa stood alongside her emotionless.

"I'm sorry I yelled at you," Charleigh said. She took Lexa's glasses from her face, hoping they would provide some level of magnification. It didn't work though because Lexa was practically blind without them.

Charleigh pushed them back onto Lexa's face and made a mental note to help the woman look for the website that provided cheap contacts since she'd run out.

Her eyes fell back to the counter, and she took the hand Charleigh was prodding. She cradled it against her chest.

"I promise I won't change anything else. I promise to keep my stuff in the room, and I won't move anything else. I will put the books back, just I can't do it alone. I wasn't paying enough attention when I took them down."

Charleigh reached over to touch her, but she pulled away. The air in Charleigh's lungs crystallized at not being able to touch Lexa. Never had the woman shied away from her contact.

"It will be fine," she promised. Even though it wasn't fine. "We can just throw them back on the shelf."

Lexa's eyes shot up, narrowing at Charleigh. Her bloody hand gestured out to the bookshelves. "If it was just fine and we could just throw them up there, then you wouldn't have thrown a tantrum over me helping you have some form of organization in your life."

Charleigh backed away. Her body tried to become one with the pantry that stopped her from being able to move anymore.

Lexa took a step toward her. Her arms were flying in different directions. To herself. To the kitchen surrounding her. To the living room.

Her voice was so loud that Charleigh could only see her lips moving over the blood sloshing in her ears. She didn't hear anything Lexa was saying. She didn't hear it because Charleigh was concentrating on the pitch in Lexa's eyes. Her inner demon was trying to crawl its way out in full force.

"Are you even listening," she shouted at Charleigh, and the smaller woman realized how close Lexa had gotten. Her body was less than a step away, and Charleigh was scared. She held up her hand and she begged.

She begged Lexa to just step back.

She begged Lexa to just take a breath.

She begged Lexa to just stop yelling at her.

Lexa looked down at the woman and stepped forward. Instead of breathing, she appeared to be smoking like a volcano. Instead of yelling at Charleigh, she was screaming.

"Are you always this unfucking grateful when someone tries to do something for you?"

Her hand hit the cabinet door above Charleigh's head. The particle board cracked. Pieces of pressed wood rained down over Charleigh's hunched body. She ducked as she sank to the floor. She dropped to her knees and covered her head.

She hid from Lexa. Hid from the world. Hid like an ostrich, hoping if Charleigh couldn't see Lexa, then Lexa couldn't see her.

Hands pulled the smaller body against Lexa's chest. Blood smeared against Charleigh's arm as Lexa cradled her.

Charleigh's body shook in rhythm with Lexa's apologies. Endless words of "I'm sorry," and "I don't know why I just lost it," and "I promise I will never do that again."

It was too little.

It was too scary.

It was too much.

"You need to leave," Charleigh said.

She pushed at Lexa until her ass hit the ground and she scrambled back. Her feet slipped in the shoes until they came off and her naked soles were able to find purchase against the wood toward the back door.

"Get out of my house," Charleigh yelled, working at the wobbly knob on the kitchen door. She didn't get it open to escape before Lexa backed away.

The ball player's movements were calculated and swift. The books thunked against the floor. Drawers from the dresser in the bedroom slammed closed, and then the closet doors shut. The huge feet pounded into the floor as she gathered the things they'd collected from Emma and Danaya's house before the two left the country.

Charleigh didn't know where she would go. It bothered her, she even cared. She shouldn't care about her like this. She shouldn't care after Lexa screamed at her and almost hit her. She shouldn't care.

But she did.

Charleigh got up from the floor and moved to the doorway.

Lexa was taking the final steps to the door when the floor creaked under Charleigh. She turned with two suitcases in her hands and a duffle bag over her shoulder. Looking at Charleigh, she set the suitcases down and reached into her pocket.

She pulled out her keys and twisted the ring in her hand. Without stepping forward, or even looking Charleigh in the eyes, she set the small bronze key on the coffee table.

"I didn't mean for any of this to happen." Her words were quiet and inflection non-existent. Another dip in Roller-coaster Lexa.

Turning away, Lexa twisted the front door handle. The door was open when Charleigh said, "You really scared me."

Lexa's breath rushed from her lungs. Her shoulders gave a little more as the darkness crept toward them outside. The fields across the street swayed in the breeze.

They both knew she had nowhere to go. They knew Lexa didn't know how to be on the bottom. And that was the thing. That was just Charleigh's problem when it came to Lexa.

She knew.

She knew what it meant to have no place to go. What it meant for the world to be doing the breaststroke, while she struggled just to stay afloat. Everything that should be easy. But it wasn't. It wasn't because, at the end of the day, there was barely anything left in the account if it wasn't negative. At the end of the day, missing another meal, followed by a bedtime story. She'd miss it all because she couldn't figure out how to swim like everyone else. So, she kept treading and hoping. Hoping that one day someone would stop and explain the breaststroke that seemed to get them to shore. Fuck the breaststroke, she wished someone would teach her how to dog paddle.

And she knew that was how Lexa felt at this moment.

And she knew that was how she decided to try again.

And she knew that was probably stupid.

She'd never been known for her long-term planning skills though.

Charleigh navigated around the rubble of her past to where Lexa stood. Took the steps to where Lexa waited for Charleigh to kick her out again. Reached out to touch her, and this time Lexa didn't brush her aside. This time she turned with defeated eyes.

Lexa's voice wavered when she told Charleigh, "I'm at an eight."

"What's an eight?" Charleigh asked.

"A freak out meter. Ten bad. One fine," Lexa explained. "The shrink. She said to measure the freak-out. Put it in my journal."

Charleigh nodded. She'd never heard of a freak-out meter, but she added it to her teacher toolbox to use with her kids in the future. Then she said, "I think I'm at an eight too."

The bags dropped when Charleigh wrapped her arms around the woman's neck. Lexa leaned down and pulled Charleigh up around her waist. Lexa's knees hit the floor, and the house shook under the aftershocks of their combined pain.

"I'm sorry," Lexa said again. Her face rested atop Charleigh's bust.

"I'm sorry," Charleigh echoed, her cheek resting against Lexa's head.

"I just wanted to do something," Lexa explained, and Charleigh nodded against her head.

"I kept them in the order I read them. Each a memory leading back to my dad," Charleigh whispered.

"Can we fix them?" Lexa asked. "Like could you remember which one you read first."

She knew if she thought about it hard, it would be possible. The problem was going through every memory would remind her of everything she'd been through. Unbottling each of those memories meant reliving all of the worst moments of her life. A task dangerous for both of them. There would be things she'd have to explain when the feelings wouldn't just go back into the bottle without some lubrication. So, Charleigh shook her head, and she stared at the change of her patterns being forced upon her.

She'd thought everything she was doing was to help Lexa move on with her life, but, in a way, Lexa was forcing her out of her routine. Teaching her how to cohabitate with another human being.

25

Even with a budget, money was running out. There was no way to make it nine months when the cost of Lithobid was $ 859 for just 30 pills. That didn't matter as much now, but Lexa had other expenses as well. Like her agent's fee, doctor's visits, and the insurance on her car. She could barely afford groceries, and that was with Charleigh covering all the other bills. The woman who couldn't put food in the cabinets was now paying for the roof over Lexa's head, something Lexa couldn't accept anymore with the fog cleared from her head.

"Look, Lexa, I can't promise anything, but I know Melbourne has potentially lost their guard and may be looking to replace her. They are working with the rookie but have lost every preseason game. I can see if they would be interested in giving you a half-season contract," Lexa's new agent explained.

Lexa looked over the corn fields surrounding the tiny chain link fence. She needed to get out of here.

'Start over,' Sylvia said. She'd known her drop was coming and took away all the resources she would need to do just that.

'Don't hurt Charleigh,' Sylvia threatened. But living off the woman's poverty level salary was putting more strain on Charleigh, who'd lost more weight with Lexa's inability to sleep.

With money, Lexa could get Charleigh a car before Danaya came back. Russia was out because of their homophobic policies. China paid more, but all the teams had their allowed one American already. Australia paid like the U.S., but it was her best bet at ceasing to be a burden.

"Make it happen," Lexa said. "As soon as they need me. I'll be on the plane."

"You sure? I heard you wanted to take a year off. It's been three years playing non-stop," the female on the other end of the line said. "Maybe you need a rest."

"Don't you work off commission?" Lexa snapped. Her hand wrapped around the pill she'd pretended to take before Charleigh left that morning.

"I'll make contact. I should know something soon since their offices are just opening."

Rexa pawed at the kitchen door, telling her Charleigh was home.

Getting up, Lexa let the dog through the door first. Her nails clicked along the floor as she made her way to Charleigh, who greeted Rexa with a smile. It had only been a week since Charleigh went back to work after Fall Break from her school. Two days since Lexa fucked up her books. There was nothing Lexa could touch in the house without messing up some sacred heap of chaos Charleigh branded as her sense of self. She still hadn't even opened the door to the room Charleigh would shut herself in each night while Lexa showered.

She moved into the kitchen and pulled the chicken from the bowl of water to begin dinner. The only thing she was allowed to do in the house was cook. It was something to do, that at least made her useful since the woman wouldn't eat if nothing was made.

The floorboards creaked upon Charleigh's entrance to the kitchen. Lexa looked over her shoulder where the blonde leaned against the doorway.

"Hey," she said.

"Hey," Lexa echoed.

"What'd you do today?"

Lexa shrugged like she'd done over the last week. She had to play neutral, so Charleigh didn't know about the pill she'd pushed into her pocket.

"Nothing." That wouldn't be good enough. She knew that. Knew Charleigh would ask follow-up questions like a nosey parent if Lexa didn't say more. "Went for a run. Read a few chapters of the lesbian book with the wine."

The chicken turned red as she sprinkled the mixture of spices she'd stolen from Emma's house before they were packed away. She'd only had half of the ones she'd seen on the recipe video, but she'd spent the better part of the morning on the phone since the medicinal-induced fog finally started to lift enough for her to realize she had to get out of this house.

Charleigh lifted herself onto the counter. It was unsanitary, but the last time Lexa made a comment about it, Charleigh rolled her eyes. Today, her legs dangled over the cabinet Lexa needed to get in.

She nudged the midget leg with the door until Charleigh gave her the space she needed. The pan should have been on top, but it wasn't. Lexa had to squat to search for it since Charleigh put the dishes away last.

'Why can't she just put them away correctly?' Lexa asked herself.

As she dug through the pans no longer arranged by size, Charleigh rambled about school. Again. Like it was the only topic Charleigh knew anything about or ever wanted to talk about.

"So, one of the kids put his name into Kahoot as GMO and you know I hate it when they don't put their real name in, so I was, like, who is the genetically modified orgasm? I was so embarrassed, and the kids were laughing so hard."

Her fingers reached over to pinch some of the flour mixture Lexa prepared for the fried chicken. Lexa pulled the plate away to keep her unwashed hands from their food.

The blonde didn't appear phased. She laughed. "I can't believe I said orgasm in front of twenty teenagers today."

The fork stabbed the chicken breast harder than Lexa intended. It was all she could do to keep her cool though, especially with the doors on the top of the pantry now removed from the hinges so Charleigh's case manager wouldn't see the damage when she came to visit. Covering the breast with the egg paste, she tried to find it in her to care about a stupid teaching game. When it was covered, she dropped it into the flour mixture Charleigh had managed to touch while she'd been focused on the first step.

After a deep breath, she reminded herself to be a zero. Zero meant Charleigh wouldn't ask questions about the pills, and she wouldn't scribble notes into the composition book where she kept Lexa's safety plan and prescriptions. The book that sat alongside the other one Charleigh kept all the receipts for the clothes she bought her daughter and notes about her visits. Why the woman was able to track every little detail but not put the pans in order by size had Lexa thinking Charleigh was the one who needed to see the psycho doctor to get some goddamn Adderall or something.

"Yeah, that's awkward," Lexa said when Charleigh's laughter stopped.

Charleigh slid down from the counter. "Sorry, I just thought you'd want to hear about my day."

The fridge slapped shut and Charleigh popped open a can of Dr. Pepper. Lexa rolled her eyes. She didn't understand why Charleigh bothered with the soda; she only ever took two sips before she left it someplace for Lexa to clean up like she was a damn maid on top of being the woman's personal chef.

The can hit the table, and Lexa could feel the woman's eyes on her.

'Just don't say anything. Don't pick a fight,' Lexa told herself.

Her blood traveled in waves. The first wave of irritation hit when the chair legs scraped against the floor too loudly. The second hit when Charleigh asked, "So, what do you want to do tonight?"

"I dunno."

Charleigh beside Lexa's arm. She was watching each move as though she'd learn to cook something that didn't come from a box.

"We could watch a movie," Charleigh offered.

"Eh." Lexa felt like she had finished Netflix and Disney Plus.

"We could go to the park and play basketball," Charleigh tried.

"What's the point?"

Charleigh leaned back against the counter. She looked up playfully. "You could work on your free throws."

Lexa's eyes rolled at the jab. The woman had no idea what it was like to shoot a ball when thousands of people were watching, waving signs around, and even booing.

"What's your problem?" Charleigh said, her eyes centered on Lexa's face.

Lexa dropped the breast into the oil. The bubbles turned the golden liquid into a dingy white. She felt her body frying internally. She checked her arm to see if her skin rippled with the rising heat.

"Nothing," she said, both as a confirmation she was not internally cooking and a lie to the woman's question.

Charleigh's eyes finally looked away. She stared at the can in her hand. "Your cheeks turn pink when you lie."

Lexa squeezed the fork in her fist. Her knuckles turned pasty, so she slowly set it against the counter. She had to avoid flailing so Charleigh didn't tell her to leave again.

'You're out of chances,' Sylvia had told her.

Closing her eyes, she breathed out. Counted her freak-out meter down until she hit three. Three wasn't neutral, but she couldn't get there without the fog.

"I'm not sure what you want from me," she said slowly to hide the emotion the woman tried to medicate away.

With a scoff, Charleigh snipped, "How about a human conversation?"

"There's nothing to talk about," Lexa stated. "I have done nothing all day. I had to cancel my hair appointment. Emma and Danaya are overseas, so I can't practice with anyone. I'm alone in this house all day, and you come home talking about your stupid job like I'm supposed to care."

The honey eyebrows rose on Charleigh's face. Her head leaned back as she looked at the ceiling. "Wow."

Lexa dropped the fork against the counter after she added the second breast. Her lips curled into a snarl, a three rising to a six.

"Don't wow me. You have no fucking idea what it's like to be here wondering when I am going to fuck something else up. Walking around, picking up the shit you leave everywhere. Waiting for you to kick me out because I touch something that has some fucking cryptic meaning to you."

Charleigh set the can down. "This is my house. I pay the fucking rent and utilities, so I can leave my shit where I want it."

"What are we even doing?" Lexa snapped.

The laugh that fell from Charleigh's lips made Lexa feel sick. "I don't know, Lexa. Keeping you from being homeless. Getting you regulated on your meds. Fucking U-hauling without any of the fun shit. Living like we're the last two humans on Earth because no one wants anything to do with us. Pick one I guess."

"So, I'm just here in your house. I'm not your girlfriend." Lexa turned to face the woman who was too close. "Are we even friends? Or am I just your project?"

Charleigh's arms wrapped around her body. She studied the worn floorboards. "You're not my project, Lexa."

"Then what am I to you?" Lexa gestured to herself. "Am I your fucking maid and cook? Or am I just a charity case to make you feel less shitty about your status in life? Like, what am I doing here?"

"Look, I get it," Charleigh said calmly. "This is complicated. I... haven't lived with anyone besides Mona, and she's messier than I am. We lived off take-out and Egos because when we were with Marcus that's all we ever ate. But... I will try to put my stuff away when I'm done with it. I didn't realize it was such a big deal."

The chicken breasts in the pot floated in the bubbling oil, dancing around each other. The salads in the refrigerator sat in separate bowls, their ingredients not to be mixed, because if it wasn't a cucumber, it wasn't allowed to touch Charleigh's lettuce, which she wouldn't eat anyways. Everything was in its own space. And Lexa needed her own space, so she could show the woman the fun times they missed with this arrangement. She'd stop being a burden and show Charleigh she could provide for her and the kid she couldn't even meet Sunday when Charleigh went for her scheduled visitation.

She checked her phone. The text from her new agent was simple: 'Melbourne is a go. You leave the week of Thanksgiving.'

'Play nice for a month,' she told herself. Then, she could come back and be the woman Charleigh wanted. The one the blonde needed, and they could be a family. A real family with a kid and everything. Maybe even more kids. Like a do-over for Charleigh since she missed everything with the first one.

"I'm sorry," she said with her back to Charleigh. "You should be able to leave your stuff where you want."

"I wish you would just tell me when things come up," Charleigh said, wrapping her arms around Lexa. "I don't want to add to your stress."

Lexa reached over and turned off the burner.

She turned and picked up the woman, setting the blonde on the counter and fitting her body between Charleigh's legs. A kiss pressed to the freckled nose.

"I'm sorry we missed all the fun stuff. I'll make it up to you."

Charleigh met her kiss. The first time since the night of the party. Their tongues soothed away the sharp-edged words they'd been using to hurt each other.

She carried Charleigh to the living room. Their bodies melded together as they shared the air between them. Lexa sat down on the couch and held Charleigh's core against her.

Dinner was forgotten when their shirts were discarded. Charleigh's breasts in Lexa's hands and mouth brought a smile to the dark lips. She hummed against the woman's perked rosy bud. Memorizing the texture for when she'd lay in her Melbourne loft alone at night.

She'd catalog the details of Charleigh's gasps for later use, so she wouldn't make the same mistakes she'd made with Sylvia. But for now, she'd take her time exploring every inch of Charleigh like a map she'd use to find her way back home.

Charleigh's fingers massaged her scalp as Lexa played with her nipples. Her head was thrown back in pleasure. Lexa lifted them off the couch and flipped their position. Pulling Charleigh's pants from her body, Lexa kissed her way down the lightning bolt marks of her abdomen.

On her knees, she inhaled the sweet scent. Licked up Charleigh's dripping core. Then she heard Sylvia's voice playing once more: 'At least with me you'd be smiling afterward.'

She looked up, finding Charleigh's gaze locked on the ceiling. She wasn't not enjoying Lexa's tongue moving around her clit. Sitting back on her heels, she replaced her tongue with her thumb. Watched Charleigh carefully to see if there was something that made her eyes close. It was taking too long though.

"Is there a way to make you scream?" she asked, for the first time doubting her ability to please a woman.

Charleigh looked down at her. She bit her lip, then slowly put her hand on top of Lexa's. Her index finger pressed down on the thumb resting atop her clit.

"Pressure, like this." She stroked the top of Lexa's thumb from top to bottom.

As a team sports player, she'd spent her life following someone else's playbook. By running the play Charleigh had given her, she felt the woman's thighs quivering around her head when her tongue replaced her thumb. Giving the woman what she wanted had her moaning and pulling Lexa's hair. She was able to taste the subtle shift as Charleigh's clit fully presented, where she paid homage to the one who'd shown up in the storm.

Slowly and deliberately, she made the experience only about the woman shaking under her touch. Took the time to draft similar plays as she brought Charleigh to another edge and licked within her as she tumbled over. She wasn't done with two, but her knees were at war with the floor.

Cradling the woman against her chest, she took Charleigh to bed. Laid her down, then searched through the drawer of toys. The vibrator on top looked like something the woman enjoyed. She lay behind Charleigh, pulling her close.

"Show me how to use this one to make you see fireworks," she asked softly.

Hand over hand, she dedicated her time to learning. The teacher knew what she wanted and didn't hold back giving Lexa a lesson on how to make her scream.

And screaming she did until her voice was hoarse and her body soaked in sweat. Selfishness wasn't in Charleigh's vocabulary though. Even exhausted from her string of orgasms, she pulled on the strap to give Lexa the blue dick she'd once been promised.

Please and thank you were only a few of the words exiting Lexa's lips. She clung to the thin hips driving into her like the true boss of the house. With Lexa weak from her climax, she lacked the energy to fight Charleigh to give her another chance to please her. She let her legs fall open for Charleigh's tongue to take her time slowly building Lexa up again.

A sex-caused fog was the only one Lexa wanted to experience. She held Charleigh against her chest when the woman finally passed out. Without her meds, the insomnia was back, but she needed the time to think. Time to plan the rest of her stay in the house. She'd make the next month about etching positive memories to erase all the pain she'd caused. Erase the cruelty of rutting against the blonde's face in search of selfish release. She'd show her she loved her, then come back from Melbourne with the money they needed to be a family.

26

Six outfits. Not a single one pink, and no flowers. Danaya had also shipped a pair of purple Jordans a six-year-old had no business owning, but Charleigh wasn't going to argue. Not when she would never be able to do it herself.

The composition book's binding was worn. Two years of notes that began after the state's ADA had said she hadn't participated in the case. A lie she had no way to fight. It was the last court hearing held in person because the world shut down, and her visits had been transferred from in-person to video conferences. Since then, she'd made sure every phone call she was granted was logged with the time the call started and the time the call ended, along with notes about what she and Joey did while talking.

Charleigh flipped to the latest page. She double-checked each item in the plastic Carter's bag with the tags still on the clothes and receipt. Lexa had insisted on purchasing the items new, and Venmo'd Charleigh the cash so the receipt would have her name on it. She'd remember to take a picture of Joey holding the bag, so if Grace lied again, she'd have the proof.

When the front door opened, Charleigh tucked the notebook under the throw pillow. She picked the stray dog hairs off the clothes. Then, she returned the articles to the bag, tying the top shut.

Lexa pulled the earbud from her ear and wiped the sweat from her forehead. The nausea seemed to have finally passed, making sleeping easier for Lexa and herself. Lexa leaned down and pressed a kiss to Charleigh's lips.

"Are you sure I can't go with you?" Lexa asked. She stripped off the tank top. Her abs glistened in the mid-morning light.

Charleigh nodded, tucking her hair behind her ear. She pressed the floral print dress down, trying to keep the wrinkles from it. She owned three dresses, identical in modest cut and similar in prints for visit days.

"I... I have to clear guests through my case manager and since... since your arrest... she won't okay it," Charleigh explained. "I also.... I pretend to be straight when I'm with my mom."

Lexa licked her lips, then pointed to the hallway. "I'm going to go take a shower. Are you going to still be here when I get out?"

Standing up, Charleigh hooked the bag around her wrist. "I'm actually going to head out. She lives near Danaya and Emma's old place, so it's about a thirty-minute drive," she said.

"Okay, well... I'll see you when you get back."

"Yeah... see you later." Charleigh turned to the door but stopped. "Hey, Lex."

When Lexa turned back to her, Charleigh almost lost her nerve to tell the truth. She licked her lips. "Uh... so, you should probably know that I'm usually really sad when I get home. Mona will probably stop by like she usually does. Try to be nice to her."

Lexa closed the distance between them. Her arms wrapped around Charleigh tightly, holding more than her waist, making Charleigh feel at home. The athlete's body smelled like outside. It made the mother miss the days she'd spent breaking a sweat in the driveway, so she'd be ready for the freshmen basketball team. She'd never got her shot after being picked up by Alex in the van a week before tryouts and sent to a school without sports.

"I'll be nice, and I'll cook us all dinner," Lexa promised.

"Don't forget to drink some water," Charleigh reminded, earning her a pouty groan.

It was a good way to leave the house. A simple kiss and warm smile, like maybe it could all work out.

The house hadn't changed in the ten years she'd been banned from within. Even the flowers in the bed were still the same annuals Grace Marshall planted every year. But the buds had blossomed and wilted. The colder nights wiped away any hint of warmth from the porch that looked similar to the others on the street.

She rang the bell, clutching the bag in her hand. Her heart beat wildly against her chest as she listened for the sound of Joey charging toward the door. She didn't come though, even when the door opened.

Grace loved the look Charleigh faked on visit days. Having seen the difference between Lexa's world of wealth and what she'd considered rich with her mother had made her look at everything a little less envious.

Grace's ironed dress wrapped around every protruding roll. The sleeves covered her forbidden weathered shoulders as the dark eyes stared down at her once daughter. Charleigh had never heard the woman tell her she loved her. The child she'd adopted through the church when her place in heaven was called into question for not giving her husband a legacy. There were supposed to be more of them, her dad had once explained. A house of children like the other members of the church. Families of six or seven modestly dressed humans, but he'd given up hope when the woman he'd married couldn't look at the girl whose hair was the wrong color and eyes the wrong shade to hide she didn't belong to them, even though the secret was kept.

Charleigh smiled, her eyes glancing behind her mother to catch a glimpse of her doppelganger. She thought she saw her on the stairs, but the door shut too quickly for Charleigh to be sure.

Without a word, Grace clicked play on the phone in her hand and held it in Charleigh's face. A YouTube video played on the screen.

The crystal-clear video began with Charleigh smiling as she tipped a shot glass into her mouth and slapped it against the table. The video cut to her standing over Danaya, alcohol spilling from her breasts, coating Danaya's face as the woman tried to catch it under the bouncing bust.

Charleigh's stomach fell from within her, and her diaphragm collapsed without the support. Her lungs couldn't work when she tried to breathe as her clothes were stripped from her body on the screen.

She closed her eyes when she heard her voice in the speaker. "Fuck me like I'm Lexa Jenson's whore."

The video played the full five minutes. Every slap on her ass caused the speaker of the phone to scratch. Her voice was so loud as she begged Lexa for more. Then it cut to Sylvia pressing against her on the counter. Her finger was running over Charleigh's lip.

"We could make rules. You and me," Sylvia said, and Charleigh could remember the touch. Remember the fear she'd had for the woman pinning her to the counter.

The bag slipped from Charleigh's fingers. The shoe box smacked against the ground, echoing against the entryway's walls.

"Please stop," she whispered.

She swallowed the tears threatening to fall even though the video wasn't stopped. She watched herself walk off-camera as Lexa and Sylvia stared at her naked body. It wasn't stopped until Sylvia's tongue ran up the roof of her mouth and the woman's promise for more rewards if she was a good girl was said aloud.

"The visit has been canceled," Grace stated. "All visits are canceled. Your little adult video has gone viral, and the case manager has agreed you cannot possibly provide a healthy environment for Joey."

The door slammed in Charleigh's face before she could explain. She banged on the barrier; her fist bruised as she beat against the wood.

Screaming as her freeze turned to fight, she cried out, "You can't cancel my visit!"

She pressed the doorbell over and over again.

"You can't take her away! I'm going to fight you!" She smacked the wood again. "If it takes everything I have, I'm going to fight you because I. Am. Her. Mother!"

The door didn't open though. She didn't hear the little feet slap against the floor to come to greet her. She only saw the silent tear-stained face staring back at her from the window. Joey's little hand pressed against the glass with the curtains covering the back of her body.

Joey was yanked from view as Charleigh heard her daughter crying for her within. The screaming didn't last long, and she'd lived with Grace Marshall long enough to know if the woman deemed the tears pointless, she'd give a reason for them to be falling. It's where she'd learned to give up, and Joey was learning it now without her grandfather there to tell the girl she mattered.

The bag of clothes and new shoes lay on the concrete alongside where Charleigh had fallen. Tiny rocks dug into her knees as wrinkles set into the dress, she'd never fit in.

When the well in her soul ran dry, she stared at the car that had ended her relationship with her daughter. If it wasn't for the car, she'd never have been at that party. If it wasn't for Lexa, she would have never had to make the deal for the car, and she'd be at the park with Joey.

It was Lexa's fault.

She didn't delete the video. She'd recorded her and left it there for Sylvia. Sylvia and Lexa had ruined everything. Made her into nothing to the only person who mattered.

Nothing. That was all she'd ever be.

27

The door to the house opened without a knock. Lexa had barely enough time to duck into the bedroom before she heard voices in the living room. Pulling her shorts up, she cinched the tie.

"I don't know why, but I expected it to be bigger," an unfamiliar voice said in the living room.

"Well, your mom has gone out of her way to make sure Charleigh was isolated from everything and everyone." That voice Lexa would recognize anywhere.

She turned the corner to greet Mona and her guest. 'Nicely,' she reminded herself. The way she'd been instructed to. The floorboards creaked under her weight as the house protested her presence as usual.

But she didn't get to be nice. She froze in the narrow hallway.

Her throat closed, unable to swallow as she stared down the barrel of a handgun. With fingers spread out, Lexa slowly moved her arms away from her body, so there was no question she was unarmed.

"Jesus, Evie," Mona growled. "Put your fucking gun away. It's just Charleigh's girlfriend."

The gun lowered from her face, but Lexa still couldn't breathe. She stared at the woman holstering the weapon on her hip. A pregnant belly protruded over the top of her jeans. The woman's gravelly voice hissed, "You didn't say anyone was going to be here. She scared the shit out of me."

"Lexa, you good?" Mona asked, moving in front of the other woman. "Sorry, dude. We didn't realize you were going to be here. I just knew it was Charleigh's visit day, and she is usually pretty fucked afterward."

Lexa couldn't stop looking at the weapon. The roots her feet had grown withered from under her, but her heart hadn't slowed.

She looked up at the woman whose eyes narrowed at her. "Didn't I arrest you at Echo's bar?"

"You just pointed a gun at my head in my fucking house," Lexa said. Her hands dropped. "You walked into my house and pointed a gun at me."

Mona held up her hands. "Lexa, look I know that you are freaked out right now. We're sorry. Charleigh never said you were living here."

Lexa stared at the woman behind Mona. Her chin raised and her eyes unblinking. Nothing about her face said she was sorry. And it hit her. This wasn't just the cop who arrested her. She was the bitch who stole Charleigh's sister from her side. The brat of the boss who treated Charleigh like shit.

Lexa's finger jabbed toward Evie. "What the fuck is she even doing here?" she growled. "Charleigh doesn't need her. Apparently, she doesn't even need you since you just ghosted her for the past few weeks."

Mona shook her head. "Look, I know that everyone is a little tense right now. I didn't tell Charleigh I was bringing Evie because she would have said not to come."

"Because she's part of the family that ruined her fucking life," Lexa roared.

"Yeah, I know. I know better than anyone because I was there for everything. I was the one that was there, but Charleigh... Charleigh's not alone. She has you and she has me and she has our co-worker Parker, who is also on her way. We didn't know you were going to be here, and Parker and I were talking, and we figured we needed to stop living in these silos. So, she is coming with her girlfriend, and I brought Evie, and Landon is going to be here later."

Mona held up a bag of wood. "We were going to light a fire in the pit out back because fire calms Charleigh. She watches it and she sings. Lyra is bringing her guitar. See, it wasn't supposed to be like what just happened. We are all just here to be here for Princess. Please, dude, don't make this into a thing."

Lexa sucked her teeth. "I promised to be kind when you showed up. I'm not fucking up another promise. But don't you ever point that fucking gun at me again."

Evie looked down at where her hand held her belly. "They tell us in the academy: 'It's better to be judged by twelve than carried by six.'"

"You know what's better than all of that?" Lexa didn't wait for an answer. "Not shooting innocent fucking people in their own house when you're the one breaking in."

Mona whistled. "She's kinda right," she told her girlfriend. "And I told you to leave the gun at home."

"Don't start with me," Evie growled. "You bring me out to the middle of a fucking field. What if a bear comes for us?"

"A bear?" Mona rolled her eyes and then cast Lexa a look. "This fucking psycho tried to sacrifice me to a raccoon when we went up to Payson last spring, but she's talking about a Glock stopping a bear in the middle of the Phoenix Metro area."

Lexa agreed the woman was ridiculous, but she was too pissed to find anything amusing. She barely managed to unclench her fists. Her breathing was just starting to regulate and the pulse in her ears had faded.

They didn't get a chance to move on with Mona's plan. They couldn't when the front door slammed open. The knob hit the bookcase causing books and trinkets to fall from the shelves.

Charleigh's face was beet red, the vein in her neck pulsing. Her eyes ran over the women in the room landing on Lexa.

The roots in Lexa's feet melded with the floorboards again as windows rattled in their crumbling frames with Charleigh's scream, "HOW COULD YOU?!"

The family photo from the end table flew at Lexa's head. The cord from the lamp snapped as it was torn from the wall and launched next. Both deflected by the woman rooted in the hallway with nowhere to go.

"I fucking begged you," Charleigh cried.

Shattered glass littered the floor as the woman ran across it. Her tiny fists hit Lexa in the chest.

"How fucking hateful do you and your bitch of a wife have to be?"

The fight within the woman dissolved as Lexa grabbed her wrists to keep from getting hit. The bones in the thin arms turned to jelly when she sank to the floor. Her knees bled in the floral dress when she looked up at Lexa. Tears streamed down her face.

"Why would you do this to me?" she cried. "I did everything you asked. Why, Lexa? Why?"

Words came to Lexa, but her tongue wouldn't move. She couldn't say anything as the gun in Evie's holster stayed in place. She swallowed when Charleigh's face fell from her upward gaze. Her shoulders shook and animalistic cries broke from her lips.

"Guys, we have a problem," a new voice called out before making it up the steps.

A petite redhead stopped in the doorway. She scanned the room while everyone stared at Charleigh still sobbing. Without a word, she walked carefully around the largest parts of the glass to the weeping blonde. She pushed the basketball player back and squatted before Charleigh. Cupping her face, Parker waited for the red-rimmed eyes to meet hers.

"You haven't lost yet," she said. "I saw the video. I know. I know how betrayed you must feel right now, but I need you to hear me when I say you haven't lost yet."

Lexa looked at the back of the red hair. She remembered the woman from the bar. Echo's tits, Kayla had explained. She tried to understand why Echo would release her own video of the bar fight.

"She wouldn't let me see her," Charleigh choked on each word. "She slammed the door. Wouldn't let me see her. Said no judge would give me custody after a sex tape went viral."

'Sex tape?' Lexa had stalked every element of Charleigh's media presence in the days she'd waited for access to the Instagram profile. There was no sex tape.

Parker ran her thumbs under Charleigh's eyes, turning the streaking eyeliner into war paint. "Which is illegal. You haven't lost yet, and Lyra is on the phone with the ADA of your case. She works with him. We got your back."

It hit Lexa like a ton of bricks as Mona's speaker played Charleigh's voice begging to be her whore. She looked at the blue eyes staring up at her.

"I didn't," Lexa said. "I swear, Charleigh. I didn't."

"You filmed her having sex with you?" Mona yelled. The bag of wood hit the floor. Mona's body barreled past the women on the floor toward Lexa. "You fucking pervert."

Lexa sat in her car outside the house she'd shared with Sylvia. Her lip was busted open, and her eye was already swollen. She hadn't fought back when Mona attacked her. She'd taken the woman's punches and the kick to her stomach, robbing her of the air in her lungs.

It only ended when Evie tried to stop her and the door to Joey's room was busted through the frame. The purple bedroom glowed in the dark with hundreds of stars and planets.

Lexa fled the house before she could be hit again. How she ended up in Scottsdale, she wasn't sure. But she staggered from the car. Her ribs ached where the Doc Martin boot had landed.

Her hand slapped against the glass door as she screamed, "Open the door, you fucking bitch!"

She stepped back when the door swung open. Sylvia's eyes widened as she took in Lexa's face.

"What the hell happened to you?" she asked.

Lexa coughed. The blood coated her tongue.

"You pretended to give a shit about her." Lexa pointed her finger at Sylvia. "You're a fucking monster. You fucking ruined her life because she didn't fall at your goddamn feet and worship the money you stand on."

Sylvia rolled her eyes. "I have no idea what you are talking about, Lexa. Are you off your meds again? The paranoia kicking in? Jesus, are you ever going to change?"

"I didn't fight you when you robbed me. But I'm going to fight you now. I'm going to fucking ruin you to the point that no amount of Daddy's money will ever buy your way out. Because I fucking know." Lexa beat her hand on her heart. "I know what type of snake you are. And I'm going to fucking make you pay for releasing the video of me and Charleigh having sex."

Sylvia's head tilted. "What video?"

"Don't fucking play innocent," Lexa choked. She spat the blood in her mouth onto the doorstep. "You told me if I gave you what you wanted... if I gave you the fucking divorce that left me with nothing that you wouldn't hurt her. And you still did it."

"I didn't release any video of you and Charleigh having sex." Sylvia's arms folded across her chest.

"BULLSHIT!" Lexa stepped into Sylvia's space. The blonde was barely taller than her, but she didn't care. She stared into her tar-filled soul. "I shattered my phone. I couldn't delete it in time, so you fucking sent it out because she chose me. She chose me over you!"

Her fists shook at her sides, but she didn't hit the woman. She'd hit her image; it was the only thing Sylvia ever gave a damn about.

"They took away her visitation, Via. They took away her visitation and they are going to terminate her rights because of you."

Lexa searched Sylvia's stoney expression for a hint of remorse. The tiniest glimpse of guilt. But Sylvia's lips sat in a straight line.

Her tone never wavered when she said, "I didn't release a sex tape of you or her. There is nothing I would gain from doing so."

"Then who would do it? Huh? Who had access to that video? The video that you fucking watched." Lexa smacked her chest again. "I never even saw it!"

"Kayla." Sylvia closed her eyes. She shook her head and inhaled as much air as possible. "I told you I thought you logged in to watch you sleep with other women. It wasn't you though. She told me. She told me she did it. She used your username to log in and she would change the footage. It's why I didn't know you were sleeping with her. She deleted every record of you two together because she knew. She knew I would cut her off if I found out. Which I did. I cut her off months ago, but she showed up last week. Said she needed money, and I told her no. I told her I wanted nothing to do with her after she betrayed me."

Lexa pounded her fist against the door frame. "Don't fucking lie to me!"

"I'm not lying to you, Lexa." Sylvia stepped out of the doorway. "Come inside. You need some ice, and I need to call Simmons."

Lexa stepped away from the house. "I'm not going in there with you."

"Then where are you going to go, Lexa?" Sylvia rolled her eyes again. "Back to Charleigh's? Did she do that to your face, or did she have one of her other trashy friends beat your ass?"

"Like you fucking care where I go." Lexa spat another loogie of blood out. "You don't give a shit about me. You just want to hurt me for defying you. Well, you fucking won."

She stepped back again and threw up her arms. "You fucking won this round. But we're not done."

"We are done," Sylvia stated. "I didn't have anything to do with this because I am done with you. The only thing I can say is at least now you know what it feels like to have your world shattered. To have the world see your life crumble before you even knew it was happening."

With bloody teeth, Lexa curled her lip. "I hope you die alone and fucking miserable, and your worst fucking nightmare comes true. I hope you die, and all your fucking money goes to the sister that ruined our fucking marriage."

"You've lost your goddamn mind, Lexa," Sylvia snapped.

"Have I?" Lexa's wicked laugh echoed off the walls. "Why else would you be in such a rush to get married again? It took me a minute, but it came to me. Because if something happens all this becomes hers. The little girl that tore your fucking family apart because your mother was a cheating whore."

The masc of indifference Sylvia had mastered before Lexa met her cracked. Sylvia licked her fangs, showing the blood-sucking bitch she tried to never let anyone else know existed.

"Well, I am my father's daughter. I guess that's why I married a cheating whore myself."

The door slammed in Lexa's face. Sylvia left her standing on the porch to bleed out with the blow she'd dealt. But Sylvia's truth didn't bother Lexa. She knew she was a cheating whore.

As Lexa made her way back to the car, she pulled the phone out of her pocket. She stopped the audio recording. She'd need it to prove to Charleigh that she didn't make the video. To prove to the woman that she was going to fight for her. Even if it was the last thing she did before she left.

She'd make sure Joey came home. Then Charleigh wouldn't have to live in that house alone. Echo's Tits had said what Charleigh's mom was doing was illegal. She would get a lawyer, and she would make sure Charleigh wouldn't have to curl up on the floor and make wishes on fake stars that never came true.

28

Around the fire pit, Charleigh listened to the depth in which the Greyson girls and son-in-law-to-be were embedded into the child welfare system. She learned the lengths to which they had previously used their connections to who they felt deserving. It hadn't surprised the broken-hearted mother, just reinforced her understanding of how much Dilynn had fucked her over for the past three years.

The intended calming circle was abandoned for a strategy session as all the couples plotted the various avenues of Operation Rescue Joey. Plan A was quickly voted down, and then Plan B, C, and D all posed too many risks according to various players.

The conversations were simultaneously scribed, then cataloged in Charleigh's head as her internal voice shot questions at her about where Lexa went and if she burned Sylvia's house to the ground would the woman still want to marry her? The question about whether Joey would remember her sitting on the driveway before her mother had silenced her cries made her eyes fall from the fire to the ground she wished she was buried within.

As they talked, Charleigh watched the wood disintegrate in the hellish bath. The flames carved away sections at a time until the dried pulp fragmented into ash. Pieces floated into the air around them and choked in the smoke until the last of their energy was suffocated.

Charleigh's throat was raw and sore from screaming, and her eyes felt heavy from the tears she'd managed to hold in. Unwilling to give anyone associated with the Greyson name any more fuel to burn her alive, she sat breathing shallowly on the plastic lawn chair.

She didn't speak to the uninvited guests nor sing to the chords Mona played. She didn't try to convince Mona kidnapping Joey from her after-school program was a bad idea. Mona didn't need her when Landon and Evie had assured Mona, she was too pretty for prison. And Parker had added Mona was not lesbian enough to let loose behind bars, and she would know since Parker spent her teenage years in juvenile detention.

She stared through Parker when the woman probed Charleigh with gentle questions. Each question was aimed at getting Charleigh to verbally acknowledge the ache in her chest so she could process her anger, while Lyra had spent most of the evening texting friends to get Charleigh a new lawyer.

The night ended early with Parker having to go to her second job at the bar and the pregnant duo unable to sustain the late nights like Charleigh was accustomed to with weeks of holding Lexa's hair out of the toilet.

Mona wrapped Charleigh in a tight embrace when she walked the royal family and court to the cars.

"You're not alone," Mona reminded her.

Parker echoed the phrase while she hugged Charleigh next. But when the gravel crunched under their tires as they all pulled away, the truth settled like a biosphere around the house, disassociating it and her from the rest of the world.

Charleigh stepped over the boards that would summon the monsters sleeping under the furniture. She knelt before the couch and pushed up the cushion. She reached through the hole that had been left by the missing spring. The glass bottle rolled away when her fingers grazed it.

The couch fought her for the bottle. The glass base lodged into the space. She considered going after the spare at the top of her closet, but she'd given up enough to others already.

She kneed the couch, the cuts in her skin silently screamed at the impact. But the couch gave up under the assault.

Her body fell backward with the pain relief in hand. A heavy bottle of peach bourbon she'd lifted from Mona's collection before the woman cleaned out their apartment and drove her to weekly AA meetings.

Rexa lay on her bed, big eyes watching as the cap came off and the mouth of the bottle raised to Charleigh's lips.

Charleigh's freckled nose didn't scrunch under the burn. Her throat didn't protest as she allowed more than a shot to run down it.

Her head leaned back against the couch. She twisted the bottle in her hands. It made her think of Danaya. The disappointment she'd hear in the woman's voice when she'd have to tell her Joey never got her shoes. Luckily, she didn't have a phone to talk to the woman. Not after she'd finally fully destroyed the birthday device, throwing it at Lexa when the woman ran away. Maybe Danaya would forget by the time she came back to the car she wouldn't need anymore.

She took another drink and looked at the dog. Rexa had saved her from the loneliness of the house. Gave her a reason to get up each morning and would keep her warm with Lexa now gone.

"It's just you and me, Rexa Pawson," Charleigh told the dog. Taking another drink, she studied the pit bull. "I shoulda given you a better name. You deserved a name better than Lexa fucking Jenson. What do you think? You want a new name?"

Rexa's lips shook when she let out a heavy sigh.

"Yeah. I know, I suck as much as she does." Charleigh stared at the bottle. "Sorry you got stuck with me. You deserve better than being with a piece of shit too stupid to see what was right in front of my fucking dumb face."

Getting up from the floor was easy. The bottle became lighter as she chugged the contents down the hallway. Her fingers dragged along the wall until she reached the broken door. The cracked frame would lose her the deposit, but it didn't matter. It would be repaired like she wasn't even there.

There was nothing to trip on as she went into the room. Nothing to lay on but the floor. The floor knew her though. The only space in the house that didn't talk back. Didn't protest as she cradled the half-empty bottle in her hands. And didn't pull away when the tears and alcohol created a pool against its surface.

The cold air bit at her skin, but the anger warmed her blood. She'd missed the feeling of being warm— the only benefit she could now find of Lexa lying next to her. The pain Sylvia had promised was numbed when the burn of the drink subsided.

Sylvia promised the hurt, and Charleigh ignored her. Ignored the email to rescue her from the woman who had torn her to pieces. Sylvia never would have released the sex tape if she'd left Lexa. If she'd taken Sylvia's offer, she would have hated herself, but Joey would be coming home instead of learning to swallow her tears.

'Why did Sylvia put herself in the video?' a voice in Charleigh's head asked. Her mind replayed the video again. The words were right, but it was all wrong.

Sylvia was a liar. She'd lied to Lexa about the counter and used Charleigh to get the divorce she'd wanted. The promise to get Joey back was also a lie. It had to be a lie because otherwise, she'd never release the video.

'Why was Danaya in the video?' the voice asked next. But Charleigh was too tired to answer another question when she hadn't found an answer to the first.

The bottle rolled from her fingers as the darkness seeped in through her ears and clouded her mind. She curled into a ball as sleep pulled at her senses.

Her body was prodded awake by the dog. She wasn't supposed to sleep in this room. Only Joey was supposed to sleep in it. So, she followed the pup to the bed that smelled like Lexa's honey hair cream.

She held the satin-covered pillow of the traitor who ruined everything she worked for and then ran away like a coward when no one was looking. She cried the tears she'd held back for Lexa's betrayal while she wished on the stars she couldn't see. Then, she prayed to the God who abandoned her like everyone else Joey hadn't been slapped across the face to make the pain real and the tears justified.

29

With nowhere to go, Lexa found herself pulling into another place she wouldn't be welcomed. The parking lot was mostly empty when she put the car in park. She'd been formally trespassed from the premises and there was a good chance she'd find herself back in jail for entering, but she had to start atoning.

She waited until the bar's bouncer dipped inside momentarily, giving Lexa time to slip into Echo's Escape.

Cheers of women didn't welcome her this time and the music didn't beat against her. Her presence went unnoticed by anyone but a server from across the bar who squinted in her direction.

She knew she didn't have time to play ghost, so she searched for Echo behind the bar. Then she looked around the dance floor until she heard the woman's heavy laugh on her right.

Lexa saw Echo before the bar owner saw her. She held up her hands in surrender as she approached the high back table where Echo chatted with a woman pulling at the floral top too formal for the rustic setting.

The goofy smile fell off the bar owner's face when she caught her first glimpse of Lexa. Echo's beer hit the tabletop, and the dark eyes centered on Lexa. The woman rose to her full stature with tattooed biceps flexed as she prepared for a fight.

"I have already had my ass kicked tonight," Lexa stated with her hands still in the air. "I'm not looking to fight you, drink in your bar, or meet anyone."

"Then why the fuck you here?" Echo asked. A crease formed between her eyebrows as she stared at Lexa.

Lexa let her hands fall to her sides. "I did a lot of shitty stuff and a lot of it happened here. I... I just needed to tell you I'm sorry. I know it doesn't make up for hitting you or fucking up your place of business. I know that the money my ex-wife gave you doesn't buy forgiveness either. So, I'm sorry."

She dipped her head and tried to breathe. Her chest still ached with each breath.

"You get your face bashed in by my sister's friend?" Echo asked. When Lexa didn't answer, Echo clarified. "Charleigh. The little blonde that you just went viral for videoing her fucking you and your wife."

Echo scoffed. Her hand waved dismissively at Lexa as she said, "All you rich people are fucked, you know that? Like, why you always gotta tear apart people that don't got shit?"

"Via didn't...." Lexa tried to swallow the shame, but it caught in her throat. "It was edited to hurt Charleigh. Charleigh and I had sex, yes, and Sylvia kissed her. But it wasn't because they were.... She just kissed her to hurt me for hurting her. Because Kayla and I kissed here. I.... This is fucking stupid, and I don't know why I'm telling you, but I just want you to know that we didn't.... She didn't, like, take advantage of Charleigh in how you think. I didn't take advantage of her. I mean, I kinda did but not like that. I took advantage of her kindness and her willingness to be there for me. But I didn't make that video."

She looked around the bar. The barmaids each took extra steps to avoid coming near her.

"I should just go," Lexa said. Not sure where her car would take her next.

"I'm going to let you stay," Echo stated. She walked to the bar and set a bottle of water on the wooden top. "Mainly because I want to know more about what happened."

Lexa took the water in her hand. She hated water because it reminded her, she needed to take her meds. Sylvia's jabs about her being off her meds reminded her she'd fucked up again.

She pulled the pill from her pocket where she'd hidden it earlier that morning. She rolled it between her fingers, then looked at Echo. Licking her lips, she explained for the first time to someone aloud, "I... uh... I have Bipolar Disorder I. This is supposed to help me be stable, but it stops me from feeling a lot of things. Last week, Charleigh.... I messed up her bookcases and I broke a frame of her kid. I got cut while picking up the glass and I couldn't feel the panic, so I stopped taking it."

Echo leaned against the counter and held out her hand. Lexa wasn't sure why, but she dropped the pill in the woman's palm.

"You've been off this all summer?" Echo asked.

Lexa nodded, watching as the pill was studied by the other woman. She opened the bottle of water and took the pill back from Echo. Without thinking about it too much, she took a sip of water and dropped the capsule into her mouth.

"I take Paroxetine for PTSD," Echo offered as Lexa chugged half the bottle. "When I was a kid, there was a lot of violence. I grew up in the system until I graduated from juvie, and I got out. I thought it was all behind me, but then I had kids. And... uh... the secondary trauma just made the nightmares worse. I started seeing someone and... I know what you mean when you say it makes you feel like nothing sometimes."

"When the cocktail is right, it's not as bad," Lexa admitted.

Echo dug in her pocket and slid a card to Lexa. She tapped it into the bar top. "Her name is Dr. Rose. Works with the LGBTQs. You should call her and maybe it will help some."

Lexa picked up the card and studied it. "I didn't think anyone actually named their kid Monica."

"So, do you know who made the video?" Echo asked shoving the hat on her head.

Lexa had cheated in Echo's bar with Kayla. Busted Echo's face up for interfering with Charleigh, but seeing Sylvia's championship hat on the woman reminded her of the jealousy she'd always felt for the soft masc. It was part of why she still wore Sylvia's sweatshirt. She'd had to steal that sweatshirt, while the bar owner was given the hat. She knew Sylvia and Echo had never been more than friends, but Kayla had once told her to watch out for Echo in the beginning of her relationship with Sylvia. That the tattooed woman would always mean something to Sylvia, and the hat was just a reminder of that truth.

Sylvia's half-sister was a snake-like siren though. The type of woman who belonged in that horrific play by Shakespeare Lexa had to stand on stage and act out her twisted monologue.

"Kayla released security footage from my house." Lexa twirled the water bottle cap between her fingers. "I blocked her from everything after I went to do this meet and greet at the school. It was for Charleigh, and it took some time, but I fucking love her. I fell in love with her."

"Why was Via in it? Or Danaya?" Echo asked.

"Via cut her off," Lexa offered. "I think Danaya was targeted because she was why Via left. We'd seen Kayla at a restaurant a few weeks ago. She'd said she would get Charleigh back for stealing her girlfriend and the cunt that stole her sister. I thought she was talking about me... but I think she meant Danaya."

"Kayla was always a twisted bitch," Echo admitted. "Like obsessive. She fixated on my friend and turned a bad situation into the worst. Henry was like a little sister to me, and she'd always had a drug problem. Born addicted to the shit and I could never prove it but the night Henry ODed, she'd said she was going to end things with Kayla."

"I remember that name," Lexa said. "Kayla talked about her when we were in treatment together. She'd said Sylvia forced her to self-commit because she was depressed when her girlfriend died."

A barmaid called out a short order to Echo. The woman moved around the bar, gathering the drinks and sliding them to the woman in the loose-fitted jeans. The lesbian in Lexa couldn't help but notice the way the woman's tits hung out of the strategically sliced shirt.

"Is it, like, a requirement for all your employees to always have their boobs popping out?" Lexa asked.

Echo snorted and shook her head. "I don't have a dress code. Well, closed-toe shoes, but Parker, my sister, breaks that shit all the time with her stripper heels."

She pointed to another member of her staff with close-cropped hair and a fitted t-shirt. "Xio, the hey mama's lesbian over there, pulls in as much as Parker as just a barback. I tried to get Charleigh to come to work for me because, between Princess Parker, Charming Charleigh, and Explicit Xio, I would be able to pack this place better than any NWBA game win."

"Sorry to burst your bubble, but Charleigh goes to AA meetings," Lexa stated. "Plus, she shouldn't have to work two jobs. I'm going to make sure of that."

Lexa took another drink of the water. She watched as Echo casually wiped down glasses and filled drink orders. The woman disappeared into the back kitchen momentarily and sauntered back with a smile on her lips when she looked at Lexa.

"Are you always this forgiving?" Lexa asked.

The song changed while Echo studied the burnt-out strand of Christmas lights around the rafter above Lexa's head. Then she took a sip of her beer.

"I think it's the meds. Like even when I'm mad, I can't be mad." Echo wiped the bar top, even though Lexa couldn't see anything wrong with it. "To be clear, I'm still mad about what happened here. I'm mad I let you come in here so many times and do what you did because I knew you were married. But I always reminded myself I bought this place so people could be who they wanted to be. And if you wanted to be a cheater, then who was I to stop you."

"You almost did that night. When I saw you with Charleigh," Lexa admitted.

Echo licked her lips. "Parker knew her from work. Said that she was quiet and a little awkward but overall, a sweet person. Charleigh had said she needed to dance and then she was going to head home, so when I saw you looking at her, I went and gave her that dance and hoped she'd go home."

"Kayla once told me you were waiting for Via to leave me. Said you loved her, and that she was always flirting with you. So, I... I saw you with Charleigh and wanted to make you pay for flirting with my wife. Ex-wife. We're getting divorced," Lexa admitted. She peeled the wrapper from the bottle. "When you left her on the dance floor, I stepped up to make sure she went home with me. She was dressed like a fan, and I thought this one would choose me. Choose me over you. Told myself I was a big star, and I wouldn't get shown up by you, because Via never flirted with me. But she did with you. I saw it even before Kayla pointed it out. She and you laughed together, and she was always taking pictures with you. Only pictures she took with me were the few times we went to events together."

"I'm married, and I'm not a cheater. That's my fucking wife," Echo growled. She licked her teeth as though the words had left a bad taste in her mouth. Then she looked up. "Sorry, I just found out my suspicions were not just paranoia."

"I'm sorry," Lexa said. And she was, but it felt weird to be sorry when she'd done it to Sylvia.

"Why do you all do it?" Echo's fingers pressed against the bar top until her knuckles turned white. "Do you all even think about the fact that you guys married us? That we, like, blame ourselves when you find some other chick to fuck?"

Lexa smashed the wrapper from the bottle, crushing it into a projectile. She didn't get a chance to answer before the bottle was slapped from her hands across the bar by a seething redhead.

"What the fuck are you doing here?" Parker snapped. Her glare moved immediately to Echo. "She busted your face open. Fucked with Charleigh's heart and fucked up her life. And you just let her back in here?"

Lexa shook her head. She pulled the phone from her pocket and set it on the bar top. Without looking at Parker or Echo, she played the grainy recording of Sylvia's testimony.

"I didn't know about the video." Lexa licked her busted lip, praying Echo's Tits wouldn't force the cut open again.

Parker folded her arms across her chest. Her huge fake boobs protruded from the top of her corset top as her jaw ground.

"I fucking hated that bitch Kayla the moment I saw her," Parker stated. Then she pointed at Echo. "You're still on my shit list."

"What'd I do?" Echo whined.

"I don't know, but I'm mad at you," Parker growled.

Echo rolled her eyes, then wiped the water from the bar. Lexa only caught the, "fucking crazy ass..." of Echo's grumbles before the fiery woman shot her a look robbing Echo of the remainder of her sentence.

The dark eyes narrowed on the woman. She pointed to herself as she countered, "I didn't do shit. You're just mad at me because you're not mad at her anymore and your hellfire has no one to rain on. Why don't you yell at your ex? She's on the patio waiting for you."

The cap to a Heineken popped off, and Echo slid the beer to Parker. "And tell that bitch she'd better pay for her drinks tonight. You come here to work, not buy other bitches' booze."

Parker licked her teeth, turning her angry eyes back to Lexa. "So, what are you doing here?"

Lexa shrugged. She took the new bottle of water that Echo handed her. A plate of crinkle fries was also pushed in front of her. Echo nodded to the plate she'd received from the kitchen. "They taste like shit, but I know you're supposed to eat with Lithium. If you puke in my bar, you're cleaning it up."

The fry squished between Lexa's fingers, and she wasn't sure if the pill or the food would make her more violently ill. Lexa looked up, "You poison them?"

The boom of Echo's laughter reminded Lexa of the nights she and Sylvia had come here. Before there were rumors of her infidelity, they'd come after every game. Sign autographs and dance. Pose for photos so the business would pick up. Lexa glanced around, realizing the bar wasn't even half as busy as she remembered it used to be.

"Poison is for pussies. Way too easy." Echo turned the bottle opener in her hand like it was a knife. "I prefer blood when I murder."

"You don't murder bugs," Parker shot back. She pointed to herself when she met Lexa's gaze. "I on the other hand have murder in my genes. So, tell me what the hell you are doing here?"

Before shoving the soggy fry into her mouth, Lexa explained, "No place to go, and all my stuff is at Charleigh's house, so I just drove and ended up at my ex's house. Then, I drove some more and ended up here."

"She apologized," Echo stated. "And Via cut me a check two weeks ago for the damages."

"We hate her too." Parker huffed out a breath like a pissy bull ready to charge. "You saw the video. Charleigh was fucking terrified when that rich woman had her trapped against that counter. And that kiss. Don't even get me started on how clearly one-sided that was."

"Parker, chill," Echo said. "Whatever is going on, we have minimal information. And we both know that I have spent more time talking to that girl than you have because you're just as antisocial as she is."

Lexa pulled the wrapper off the bottle again. "You told her you guys could fix it."

"Yeah." Parker sat on the stool alongside Lexa. "I don't think she believes us though. I mean, I can't blame her with how much Dilynn fucked with her head all these years."

Echo choked on her beer. "Dilynn. Dilynn Greyson fucked with Charleigh's head. No way. That woman goes out of her way to be nice to everyone. I mean, she gave you a job."

"No, she goes out of her way to make everyone believe she's sweet and she cares so much but there's just so much more." Parker strummed her fingers against the wood before she looked up at Echo. "When Charleigh got sick in the middle of class, I went to check on her as she was leaving but before I even got to the office, I saw Dilynn jump from her car and cuss Charleigh and Alex out because Charleigh got caught in the rain and Alex gave her their jacket. She didn't have shit to say when they loaned me their boots, but she made Charleigh feel like shit until she gave the jacket back to Alex. *And then,* Dilynn screamed at her for showing the kids her tits because her shirt was wet, which was why she was wearing the jacket in the first place."

Parker held up her manicured finger. "And don't even get me started on what happened when Mona came to tell Evie and Landon that she was pregnant. Dilynn ripped into Charleigh and accused her of trying to destroy their family before she even knew who was pregnant. Like, she heard the words I'm pregnant and her face turned into a tomato as Evie charged the door with her fucking gun and Dilynn went ready to bury the body."

"Damn." Echo pushed the hair from her face, then pulled Sylvia's hat back on. "You sure Lyra is worth all this crazy?"

Parker sighed, then rolled her eyes. "I mean, if I can get her to cut the figurative umbilical cord, then yes. The fact that you are going to move into that house down the street honestly is the only hope we have because I am not down for the family commune they are building. I already think it's weird as fuck that Mona even agreed to move in with Evie. Like I lived with that girl in juvie, and she is fucking terrible, and Lyra says she has only gotten worse throughout the years."

Lexa uncapped the water bottle. Her tongue felt like sandpaper again, and her stomach was already starting to twist. She made a mental note to call the doctor tomorrow to schedule an appointment. There wasn't any more weight for her to drop if she was going to function for Melbourne.

"How was she when you left?" Lexa asked Parker. "Charleigh, not whoever else you are talking about."

Parker tapped the bar, then leaned over it. She pulled a bottle of rum from the tray and set it on the counter. Echo set a glass alongside the bottle with ice in it and held the fountain dispenser at the ready.

As the drink was constructed, Parker said, "She was quiet. Like the fight had been officially beaten out of her."

Lexa sipped the water. The Heineken between them called to her until she pushed it back to Echo. "It's like it's talking to me."

Echo moved the beer to the other side of Parker and pointed to it. "Your ex is still waiting on you."

"Fuck her," Parker snapped. "She was there when Lyra and I got back together. She needs to stop coming here every fucking time I'm working. It's bad enough that now I have to see her at the fucking wedding because she's besties with Evie."

"Did Mona stay with Charleigh?" Lexa asked.

Parker took a drink. "No, she went home with Evie and Landon. Apparently, they have all officially moved in together and are setting up house."

Lexa looked at Parker. She raked her tongue over her teeth. "You guys left her alone?"

The stool Lexa had been sitting on screeched against the concrete floor. She pulled her wallet from her pocket, then a twenty-dollar bill from the leather. Slapping it against the bar, she said, "I can't believe you guys left her alone."

Parker stared at Lexa gripping the plastic bottle in her hand. "What am I missing?"

"She's a recovering alcoholic," Lexa spat. "You honestly don't think she doesn't have a bottle hidden in that house for if this happened. Or worse, if what you say is true and she thinks there's no reason left to fight, then what's her fucking point anymore?"

Parker swallowed. She looked at the glass in her hands. "I didn't—"

"I know," Lexa said. "I know you didn't think about it because you aren't actually her friend. You don't even know her."

The door slapped against the frame as Lexa made her way to the car. She didn't turn around when she heard someone chasing after her.

"I asked Lyra to get the ADA on Charleigh's case to switch out for her."

Lexa turned to Parker. The woman looked up at the sky, then at Lexa. "I bribed her is more like it, but that doesn't matter. Charleigh is going to have a real shot when she goes to court in January. Her mother's lawyer has submitted a request to terminate Charleigh's rights. Lyra won't agree to it as the ADA, but Charleigh is going to have to show up and be sober, and..."

"And?" Lexa parroted, tired of waiting for the rest of the sentence.

"You shouldn't be with her in court. You shouldn't be living at the house with her," Parker said. She folded her arms around her body as the skin prickled in the breeze. "Your image is shit, so whatever you do tonight, you need to support her, but tomorrow you need to find a different place to live because she is going to have to show that judge, she can do this and you being there will only raise safety concerns."

A rock kicked easily away from Lexa. She watched it bounce against the asphalt.

"I got a contract in Australia," Lexa confessed. "I'm leaving in a few weeks, and she doesn't know yet so please let me tell her... because... Because she's going to hate me when I tell her, but now I can explain it's so Joey can come home."

Lexa left Parker in the parking lot, driving through the city until the stucco and concrete turned to dark fields of corn. She'd almost missed the brick house; the taillight of the Charger just barely caught her attention.

Rexa didn't greet her as she quietly entered the house. The cushion to the couch was sideways, and Lexa saw the hidey hole in the base. The cap to the booze lay on the coffee table, but Lexa didn't see the bottle.

She found the woman curled around her pillow in the bed they'd shared. Lexa pulled the covers over the thin frame still in her sweats and t-shirt. The smoke of the campfire covered Charleigh's normal scent as Lexa pressed a kiss to the woman's head.

Rexa huffed softly from beside Charleigh. The dog's head leaned against the woman's back, taking up the remaining space on the cheap mattress. Lexa scratched softly behind her ear, and told her, "I'll sleep on the floor."

She pulled the flat pillow that smelled like Charleigh from the head of the bed and curled up alongside the mattress on the floor. Her body blocked the monster's gateway under the box spring, sealing off the entrance to any wishing to terrorize her woman's dreams.

Wrapped in Sylvia's sweatshirt and under Charleigh's pile of worn t-shirts, Lexa allowed the emotionlessness to settle in her body and prayed the violent nausea would hold off until morning. She needed to stay by the bed, so Charleigh didn't wake up alone.

30

The alarm clock's screaming jarred Charleigh from her sleep like an ax to the skull. The splitting sensation made her insides twist. She rolled from the bed trying to get to the toilet, but her feet didn't hit the floor. They stomped on the body lying alongside the bed.

Lexa cried out. Her body twisted, trying to stop the assault that hit her in the hip and the ribs probably bruised from the boot the day before.

With no steady ground, Charleigh's body careened forward. She caught herself on the closet door as her stomach heaved. The alcohol burned as it filled her mouth and tried to force its way past the hand holding her lips closed.

Charleigh ran to the bathroom, not even getting her head in the toilet before she let go because more was coming up. Toilet water and vomit splattered back at her. She retched again, unable to even wipe her face clean.

She hung over the toilet with her legs locked, trying to keep from getting hit again. With eyes watering, Charleigh felt the sweat soaking through the t-shirt on her back. Nothing could stop her body's fight against the alcohol. Her legs shook as another wave hit her.

Lexa's fingers combed the hair from Charleigh's face, holding the sweaty locks back like Charleigh had been doing for her the past several weeks. She tried to wave Lexa away, but her hand returned to the porcelain to hold herself from falling into the bowl as she leaned closer to the toilet.

"Get it all out," Lexa told her softly.

Charleigh's body lurched forward once more. All her strength was used against her will. She puked until there was nothing left in her, and even then, her body tried to vomit some more. She choked on the mucus from the tears beginning to fall, but the quaking eased when she lowered her body to the ground. She rested her face against the seat.

With the alcohol gone, the fuzziness in her head cleared. Her mother's voice ricocheted off the walls of her skull. The woman's voice tells her to rid herself of her sickness. Reminding her of her wickedness as she shoved the liquid into her mouth to cleanse away the filth. Telling her she wasn't good enough for God.

The words tried to escape through the hole the alarm created. She couldn't let them go though. She couldn't let her mother walk away again. She needed to explain the video wasn't what happened. At least not all of it. She needed to hear the voice so that she could get on the right path again. She could commit to being whatever the woman wanted if she wouldn't shut the door in her face again.

Charleigh held her hands to her head and whispered, "Please don't go."

The tap in the shower turned on. Steam quickly filled the room as Lexa promised, "I'm right here. I'm not going anywhere."

The room twisted and what should have been up and down was sideways. Or she was sideways. She wondered if gravity only worked when life didn't suck.

Lexa guided Charleigh up from the seat into her lap. Charleigh's head bobbed; her eyes closed to keep the cabinet from dancing anymore.

The fingers that hadn't deleted the footage pulled the shirt from her chest and the pants from her legs. Stripping her back to the state she'd been in the video. To the state that ruined her chances of getting her daughter back.

The water was still too hot when Lexa guided Charleigh into the shower. But the burning made it better. Moved the pain to the outside where it was tangible. Fixable. Her body's emotional pH slowly began to neutralize.

Lexa kept an arm around Charleigh's waist and stood behind Charleigh as the water washed away the tears, snot, and sweat. The hoodie and jeans scratched against her flushed skin, adding to the discomfort and reminding her of her place in this world.

The blonde leaned her head against the shower wall. The tiles were cool and made the room sway a little less. Her fingers ran along the grout until she turned away from the nozzle to the woman holding her.

The agile fingers brushed the hair out of Charleigh's face again as her arm held the woman against her. Lexa's hands were so strong, but Charleigh didn't think even Lexa could hold her through this.

Everything just felt too heavy. Every molecule in the steam-filled air squeezed her. Her knees threatened to buckle as the weight of her world was too much to hold anymore. Everything was tightening, crushing her as her insides tried to adjust to this newfound pressure.

Charleigh turned to the side quickly, and her stomach spilled another load of bile toward the drain. She wondered if Atlas ever struggled under the weight of the sky as she watched the vomit circle the drain and disappear in the darkness she belonged.

When she leaned back into the tiles, Charleigh asked Lexa the question she'd never gotten an answer to.

"Why?"

Lexa's lip trembled and the lids of her eyes drooped. She shook her head, and her chest waivered slightly.

"I swear, I didn't know," Lexa promised. When her cheeks didn't turn pink, Charleigh knew the woman couldn't be lying. "I went to Via's last night, and I confronted her. I have a recording of it. She didn't know either. She says Kayla did it. She did it to hurt me and Via."

Charleigh felt weaker than she'd ever been before when she saw the scab on the swollen lip. She'd brought Lexa home to help her. To teach her how to float. But instead of helping her, Lexa was holding Charleigh up. Holding her up after she sat on the ground and let Mona beat the shit out of her. Holding her up as the sky fell around them. A self-made apocalypse of stupidity that had both times begun with a bottle of booze.

"Charleigh," Lexa said. "I need you to look at me."

She stared into the rich earthy tones of Lexa's irises. Looked into the depths of umber and hickory, in which she wished to be buried. Charleigh got lost in her eyes, but Lexa's thumb was strong as it stroked her cheek. Pulling Charleigh back to the moment. The moment when the hot water was running out, and the chilled air caused her nipples to scrape against Sylvia's sweatshirt still clinging to Lexa's body.

Her hand dropped from Charleigh's face to her hip. Both hands holding Charleigh grounded. Hands so strong as though she could hold the universe from sucking Charleigh up in the nothingness where she felt like she belonged.

"Charleigh," she whispered. "I need you here with me. I need you to help me fix this."

Charleigh shook her head. She shook it because Lexa couldn't fix anything. She knew she was nothing. She was incapable of being anything more than nothing, and Joey deserved more than nothing. She deserved a mother who would fight for her. Not just give up.

"I can't fix it," Charleigh told her. "I'm not strong enough to fix it."

Lexa shook her head. "No. You're the strongest person I have ever met."

She scooped Charleigh up into her arms. Cradling the aching head against her sopping chest, then she carefully set Charleigh on the bed.

Her skin pebbled from the cold morning air. Lexa picked up a towel from the laundry basket and wrapped it around Charleigh before she pulled her wet clothes off and left momentarily to drop them in the bathtub.

Once Lexa had dressed them both, she held up her phone. "Call into work," she said. "Tell them you're sick."

Charleigh did as she was told, minus the calling part. She sent a text to Alex Trikru with instructions on where to find her emergency sub plans. Then she held the phone out to Lexa.

Lexa shook her head. "That is yours. I gave it to you, and I should have never taken it back. I will pick up a new one today because I have to go somewhere. I'll switch out the SIM cards before I leave."

"I'm sorry I let Mona hit you," Charleigh said. Her fingers twisted the shirt hem. "I was so angry."

Lexa knelt before her. "There are a thousand reasons I deserved the beating your sister gave me. She was right to kick my ass. You were too drunk that night. Emma told me so, and I knew it, but you said you wanted me, and I wanted to make up for the last time. But I know...."

She closed her eyes, and she said, "I watched the video last night. I watched it and I saw your face."

Charleigh swallowed the guilt. She'd never thought Lexa would know she'd stared blankly at the window as Lexa rutted into her too hard. Or know she closed her eyes to keep from crying at Lexa's demeaning taunts. Or know she gritted her teeth to keep from screaming out in pain every time she'd been pulled up by the roots of her hair.

"I never want you to pretend to enjoy sex with me," Lexa confessed. "I want to make you feel good, not like you're a toy. I should have never even asked you to choose between being a whore or a princess. You're not a whore to me, and you asked me so many times not to call you princess."

"I'm sorry," Charleigh whispered. "Just wanted to give you what you wanted. I just wanted you to have everything you wanted, and I thought I could be what you wanted. But I couldn't really and now.... I know you chose me over Sylvia because of Joey, and I can't even give you the family you wanted."

"No," Lexa said. "No, you don't have to be sorry. I'm sorry. I'm sorry that I made you feel like that. Look, I wish I had the courage or the clarity to say this before."

Lexa took a deep breath. She sat back on her heels so for the first time she had to look up at the woman.

"This world that you think I belong in is not mine. It's Via's." Lexa gestured to the walls surrounding them. "I grew up in a house not bigger than this one, wearing dresses like that floral crap you had on yesterday."

She took a deep breath, then looked up at the ceiling. "After my first season in college, I met Kayla in the hospital when I had my first manic episode. I was diagnosed with Bipolar Disorder I, which is basically the worst one because everything is more intense. We were discharged. Well, she was discharged, but I.... I let her convince me I didn't need to be there anymore, and I left with her. That's when she took me to meet Via."

Shaking her head, she continued. "Via knew from the beginning, and she regulated everything I did. I think she did it because she couldn't help Kayla."

Lexa's shoulders shrank inward. Her fingers squeezed her thighs. When she looked up, Charleigh held out her hand for Lexa to hold.

"I fell in love with Via because she was exactly what she told you. She was everything my mother wasn't. My mother looks like you and Via. When she was depressed, she wouldn't look at me, and when she was manic, she tried to fix me. She hated that she couldn't make my hair lay flat, so she fried it with chemicals. She hated that I had shit-colored eyes instead of blue like hers. She said I came out looking burnt instead of lightly toasted, which is why she never had any other children." A tear slid down Lexa's cheek, but she wiped it away before it could fall from her chin. "She hated that I needed glasses, so she broke them every time I forgot to hide them. My feet were too big. I was too tall. Really, she hated everything about me, so I hated everything about me. The crazier she got, the more my father traveled until it was like he wasn't there. And when I came out, he washed his hands of me completely. Said he didn't make no faggot, and my mother must've tricked him. He left her, and then I left her when I went to college."

She chuckled painfully when she added, "I guess that is about ten things you should have known about me before I crashed into your life."

Charleigh opened her mouth but closed it when Lexa squeezed her hand.

"Look, what I am trying to say is, I don't want you trying to change, so you can fit into a world that doesn't even belong to me." She held Charleigh's hand between her own. "I don't want you worrying about shiny pots or fancy kitchens because I have neither of those things. I just want you. I want you the way you are. And I am hoping... I'm hoping you want me."

"What if I can't give you the life you wanted?" Charleigh asked. "What if we can't get Joey back?"

Lexa got up on her knees. She wrapped her arms around Charleigh and promised. "We're going to get her home. There are a lot of things that have to happen first, and I need you to trust me. But I'm going to fix this. I am going to get a lawyer today. That's where I have to go. I have to go see a lawyer so that we can fight. But I'm coming back."

Charleigh nodded. She nodded even though she didn't want Lexa to go. Not wanting to be alone in the house again. The long finger was under Charleigh's chin, and she raised her head once more.

"I will be back," Lexa promised again. "Before I go, though... I need to know where the bottle is."

Charleigh shook her head. It was her safety net. It's what she had to take away the pain when everything was too hard. She'd need it when Lexa decided not to come back. Chose to break another promise, since she'd broken all the others.

Lexa was there though. Lexa was there and not letting her shy away. The creases in the corners of the woman's eyes were soft when she said, "I know why you have it. I get it. But you don't need it. You don't need to keep away the darkness because I'm here. You're not alone. I'm not going to leave you here. We're going to get Joey back, and we are going to leave this place and start over. Wherever you want to go. I'll ask them to trade me. I'll buy out of my contract, and I'll get a job coaching. Whatever you want."

Charleigh's heart hurt that the woman knew the true meaning of loneliness. So, she told her, "I left the bottle on Joey's bedroom floor."

Lexa nodded, and then asked, "And where is the spare?"

Charleigh closed her eyes and swallowed. Swallowed the bile that was threatening to rise again. Rise at the thought Lexa knew so well to ask for the second spot. The second storage of her weapon of self-destruction.

"The basket in my closet. Under Joey's baby clothes, I never got to see her in."

Lexa stroked her face, and her lips met the tip of Charleigh's nose.

"Thank you."

The lip Charleigh had been picking at began to bleed. She sucked it between her teeth. She knew what it was like to never live up to the expectations of a mother who couldn't see herself in her child. A mother who would subject her little girl to anything if it meant she'd fit.

Charleigh licked her lip, and she felt the exhaustion seep into her mind again. The room tilted slightly on its axis as the memories of Grace Marshall's words returned.

"I told you the truth that day at your house." Charleigh's stomach ached once more as her guts twisted. "My mom hates me. She was the person who told me I was nothing. I would always be nothing. A sinner and God hated me. That's why I got in the Greyson Academy van. I wanted to be more than nothing."

"I get it," Lexa said. "Our parents were fucked."

"I'm more than a teenage tragedy," Charleigh whispered more for herself than Lexa.

"And I'm more than a busted ball player," Lexa added. "And we're going to prove to this world that we are more."

She let Lexa hold her. Hold her like she should have been allowed to do last night when everyone else sat around the fire in someone else's arms.

The house didn't creak or groan when Lexa tucked Charleigh back into bed. The floor didn't protest when Lexa got up to retrieve the bottle hidden in the closet.

The drain of the bathroom sink guzzled the liquor. Then the second bottle was dumped down the drain as well.

Charleigh's stomach grumbled but the events of the morning left her exhausted. Sleep overcame her before the front door closed and locked once more.

31

As she waited on the pudgy pimple-faced boy to finish installing the film over the screen on the cheapest iPhone Pro, Lexa stared at the Whole Foods across the street. Her stomach growled, so she added groceries to her list of things to do before heading back across town.

Lexa's finger ran down the to-do list she'd written on the back of a Starbucks napkin. She tore the corner of the napkin through the drive by the long-term AirBnB that would accept her immediate occupancy.

She studied: meet with the lawyer. It should have taken longer to convince Todd Simmons to take Charleigh's case since he was Sylvia's lawyer. She'd expected to have to explain to him the details and why it wouldn't be a conflict of interest, but the phone in his office had rung. His eyes grew at the caller ID, then he waved her toward the door.

"Pay the retainer with Emily at the front desk and I will schedule a meeting with you and Ms. Marshall." Then he'd answered the call, "Yes, ma'am. I will be leaving shortly. The deed has been transferred and..." He waved at Lexa to move faster, so she did.

She tore through meet the lawyer, then tapped the napkin over the last errand on the list: replace the cellphone. She traveled to the store where she'd originally set up her phone plan in North Phoenix, passing by Danaya and Emma's condo. She hadn't heard from them in a week, and she wondered if they knew she'd fucked up again.

The kid handed her the phone, and the email app reminded her of Emma's recipe. The recipe for real Mac and Cheese was in there. She opened the list. The very, very long list of specifics. She wondered if all the different types of cheeses really made a difference, but Emma was always specific. She couldn't mess it up though; she needed Charleigh to eat something that warmed her insides. So, she moved through the list in order, knowing that even the spices would have to be purchased.

Various cheeses sat in rows on the cooler shelves. She searched for Gouda, not even sure what it looked like. Irritation rose in her as she picked up package after package, her glasses too filmy to see out of properly. She almost choked on the price when she finally located the wedge of cheese. Eight dollars seemed a lot for a hunk of moldy cream.

She tossed the pack into the cart alongside the noodles labeled as homemade and the block of overpriced sharp cheddar. She still needed cream, and the total was already running high with the vegetables and meats she'd gotten to stock Charleigh's refrigerator. Even though she wouldn't be living with Charleigh, she was determined to spend as much time with the woman as possible before she left. Needed to make she Charleigh ate enough to stop her bones from trying to rip through her skin.

The phone screen had locked by the time she went back to the list, but the TikTok notification sat begging for her attention. She hadn't bothered to listen to any of the five voicemails Sylvia left her last night or read through her 14 text messages. But Sylvia was live streaming on TikTok.

Lexa knew she must be doing damage control after the world had been led to believe they were sharing women. Lexa placed an earbud into her ear and opened the stream to Sylvia sitting in the yard of their once-shared home.

Sylvia took a sip of water. Her eyes read the comments only visible to her, and she chewed on answers before speaking.

"I had a good season, but I missed my home. Since my contract has ended and I am now a free agent, I decided I wanted to come home. After careful consideration, I decided I would like to enjoy the game in a different capacity. As the new owner of the Phoenix Devils, I look forward to watching the sport grow."

Carts pushed around Lexa as she stared at the screen. Lexa swallowed her new reality of being completely unemployed for the upcoming year. Not with her career now in her robbing ex-wife's hands. The hands she'd promised to ruin last night.

Sylvia's eyes stopped smiling as she answered the next question. "I understand many people are interested in discussing the doctored video recently released. The woman in the clip is a victim of someone taking advantage of a security system meant to protect the people within my home. My legal team is pursuing action against the individual who chose to hack into my security system and throw together clips to tarnish the woman's image. What happened in the video was framed to hurt the woman.

'I understand many have opinions regarding what they saw. Lexa and I are not in a throuple, and we did not have a threesome with the woman in the video." Sylvia's eyes moved over the screen. She glanced up at the camera, and Lexa felt like Sylvia was looking at her. "Lexa and I have filed for a divorce, and it was not the result of the relations she shared with the woman in the video."

Sylvia sighed and shook her head. "If you wish to do anything to support me, then the best thing possible would be to let the video be allowed to fizzle away. Leave the woman in the video alone as anyone could imagine how violated she already feels. This is all I will say on the matter."

Hearts and roses rose up the screen. Sylvia smiled at the camera she was not holding herself. Lexa had no doubt there was an entire PR team present for the simple video.

"I do not have any intention of trading my former wife to a different team or canceling her contract. Lexa is a truly gifted athlete, and she will continue to lead the Devils for the foreseeable future. With Danaya and Emma at her side, I do not doubt bringing home a championship next year. However, if Lexa wishes to pursue a contract with a different team, then I will support her decision."

Sylvia smiled, but it was her media smile. "The loss to Dallas was disappointing, however, I do not wish to dwell in the past. I look forward to Emma Delango and Danaya Tanzon's return next season alongside Lexa."

Lexa breathed out. At least she hadn't been fired or traded. She chewed on her lip, then licked away the blood where the split had broken open once more.

"Yes, I am aware Lexa will be leaving for Australia in a few weeks. My sincerest hope is she will return ready to bring back another championship next summer." Sylvia smiled into the camera once more. "No, she is not leaving because of the video. She has been planning to play overseas like she has done since first being drafted into the NWBA."

Sylvia took another sip of water, then smiled professionally into the camera. "One of the major challenges I hope to tackle first will be regarding compensation. I wish for my players to not have to spend their off-season overseas, so when Emma, Danaya, and Lexa return to the States, we will be renegotiating their contracts to ensure they are provided the rest needed to keep them healthy. I know we have the talent needed to bring home not one, but many titles moving forward."

Her ex-wife was still talking when Lexa closed out of the livestream. She'd ignored Sylvia's messages for a reason, and she was not going to let anything the woman said distract her from finding all the ingredients needed to make Charleigh a dinner she'd love.

Lexa opened the recipe again. As she read the ingredients, she checked the cart to make sure she had each one. With everything accounted for but the heavy cream, she logged into the bank account to check her balance.

If she'd done the math correctly, she should have $1,156. Her stomach churned as she looked over the basket of food. There was no way it would be that much, but when the wheel spun around and around, she worried for the first time in her adult life she'd have to put something back.

A cart pushed up behind her, blocking her in. She gave the brunette a side-eyed glare as the woman barked at the child with her. "Josephine, enough. I just need ten minutes of you not talking to get this done."

The bottom of Lexa's t-shirt was pulled softly. Just enough to tear her eyes from the screen still loading.

"Josephine Marshall, do not touch other people's clothes," the older woman hissed. The child's blonde head was pulled from Lexa's periphery.

Lexa turned from the cooler where the cream awaited her to the large blue eyes staring up at her. She knew those eyes like she knew that name. Grey and blue and beautiful.

The little girl's wrist was clutched by a woman scanning over the various yogurt options. When Joey moved toward Lexa again, the woman jerked the girl back to her side.

"Stop fidgeting," the woman growled.

But the little blonde ringlets bounced as she tugged at the woman's hold on her. She pointed at Lexa. "Gamma, it's her. It's Mommy's favoritest person in the whole wides world! I tolds yous I saws her. I tolds yous it's hers. It's Lek-sa Jenisen."

Joey's little body bobbed up and down as the woman's cold eyes ran up Lexa's overtly gay attire. Lexa's brows cinched in the middle as she stared at the woman's hand on the child. When the fingers released the girl, Lexa felt her skin flush as the fingerprints on the freckled wrist shifted from red to peach.

With a tentative step forward, Joey leaned her head back to look at Lexa. Her lips spread into a giant smile.

Lexa knelt to the child and took the little girl's outstretched hand in her own. She soothed away the evil witch's print on the freckled wrist as she listened to the girl.

"My mommy loves you," Joey said proudly. She continued to hop as she spoke. "She tooks mes to sees you plays the bounceketball. We didn't gets to sees you afterward, but we gots to takes a picture withs the others lady. The ones with yellow hairs like me. Sylveria helds ups so I was so, so bigs, and I gots to touchs the hoops, and Mommy said thats thats lady was verys nice becauses she helpeds her goes tos college."

Lexa's head tilted. Her mind replayed Sylvia's words about taking her chance with the mother. Charleigh had never mentioned meeting Sylvia before, just that she'd gotten a scholarship. But Sylvia had known her as an adult. More than seeing her in the stands. It hit her then. The preseason game: Mother's Day weekend. She'd skipped the event because the trade had just been announced and her plans of being a mother were leaving for Chicago with her wife.

"Josephine, we have--"

Lexa held up her hand, blocking the woman's words from the child. Luckily, Joey didn't care what her grandmother wanted. Her attention was entirely focused on telling Lexa everything about meeting Sylvia.

"Mommy thanked hers for hers schoolership and Sylveria tolds her that's she was prouds of her. She huggeds my mommy ands she tolds mes my mommy's specials and thats I'm goings to go to colleges somedays like mys mommy. Mommy crieds ands said thats Sylveria changeded hers lives and thats she owneds her. She says shes was going to pays Sylveria back somes day big big. The yellow haired ladys was so so nices. She saids I was smarts like my mommy ands thats I was goings to grows up to be prettys like her too. Mommy turned so reds and even redders when she saids mommy was wearings the jerseys with the wrongs name, and Mommy laugheds but she looked like a tomatos. She saids we hads to goes because Gammas woulds be mads thats we was lates and Sylveria was sad for Gamma beings mads."

If Lexa hadn't watched her ex propose to Joey's mother, the jersey name would have been a joke. A joke she'd told hundreds of women as a way to remind them she wasn't Lexa Jenson; she was Lexa Winters.

"She told Sylveria that she was sorrys she was leavings and Sylveria promised she's comes back and theys have plays dates when she gots backs to talks about my mommy's lives after she finished the scoolarships," Joey heaved in a quick breath and kept talking. "Ands. Ands. Ands I tolds her I's gonna play the bounceketball like hers. I tolds her thats I's goings to be likes my mommy's favorite. I's going to be like Lek-sa and I's goings to be numbers 1 and that my mommy wasn't wearings the wrongs name because she was a Jenison lover. And Sylverias saids yous was the best and that I had to practice so she could give me a jersey withs my names someday because shes going to buys the Devils, and I's going to play for Sylveria's Devils."

Lexa smiled at the child who rambled like her mother. Words fell out between giggles and smiles. The fear of fidgeting was lost as she kept talking.

"Ands... ands... Ones days my mommy is goings to takes me to see you plays again. She saids when I'ms bigger I cans go tos thes games, ands I wills brings my balls so you cans sign it. I's sorrys we didn'ts gets to sees you when Sylveria holds me up. You wouldas sees hows goods I am. We waiteds forevers but we couldn'ts waits anymore because we had to takes the trains back. The trains was so much fun, but Gammas was mads because we weres lates because wes was trying to gets you to signs my jerseys. I have a jerseys with a numbers won ons it likes you. Its not a reals reals because thoses costs sooo much moneys but mommy sewed the wons on it and she useds her sparkles and she put Jenisens ons it so I could wears it when we practice. My favoritest color is purples and she makes my jersey purples likes yours but whens we saws you yous was wearing white and not purples. Do you likes purple or whites because I likes the purples but its okays to be different. Mommy says you can likes whatevers you likes and no ones can tells you whens to likes. I don'ts like pinks so I askeds my mommy for purples because yous wears the purples when you goes aways but its okay if you don't likes purple."

The child moved her hand in the air like she was dribbling the ball. Then she passed the imaginary ball to Lexa.

"Sees. I cans do the dribbles and the passes. I so goods at the passes and Mommy said I going to play the bouncesketball."

Lexa passed the imaginary ball back to the child when she took another moment to breathe. Joey pushed the ball up in a fake shot and ended with her wrist flicking in the air.

Then, Joey leaned in close and whispered loudly to Lexa, "Gramma said no bounceketball because she thinks girls can't play the bounceketball. But I do. I do. Mommy said I play the bounceketball when I go live with her but Gamma says I can't see Mommy anymore, but she tells fibs 'cause she says girls can't play bounceketball but you and Sylveria are very pretty girls."

Joey doesn't seem bothered by the fact Lexa still hadn't said a word. She just kept talking and bouncing until she turned to Grace's scowling face.

"Gamma! She's real and I gots to meet her!" Turning back to Lexa, Joey wrapped her arms around Lexa's neck so quickly, it sent Lexa to her butt. The arms around her neck squeezed tightly, as she told Lexa again, "You're my mommy's favorite."

Lexa's voice cracked as she pulled back from the child's embrace and looked into her eyes. "You know, I am pretty sure that you are her favorite. I'm just her second favorite."

The little girl twisted her mouth just like Charleigh did when she was thinking really hard. After she nodded a few times, she said, "She loves you a lot. But she told me... she told me I was her most favorite."

The blonde brow furrowed when she looked back at Grace. Her large blue eyes stared up at the disapproval from the woman. The blonde ringlets fell over the child's face when her chin dropped, and she pulled on the dress covered in tiny pink flowers.

"I's sorry," she whispered. "Wes supposed to follows the rules when wes at the store. Nos running or jumping or hopping. Nos touching anything. And nos talking to strangers or theys steals me away."

Lexa looked up at the woman. Her nails dug into the flesh of her palms as she rose back to her feet. She licked over her teeth and reminded herself not to make a scene. Not in front of the child already afraid she was in trouble.

Grace Marshall straightened her back, but no matter how high she raised her nose to appear above Lexa, she still had to look up at her. She dropped her gaze to Joey, standing motionless next to the cart.

"Go get the string cheese, Josephine," the woman said without a please or a thank you.

As the dressy sandals dragged across the vinyl wooden floor to three coolers down, Grace cleared her throat. "You can tell that woman I already contacted my lawyer," the woman said coldly.

Lexa focused directly between the dead eyes, and smiled, "Funny because I contacted mine as well. He told me some interesting information, like by denying Charleigh's visit, you broke the law. He also said visitation is standard 2 hours a week as a minimum, but Charleigh has only been allowed to see Joey 2 hours every other week. He said he would ensure that all the time you stole away from her is returned. And that's just the start."

The fear widened in Grace's eyes before she could mask it. Taking a step forward, Lexa quietly covered the woman's upturned face with a promise, "Put your hands on Charleigh's daughter again and she won't just get custody, I'll file an assault charge on you."

Grace's knuckles turned white as she clenched the handle of the shopping cart. Her face tried to remain impassive as the little arms threw into the cart a package of string cheese.

Joey pulled herself up on her toes and peered into the basket. She counted the items quietly to herself.

Looking down, Grace told Joey, "Go get your juice boxes, Josephine." The woman pointed down the aisle where both women could see her. Joey nodded silently and walked slowly toward the shelves. She pulled packs of juice boxes out from the shelf and stacked them on the ground.

"You and her are disgusting. No way a judge is going to give abominations like you custody of a child," Grace hissed.

Lexa stood up straighter. Her voice was low because she could hear the six-year-old teetering toward them with three stacks of juice boxes in her arms. "She is kind, smart, and caring. You tried to make her believe she's nothing, but I will spend the rest of my life proving to her you're the liar and the sinner. You know anyone that teaches their child they're worthless doesn't deserve to be a parent."

Joey was back then, so Lexa put on a smile and knelt next to the subdued girl. "Joey, I am so happy I got to meet you. I will make sure your mommy has tickets for you to sit in the front row of our first game next season."

The little girl smiled and looked up at her grandmother, "Gamma! Her knows my mommy's name for me! Her knows my reals name!"

Lexa returned to her cart and walked away before she said anything else. The Lithium had kept her balanced, and she wondered if maybe she was finally starting to regulate.

Pulling the phone out of the child seat, Lexa glanced down at the account that had finally opened. She blinked because it couldn't be correct. But it was. It was the correct bank account number, and it had $101,685 within it.

Lexa scrolled past the new charges she'd made to the transfer notice. The transfer of funds for $95,152. Simmons hadn't charged her card either, which was weird, but it didn't matter. She'd worry about that later.

She stood in the cereal aisle, staring at the balance. Then she stared at the one week's worth of groceries she picked out, contemplating what she could do since she didn't have to worry about the cost of cheese.

32

A semi-circle of sophomores and juniors faced the statement scrawled on the whiteboard: Power comes from others believing you're better than they are. It was the last class of the day, which already meant the energy level was high. The students' conversation grew louder as Charleigh drew lines between the names of the kids on her tracker sheet and put a tally mark for each time they contributed.

She'd managed to pretend she'd not received the notification of Sylvia's live stream after Lexa left her with the cell phone on Monday. Work became her escape as she desperately tried to cling to the last fibers of her sanity. The kids distracted her from thinking of Lexa leaving, while Lexa spent her time and probably her advance from the Australian team to purchase Charleigh's forgiveness, which she hadn't asked for yet. Tuesday, Lexa replaced her couch with guilt money. When she got home Wednesday, a twin bed was set up in the bedroom with all the stars. It at least hid the stained hardwood. And in all the redecorating, Lexa still hadn't bothered to tell Charleigh she was leaving.

She knew it was happening because Lexa's clothes slowly began to disappear from her house until there was just enough for Lexa to change into each morning before Charleigh left for work. So, she went through the days preparing for the familiarity of disappointment when she'd awaken to an empty bed without Lexa there to keep her warm as the nights grew colder.

Kinsley sat through her second class of English for the day to earn the course credit she'd been deficient upon enrollment at the school a year ago. She practically bounced in her seat as she explained, "No, that's not what Machiavelli is saying though. Yeah, he argues for fear being more important, but he is not arguing that fear is the most important."

"Like in *The Hunger Games*," a lanky adolescent human said, pushing the bangs back from their eyes. "Even Snow knows the importance of love. He rules through fear, but at the same point he makes the people love the game and even knows they have to leave the smallest element of hope at the end."

"He's a villain though," Olivia whispered. The hooded fifteen-year-old sat with her eyes glued to the picture she'd been shading in. The small metal case of pencils Charleigh gifted her lay open, allowing her to escape the animated movements from the rest of the class. Unable to hear her well, the kids stared at the girl who'd beat a murder charge.

Kinsley's leg shook a mile a minute. When everyone continued to stare at her friend, she said loudly, "She said he's a villain." Then she countered, "But he didn't realize it at first. I mean it's like that quote about people not realizing they are a villain. Like, they believe what they are doing is for the best for their people."

Kinsley looked to Charleigh for help. "What's that quote again?"

Charleigh laughed lightly as she flipped on the document projector. She searched through some of the quotes they used frequently in her course. When she found the right one, she put it under the camera so everyone could read it again as Charleigh read aloud.

"Jim Butcher wrote in his book Cold Days that 'No one just starts giggling and wearing black and signs up to become a villainous monster. How the hell do you think it happens? It happens to people. Just people. They make questionable choices, for what might be very good reasons. They make choice after choice, and none of them is slaughtering roomfuls of saints, or murdering hundreds of baby seals, or rubber-room irrationality. But it adds up. And then one day they look around and realized that they're so far over the line that they can't remember where it was.'"

Charleigh didn't get the chance to contribute more before Kinsley was out of her seat, pointing to the words illuminated on the wall.

"Like Snow probably doesn't even know where the line is anymore. We got some hacked-up director's version in the film, but Collins never wrote that."

Lamont stood as well and picked up a slim white book. He held it up like a Bible, waving it as though he was delivering a sermon. "I get what you're saying, Kinney, but Machiavelli is telling the prince that the only way to gain respect and retain it is by instilling fear, and fear causes rebellion. That's what Katniss became a representative of. The discontent with fear-based leadership."

Casper was up next to his best friend, "And Rand argued that the fear-based leadership failed as well due to the people who walked away from their jobs because of the fear of government. I mean it won't stop people from breaking laws." He held his tattooed hands up and signaled around to the other students. "Every person in this room felt that rules were pointless. We broke them and our fear-based legal system didn't do anything to fix the problem. They didn't care why we were breaking laws. They just cared that we had consequences."

Kinsley returned to the circle and the boys flopped back down in their seats. Once everyone was quiet, Olivia whispered, "People die, or they just go away. People change to be safe. You choose which monster will take better care of you because no one here has any power. We're just the ones the rest of the world forgot about. So, we just gotta choose who will hurt you the least and do what you can to not get stuck in the middle of their war. Love isn't forever, but fear doesn't go away."

The tiny egg timer blared. Olivia's hands quickly rose to cover her head when Kinsley jumped at the sound. Charleigh sighed, and flipped off the projector, knowing the momentum they'd gained would be lost by tomorrow. Discussion and engagement like this were golden. The type of lesson Dilynn wouldn't have been disappointed in, but bells ringing to interrupt them never failed to ruin the start of a good thing.

The kids grabbed their bags and notebooks as Charleigh reminded them, "Tomorrow, we're talking about the next section so DO NOT FORGET TO READ IT." But most of the teens were gone before she finished her sentence.

"Bye Marshall!" and "Love ya, Marsh!" were called back as the remaining students left for the day.

Kinsley and Olivia were the only students lingering. The older girl whispered something to the younger hidden by her hood. Olivia nodded, then said, "I have a session with Ms. Parker."

"I'll wait for you in the truck," Kinsley promised, then hugged the girl. The embrace wasn't reciprocated, but the younger girl didn't shy away from the contact, which was progress.

Once they were alone, Kinsley moved to help Charleigh gather the work from the baskets she'd be taking home to grade as some other element of her life was replaced. They worked in silence until Charleigh could no longer handle the waves of tension rolling off the teen and smashing against her.

"You okay, runt?" Charleigh asked.

Kinsley pushed herself atop a table, her fingers playing with the tear in her jeans. "Are we sisters?"

Charleigh studied the white strands Kinsley twisted between her fingers. "I mean, if you want that then yes. I heard the meetings with Phyllis and Tamika are going well though, so it's okay if you don't feel that way too."

Kinsley looked up with just her eyes. "So, since you're my sister. I need to talk to you like sister you and not like teacher you."

Her mind raced through the worries cutting between each other. They weaved around one another, slowing the different topics until her mind fixated on the one thing she'd always feared for the girl.

'Please, don't be pregnant.'

"Look I know you love that bitch, but seriously she's no good," Kinsley stated. Her face glowed with a pinkish tint, threatening to break through the layers of contoured foundation. "She's always in trouble and is a cheater and like Olivia said, you gotta choose a leader that is least likely to hurt you. You choose her... you're choosing the villain. There's hundreds of other women out there. Like Olivia's mom, Echo. She's getting a divorce and she's scary but good scary. You should go out with her because she's not a cheater. Olivia said her mom said you were really sweet and cute and so as your sister, I'm telling you, you need to dump the cheating bitch and look for someone else."

Charleigh couldn't figure out how Kinsley even knew about Lexa. They'd stayed at the house. Mona promised not to bring it up to Marcus. Parker also followed up Lyra and Evie were sworn to secrecy, so even Dilynn and Alex wouldn't know.

When Kinsley flipped her phone in her hands, Charleigh's insides turned to mush. The heart in her chest barely seemed to move as the truth filled her with toxic fumes.

"Did you see the video?" Charleigh whispered.

The girl's eyes shot up, and she audibly swallowed nothing. Slowly she nodded, then explained, "Yeah. Your mom was at the house Saturday. She showed Marcus and then started talking about the school. She said she knew he was a liar. That this place wasn't what she was looking for. Said she was going to bring their whole scam down."

'She wouldn't,' Charleigh told herself.

"She was talking about going to the news unless they fired..." Kinsley was still talking but Charleigh didn't hear the actual words.

She couldn't when she knew what was coming. The day's excitement faded too quickly as the foundation below her began to liquefy. She could barely breathe, and she realized the floor of her classroom had become equivalent to the Swamp of Despair. The tiny fibers of herself she'd tied to various places in the room began to snap one at a time, and she only sank deeper.

There was no way out, but she tried to breathe through the panic attack. Gasping as she held back the tears, her system was shocked by the cool hand taking hold of her bicep. It didn't belong to Kinsley because she was looking at the teen's face, red with rage.

Charleigh's hands flew up to halfway block whoever may be trying to hurt her and at the same time pushed them away to give Kinsley a chance to escape. She barely managed to free herself from the touch when she felt the panic fleeing as her rage came charging into the battlefield she was thrust in the middle of.

Without thinking about Lexa's promise her ex had nothing to do with the video, Charleigh's hand collapsed against the right side of Sylvia's face for not deleting the video. She opened her mouth ready to unleash the rage she'd accumulated for the woman's stupid games. But her tongue shook loose all the ammunition she'd loaded on the tip as her head snapped to the side and her face exploded into white pain.

She reached up and touched her right cheek. It stung, but Sylvia's glare stung just as much when she stared down at her with her chest puffed up ready for a brawl.

With teeth gritted, Sylvia hissed, "Are you done?"

Charleigh stared at her, unable to make words. She was pushed to the side, Kinsley's smaller body inches away from Sylvia. Small fists shook before she launched toward the intruder. Her battle cry was fierce, but the first attempted punch was caught. Kinsley cried out as Sylvia wrenched the teen's arm behind her back and shoved her away.

A tear leaked down Charleigh's face, but she pulled the younger girl away when Kinsley rushed to try to hit Sylvia again. Kinsley had been hit enough in her life, so Charleigh put herself in the line of fire and ducked her head to take the next punch Sylvia delivered.

"I'm sorry I hit you," Charleigh said behind her hands held to block the blow she knew was coming. "I don't know what you want but whatever it is, I'll give it to you. I will give it to you if you promise that it's done. That once I pay whatever debt I owe you, you'll stop coming after me. Lexa's leaving. If you want me to cut ties, I will. I swear. Just leave me alone."

Charleigh couldn't stop the tears from falling, and before long she couldn't stop her body from falling either even though the strike never came.

The older woman didn't catch her. She simply reached forward and tapped Charleigh hard enough to send her backward into one of the classroom's armchairs.

Charleigh wiped the tears from her face. Just touching her cheek sent another sharp pain up through her head.

She looked up to find Sylvia taking in the room. Her perfectly proportioned nose turned up at the faded couch across from Charleigh. With a shake of her head, she took a seat on a more appealing desktop.

"I can see why Lexa would love you," Sylvia stated. She waved a tight circle in Charleigh's direction. "We're nothing alike. You are exactly like Dilynn though. I bought her this couch when she first started teaching. Provided the materials and the tools so she could build those pallet bookcases. Took her to the hospital when she drilled through her finger. She was ridiculous because I would have just bought some like I bought most of these books."

Charleigh chewed over the details of the room she'd grown up in. Everything but the posters on the walls and the newer books had come from Dilynn's original classroom. None of it would be able to go with her when she was fired, but maybe that was a good thing. Leaving everything that was a Greyson behind at the same time as Lexa was leaving might be the first step to actually growing up.

It didn't change how scary it was though. Everything she'd thought made up who she was were just things. Props in a play where she read the lines of the part she was cast. She'd been given a script her entire life to follow, and Sylvia was there because she had a new role for Charleigh to play. That much she was sure of.

Sylvia nodded to Kinsley, then asked, "Who's your guard pup?"

Kinsley moved to step between them again, but Charleigh held up her arm and blocked her enough to stop her.

"She's my sister," Charleigh declared. "We have the same foster father."

"You are something else." Sylvia sighed and looked up at the ceiling. "I told her when she was ready to know you, I would find you. Then I saw you when I gave you the scholarship and I knew. I knew, and I assumed she knew too. I mean, it's like deja vu. I had hoped when you got out of this place, you'd never come back. You'd take your kid and start over."

With a shake of her head, Sylvia asked, "After everything you went through here, why come back here?"

Charleigh glanced back at Kinsley. Most of her past hadn't been shared with the kid. She'd kept it locked up from her to ensure the boundaries didn't blur. "Kins, this is not to leave this room."

"You don't owe her shit. She's as bad as that cheating slut," Kinsley snapped.

Charleigh licked her lips, then took a deep breath. The exhale was slow enough to stop the need to cry. She put a cork in the bottle of her emotions, then told the girl, "You don't repeat this to anyone. Not Bastian or Olivia."

Kinsley's eyes fell to the floor when Charleigh turned back to the woman whose house she'd invaded. Whose life she'd disrupted.

"The deal was I would come back and work here after college. Greyson and Trikru promised to take care of Joey if I went to college. They said she would go home with me when I came back and worked for them."

Charleigh licked her lips once more. Her tongue was dry, but her chapped lips were drier.

"They promised me a stable job and enough to provide for us both. It was the only way they agreed to keep her, because otherwise I would have had to leave the school since there's no family housing, and I didn't have anywhere else to go. My mom unadopted me because she found out about the pills and drinking, and the boys. She said she should have expected me to be a whore like the slut who gave birth to me. That's how I found out I was adopted."

Charleigh glanced at Kinsley, finding the girl staring at her. She offered the teen a half smile before she continued.

"I was going to have to go live at a group home, and I probably wouldn't have been able to finish school—" Sylvia let out a heavy sigh, and Charleigh could tell she was growing bored. "Sorry, I thought you wanted the whole story."

"I want to know what happened. I want to know why the kid isn't with you if you did what they said?"

She could feel Kinsley's eyes on her. The stare pricked her skin as she disappointed someone else.

"I didn't show up to sign the guardianship papers because I... I went to find my birth mom, and I couldn't. I couldn't just walk in there and see her. I got really, really drunk, and I didn't want them to know that I fucked up again. My mom... I mean, Grace, well she took them to court, and they didn't stop her because I didn't show up to renew the agreement. I thought for a while that Greyson knew and she didn't fight because she hated me."

Charleigh met Sylvia's gaze. "Are you why she hates me? Is that why she gave me up? Because you didn't want kids?"

Sylvia's brow scrunched, and her eyes scanned over Charleigh's face. Then a slight smile curled up her lips. "You do math as well as she does. I met her when she was seventeen. You would have been two."

"I wasn't adopted until I was three," Charleigh said, staring at Sylvia.

"It was a closed adoption when you were born," Sylvia stated.

"The first family gave me back because they found out they were going to have a real baby. My dad and Grace.... They were round two."

Sylvia stared at Charleigh impassively. It was a mask of indifference Charleigh wished she could have mastered.

"Why was she able to fight for custody if she unadopted you?"

Charleigh's gaze dropped to the floor. She'd once asked her case manager the same thing. A woman who was barely out of college herself. The first case manager she had was competent enough to get promoted quickly.

"She told them she wanted to fix her mistakes. Said that she knew it was important for me to have a relationship with my daughter and she was best suited to ensure that because she raised me." Her eyes rose back to Sylvia. "She said it was her goal to fix our family, and the judge bought it. Said Greyson and Trikru only knew me from the school and didn't have any actual relationship with me. But it all happened because I didn't show up to sign the papers. It was my fault. All of it was my fault."

Sylvia's eyes stared upward, then she pushed a stray hair behind her ear. She looked back at Charleigh. "Have you thought about my offer? Since Lexa is leaving, I mean."

Charleigh didn't know how to respond to the statement, not after the woman had described her relationship with Dilynn. She didn't have a chance to point out how weird it was because Mona rushed into the room.

"Princess, your mom is here with Dilynn and Alex. Marcus just went into the office, and I heard Dilynn yelling a lot of fucks. We need to, like, escape through some fucking pod or something. Like, light speed..." Mona paused, narrowing her eyes at Charleigh's cheek. "What the fuck happened to your face?"

Sylvia stood, pressing the folds from her pants. Mona squinted at her, then looked at Charleigh's face. "Did she fucking hit you?" Mona growled.

Sylvia rolled her eyes but looked back at Mona. Her voice snipped, "Is there someone else that is going to come in or can we get to the part where you are going to do exactly what I say?"

"Fuck that!" Mona protested. "You get the fuck away from her before I liquify your stuck-up ass."

"I know you," Sylvia stated dryly. "You're the science nerd who ruined my Louis Vuitton pumps during my walk-through last year and didn't even apologize." Her gaze shifted to Charleigh. "Is your sister always so violent?"

"I'll show you violent," Mona growled.

With a sigh, Charleigh knew the only way out would be to listen to another one of Sylvia's offers. "Just tell me what you want from me."

"I came to fix this just like I have been fixing shit for Lexa and Dilynn for years." She looked over Mona and Kinsley before turning back to Charleigh. "I have an extensive history with your... employers." Her eyes ran over the room once more. "I plan to use it to our advantage, but I can't do that if you've given up. So, get up. Show me I'm not wrong about you."

Charleigh sat baffled. Sylvia couldn't just expect her to snap to attention. So, she sat in the chair still contemplating if it was better to take Sylvia's offer or to just give up. Giving up, turns out, wasn't an option because Sylvia didn't like to be wrong.

Her body was pulled from the chair when Sylvia's hand locked on her arm. Once her feet were under her, Sylvia shook her slightly as she commanded, "Shoulders back. Dilynn will never believe I allow you to slouch in my presence."

She turned to Mona and Kinsley, demanding, "You two need to leave."

"I'm not going anywhere," Mona snapped. Her hand rested over the small protrusion of her abdomen that had popped out overnight.

"Me either," Kinsley chipped in.

Sylvia looked down at Charleigh. Her voice left no room for argument. "They need to leave."

The front door to the building opened. The house protested the intrusion, but their cries were ignored by the group of people who'd stopped to argue once inside the doorway.

"I'll be fine," Charleigh lied when Mona shook her head, but Kinsley pulled Mona's arm. The girl never had a reason to doubt Charleigh's instructions, so Charleigh nodded to the rear door she'd used regularly to escape.

The back door closed silently as Dilynn's voice bounced off the walls of the hallway. "You do not dictate what is happening at my school and your threats are nothing more than slander that I will gladly take to court. One reporter calls me, and I swear you will spend the rest of your life fighting me, and I'm not Charleigh. I have the money to fight. More money than you can ever dream of having."

Sylvia stood too close to Charleigh to be deemed anything less than intimate. Her breath was minty sweet, and her eyes seemed to be searching Charleigh's very soul. She whispered, "Follow instructions explicitly," as she stared down at Charleigh.

"You better not kiss me again," Charleigh hissed when Sylvia's gaze dropped to her lips. "You had your tongue in my biological mother's birth canal, so that is gross."

Charleigh worried she'd given Sylvia an idea she hadn't previously had when mauve-painted lips pulled up into a slight smirk and the stern eyes crinkled in the corners.

She reached up, taking hold of Charleigh's chin. It was lifted as though to challenge Charleigh immediately or test her obedience.

As the administrative posse entered the classroom, Dilynn's voice froze mid-threat.

"You have nothing to worry about, Princess," Sylvia said loud enough to be heard by everyone. "I will take care of everything. I'll take care of you because you matter to me."

"Sylvia?" Alex asked. Their lips straightened in a thin line. Then, they rubbed the close-cropped hair at the bottom of their neck. "What are you—?"

"Why didn't you call to say you were coming?" Dilynn asked, shifting her gaze back and forth between her former lover and the kid she'd tossed aside. The freckles on her face were more prominent than usual as she stomped into the room, "I didn't see you come in and no one said—"

"I own more than half of this school," Sylvia stated dryly. "I don't need to check in when I come to see it or—"

Dilynn cut her off. "You are a silent part—"

"Dilynn, be a dear and let the grown-ups talk," Sylvia said, looking at Alex. "I thought after all these years you'd finally get control of that. Still sounds like a little bitch, always yapping. And you know I never liked dogs."

Alex stepped in front of Dilynn. The nervous energy of their being had fizzled, replaced with a cold commanding stare. Their fists clenched as Alex demanded, "You will apologize now. Whatever game you think you are playing—"

Sylvia turned back to Charleigh. Her finger ran down Charleigh's cheek as she smiled warmly. "Show Alex what a good girl looks like, Princess, and go get Mr. Simmons from the office. He has the contracts."

Charleigh fought the urge to hit the woman again. Fought even harder to not snap at being called a princess once more. She was going to kick Mona's ass when that baby came out for adding that word to Sylvia's list of things she could refer to her as.

Marcus cleared his throat, "I could... I could go get him." Sweat trickled down his temples as he stood hunched in the doorway.

Sylvia didn't tear her eyes from Charleigh, and she waited to be obeyed. With a shallow swallow, Charleigh agreed to play her new role in this new act.

"Yes, ma'am."

The back of Sylvia's hand stroked the flesh beginning to bruise. "Good girl," she praised before turning back to Alex.

The last thing Charleigh heard on her way down the hallway was Sylvia's boasting. "She's only been mine for three months, and she's so compliant. Polite and obedient, it's absolute bliss. Not to mention it's like a do-over. Action Figure, you never knew Dilynn when she was younger, but Charleigh is her mother, only sweet. So eager to please, like someone had already broken her down so many times she just needed one person to look at her like she was worth fighting for."

Charleigh had never traveled the path to the office so quickly before. The lawyer was already at the door, checking his phone. He barely glanced up when Charleigh asked, "Are you Mr. Simmons?"

"Yes," he grumbled. He tucked the phone into his pocket.

Charleigh pointed toward her building. "I'm supposed to take you to Sylvia."

He nodded and left the office with her. His strides were longer than hers, so Charleigh had to move twice as fast to keep up with him. As he walked, he explained, "Ms. Winters told me to tell you, she's running a give and go. She said it's basketball and you'd know what it meant."

"A give and go? That's, like, she has the ball, and she hands it off and runs out of the play. I fake the shot, but pass back to her without—"

"We don't have enough time to go over the details." He reached into his pocket and pulled out a business card. "Tonight, you are to go straight to Ms. Winter's house in Scottsdale. She said to remind you that it's the house you always dreamed of living in with your daughter. We have paperwork to sign. I will begin submitting motions to the family court on your behalf. Ms. Winters has other matters to discuss with you as well regarding your contract with her."

Charleigh stared at the name on the card as she tried to keep up. Her toe snagged on an invisible pebble, and she stumbled into the man. Mr. Simmons caught her quickly and pulled her back into step with him.

"When we go inside, you must do what she says," he explained.

"Like she says jump, I ask how high?" Charleigh rolled her eyes.

Mr. Simmons stopped just outside the door. "No, you jump. No questions. No back talk. She has to prove you're a better sub than your boss."

'Sub?' Charleigh almost gagged on the silent word.

Her students' conversation came to mind. Sylvia was a Machiavellian. Probably a direct descendant of the man. She made a mental note to ask Sylvia about her family tree one day. Rich people always knew that kind of stuff.

"If you play this right, we will get your daughter home before Christmas," he said with the door handle in his hand. He waited for her to nod, and then he held the door for Charleigh.

When they returned to the room, Charleigh's eyes immediately fell on Marcus. His eye bags hung lower than usual, and his jaw was scruffy from not shaving. He glanced over at her and shook his head.

With a low voice, Marcus said, "Charleigh, we need to talk with you about—"

"Princess, come here," Sylvia commanded.

She'd done a lot of stupid shit in her life. Pretending to be Sylvia's sub to get her kid back, really couldn't even make the top fifty bad decisions. Hell, committing to be Sylvia's sub wouldn't even make the list, which is probably in the contract.

'If I do what she says, Joey comes home,' Charleigh reminded herself.

She walked across the room with her eyes fixed on Sylvia's face. She stood beside the woman, and an arm came to rest over her shoulders. She took a deep breath, tasting the rich perfume that smelled like Lexa's sweatshirt. It felt weird that she already associated the scent with safety. Maybe Lexa was only in her life to prepare her for her new reality. She was Sylvia's now. Like Lexa promised to make her hers, but she'd lied, again. Danaya said Sylvia didn't lie though.

Charleigh wouldn't let her mind wander down the rabbit hole of what this day would cost her. It wasn't like she had any dignity left, so whatever fee Sylvia demanded, she would pay, even if it meant becoming Sylvia's pet. Joey had to be more important than anything else. Sylvia at least treated Joey kindly. Told her kind things about Charleigh, even though they weren't true.

"As I was saying, I am back from Chicago, and it's time we revamp this place. Charleigh and I were discussing the lack of athletic facilities for the students, and I feel we should break ground in November. We should discuss—"

"Why do you have your lesbian hand on my daughter?" Charleigh's eyes shot up. Grace Marshall's mouth shifted, grinding her teeth. "You were that pervert in the video. You and that other woman. The colored one."

Sylvia sighed loudly. She ran her eyes over Grace's ill-fitting dress. Unamused with the interruption, Sylvia snipped, "Who are you and why are you speaking?"

"I'm Grace Marshall, and that," Grace pointed at Charleigh, "is my daughter."

With a slight tilt to her head, Sylvia narrowed her eyes at Grace. She licked her teeth before she said, "You signed away your rights to Charleigh when she needed her mother. You unadopted her. Said horrific things to her. So, let's just be clear, she's not your anything."

Sylvia's gaze shifted to Dilynn, "And she's not yours either. I told you to come to me when you were ready to find her. You didn't. She's mine now. And you broke your word to her and me, which has consequences."

Turning back to Grace, Sylvia stated, "You need to leave since you have no reason to be on my property."

Charleigh's chin dropped to her chest. The blonde waves fell around her face, and she counted to six. One memory from each of Joey's years on earth.

Alex stepped into Sylvia's space. "This is not how this is done," they stated. "You do not... You can't just... She's a child."

Sylvia's grip on Charleigh tightened. She clicked her tongue, then said, "She's an adult. Older than Dilynn was, and I am not here to debate mine and Charleigh's relationship with you. I am here to talk about the school because it's important to Charleigh."

Marcus cleared his throat. "Actually, we are here to talk about the video. The video of Charleigh and your... well, you too... because she was... because of the sexual nature of the video."

He wiped the sweat from his temple with a handkerchief. "The video is detrimental to Charleigh's credibility with her students, and it was brought to the school board's attention."

Sylvia stared into Alex's eyes. "It is troubling when videos of sexual acts become public. After all, we all know how violating viral videos of intimate acts can be for a person. Or people. I would think that whoever released this video had a direct intent of causing Charleigh harm. Someone who has a grudge against her. As someone with shared interests in protecting Charleigh, I would think you'd be trying to defend Charleigh rather than shun her."

Charleigh understood why Lexa was so upset with Sylvia talking about her like she wasn't in the room. Situated under Sylvia's arm with her name falling repeatedly from Sylvia's lips made her feel like a dog beaten into submission.

"The nature of the video in the heated political climate could threaten our ability to provide the safe environment our students need," Dilynn stated from behind Alex. "You and Charleigh both know we provide rehabilitation services to youth who are questioning their sexuality and have made mistakes. Because keeping *all* students safe and the reputation of the school as a place where parents can ensure their students are not being influenced by sinful thoughts, the board voted to dismiss Charleigh. We have no choice but to terminate her contract immediately. I am trying to..."

Dilynn's words crushed the space in the room like a beer can. Humiliation folded every cell in Charleigh's body while acidic blood burned through her circulatory system. She felt like she was burning from the inside out, but Sylvia was next to her. The long arm kept Charleigh in place as the room faded in and out of clarity.

"Well, I had been worried about that. I thought that you would have fought for her, but I guess fighting for her was something you two gave up on a long time ago," Sylvia said. "I thought when we built this school, we had shared values. I was wrong."

"Our values have always been centered on helping our students live a true life. Sylvia, you know that being in a same-sex relationship is not something we can support here. That is not why parents send their children here."

Sylvia pulled Charleigh into a tight embrace. She pressed her lips to Charleigh's head. "I know you're disappointed, honey. Don't worry."

Charleigh leaned back and looked at Sylvia. The eyes staring back at her weren't cold, they pulled her into the clear water that didn't try to drown her. They didn't dilate in desire but kept steady.

"I'll build you a new school if that's what you want," Sylvia promised. "You deserved better than this. Better than bullies and broken promises. Plus, now we can pretend she doesn't exist, like she did to you for far too long."

Sylvia released Charleigh and held her hand out to Mr. Simmons. She didn't blink when his briefcase slapped against the desktop. The clasps snapped open loudly, and then the papers shifting broke up the silence. Mr. Simmons handed Sylvia a thick stack of papers.

As she handed them to Alex, she said, "As the majority owner of the property, I will be placing the land owned by the Winters Trust up for sale next week. Here is a copy of the listing. As you know, this area is prime for residential development, so I expect to select a buyer by the end of the month."

Sylvia's thumb ran over Charleigh's lower lip. "Princess, I know you're sad, but I promise I'll make it all better. I'll destroy every single one of them for making you believe you did anything wrong because we all know whose fault this is. Gather your things and meet me at home. Mr. Simmons has information regarding our custody hearing, and I need you to choose the paint color for Joey's room. I want it ready when she comes home."

Her hand was on Charleigh's chin once more, and she winked at her. Then she pressed a gentle kiss to Charleigh's lips. Charleigh let Sylvia's lips part her own and kiss her in earnest. Squashing any doubts the others may have had that she belonged to the scariest person in the room; the one with all the power.

As quickly as Sylvia came, she was gone with Mr. Simmons at her heels. Not bothering to say farewells to Alex or Dilynn. However, she didn't need to.

Alex stood straighter. The papers crinkled in their fist. Their body whipped around to their wife, and they sent the papers flying toward her.

"Are you willing to lose everything we built? Everything we've done," they snapped.

Dilynn had found a seat on the ancient couch. She flipped through the real estate documents as she said, "I don't understand."

Grace stood straighter; her arms crossed her chest. Without saying goodbye to her daughter, she stomped from the room. The door slapped behind her.

Charleigh looked around the room. There was so much stuff, and she only had one box. Picking it up, she started to put stuff on her desk in the box. She stopped at the photo of her and Mona, holding it in her hands.

"I know that all of you hate me." She glanced back at the three adults she'd once thought cared more than anyone. "I know I disappointed you over and over again, but I don't want this place to go away. This place is special. I will talk her out of selling. Maybe then, you'll finally forgive me."

Dilynn closed her eyes and breathed in as the building settled. She looked at Charleigh, then said, "I knew I saw her car here before you got the Charger. Why didn't you tell me you were seeing Sylvia?"

"You told me I wasn't allowed to date anyone," Charleigh reminded her. It was the truth, but the lies that came about Sylvia to her tongue slid off easily afterward. "I thought if you didn't know, you'd go with me to court like you promised. I didn't want her to do the legal stuff because... because I wanted to show her, I was capable of being good enough for her. I... I also thought you would want to see your granddaughter more than you could hate me for being born. But that wasn't ever going happen, and I was going to leave at the end of the year anyways to make it so you didn't have to see me ever again."

Alex studied Charleigh closely. With narrowed eyes, they said, "Sylvia's ex-wife and you were having sex in that video."

Charleigh couldn't look at them when she twisted another tale. "We met after a game. Marcus and Mona get me season passes for Christmas each year, and I met them when my car was having trouble in the parking lot. Lexa and Sylvia were together, but they had an arrangement. Lexa decided to leave Sylvia though, and I... I enjoyed being with Sylvia. She is nice to me. She checked in on me when she was in Chicago, and when she came back, she said she wanted more. No one has ever wanted me, so it made sense. We just make sense."

Marcus looked at the ground, "Look Charleigh, I'm sorry. Maybe you could come to family dinner tonight and we could talk about all of this. Your mother was here, and the plan wasn't to go this far. Your contract is terminated, but it was just to buy some time to deflect her attention. So, we could keep pretending to be a conversion camp." He wiped his brow. "I got some savings put away so I can keep you afloat until—"

"I appreciate the offer and all, but I know you never really wanted to be responsible for me. So, it's all good honestly. I'm Sylvia's Princess now. You and Mona won't have to clean up my messes anymore," Charleigh said, cutting him off. "Sylvia told me to come home, so I have to go. She'll be upset if I disobey her."

Wiping the sweat from his forehead, he nodded. "Oh... well, no matter what, just know you can come home if you want to."

"It never really was my home though, you know?" Charleigh told the box as she placed the photo of her and Mona within. "I get why you took me in, and I hope you know that you probably saved my life because she was going to kill me. Between the ipecac she gave me to vomit the sin out to the search for someplace she was trying to send me to get, like, electroshock therapy, I wouldn't have made it. All of you saved me with this place. But it's time I stop pretending I belong here. I really shouldn't have come back when Joey was already with my mo—Grace. You all got your kids and your lives, and I'm going to stop messing that up for you. Going to stop being the reason you get pissed off whenever you come in here because this is your life. I shouldn't have tried to pretend to be you."

She glanced over to find Dilynn's eyes staring at her. For once the woman wasn't angry when looking at her.

"I'll send you photos if Sylvia is okay with it. I'll ask her about letting Joey visit with you." Charleigh licked her lips. "It might take me some time, but I'll get her to understand you love her. She'll understand, I'm sure because she loves you. She has never said anything but good things about you."

"You'll always be family, Charleigh," Marcus promised. "I know I'll never be your dad. But I will always think of you as my daughter, so whatever happens between you and Ms. Winters... I would like to be in your life. If you two get married, you know, I want to be there."

"You should tell Mona that," Charleigh said, not looking at the man. "She was the one you said you were going to adopt, not me."

Alex's fists squeezed until the blood drained from their fingers. They looked at Charleigh with the same rage they'd had for Landon.

"I won't fight it," Charleigh said, turning back to Dilynn. She looked around the room she'd grown up in. "I know you never really wanted me to come back. And I embarrassed you over and over again like Mona said. I hope you know I never meant to end up like this. I thought... I thought I could actually make you proud, so I'm sorry I let you down."

Dilynn looked up at Charleigh. Her eyes ran over Charleigh's face and zeroed in on the bruise on her cheek. She got up immediately, reaching out toward the younger woman.

The fingers ran carefully over the bruise, and Charleigh couldn't stop herself from leaning into the warm hand cupping her cheek. She closed her eyes, inhaling the scent of Dilynn's perfume. She'd searched for years but was never able to locate its match. So, she breathed in as much of it as possible, knowing this was the last time she'd ever see the woman again.

"Did she hit you?" Dilynn asked so quietly, pulling away.

Charleigh's fingers grazed the sensitive flesh, realizing she too hadn't come out of this unscathed. Sylvia won this battle with fear. A battle that would steal her friends' and family's jobs and Kinsley's education. And even though Dilynn hated her, the ice queen wasn't President Snow. She took care of everyone else, and maybe, Charleigh could finally prove she was worthy of Dilynn's care and love.

"I definitely deserved it," she told the tearful eyes looking back at her. "But you don't deserve to lose your school over my mistakes, so I'll do what she wants, and I'll get her to understand that you had to fire me."

33

Dinner was ready over a half hour ago. The lasagna's cheese had solidified into a shell as Lexa paced the living room, waiting for Charleigh. The stain on the floor was wearing away as she walked five steps to the recliner and five steps back to the bookcase. Lexa had called five times between her twenty-two text messages.

Charleigh was always late coming home from work, but never this late. Her freak-out meter was at a ten as her mind ran through the various scenarios. Ones featuring the Charger stuck in a ditch, under a truck, or on fire. She'd briefly gone outside to check the sky for smoke. When she found none, her imagination returned to Charleigh being hurt and alone somewhere.

The vanilla pumpkin Scentsy cubes, she'd picked up at Target to make the house smell homey, were suffocating her. The oven had made the inside also too warm, and her mouth was too dry because she'd taken her meds.

She'd done what everyone said needed to happen. Taken her meds on time, and she was still at a ten.

A ten felt like the walls were caving in on her because Charleigh was the one who held the walls up, not Lexa. She needed her to come home, so Lexa could start talking about their future. She could tell her she got her money back and that she'd seen Joey. They would call Simmons together since the bald penis hadn't gotten back to her yet. If Sylvia had pitched a fit about him representing Charleigh, then they would call someone else. They would fight for their future family. The future that was non-existent if Charleigh didn't exist anymore.

With shaking hands, Lexa kept repeating, "She's just late."

When a car drove by and didn't pull into the driveway, she slid down the wall to the floor. Clutching the roots of her hair, she tried to take a deep breath.

"She's just late and her phone died."

Her head hit the wall with a thud!

"She'll be home any minute and will freak out if you are losing control."

She let go of her head. There was no need to hold her head because that was a solid sign she was losing control. Charleigh would think she'd not taken her meds.

Her fingers clenched as her nails dug into her palm. It hurt just enough for her to know she was human, but the pain was nothing compared to the emptiness that would be there if something happened to Charleigh. She clenched her eyes as hard as she clenched her hands.

She started counting back from ten to calm herself down. She promised herself to be in the chair when she got to five.

'10... I am just PMSing, and Charleigh has made this drive countless times before.'

'9... Nothing has happened to her. I am panicking because I am afraid.'

'8... I am afraid of being alone, and I fixated my fears on losing her.'

'7... She is becoming my new Sylvia, and I am giving her too much.'

'6... Charleigh loves you, she said so. Don't ruin what you built.'

'5... You can't lose yourself again. You can't depend on her.'

'4... You made it to five so get up and move your ass over.'

'3... Don't get power-hungry. You will ruin everything.'

She didn't make it to two, because gravel crunched in the front of the house.

Lexa pushed up from the floor. Hands wiped at her face. She slapped her cheeks to make sure she had color. Put a smile on because she can't show the woman she was freaking out.

She moved to the door and threw it open, but the car was wrong. It's not the little blonde of sunshine she depended on getting out of the car. It was the redhead with giant tits who belonged to the bar owner. Echo was there too though, pushing her hat on her head and taking Parker's hand.

Lexa looked over them toward the minivan that had given her false hope. She scanned the street for another set of headlights, but the road was dark and soundless.

"Lexa," Echo said calmly. "Can we come inside?"

"Where's Charleigh?" Lexa asked Parker. She'd know where she was. They worked together. She had to know why Charleigh was at the school so late. "She never charges her phone. She... she probably forgot she had a meeting. She had a meeting, right? Did that bitch Dilynn yell at her again? I swear, I am going to file a lawsuit against that woman."

"Lexa, Charleigh got fired today," Parker said. "Her sister Kinsley said your ex-wife came to the school—"

Lexa didn't wait for Parker to finish her sentence. She left the door open and went in search of her keys. She'd set them on the kitchen table. Or she thought she had. She looked at the counter, cleared away from all the dinner mess.

"Where the fuck are they?" she asked herself.

Echo stood in the living room, her head on a swivel taking in the room that said so much about the woman who lived there. Parker blocked the kitchen door, so Lexa couldn't continue her search.

"Hey Lexa, we need to talk to you," Parker said.

"I need to find my keys. If she got fired, I need to tell her it's okay. I need to tell her I got a job, and I will take care of her," Lexa said, turning from the redhead. She searched the kitchen again. Opened the pantry and then the refrigerator to see if she'd put them there by accident. "I was going to tell her. I was going to tell her I had to go but I would be back. But now she can go with me. I'll take her with me to Melbourne and we will be fine. It will all be fine. We'll get Joey and she can go to school there."

"Charleigh isn't at the school. She finished packing up her stuff an hour ago. She's with Mona," Parker explained.

Lexa spun around. She nodded so the woman saw she heard her. Her fingers pulled at a tight twist, as she thought about the fact Charleigh hadn't come home. She probably thought Lexa would be mad. Always so worried about disappointing everyone.

"Mona will make sure she doesn't get drunk," she said to herself. She nodded once more, glancing at the ruined food. "Yeah. That's good. She can't drink because she has to stay sober for court."

She grabbed the aluminum foil she'd used to cover the lasagna while it was in the oven. It would heat up well if she didn't leave it on the stove too long. It would be fine, and Charleigh and she could eat it after the blonde was done crying.

"Where did they go?" Lexa grimaced as a new thought crept up her spine. She turned to Parker. "She didn't go to beg her boss, did she? Because she doesn't need that stupid job. I can support her. I got a job. I just hadn't told her yet, but since she doesn't have to work there. We can get Joey, and I can take them with me to Australia. I can take care of them there."

Parker glanced at Echo as Lexa returned to her search. She checked in the sink, and then inside the cabinets for her keys. They had to be somewhere.

"Just tell her," Echo said. Her hand pushed the overgrown bangs from her face, and she put the hat back on her head once more.

Lexa froze. Her hands pressed to the countertop. "Tell me what?"

The floor under Parker creaked as she shifted her weight from side to side. "Charleigh didn't go to beg for her job back. She is on her way to your ex's house."

The five-layer lasagna no longer looked appetizing. The marinara sauce had dried at the edges and the noodles drooped in the casserole dish for two. Charleigh had never had real lasagna before, so Lexa found a recipe to surprise her. Surprise her with the tickets for her Winter Break to come to Australia and see her play. One for her and one for Joey, so Charleigh would know when she told her. Charleigh would know that her going was temporary and they would spend Christmas together.

But it turned out Lexa was the temporary one. She should have seen it coming. Should have known Sylvia would be the one Charleigh would choose. She could give Charleigh everything she'd never had. Stability and devotion. Charleigh would never have to question if Sylvia was devoted to her, but she would always question Lexa. Lexa and her chaos.

"Lexa, did you hear me?"

Lexa scraped her tongue over her teeth. She'd forgotten two of the waters on her schedule and her throat was raw.

"Why?" she whispered. She closed her eyes, so she didn't mishear.

"Kinsley said she had to sign a contract with Sylvia. Said Sylvia came and she threatened to close down the school, so Charleigh had to give Sylvia what she wanted so that Sylvia wouldn't sell the school," Parker explained.

Parker's fingers carded through her hair, pushing it out of her face.

"Look, I don't know what happened because I was in a session with a student, but my boss, Alex, came in fuming. And they are, like, the calmest person ever. But they were asking me questions. A lot of questions about Charleigh and if I knew who she was dating. But before I could answer them, they said Charleigh said that she'd been with Sylvia all summer. They didn't believe her, though. They said she wouldn't look at them when she told them she was in a relationship with Sylvia, and they weren't buying she would have a threesome with you and Sylvia."

Lexa licked her lips, but her sandpaper tongue did nothing to soothe the cracks splitting open. She asked, "What did you tell them?"

"I didn't want to tell them that Charleigh had lied to them, so I just said I didn't know anything about who Charleigh was seeing." Parker let out a heavy sigh. "Which, I mean, I don't really know what is going on because I didn't even know she was seeing you to begin with. And with your ex just showing up and claiming Charleigh publicly, like I don't know if they are a thing or not a thing, or if you and she and Sylvia have some three-way relationship like Mona and her people. I met them a few weeks ago and you twice in less."

Lexa looked at the crack in the ceiling. The lightning bolt ran across the plaster. She couldn't be sure, but she felt like it was growing as she stared at it. She pressed her fingers into the chipped laminate countertop, trying to feel the house coming apart. The house Charleigh would be forced to leave if she took Sylvia's offer. Because Sylvia rode to her rescue, while Lexa played the dutiful housewife.

The fog in her head thinned momentarily to show the forest of lies surrounding the two blondes in her life. Was it all just a game to get back at her? Phyllis had sent Lexa to the school after the bar. Phyllis was Sylvia's agent too. Sylvia had known it was Charleigh, she knew Charleigh. They'd met before, and Charleigh had never said anything about it.

But the window closed, and Lexa knew it couldn't be real. Sylvia wasn't a villain. She'd never been a villain, and Charleigh didn't stand up to anyone. Ever.

But she'd lost her job and her visitation. Lexa had told her she was going to fix it, but what if Charleigh didn't believe her? The woman had no reason to believe her, and Sylvia had come in to save her. Come in and propose to her again, and...

"Did Sylvia tell Charleigh I was going overseas?" Lexa asked.

Parker sighed once more. "No, but she already knew."

Lexa turned to Parker. Her nails found the same trenches in her palms she'd spent the last half hour digging. Lexa bellowed, "You fucking told me you wouldn't tell her!"

Echo stepped toward Parker. She placed a hand on the smaller woman's shoulder, and Lexa knew now why Echo was there. Parker was scared of her. And she should be.

"How fucking dare you," Lexa growled. "You said you wouldn't tell her, and then you told her the first chance you got. You're no better than the rest of that fucked up family you're trying to sleep your way into. That's why you brought your bodyguard? So, she'll keep me from kicking your ass for trying to ruin my relationship?"

Parker narrowed her eyes on Lexa. Her chin rose as her shoulders straightened. She held up a single finger as she spoke, "If you think I'm going to stand here and let you talk to me like that, you have another thing coming to you. Because I didn't bring a bodyguard. I brought someone to keep my demon ass from murdering you. I came here so that you can get your shit together before you do something stupid and hurt yourself or her."

The teeth in her mouth ached, but Lexa couldn't stop from grinding them. She checked her volume, as she said, "Then who the fuck told her because I only fucking told you. I told you in a dark parking lot where no one else was."

The eye roll made Lexa feel like she'd missed something. But Parker's face hid none of her emotion as she stared at Lexa like a moron. When Lexa didn't read Parker's face, the words hit her in the chest.

"She saw it on fucking TikTok with the rest of the world when your ex announced she'd bought the team. Charleigh came in to see me on Tuesday about a job at Echo's. Talking about how you'd said you were going to get a lawyer for her, but you were leaving so she needed a job to get one herself.

Something about taking your ex's sister to court for defamation and then getting her kid back."

Parker took a deep breath. "Apparently though, your ex showed up today with a lawyer, threatened to close the school, and made my bosses think she basically owns Charleigh. Oh, and beats the shit out of her because somehow between lunch and getting fired, your girl ended up with a black eye."

"Who the fuck hit her?" Lexa growled.

"Your fucking crazy ass ex-wife," Parker snapped.

Lexa looked at the counters again, then realized she hadn't checked the living room. She moved through the door and passed the fiery therapist toward the keys on the coffee table. She growled to herself, "I'm gonna kill her."

Echo stepped in Lexa's way with a hand up. "Hey, Lex... I'm going to need you to take a breath."

"Take a breath?" Lexa's eyes centered on Echo's eyebrows. "Via gave her a black eye and you want me to take a breath? I know you've always been in love with her, but you have got to be shitting me right now. You clocked me and had me arrested for holding her against a railing and now you want me to breathe when Charleigh is walking into Via's fucking lair?"

Echo licked her lips. "You were trying to rape her in my bar. Parker left out the part where Kinsley told us Charleigh hit Sylvia first. Like no words, turned around, and BAM! So, how about you take a breath, and think about what Sylvia wants from Charleigh that would require a contract? If you know that before you get there, you can prepare to talk her out of signing it or you can prepare to support her."

"You were there?" Lexa asked. "At the school?"

"My kid goes to that school," Echo said. She nodded to Parker. "She sees Parker for therapy. I went to pick her up, so I was there when Kinsley came in to tell us what happened."

Lexa pulled at the root of her twists. The twists Charleigh had learned how to do from a three-minute YouTube tutorial on Monday when Lexa had brought her a comb and asked her for help. Her body had been relaxed then, sitting on the floor as Charleigh broke in the new couch. Her nimble fingers carefully detangled the dreads Lexa couldn't get to on her own and soothed her scalp with oil. Being extra careful to not tear a brush through it. Charleigh had known that Lexa was leaving. She could have hurt her, but she didn't.

"She said if I hurt Charleigh she was going to marry her. She would marry her, so I had no one left to help keep me sane."

Her eyes fell along with her hands. Her mind was unable to keep up with the ideas peeking out through the fog and dipping back into the haze. She hit herself in the head, trying to shake them free from the haze. "Stupid fucking meds. I can't fucking think right."

Echo's hand stopped a second blow from making contact with Lexa's skull. "Lex, let's sit down for a minute. Charleigh is a smart girl. She wouldn't just go there and get married. She can't. Your divorce isn't even finalized yet, is it?"

Lexa looked at the warm chocolate eyes looking back at her. The woman's brows rose, and her mouth twisted, because they both knew the answer since they were both in the middle of a divorce.

"No."

"Okay, so let's just sit down and catch our breath. You can't go there to start a war. Charleigh is.... She's going through some really tough shit and we both know Via. She isn't going to hurt Charleigh for something you did, and she isn't going to force her into anything she doesn't want to do."

"What if she thinks this is the only way to fix things?" Lexa asked.

Parker smiled softly and led Lexa by the hand to the couch that didn't have Charleigh's butt print on it. Another part of Charleigh she'd changed without asking. But she had to get rid of the hiding space while she was away.

"Mona is with her. And if there is anyone in this world that cares about Charleigh more than you, it's Mona."

Lexa's voice cracked when she asked, "Why did she go?"

"To save the school. To save mine and Mona's job. Her dad Marcus's job. To save her sister's future. She's not going to hurt you; she's going to keep everyone else from getting hurt. So, let's take a minute, and then Echo and I are going to go with you to be by her side because she is not alone. And we'll show her that even if you are in Australia, she'll still not be alone."

"Plus, I got to get her to agree to come work for me," Echo said with a shrug. "She's going to need a job if you all are going to court to fight for rights."

34

The size of the room hadn't changed since the last time Charleigh stood alongside the breakfast counter, but she felt smaller in the space now dramatically changed. The room was now fit for a family. A space where her daughter could be a kid, instead of worrying about Joey breaking one of the glass sculptures, which had been removed.

When they'd followed Sylvia within, Charleigh couldn't keep from running her finger over the soft cream couch. The stiff leather with cold metal legs had been replaced with a sectional whose cushions looked as though they could give her the hug she was in desperate need of. Sitting atop the couch were throw pillows for every color in the rainbow surrounding one that said, 'Family.' Grey walls had been repainted to a warm blue and the artwork of seductively posed female bodies had been removed. Frames awaiting family photos strategically lined the base of the walls, and it was clear Sylvia was renovating every aspect of her life now Lexa was no longer her wife. Those were the least shocking changes Sylvia had made to the house over the last few weeks.

The greatest shift in the home was a reminder to Charleigh as soon as she entered that she was here to sign over her life to Sylvia so Joey could hit the figurative lottery. In place of the bar, where Charleigh had found the supplies she'd needed to make Lexa's party a success, sat a child's playhouse. Within the colorful structure stood a play kitchen stocked with more kitchen tools than her own held. It would be a place Joey could play bakery within as she learned to feed her child in the kitchen.

Sylvia dished three plates of something orange with too many vegetables. She even took the time to wipe the edges of each plate, making it look like it came from a restaurant, and then she slid two of them in front of Mona and Charleigh. With a glass of wine in hand, Sylvia spread out an array of carpets.

"Which do you think would go best in the master bedroom?" Sylvia asked. "The hardwood echoes too much."

Charleigh looked at the options and shrugged. "Why don't you just pick out a rug? Then you could at least clean under it regularly and you can replace it when you're tired of it."

Sylvia hummed to herself, then tossed the swatches into a pile of other samples she'd been trying out. After the swatches was a catalog from Pottery

Barn. The kind Charleigh would get in the mail, just so she could play make-believe.

"I like the four-poster, but I think it would interfere with the ceiling fan," Sylvia said. She flipped a couple of pages and pointed to a wall-length padded headboard. "This is in style right now."

Mona snorted, drawing Sylvia's cold grey eyes toward her. Not one to ever give up the chance to say something snarky, Mona threw in her opinion.

"Looks like a padded cell, but the other one could be used to hang yourself from. I guess it depends on if you want it to be quick and simple or have a lock you up and throw away the key vibe."

Sylvia's eyes crinkled in the corners as she watched Mona shift the food around her plate. "There are other options," she said with a hint of amusement.

She flipped a few pages and pointed to a pewter frame. "If you prefer a metal frame, I can think of a dozen configurations your body could be secured in."

After another couple of pages, Sylvia gestured to a different frame.

"There's the sleigh bed. I have found it gives fantastic leverage and would get your ass in the perfect position. Even the most clueless lover would be able to hit the g-spot every single time."

Mona coughed into her napkin, "Lexa."

"The bed you have already is nice," Charleigh said. She meant it as a good thing, then she bit her lip.

Mona cast a side-eyed glance in Charleigh's direction. She used a piece of tofu as a microphone as she said quietly, "Smooth, Chucky. Real smooth. Wanna mention that the mattress bounces back really well for all the sexcapes you're going to be providing?"

'Just shut the fuck up,' she said to chastise herself. There was no point in her trying to do the speaking thing. Her life was no longer about speaking, it was about doing what Sylvia wanted when Sylvia wanted it. And Sylvia didn't want any more reminders Lexa had had her first in that room. It was why she was buying a new bed.

Sylvia took another sip of her wine. She must not have liked her homecooked meal, because she flipped the page.

As the options continued to be placed before her, Charleigh struggled with the reality of Sylvia's proposal and decision. She'd thought there was still time to talk to the woman, but maybe the kiss had been a promise and not a skit.

The weight of the marriage on Charleigh's tongue kept her from doing more than staring at the colorful concoction with the occasional nod or tap of her finger on the image.

She'd decided to agree to the marriage under two conditions: Joey and Rexa got to come with her and Greyson Academy remained open. Charleigh had listened to Mona's disagreement with her decision the entire way over, but she'd promised to be supportive. Even so, she also offered to burn the school down if Sylvia promised not to press charges, so Charleigh wouldn't feel obligated to save the hell hole. But she'd promised Dilynn and Alex she would save the school. So, there was no other option, until there were hundreds of options put before her.

Paint pallets with coordinating textiles for the four guest bedrooms, for the guests she'd never have. Bed frames and nightstands to match, then to put a writing desk in the room or not. The only room somewhat interesting to Charleigh was the remodel of the office into a library. She needed to choose what type of rolling ladder would look best to make the highest shelves accessible.

Every inch of the house was being rebranded, just as she would be to meet Sylvia's standards. Because Charleigh did not doubt that she would be next. Going to the store in sweatpants and a baggy t-shirt would cease to be an option. She wondered if she'd even be allowed to go to the store, or if Sylvia had someone to do it for her. Would her life really be submissively tied to that bed now Sylvia would be staying in Phoenix?

Charleigh swallowed the new truth. She'd never leave the state. Never live in a place with trees or see a place not chosen by the woman selecting her future from catalogs.

Mona used her fork to move all of the bell peppers to the side of the dish. The tofu squished under the tines, then wobbled as it was speared. Mona held it up, her brows nearly touching as she squinted at it.

"Never thought I'd appreciate Evie is a carnivore, but I guess the impossible is possible," she whispered as she added the tofu to the edge of the plate with the peppers.

Sylvia had finally begun to eat but set her fork down as well. The home-cooked meal she'd prepared was gone to waste on the younger women who had twenty-seven different ways to make a pack of instant noodles but felt sick at the sight of tofu and vegetables.

She smiled into the mouth of her wine glass. After taking a sip, she set the glass alongside her plate. "If you two would prefer, I can order some takeout. I know veganism is not most people's choice."

"No... uh, thank you for the food," Charleigh whispered. She'd have to get used to the food. It would be the least she could do for the person who brought Joey home.

She raised the fork to her mouth and tried to smile through the burn. Whatever the orange sauce was, it hated her as much as she hated it. But she swallowed and scooped up a second bite, so Sylvia would see she would be as obedient as she wanted her.

Sylvia stopped the fork's ascent. "You don't have to eat food, you don't enjoy."

When Charleigh looked at her, the woman pressed the fork back to the plate. "We'll go out after Mr. Simmons gets here with the contracts."

She set a different catalog before Charleigh. The page flipped to a room filled with pastel pink and white furniture. Pottery Barn for Kids provided a perfectly floral pink room for a little girl who wasn't Joey.

"This set is on backorder, but my understanding is it's very popular. If we order now, I'm sure I could jump the waiting list."

Charleigh's upper lip curled over her teeth. With a slight chortle, Sylvia flipped the page. "Or we could go with something not so flowery, I wasn't sure if she liked pink, or you if wanted something more gender neutral. This one is more forestry, but we could dress it up to be a fairytale land."

"She likes purple," Charleigh whispered. "And basketball. She likes purple and sparkles and basketball."

Sylvia smiled and flipped a few pages. She tapped against a four-poster bed. "We put up a mini hoop off the top post. She could work on her bounce and her shot. I never was allowed to jump on the bed when I was a kid, but Joey liked to bounce the last time I saw her. I think she would probably love to jump on the bed, and you have to let her."

Mona squished her lips together and shook her head. She set her fork down. "I'm sorry, but this is weird. Like, are you really doing this, Charleigh? Don't get me wrong, she's gonna take care of you, but this is fucking crazy, and you know it. You don't know her. What if the only room she isn't letting you decorate is a fucking dungeon?"

Charleigh closed her eyes, remembering the commitment she made—to follow Sylvia's instructions, so Joey could come home. Even if this was the home she came to, at least they'd be together.

"I'm sorry, Ms. Winters... could we—"

"Sylvia," the older woman corrected Charleigh.

Charleigh tucked her hair behind her ears. "Sylvia... I'm sorry. I don't mean to be rude, but could we please talk about the contract Mr. Simmons is bringing?"

"Yeah, and then we need to talk about you putting your hands on Charleigh because that shit better never happen again," Mona said. She flipped the butter knife around in a circle. "I don't care if I do life, you hit her again and I will liquefy you."

"I have no intention of hitting Charleigh. It was honestly a reflex since she hit me first," Sylvia stated. "I know all of this is very rushed. The reality is the time crunch of our situation is a matter of urgency, and I want things ready for Joey when she comes home. This house should not feel like it is being thrown together, it should be stable from the moment she walks into the door, and then we can—"

"I can't marry you," Charleigh practically shouted.

She felt instant relief as the words came out. The food on her plate ceased taunting her that she had no chance in hell of surviving the woman's expectations.

The glass of wine froze in midair. Sylvia examined Charleigh like the paint pallet. Eyes ran over her face to her hands holding on to the counter as she waited for Sylvia to blow up.

When Sylvia said nothing, Charleigh's brain vomited her thoughts over the dinner she'd barely touched.

"I can't marry you and it's not that you are not beautiful because you are. You are so beautiful and so powerful, and at times that combination is very intimidating but after listening to you talk to Greyson and Trikru, I have a feeling that has gotten you far in life. But I can't marry you because you have a lot of money and you stepped up to save me when Lexa has done nothing but lie to me, but that's not the point because I need you to know that I can't marry you.

"I was going to come here to say, 'Yes, I will do whatever you want.' But I have been saying that for years and it has seriously gotten me nowhere. I mean, I did that with Greyson and Trikru, and they never did what they said they were going to do when I did what they wanted. I did it for Lexa over and over again, and I don't want you to think that she hurt me because this time I expected it. And I need you to know that I think you're amazing, and you are right you were never the villain. I get why you took Lexa's money, and I am sorry she hurt you and I know I already said this but I'm sorry that I had sex with her in your bed and if I were you, I would definitely replace that bed if you were serious about how many women she had sex with in it. I mean Danaya and Emma once joked about having sex in my bed and I was like, nope."

Charleigh ran out of air, but as soon as her lungs were filled, her body spit out more words.

"If I tell you I will do whatever you want, then I have to mean it and I don't know what you want but I don't think you actually want me. I mean, you don't even know me and if you did, you probably wouldn't like me because I am dumb a lot and I don't know how to cook but... but... but I really like fried chicken and macaroni and cheese, and I think I would die if you made me be a vegan and... and... I already told Lexa and now I'll tell you... I don't fit here."

Sylvia held up a hand, and all the words falling from Charleigh's lips dissolved in her mouth that snapped shut.

"I know, Charleigh," Sylvia said. "I know, you don't want to marry me, and I would never force you to marry me. I won't even try to talk you into it because the last blonde I did that with ended up telling me no."

Mona got up from the bar stool. Something had caught her attention, and the nosey human she'd always been forced her on a mission to investigate the wall of carefully placed trophies, plaques, and photos. Charleigh watched Mona study the pictures until Sylvia started speaking again.

"My offer for marriage will always be on the table for you. It is not something I extend lightly, and I did not extend it out of any delusion you currently love me. I don't even know if you would even like me, because like you said our worlds don't truly mix. But if you did marry me, I would expect commitment and a shared understanding that I would devote myself to making you happy, and I would wish the same in return. I would expect us to have as normal a relationship as possible, including sex because I don't want to be cheated on again and do not wish a life of celibacy. So, I would take my time to prove myself worthy of your love, and I would expect the same from you."

Charleigh swallowed the fear she'd had before. The woman adjacent to her smiled.

"I know you probably think I am—"

"A creepy rich bitch that lures young women into her home to bathe in their blood," Mona offered.

"Mona," Charleigh hissed. "Shut the fuck up."

But Sylvia laughed. A genuine laugh, making the space feel a little less vast and the woman a little more human.

"Look," Sylvia said, once the laughter ceased shaking her chest. "I can imagine both of you are very uncomfortable being here. I apologize Mr. Simmons is not here yet. He had to run an additional errand for me after we decided to smack each other around in your classroom. I thought things would have gone differently today and that Dilynn would have never brought up terminating you when I was offering to invest more money into her school. So, I had to adjust my plan, and he will be here shortly."

Mona picked up one of the photos and she looked at it more carefully.

"So, the marriage proposal," Sylvia started again. "It was a hasty offer and in large part, it was to warn Lexa she could not get away with treating you like she did me. That being said, I also have an obligation to you, Charleigh."

Charleigh opened her mouth, but the question she'd planned was sliced with Mona's.

"How do you know Kayla?" Mona held up a photo from the shelf.

Sylvia sat up straighter. "She's my half-sister."

Charleigh's eyebrows cinched together. She turned to Mona, and asked, "How do you know Kayla? Have a secret relationship for years with her as well?"

"We went to school with her," Mona said, staring at the photo. Then she held it out to Charleigh.

Charleigh took the frame and looked at the woman from the bar. The one she'd seen in the photos on Lexa's Instagram. The one who crashed their game night.

"I don't know how you don't remember her," Mona said. She tapped the woman's face. "She's the one that told Trikru that we were dating because I turned her down for Winter Formal. She was like two years older than we were."

Charleigh looked at Mona. "That can't be the same Kayla. Kayla's last name was..."

"Karlov," Sylvia whispered. "Her last name is Karlov. And yes, it is the same person. She was there the year the school opened, and I withdrew her, her senior year."

Charleigh stared at the photo, but every memory she'd had of Kayla in high school was hazy. She'd known the girl Mona was referring to, but she had trouble aligning her with the woman pressed against Lexa on the dance floor.

"I know you know her. She fed you enough pills and drinks to keep you fucked up for months. She told you she could give you something that would make you feel less invisible, and you were pissed at me, so you went off with her on the regular to that bomb shelter where the kids still go to get high. And the last time... I went out there to drag you home... You could barely stand up because you were so out of it, and they had left you there naked, and you had been.... And I told Alex. I told them what those boys had done to you, and that Kayla had given you the pills." Mona looked at Sylvia. "You knew."

Sylvia ran her finger over the rim of the glass. "I got the call from Alex she'd targeted you. She's not well... never has been and when Ms. Rameriz chose you over her... it was too much for her to handle."

The woman's eyes fell to the glass. She lifted it once more to take a drink, but she set it down.

"She blamed you for her heart break. I didn't learn until much later that her obsession with people is an actual disorder. She falls in love with someone, and they become hers in her mind. According to her, Ms. Ramirez was hers and then Lexa was hers. And you and I stole them from her. Well, technically in her mind you stole both of them, but then I kissed you and she felt like I was choosing you as well."

Mona held up the photo. "You knew she basically organized a gang rape, and you just covered it up with all your money, didn't you?"

Sylvia took a deep breath. "I tried to, but Alex and Dilynn wouldn't take any money. They were going to have Kayla arrested, but I promised I would take responsibility for you, Charleigh. I would give you the life my sister tried to ruin."

"So, you did use your money to cover it up," Mona growled.

Charleigh swallowed even though the lump in her throat was threatening to choke her. She looked at Sylvia.

"You gave me the scholarship because you felt guilty," she whispered. The only thing she'd felt she'd ever earned wasn't an accomplishment. Wasn't something to be proud of. Nothing about her was something to be proud of.

Sylvia tapped her fingers against the counter. "When Alex called me and told me you were pregnant, I had to do something. They said they were going to take care of the child, but they couldn't financially take care of her future and yours. So, I started the scholarship program and advertised only at Greyson's the first year. They said they would make sure you would apply, so yes, you were always going to get the scholarship."

Every breath was too shallow. The lungs in her chest couldn't inflate even though the heart already too broken to pump her blood properly was beating. She was too young for a heart attack, but it didn't feel like anything less. Tears threatened to leave tracks down her already swollen face. Fighting her body wasn't knew, yet it felt more difficult than usual. Cognitively the option of giving Sylvia Winters any more tears though was vetoed. Her emotions would not come flooding out of her because this woman was just as much of a liar as her ex-wife, the biological mother who'd thrown Charleigh away, and the monster making Joey believe being a woman meant being less.

"You said you saw me," Charleigh said, raising her chin to Sylvia's pity-filled eyes. "You said a lot of things and I believed you. I believed you when you said you weren't the villain even, but you are. You made everything that happened possible. You did it by trying to make it disappear. Just like you're still doing. I guess you didn't realize that she'd come for you too. She came for your wife, and she won. Because Lexa chose her over your marriage."

Mona put the picture down and tapped Charleigh. "We should go."

"No." Charleigh shrugged the hand off her. "I want her to know. I want her to know the truth. I didn't get pregnant from the orgy in the bomb shelter. I was high as fuck to make everything easier, but I wasn't raped. I fucked them all, including your sister because I wanted to. And not one of those boys is Joey's father."

Mona stared at Charleigh. "You said you didn't know."

Charleigh rolled her eyes. "Well, of course I did. I couldn't tell anyone the truth. No one gave a damn about me, and if I told them, then they would make me leave and I couldn't leave because I belonged to Marcus. So, I took what he gave me because I had already lost part of you, and I couldn't leave you because I didn't want him to come after you next."

"Marcus?" Mona asked.

Charleigh shook her head. "Marcus may look like a pedophile, but he isn't. And you know that."

"Who the fuck is it, Charleigh?" Mona growled. "Who the fuck hurt you and made you think you'd have to leave?"

"For someone so fucking smart, I really don't understand how you failed basic genetics, Mona. There were only two people at that school who would make a baby with blonde hair and blue fucking eyes," Charleigh hissed. "And I was half of them."

Mona's hands clenched in a fist. "When?"

"He'd wait until Marcus took you to therapy. He said he could help me do what straight girls did, so I could go home when it sunk in that I wasn't going back. Two weeks, maybe three. Every day felt so long. He said I was a princess, and I just had to learn to take care of a king. I fucking hate that name because he said it every time. Good girl and princess, those were his favorites." She turned to Sylvia. "Why are those the names you guys always go with? Like, you already have all the power, does it make you feel like you're protecting us or something as you remind us we are nothing?"

Sylvia couldn't hold Charleigh's gaze. She pulled the glass up to her lips and drained the remaining wine. And God did Charleigh want some of it. She briefly considered just pouring herself a glass, but the catalog from Pottery Barn Kids reminded her why she couldn't.

"Why didn't you tell me?" Mona asked. Her body was in the room, but her eyes scanned over, what Charleigh could only assume was, every memory, trying to figure out how she'd missed it.

When she looked up, Charleigh smiled apologetically. She needed Mona to understand how important she'd been. "You wouldn't have wanted me if you knew what I did to try and fix myself. And when I had you, for that brief moment, I didn't want to lose you. I didn't want you to be ashamed of me. Then you left me, and it didn't matter anymore. Nothing mattered so I just did what he wanted because it was easier that way. Everything was easier doing what everyone else wanted."

Sylvia cleared her throat. "Who was it?"

"His name is Kyle. He was our foster brother," Mona said. Her murder mask was set on her face, and Charleigh wondered if Mona knew how to liquefy someone.

Mona's fist tapped against the counter. She drummed out a beat, calling her demons to war. Then her face snapped up. "Does he know? Know that he's Joey's father?"

"Yes. He knows." Charleigh pushed the hair back from her face again. "He was supposed to take me to a clinic that afternoon. Marcus had given him permission to take me to the movies while you were serving your detention with Trikru. That's why I went to the bomb shelter and fucked all the boys there. So that they wouldn't start asking questions."

With a shrug, she added, "Everyone just assumed Joey was early because they thought I lost my virginity at the shelter. I wasn't sick because of the drugs though, I was sick because I was pregnant and I had been sick for a while because I was trying to make sure no one knew because he told me if I didn't get an abortion he'd kill me. So, I made it, so he didn't have to. And I knew you were mad at me, but I didn't want to die yet. That came later, with the postpartum depression."

Charleigh wrapped her arms around her chest. She'd managed to push the trauma away and lock it behind a door in her mind she didn't open. The fourteen-year-old version of herself stayed there too, in solitary confinement to keep the secret that saved her life. She'd locked her away because every holiday he was there. Every major event invited to. She held her body as she remembered Kyle's arm wrapped around her for the photo at the start of summer when the whole family had come to help her move into her first house. The house had fought for her. The railing of the porch gave out, so he fell from the stairs to the gravel. His hands and face were bloody, forcing him to leave.

She picked at her lip and considered if she should tell Mona. If she should tell her she'd found her courage. But Mona was searching her pocket for her keys, and she had to stop her. Stop her from going to prison before her baby was born like Danaya's mother had. Because a weed charge had gotten the other mother five years. A murder charge, even for a rapist, would get Mona life.

"That's why I had to get Kinsley out of the group home. I saw him talking to her at her school and I knew. Too close. He was too close to her, so I got her out before he could hurt her, and then I got him fired so he couldn't hurt anyone else. And Marcus kept him away because they were fighting. I knew Marcus would keep her safe because he felt guilty, I got knocked up."

Mona squeezed the keys in her hands. Her fingers played with the carabiner on her belt loop. "You should have told me."

"I should have done a lot of things. But like I told her, I make really dumb choices."

She turned to Sylvia. "So, I guess Lexa was right. I did steal your money for college since I didn't actually earn it."

She didn't thank Sylvia for proving what she already knew; that she had never done anything to be proud of in her entire life. By the pity-filled look on Sylvia's face, she already knew it.

"Don't worry about the contract," Charleigh said, with a nod. "I'll find a way to get my own lawyer."

Charleigh got up from the chair. She pushed it in carefully to make herself seem in control as the molecules keeping her together wildly spun around, breaking apart the bonds to flee being a part of her.

"Sit down, Charleigh," Sylvia commanded calmly. "You're not paying for another lawyer and you're not leaving. This house is yours. It's already been gifted to you."

Sylvia waved her hand over the samples and catalogs. "Thus, all the redecorating decisions. It's not my bed that I'm replacing. It's yours. All of this is yours."

35

Mr. Simmons reached out to ring the doorbell as Lexa passed him. Sylvia must've had the hinges oiled because the five-foot wide door swung open silently, allowing the voices contained within to hit her at full force as they attempted to escape.

Lexa heard Charleigh yell, "Why the fuck are you giving me a house?"

Her foot fell into the house as Parker and Echo walked into the back of her. She put up her arms, blocking their path so she could hear the explanation.

"Like, did you not just hear me? It's not Kayla's fault I got pregnant. I was just a dumb blonde whore, and you owe me nothing!"

Lexa glanced back to see Parker tuck her hair behind her ear. She too was focused on the conversation within.

"Are you done with your tantrum?" Sylvia snapped.

"I'm not a child, and you do not get to talk to me like this. I don't care that you have magic powers to get Greyson to shut the fuck up. I don't fucking belong to you, and I will never be the obedient pet you were hoping for."

"I don't want you!" Sylvia yelled back. "I never wanted you, because just like Alex said you're a fucking child, stuck in the 16-year-old mind state you had when your life turned upside down. This is why you can't seem to understand this isn't about what did or didn't happen in high school. I don't care who knocked you up."

Lexa looked at the floor. Sylvia not wanting Charleigh was a good thing. Especially saying it aloud, because she had always made it clear to Charleigh she wanted her. At least she thought she had.

"The fact is my sister attacked you, again."

'Again?' Lexa tried to think of when Kayla had attacked Charleigh. She'd sworn Charleigh had left the bar. Not been a party to the punches thrown. And the dinner hadn't been an attack.

"She made that video because you took Lexa from her. So, this is your restitution. The house and the check that Mr. Simmons should have been here to deliver to you. The contract is for the house. The check is for the black eye I gave you."

"I don't want your money," Charleigh snapped. "How many fucking times do I have to tell you and your ex-wife that I am not a fucking gold digger. I don't want anything from you but to keep the fucking school running."

Lexa heard heels click across the hardwood.

"I am never going to close that school," Sylvia stated calmly. Lexa could picture the mask falling back over Sylvia's face. Her voice grew warmer, and Lexa knew that her hands were on Charleigh again. "I just wanted Dilynn and Alex to feel for a moment what they put you through. The betrayal they caused you. And I wanted them to pay for that betrayal because they didn't just make a deal with you. They made one with me. I would take care of your college, and they would take care of Joey. And they didn't do their part, so I need them to know. I needed them to understand there are consequences for not keeping their word."

Mr. Simmons cleared his throat, but Lexa gave him the universal sign for 'shut the fuck up' with an over-the-shoulder glance back at him.

"If you'd rather not take my check, then I will sign over the property for Greyson Academy to you. You can have the land, so you can trust the school is safe. Because I understand, Charleigh. I understand why you don't trust anyone. I wouldn't trust anyone either in your position. But you can trust me to give you whatever you want."

Charleigh's groan was equal to a teenager whining with her parent. "Why is everything about payment with you? Like, do your ears not work? I. Don't. Want. Your. Money." Each word was punctuated with a clap between them.

Something in the room slammed, and then Sylvia was louder. Her voice raised an octave—a tone Lexa had never heard her speak with before. "Because it's all I have."

Lexa chewed at the chapped skin on her lip. She held her hand against the door frame so no one could pass her as she continued to eavesdrop.

"I have nothing but a barren womb and more money than the entirety of the state. So, at some point I am going to have to give it all to someone, so why not you? Especially since if your fucking mother would have just told me, it would have all gone to you anyways. I would have found you, and I would have put her and you up in a house, and when I didn't have anything, it all would have gone to you because I would have been the same type of parent to you that my father was to me. But that was then. Now, you can't be my kid. So again, why not you? Why not give everything to a girl who wants none of it, including me?"

There were never going to be kids. It wasn't that Sylvia didn't want them, she couldn't have them. Lexa wondered why Sylvia never told her. Never told her it wasn't even a possibility. She'd have understood, at least Lexa thought she'd have accepted it.

"That's why you said you want to adopt Joey. Because you can't have kids and you have no one to leave your money to," Charleigh summarized. There was no way the woman wasn't snarling at Sylvia with how her voice changed to a low rumble. "But Lexa asked you for kids. She was willing to carry them and wanted to give you a baby. And you told her no."

"I couldn't let her have a baby," Sylvia snapped. "Her mother was bipolar just like she is. I couldn't knowingly let her bring another life into the world if she'd even possibly pass on the crazy in her brain. I can't just give a child that will be unable to control their impulses enough money to start a world war if given the chance."

Lexa knew her heart should hurt. It had been running on overdrive for the past two hours, but the ache never came. Her breathing didn't change, even though the words stung.

"You knew she was bipolar when you met her," Charleigh growled. "You knew who she was, and you promised her the world. You broke her fucking heart."

"I knew that if I didn't marry her, Kayla was going to, and she would have gotten Lexa to stop taking her meds. She would have waited for Lexa to go manic and married her. And I couldn't see my sister hurt another girl. I already watched her drive one into a grave and Lexa... Lexa was innocent. You never knew Lexa when she was a baby gay. She wasn't this crazy cunt who chased after every bitch in a short skirt who would bend over for her dick."

Someone in the room cleared their throat. Then Lexa heard Mona, "Actually, we did."

Lexa searched her memory for when she could have possibly met Charleigh and Mona. Charleigh had said they had Shakespeare together, but she'd never actually met her then.

"We had Shakespeare with her our freshmen year. This dumb shit used to sketch her profile while we sat a safe stalker distance away. But then I pissed the bitch off, and Charleigh took the brunt of her anger in the hallway. But like a moth to a flame, Charleigh followed her career and crushed from the stands."

Sylvia asked, "How did you piss her off?"

"I had sent a note via paper airplane to your cheating wife with Charleigh's phone number. Said 'Call your number one fan so she'll stop filling notebooks with your pictures like a stalker.'"

Lexa remembered the paper airplane smacking her in the head during class. A bitch with a pixie cut snickered at her as the little one with blonde pigtails shrunk down in her chair and covered her face with a Devil's baseball cap. She'd seen the smaller one in the hallway afterward. Her hand came down on the pile of novels and notebooks in the girl's hands. Notes and texts flew out of order as she stomped on them and went to her last game of the season. Her first drop came later that night when she blamed her loss on the blonde bully behind her.

She'd never looked at the plane. Assumed it was another asshat making fun of her because she still hadn't figured out how to manage her hair. But it had been Charleigh and Mona, just trying to give her a phone number.

Mr. Simmons had grown tired of Lexa's eavesdropping and pushed her arm aside. Leaving Lexa in the doorway, unsure of what she was doing there anymore.

"Have you forgotten how to ring the bell?" Sylvia snapped at the lawyer.

"The former Mrs. Winters and her associates are in the entryway. They let themselves in, and I figured I would come to stop this conversation about her before your discussion forces me to return to my office for another check," suck-up Simmons reported.

Lexa licked her dry teeth as Sylvia turned the corner to the entryway. They just looked at each other, neither acknowledging Lexa had been standing there too long.

With a nod to the great room, Sylvia permitted Lexa to enter. Parker and Echo followed at her heels.

She moved to the center of the room where Charleigh stood. Her hands cupped the blonde's face and turned it so she could see the bruise running along the side of her cheek and eye socket. "Did it feel good to punch her first?" Lexa asked, trying to force a smile on her face.

Charleigh let out a single, "Ha," and wrapped her arms around her own body. Quietly she said, "I got fired today."

"I know, Parker came to get me." Lexa swallowed her fear and asked, "I heard you two fighting about not wanting to be together. Did you accept her proposal?"

Charleigh looked at the ground. Her chest shallowly rose and fell before she said, "I came here to do what she wanted because that dude told me if I followed her instructions, he'd get Joey home by Christmas. But I got here, and she made me make like a zillion decisions about decorating the house."

Lexa looked around. The hard lines and grayscale theme Sylvia kept had been replaced with the colors of Charleigh. Everything was brighter and softer, even the light fixtures were replaced with stained glass, so the ceiling reflected a rainbow haze.

"I kept thinking that next she'd be showing me acceptable haircuts and she'd throw away my sweatpants and it was like she was going to send me to a metalsmith to hammer out all my dents and scrub away my scratches. And I don't think there's enough polish in the world to make me fit in this cupboard.

So, I can't." Charleigh's head kept shaking and her voice cracked. "I can't. I can't marry her, and I just want to go home because everything is a lie. It's just so many secrets and lies, and I feel like a bug in a web of lies."

Mona snorted and looked at Sylvia. "See luring women in for the blood."

Charleigh wiped the scratchy cotton sleeve over her face, then told Mona, "Would you just shut up?"

"If you leave or don't leave, it will not change the reality that this is now your house," Sylvia stated. "It has been put into a trust in your name. The trust will pay the property taxes yearly as well as the warranty for any major maintenance. And I don't lure young women here to drink or bathe in their blood."

Mr. Simmons cleared his throat. His briefcase lay open on the kitchen island where the papers had been placed away from the plates still loaded with food.

Lexa looked at the Tofu Jalfrezi. She could picture Charleigh's face as she stared at the plate when the only vegetables she'd ever seen Charleigh eat were green beans and lettuce smothered in Ranch dressing. But then she realized Charleigh was probably starving and her frustration with Sylvia grew. If she was going to steal her girl, at least have the decency to feed her actual food.

"Ms. Marshall, I need you to sign here so I can file the petition to have your case in family court dismissed. After going through the files, the ADA... Ms. Lyra Greyson-Trikru, sent over, it is abundantly clear your parental rights have been violated and the state's initial case regarding the abandonment of your daughter is unsubstantiated. If you don't sign though, I can't file the motion."

Charleigh looked at Lexa. "If I sign it, then I'll owe her for the rest of my life. She'll always be the one that made it so Joey could come home."

"No. She won't." Lexa tapped her chest. "I paid Simmons. I hired him. I paid him a $5000 retainer fee and he promised to be in contact by the end of the week."

She turned to the man. "Did I not come to you on Monday and pay your fee?"

"Technically you came to me on Monday. However, you were never charged the fee because I was contacted almost immediately after you left by Ms. Winters and was told she would be covering all charges regarding this particular matter, and the request for the deed and other assets to be transferred to Ms. Marshall's name," he explained.

Lexa's head fell backward. "You couldn't just let me do this, could you?" she growled.

"I was holding up my end of obligations," Sylvia stated. "That's all I ever do, and for some reason, it just keeps blowing up in my face. Just once I would like someone to just say thank you."

Echo waved her hand in the air slightly. "Uh... I did. Just said thank you, I mean. Well, that and to tell your rapist wife ain't ever allowed to set her cheatin' foot on my property again. Then I think I said thank you again. And once you ordered a drink from me and I said thank you and that I think your purty. Purty awesome was my save of course."

Parker elbowed Echo in the ribs, causing the larger woman to stop talking. "You sound like a hillbilly telling a girl she gots a purty mouth."

"You said 'thank you and go the fuck to hell," Sylvia countered. "And there were more words about my whore of a wife being banned. Oh, and take my rich ass someplace else. And that my sister is—"

"I had a concussion," Echo grumbled as her shoulders fell.

Mona walked to the breakfast bar where Mr. Simmons had laid out the contracts and the check for getting slapped. She studied the legal forms, then the check, while the rest of the people in the room waited for Charleigh to decide.

"Did Sylvia already pay you?" Mona asked the lawyer.

Mr. Simmons cast a glance at Sylvia. When she nodded, he explained, "My office has a standing retainer with Ms. Winters, so she does not pay for each particular situation handled for her."

Mona held up the check and walked to Charleigh.

"Chucky, pay the man yourself. Take this $200,000 check from the white savior and pay the man yourself. And also, next time let me fight her because I coulda used $200,000."

Charleigh shook her head, and a small smile played at the corner of her lips. "You're a Greyson Princess now. You're already rich."

Mona shook her head. "Oh, hell no. I'm not going near that family money with a ten-foot pole. But you've seen the size of Landon's head. My entire coochie is going to need to be reconstructed after this kid comes out."

A hand came up when Echo gagged. Not a fake gag. A real gag with her lips in an O as her eyes searched for a trash can.

Mona ignored the retching and pointed to the check.

"You pay him. Then he's yours and you're not hers. You don't have to belong to anyone. Not this bitch that didn't even tell you she's leaving in like two weeks. Not to the rich spider with the hidden dungeon. You just get to be you, and Joey can come home to whatever home you want to bring her to. I mean if you don't want this place, then rent it out. That's income. You hit the fucking lottery and didn't even have to buy a ticket."

Sylvia lowered herself to the couch that looked too comfortable for the irritation etched into the crease running over her forehead. The cream-colored pillow encased her body as her arms covered the word 'family.'

Mona held out the check to Charleigh. She waved it slightly, as she said, "You came here because you thought marrying her was your only option. Hell, she thought it was your only option too, so she already had everything planned out for you. But this puts you in control of your life for like the first time ever. Not Dilynn or Alex telling you what to do. Not Sylvia pulling strings like you're a fucking marionette. Not Lexa or me doing shit for you. Just you."

Charleigh took the check and read over the total. A single piece of paper that would grant her freedom from everyone. When she finished, she licked her lips and her eyes moved to Sylvia. Then to Echo.

"Did you mean it?" she asked the bar owner. "The job offer? Like, I don't have any experience in the service industry, but I will show up every day and I will work whatever shift you give me."

A broad smile spread across Echo's lips. "Literally why I'm here. Well, that... and to see how the other half lives. Clearly, I shoulda spent more time flirting with Via because I picked the wrong blonde to marry. Like Jesus, Via. How much space do you need?"

Sylvia's lips pulled into a tight smile. "You know, enough to make the dungeon I'm hiding underneath inconspicuous. Where do you think all the other girls Lexa brought home are hidden?"

Mona slapped her hand to her leg and laughed. She pointed to the woman. "I fucking knew it."

Lexa reached out to Charleigh, but the blonde moved before Lexa could touch her. She moved to Sylvia and Lexa's heart started to pump too fast.

"I told you you probably wouldn't even like me. That I can be really dumb. And this is probably dumb. And I will probably regret it when my feet hurt or some drunk bitch screams at me for dropping a beer, but I'd rather be dumb and poor than rich off someone else's guilt." Charleigh's shoulders rose as she held out the check. "Keep your money and keep your house. My kid is coming home because I can do what that guy just talked about on my own. She'll come home to the room where I hung up a star for every single day she'd been away, not the one you chose from a catalog because it's popular with people like you."

When Sylvia didn't take the check from Charleigh, the younger woman dropped it at her feet.

"You don't owe me shit, and now I don't owe you shit. The debt Dilynn and Alex owed you is paid with the bruise on my face, so the school is safe, and all my friends and my family's jobs are safe. It's done. And I get to walk out of here fucking proud I didn't lay down and let you fuck me because it was easier than standing up for myself."

As Charleigh left, Mona and Parker followed. Lexa could hear them calling for Charleigh, but Sylvia stared at her. The words of why they never made it echoed back from the mountain they'd reached.

"I could have carried your egg. We could have done genetic testing or used a donor egg. There were so many options," Lexa said.

Sylvia gripped the pillow tighter. "All of them involved you going off your meds to be pregnant and who knows what you would have done to yourself or the child."

Lexa swallowed the truth. Sylvia had thought it through. She'd probably gone over every detail, including marrying Lexa so Kayla couldn't. Her vows were just another twisted form of sibling rivalry.

"Did you ever love me?" Lexa whispered.

The pillow in her arms smooshed as Sylvia's grip tightened. She smiled weakly, but it didn't reach her eyes. Her tongue licked her lips, before she said, "More than you could ever know, but I knew a long time ago that I didn't make you happy."

Sylvia closed her eyes and shook her head. "You know, Emma told me you said it was like fate put you and Charleigh together. We laughed about how ridiculous it sounded, but apparently, you and she have been crossing each other's paths over and over again. Yet, each time someone has been there to get in the way. So, I am stepping aside. No more promises to her. But that means you too. Don't be the one to get in the way this time, Lex."

The torn Devil's sweatshirt pulled easily from Lexa's body. The sports bra underneath was enough to keep her mildly decent. She stepped into the colorful room she would have loved and dropped it from her fingers to the coffee table in the house it should have been left in when Sylvia told her to leave.

She ran after the woman who didn't need her to fix anything.

The blonde stood at the driver's door of the Charger. Mona tried to talk sense into her about the check and the house. Parker told her it was okay to be angry, but she shouldn't be making decisions based on that anger.

Lexa slid around them. She used her best asset and boxed the other two out. One arm held Mona away from Charleigh, and the other pulled the door to the Charger open.

"Go," Lexa told her. "Wherever you want. When you're ready, call me. I'm not leaving you and I know you think I was, but I'm not. It's your play. You run it how you want, Coach."

The smile in Charleigh's eyes was all Lexa needed. Lexa wrapped her arm back, holding Mona from getting past her. Mona kicked her in the calf and

Parker pushed as she was smashed into Mona. But Lexa kept them at bay as Charleigh took her shot to escape their lecture.

As the Charger peeled away, the crickets' soft song settled in rhythm once more. Lexa watched the taillights disappear with a right turn.

"How can you let her walk away from that much money?" Mona yelled. The back of her hands pushed Lexa forward. "She needs it. She got fucking fired today."

Lexa turned to Charleigh's friends. "No. She needed to stand up for what she believed in more. And you know it. You know what just happened gave her something no check will ever give her."

Mona kicked Lexa's shoe. "I know. I know you're right, but it was sooo much money. And this fucking house, she could be set for life."

Parker folded her arms over her chest. "She's not worried about life. I bet you aren't either and I sure as hell know I am not. People like us don't think about a month from now, a year from now, let alone life. We are just trying to survive until tomorrow. And dropping that check on the floor like money didn't matter, you know it made her feel invincible. Like, for the first-time, she knew money wouldn't solve a problem."

"It would have solved all of her problems," Mona whined. "Like there were five zeros! Two hundred thousand dollars for getting bitch slapped. Like shit, can I get her to slap me and give me a check? Then maybe I could get Evie and Landon to move away from Mommy Dearest."

Parker chuckled. "Your dumbass moved in there to begin with. I told Lyra if she ever wants to live with me, it will never be on that street."

Lexa played with the twist that fell in her face. She smiled, as she told Mona, "Apparently Sylvia's looking for an heir. I bet if you keep talking shit to her, she'd fall for you. She always loved it when people stood up to her. It's why she liked Danaya and wanted them to draft her."

"What is with rich girls and wanting so much banter? Do you all not understand it's exhausting having to always be ready with a comeback, so you feel like a normal human?" Mona groaned.

With a shrug of her shoulders, Lexa tried to help the woman understand. "When people like you, talk back to people like us... it's refreshing. I guess that's why I get her not taking the money. I couldn't figure out what to do without it, but Charleigh. Charleigh made something out of what I would consider nothing and when there wasn't anything she still made it into something."

A smile played on Mona's lips. "In college, she wrote this essay. It was on defining the word nothing. She rambled for five pages about how nothing was, in fact, something. People just couldn't describe it because it was so original that nothing left a person with a void of words to compare it to. I think about it every time she says she's nothing. Like I knew that she knew that nothing is something."

Lexa smiled and looked up at the stars. She hoped tonight Charleigh felt like more than nothing. She whispered, "That she is something."

"Something else," Parker said, putting her arm around Mona. "She truly is something else. Now, Lexa, can you please explain why you are half-naked? I know you had clothes on before we left the house."

36

Parker's hand-me-downs lay in heaping piles across Charleigh's bed. She'd tried on at least a dozen outfits before settling on a tank top with corset strings running up the back. It had been three weeks since Charleigh left the promise of Sylvia's safety. The clothes she'd finally started to feel like herself in were put away, and the version of her from college had infiltrated her closet.

She held the phone in the crook of her shoulder as she listened to Parker tell her all the gossip from work.

"I know it doesn't feel like it right now, but you are lucky you got out," Parker proclaimed. Her laugh was wickedly amused, and Charleigh knew she was just leaving work. *"Dilynn has been storming around campus trying to put out all the figurative fires the kids have started. They put out a newspaper on Monday calling for a walkout. Oh, and someone installed a padlock on your classroom last night when Dilynn announced she'd be taking over your class until they found a suitable replacement."*

"That kinda blows," Charleigh said, trying to reach the ties behind her. "She was a really good teacher. Like all the stuff that I do in my class came from her."

"Well, the kids made it clear they don't want her in your room today." Parker paused to cuss out someone on the road in front of her before she came back to the conversation. *"Oh, and your sister took a bullhorn into the main office and declared an immediate resignation, then a series of small smoke bombs went off near each of the classrooms before the whole girl's bathroom was fuming from the vents. Alex was running around actually swearing about how Mona would never grow up."*

Pulling the straps tightly, she watched the neck of the shirt spread open over her breasts. She pulled until she was just a little uncomfortable, remembering Parker's serving tutorial on Tits for Tips. She'd be on her own for the first time without Parker to babysit her, and she wanted to be able to tell the woman that the time she'd spent wasn't wasted. Mostly, she wanted to be able to text the woman and tell her she hadn't broken a single glass or bottle for a shift—a feat she'd yet to accomplish.

"Anyways, shit was crazy," Parker finished. *"Lyra said, Mona told Evie and Landon she won't live across the street from Dilynn, so they are moving now. Just a heads up, I suggested they talk to you about renting that house Sylvia gave*

you. It would certainly piss Dilynn off, and then you could totally bank on Evilie's trust fund."

Charleigh groaned. She'd contacted Simmons to find out how to get out of being the owner of the house, but he'd explained she would have to sell it to take it out of her name. The money would then be hers still, which defeated the purpose.

"I'll think about it," Charleigh said. "I mean, with the rent money, I could pay for a new lawyer. You never did tell me what it cost you with Lyra to get her to take over my case."

"I promised to move in with her," Parker stated. *"On the condition that it wasn't at the Greyson commune."*

Make-up brushes, eyeshadow pallets, and different types of teardrop sponges lay around the counter Lexa had always kept spotless. With the woman gone, the layer after layer of powders smeared against the laminate. Applying make-up had never been of interest to her, but Parker had given her a tutorial and she'd learned the rest from YouTube and TikTok.

The knock at the door sent Rexa running on the defense while Charleigh applied the dark shadow to her lids the way Parker had shown her. She finished the corner before making her way to the door.

"Hey someone's at the door. I'll text you tonight and tell you how my first night alone went," Charleigh promised.

"Okay, bye friend," Parker said and hung up before Charleigh could respond.

When Charleigh peeked through the window, she took in the lanky form standing on her porch. The dangling DCS badge was a deliberate danger sign, setting off a series of internal alarms within her. This wasn't her usual worker, which meant the mess within would be the woman's first impression of her.

She cried out, "Just a minute," and grabbed Rexa by the collar. The dog tried to run back to the door, nails scratching the floor. The ball of muscle yanked her repeatedly trying to meet the person standing outside.

"I'm coming," she called louder as she fought against the furry hunk of sheer will and muscle. "Just let me put my dog outside."

Rexa didn't make any of it easy, but Charleigh managed to get the back door closed. She looked at the sink full of dishes and knew she was going to blow it.

As the door opened, the green eyes rose slowly up Charleigh's body. Momentarily the woman's gaze locked on Charleigh's breasts, then she looked at the tablet once more.

The lump in Charleigh's throat only grew as she stared up at a younger feminine version of Alex Trikru. The state of the house wouldn't matter, because Dilynn had sent her real daughter to finalize what Grace Marshall began, probably only to take Grace to court herself.

With the DCS badge hanging from her sweater, Sadie Trikru scrolled through a digital form as she asked, "Are you Charlotte Leigh Marshall?"

Charleigh couldn't help the defeated sigh exit her lips. Princess Greyson Number 3's dark hair spiraled down her back as her sharp jaw dropped when her gaze rose.

"Charleigh?" Sadie asked, pushing the bulky glasses up her nose. The girl scanned the form again, then looked back up.

"I... I was... Charlotte Leigh? I always wondered what your real name was." Sadie smiled and the weird flirty attitude was back. "It's like Mom's."

Holding on to the door handle, Charleigh closed her eyes. Usually, she got a call before she had an inspection, and she'd have time to prepare.

"Well, I guess we can skip the introductions," Charleigh whispered.

Her chin dropped to her chest. She wrapped her arms over herself to keep Sadie from seeing her hands shaking. "Did your sister or your mother ask you to do this?"

A long curl twisted in Sadie's fingers. She swallowed thickly before sharing, "Neither of my sisters would ask me to do anything. I was just assigned this case."

She'd lost interest in Charleigh's bust, her eyes wandering everywhere but her body for a change.

"I just opened the file, and it said you had an unscheduled visit due, so I figured I would come out since we have court in a month and a half. My supervisor informed me that your case had been with the department for several years. She said with the turnover you seemed to be slipping through the cracks and wanted me to make sure everything was in order because your mom has been calling me, like, non-stop. So, I knew that we... we need to determine if reunification was a possibility or if...."

"So, your mom sent you." Charleigh nodded and held the door to her messy house open. "Well, let's get this over with."

Sadie's shoulders straightened and her chin rose. The perplexed face went neutral as the girl stepped into the role of executioner to make her mother proud.

"The state of Arizona sent me as a representative of the Department of Child Services to perform an unscheduled visit. Is there anything in the home that could potentially harm me?"

"No." Charleigh pointed to the back of the house. "My dog is friendly but huge, and she likes to hug strangers, so I put her out back."

She flipped the switch to the light as Sadie walked into the bungalow.

Tucking the hair behind her ear, Charleigh explained, "I was just getting ready for work, and my schedule has been pretty flip-flopped, so I just want you to know that I am not usually a slob. I do have a new job though, so you don't have to worry. I am employed and I have been keeping detailed records of my tips to prove I am making enough to support myself and Joey. I...uh..." Charleigh went to the bookcase and grabbed her log. She held it out to Sadie. "I kept track of all of my visits until they were canceled a month ago. I have every item I purchased, so you can see that I... I provided seasonally appropriate clothes and shoes. I also gave my mom money to contribute to Joey's Halloween costume. I sent it to her on Venmo and I can pull up the records and show you that. I can also show you my bank statement that all of my fees have been paid."

Rummaging through her backpack, she withdrew the forms she kept with her at all times. "I also have my log for my AA attendance. And my certificates for the parenting classes I completed. I didn't miss any of the classes and the only AA meetings I missed were because my car broke down. But I have a new car so that is no longer an issue, and you will see that I went to each one of them."

Fingers tapped against the tablet glass while Sadie took notes. She looked up at all the items Charleigh held in her hands.

"I have never met anyone who has all of this documentation." Sadie took the papers and notebook and gestured to the sofa. "May I sit?"

"Yes, of course," then Charleigh held up her hands. "Wait. Let me get like a towel because Rexa sits on the couch and she's shedding like bad."

Sadie waved away the suggestion with the papers. "I'm not scared of a little dog hair."

She glanced around the room, "I like your style. This place feels very homey."

Charleigh didn't sit while Sadie went through the journal page by page. The long bony finger ran down the years of copious notes. Her eyebrows scrunched together, and she looked up at Charleigh.

"When did you say your visits were canceled?"

"A month ago. I went to my scheduled visit and my mother refused to let me see her. She said the case manager told her she didn't have to let me see her, but I went back to the usual times my mother allowed me to visit. I have photos that have the dates and the location that I was there, but she wouldn't open the door. But I was there."

Sadie looked through her notes. "You should have had at least four to eight visits since then."

"Two," Charleigh corrected. "I only get one every other week."

"You have a weekly four-hour visit or two two-hour visits," Sadie stated. She opened the journal and ran her fingers through the dates. "Who told you that you only get one visit every other week?"

"My mother sets the days and times. They are on her schedule."

"No. That is not how it works. Who the fuck was your case manager?" Sadie asked, going back to her tablet.

"Uh, the last one was Angel Damas, the month before that was LouAnn Gilder. There was a Laura Margules last spring," Charleigh listed. "I have all of their cards taped to the date that I met with them the first time in the log."

Sadie shut the book. Her tanned face stared at the tattered cover and her fingers gripped the journal so tightly, Charleigh was worried she may tear it in two.

"Charleigh, I'm going to schedule you a series of make-up visits for the time missed. I'm going to give you my card to add to this book and you will text me your availability, so I can arrange those visits on your schedule," Sadie stated. "I'm sorry this has happened to you."

Holding her arms around herself, Charleigh bit her lip. She didn't know what to think of Princess Sadie, since all prior experiences with her sisters were less than pleasant. Well except the last time, but that was only because their girlfriends seemed to be humanizing them.

Sadie handed the book and the papers back to Charleigh. She glanced around the room, then asked, "May I look around?"

With a nod, Charleigh stepped to the wall where she'd be least in the way as every inch of her home was examined.

Sadie started with the living room, looking over the photos on the bookcase. She stopped at a baby photo of Joey, smiling at the picture. Then she continued down the shelves, running her finger over the titles. She paused at a tattered copy of *Unwind*. Her lips pulled into a smile that looked exactly like Alex Trikru.

"I loved and hated this one. It was the first book that I ever read on my own."

Charleigh forced a smile to her face and nodded at the woman who moved through the kitchen. She opened all of the drawers and under the sink.

"Your daughter is... six?" Sadie stopped and looked at Charleigh. "Wait... Your daughter's name... Joey? As in Mom and Obi's Joey? Sorry, your Joey. You were the girl from the school. And you are...."

Charleigh didn't say a word or move from her spot in the doorway. She just let the younger woman put the pieces of her past together.

With a hunch to her shoulders, Sadie stopped talking and she went back to the living room where the photos of Joey lined the shelves from oldest to newest. She picked up the most recent and ran her finger over the plastic cover.

"She was only the second baby I'd ever held," Sadie whispered.

With a heavy swallow, Charleigh admitted. "I never got to hold her after she went home with Trikru. Not as a baby. I didn't get to see her until she was already walking."

Sadie set the photo back in its place. Charleigh watched the woman gather herself before she turned back with the same professionalism she'd had when she stepped into the room.

"We are going to pretend I don't know you, because if I did, then you'd get another new worker." Sadie was staring at Charleigh when she added, "And we are going to pretend that you didn't drop a bomb on my mom a few weeks ago. She's not connected to your records, and my last name isn't Greyson, so no one is going to connect the dots."

Dilynn hadn't kept it a secret after she left. That was the first thing Charleigh understood. The second was that Sadie wasn't a Greyson. How and why that happened made Charleigh feel oddly connected to the woman in her living room like Dilynn had rejected them both since the older woman even named the street her house sat on after herself. That didn't make Sadie any less of a threat. It meant she could still be a problem. A big problem, if she was still trying to earn Dilynn's love like Charleigh had attempted to do for so many years.

"Do I need another new worker?" Charleigh asked in earnest. "I mean, if your mom sent you here, then let's be real about you giving me a fair shot. I'm sure you've heard every single thing I've done to mess up my and Joey's life. And I know I'm the biggest loser to ever walk out of your mom's school, but I have done every single thing everyone has asked of me, and I am really tired of being shit on constantly."

Sadie pulled at the back of her neck. "She doesn't talk to me about anything, but she had a family meeting and told us all about you. About that you... you're her daughter and she didn't know." After a heavy inhale, Sadie breathed out, "Out of all us kids, I'm the disappointment. The reason they were all in the accident and why she lost the baby she wanted. I have a feeling she despises I ever showed up with a birth certificate proving Obi's dad had an affair that produced my mother. And I messed up probably worse than you did. Not to mention that my sisters hate me because I'm the only one who is related to Obi, so, yay, for you being a bio kid. Evie is going to torture you for-ev-er. Us being alive is, like, a threat to their existence. Plus, I'm not the smart one, or the pretty one, or the fun one. I guess, I'm the biggest loser."

"Says the woman who made it through high school and college without a kid in foster care," Charleigh offered. "I am definitely your mother's biggest disappointment."

"Well, that's just cause I'm gay as fuck," Sadie stated.

"Me too," Charleigh offered with a straight-lipped smile. "Still the one that got pregnant."

Sadie's laugh scared away some of the sadness from the room. "Well, at least I wasn't barking up the wrong tree when I tried to hit on you at Evie's house."

"Definitely the wrong tree if you want to keep your trust fund," Charleigh quipped.

Sadie shook her head, then looked at Charleigh. "So, back to why I'm here; and again, our mom did not ask me to come. Since Joey is six, you do not need locks on the cabinets, or the socket covers."

Charleigh nodded even though she couldn't breathe with the other woman referring to Dilynn as 'our mom.' Following Sadie from the living room to her bedroom, felt like she'd taken a step back in time. Like Sadie was meant to be her older sister, and she was meant to shadow the woman. It made the fact Sadie was checking her house that much weirder for Charleigh.

She'd been through these types of checks multiple times. No matter how many times they'd happened, it never made a stranger going through her drawer of underwear any easier. Especially knowing the woman touching her panties had been interested in seeing them on her. Then add to the ickiness with the fact they were related by marriage.

Sadie opened the drawer to the nightstand where Charleigh's self-maintenance devices had been tucked away. The drawer was shut quickly, and Sadie turned to the closet. Pointing to the drawer, the woman squinted her eyes and pursed her lips.

"Maybe put a child lock on that one," she suggested.

Charleigh sighed. "I figured I would just get rid of them so there was no chance she would find it. Not like she has ever been here anyways though."

Sadie's head snapped back from her search of the closet. Her fingers were running over the satin stripper dress Charleigh wore to the engagement party.

"What do you mean she's never been here?" Sadie asked.

"Like, my visitation was only permitted at the park for two hours every other week," Charleigh repeated with a little more detail.

Sadie sat down on Charleigh's bed.

"Um, dude," Charleigh said. When Sadie didn't look up, Charleigh tried again. "Look, I know you have all the power and everything, but, like, that's my bed, and a month ago you were flirting with me, so maybe don't sit on my bed."

The woman didn't move beyond a single finger running through the file. She searched for something, while Charleigh felt the last fibers of her patience being pulled to their breaking point.

"It's gotta be in, like, a handbook or something. There are some boundaries and I want Joey to come home and everything, but screwing people to make them tolerate me is what got me here to begin with, so maybe you just, like, don't."

The finger stopped moving, and her face rose to Charleigh. She tapped the screen, and said, "I have notes you had been granted overnight visits biweekly. That was over six months ago."

Charleigh shook her head. "She has never been here or to my former apartment. I go to my visits. I have only missed one and it was because my car broke down on the way. I walked to my mom's house, but by the time I got there, it was the last five minutes. So, she just let me hug her and then she took her away. She canceled the next three because Joey was sick, and then COVID gave her an excuse to stop letting me come see her for six months."

Sadie looked at the file and then at Charleigh. "Why hasn't Mom helped you with this? She knows the system better than I do, and I work for it."

"Because she hates me more than your sisters apparently hate you." Charleigh wiped the tears before they fell with her thumbs to keep her make-up from running.

"You're working nights now?" Sadie asked.

Charleigh chuckled silently and nodded. "Yep. Since your mom fired me, Echo offered me a job. It's a real job and can you please get off my bed? It's making me, like, really uncomfortable."

"Oh shit. I'm sorry. That is totally in the handbook." Sadie popped up from the pile of clothes she'd been on. "So, who will look after Joey while you're at work?"

Charleigh looked at the girl. She shrugged her shoulders. "Why would I have a babysitter? Like I said, my kid has never been here."

"She's coming home, Charleigh," Sadie stated. Then her eyes grew before her face scrunched up again. "Actually, umm... I need to see her room. She has a room or a bed, right? If she doesn't have a bed, we have programs that could get you a bed for free."

Charleigh stared at her. She'd been denied by this woman's mother for help because of that fucking bed and DCS had ways for her to get one for free. She swallowed her rage and held out her hand to the hallway.

"Her room is across the hall."

Sadie made her way to where Charleigh was pointing. Her finger ran over the busted door frame. "What happened here?"

Charleigh sucked her lips in, then popped them out. "Your sister, the mean one, and my sister got into a wrestling match and fell through the door a few weeks ago when they came to support me after my mom canceled my visits."

A groan burst from Sadie's mouth. "Evie is so mean, but she also punched my ex in the face for cheating on me. I kinda feel like Mona is like that. Like, she'd punch your ex given the chance. I am kinda looking forward to her being around because Evie is actually nicer when she's there."

Charleigh licked her lips. "Mona would definitely punch my ex for me. And she'd punch one for you because you're Evie's little sister."

Sadie entered the purple bedroom. Her body turned in a circle as she leaned back, scanning the stars. She glanced back at Charleigh. "Do you know how many there are?"

"2,155. One for every good night I missed," Charleigh whispered.

Sadie looked in the closet. The purple, sparkly clothes hung on the child's sized rail. Sadie opened the box of purple Jordans.

"A friend of mine plays for the Phoenix Devils. She bought them for Joey before she left for Italy," Charleigh explained.

Sadie nodded, putting the shoe back in the box and the box on the shelf. Charleigh stepped out of the doorway, allowing Sadie space to leave Joey's room.

"Do you have a carseat or do you need one?" Sadie asked.

"Uh, I need to get one," Charleigh said. "I can pick one up--"

"Don't worry, I have a few in my garage for this situation. I will bring one by tomorrow after I meet with my supervisor." Sadie looked back up at Charleigh. "We have to make a safety plan. Do you have time today or should I come back tomorrow?

"How long will it take?" Charleigh asked, wringing her hands together. "I want to do this now. Whatever it takes, however, I also can't lose another job. I am looking for a new teaching position, but I can't put your parents down for, like, a reference and that's all of my experience."

The room became interesting to the woman. She wound a curl around her finger once more, watching it spiral.

"I know you think she's out to get you, but she came home and cried the night she let you go. I was the only one home and I asked her what was wrong, and... and... she said she'd messed everything up. I didn't know what she was talking about until Obi came home, and they were yelling about how Sylvia was right about it being cruel to you. They were so angry, I thought for sure they were going to leave again. They always leave when they are pissed, and every time I think, this is it. They won't come back this time. My sisters think I live in the guest house because I'm dumb, but... they weren't there. They went off to college the year they got married, and I was there with them. I was there every time Obi walked out. Their walking out was part of why I never got adopted, but Mom was the one who gave me my first real home even after Obi walked out after finding out I was related to them. So, I stay at the house, so she won't be alone if they don't come back."

Charleigh didn't tell the woman Dilynn was only crying over potentially losing her school to Sylvia's revenge. What the woman wanted to believe about her mother wasn't any of Charleigh's concern if she was there to help.

"So, do I, like, wait for my court date in January now, and you, like, recommend that Joey comes home with me?" Charleigh asked.

Sadie's eyebrows scrunched in the middle. "You literally have no idea how any of this works do you?"

"Case managers usually go talk to my mom first. She tells them I'm a drunk whore, and then they hate me immediately." Charleigh wrapped her arms around herself. "You're the first one who even really looked at me. However, no one else ever sat on my bed"

Sadie snorted out a laugh, then said. "Well, you're gorgeous, how could I not?"

Her hand slapped over her mouth. She lifted it only to add, "Oh my god, I am so sorry. Please, don't tell my supervisor I said that."

Charleigh shrugged, glancing down at her chest. "I work at a lesbian bar after the internet has seen me naked. Trust me, that's the nicest thing anyone has said to me in weeks. And to be fair about everything, you are one of the pretty Greyson girls. My sister and I used to make up stories about you guys, like, you were royalty, and we'd pretend, like, we were peasants that would, like, swoop in to save the princesses and get to marry into the royal family. Stupid kid stuff, but... sorry. I just figured you should know that we never thought of you any differently than your sisters."

"Thanks. That's really sweet." Sadie slipped her tablet into her oversized bag that looked like a Dilynn hand-me-down. She clasped her hands together and swayed side to side. "Just wondering... who did you get to marry in these fantasies?"

Charleigh couldn't stop the eye roll. "You know, I should have been worried about Mona years ago when she always said she was rescuing Princess Evilee."

"And you rescued...?"

"You know this was a different game when I didn't know I was related to you," Charleigh stated.

Sadie laughed, but her hand came up to tug on her neck. Apparently Sadie didn't just get Alex Trikru looks. She got the whole package of quirks with female packaging.

"It was you." Charleigh sighed. She waved her hand in the air. "I imagined being Greyson, and well... Greyson and Trikru. Everyone always said I looked like Greyson and, you know, all the queers crushed on you because you look like Trikru. I guess this was the plot twist, right? Like, it turns out we are sorta related, so it's even more of a twisted fairytale."

Sadie's laughter was rich and warm, spreading throughout the room, growing colder by the day. It wrapped Charleigh in a hug even though the two didn't touch.

"Thanks," Sadie offered, her face flushed just enough to make Charleigh feel like she didn't completely ruin this meeting. "It's nice to know that I was chosen because I know." She looked at the floor with a far-off gaze, quietly adding, "I know what it's like to feel like the people who are supposed to love you threw you away."

The sadness crept back into the room with the shadows. The sun was falling, and Sadie's gaze told Charleigh she did understand. Even living in a castle came with its challenges. Mona and she used to laugh off rich people's problems. Like, Sylvia's confession had just been a rich girl issue, but that didn't make the pain any less. That was something Charleigh understood now.

"So, the safety plan is going to take time. I'll come back in the morning to go through it with you and we will make some decisions and figure out what support I can put in place for you," Sadie explained. She placed her tablet into her bag. "Then, basically I file my report that your home is free of any potential dangers. I will note that you have childcare for your night shifts through your sister and my sister since their pregnant asses need some practice. My supervisor will look over the report and when she approves it, then it will go to the ADA."

Sadie took another scan around the room. "I noticed Lyra is assigned to the case, which I am betting has something to do with her and Evie being pissed at Mom. They apparently had some bonfire planning session, but you know didn't bother to call the person who could *actually* fix things." Sadie waved away her words. "Anyway, she will then file for a change of custody motion. I will call her and make sure it's ready before I even meet with my supervisor. After that, we just wait on the judge to sign it and Joey comes home."

"How long does it take the judge?" Charleigh asked, trying to protect the ember of hope Sadie breathed into life.

Sadie shrugged. "I have never seen it take longer than two weeks."

"Two weeks?" Charleigh choked. Her eyes moved around the house. "She'll be *here* in two weeks?"

Sadie tilted her head. "This is what you want isn't it? You have all the requirements. There's no alcohol, and the pantry has food in it. Chemicals weren't within reach. I mean, even with the rainbow of dildos in the drawer, there are no concerns. Questions, but no concerns."

"Like... like, the judge won't, like, say no, even with the stupid sex tape?"

Sadie stared at Charleigh like she'd lost her mind. "Was it a tape of you having sex with a child?"

"No," Charleigh said, shaking her head in case her verbal response wasn't enough.

"Then, the judge would have no concern about any of it."

Charleigh wrapped her arms around Sadie's thin body. She hopped, holding the woman as she thanked her over and over again.

Joey was coming home.

37

The silent phone taunted Lexa. She felt like she was watching the seconds count down in a game she could lose. Each moment was happening in slow motion with her unable to help because Coach Charleigh ejected Lexa from the game.

The woman took the ball and was running a play with people Lexa couldn't just call to check on her. Not after Echo had texted Parker that she was staying with Sylvia until she was okay, and Charleigh's friends said she couldn't go to dinner with them because she wasn't wearing a shirt.

So, she returned to the short-term rental, where all of her things were. Everything she'd brought to Charleigh's had made it to the one-bedroom condo. A space smaller than Charleigh's tiny house, with a couch that was hard and too small to curl up on into a ball.

All Lexa could do was wait for someone to reach out to her. And waiting was never something she had been good at. She'd spent every day since she'd driven away from the house she'd shared with Sylvia with her phone in her hand. But not once had it rung.

Scared to set it down, the device became her distraction. She scrolled through TikTok, hoping it would cause her brain to rot and kill the termite in her mind that kept tunneling back to her memories of the woman who hadn't reached out in two weeks. She watched the videos until her thumb slipped and her face was displayed on the screen.

As she tried out a filter that showed her the male version of herself, she wondered if people would have seen her differently had she been a boy. If her mother would have hated her less if her hair could have been kept short? She considered briefly going back at her head with the scissors until there was nothing left but stopped herself.

With a shitty image that needed fixing, Lexa began to occupy her time with becoming TikTok famous. A part of her hoped Charleigh would see her keeping her shit together. She started small, filming back-and-forth skits about talking to rookies she'd played with. After acting out a conversation she'd had with Danaya, the younger woman came back with her own skit, setting off a battle of impersonation videos.

The younger woman had an advantage, playing on Lexa's inability to be Black enough. The final straw was a poke at the matted puff atop her head. When Lexa didn't post a response, Danaya sent her a calendar invite for the hair appointment she'd scheduled for Lexa. It was a reminder of something else Lexa needed to learn how to do for herself.

That night, Lexa stood in the mirror, bearing her soul for the viewers who'd logged into her Live. She pulled at the butchered sections of her hair as she told the world her truth.

"A few weeks ago, I suffered from a Bipolar drop."

She licked her lips, looking at the camera centered in the ring light Amazon had dropped on her doorstep earlier that afternoon.

"When you're bipolar and the drop happens, it feels like the world is collapsing around you. Well, for me it was like the ground shook like an asteroid had struck Earth. The walls were falling and everything was crushing me into the ground."

Lexa wet her hair with the shower nozzle. Carefully carved sections against her scalp to get to all the mattes she'd let develop since Charleigh and Danaya weren't around to help her. Coming to the appointment washed and detangled was an expectation, and she would have to figure out how to do it without another set of hands.

"I kept my condition a secret from everyone around me but my former wife, who worked tirelessly to help me maintain stability. Some people can function without meds, but I can't. I think there's been enough documentation from this summer proving I need my meds."

Her long fingers worked to separate the knots. She smoothed some conditioner over her fingertips to help the detangling process.

"My hair has always been a struggle for me. I have a white mother who never wanted a child who looked like me, so I spent my life afraid and hateful of my hair. I sought out styles that rejected it the way my mother had."

With the knots cleared, she rinsed the conditioner from her head. Then she scrubbed a section with a shampoo bar, building up the lather before moving on to the next section.

Looking up into the camera, she said, "If you're watching this and you have a baby with curls, please take her to see someone who can help her know she's not alone. I was so scared to go get my hair braided last time because I was worried she'd tell me I was ugly and stupid for not knowing what to do. But it was a great experience, and I left feeling like I didn't have to hate myself."

When each section was foamy, Lexa blew the bubbles still on her hands at the camera. "Tomorrow, I have an appointment to get my braids replaced, but

I think I'm going to try something new. I'm going to learn how to take care of my hair, so I don't feel like I'm not good enough."

Lexa ran the water over her hair, rinsing away the shampoo. When she was sopping wet, without a hint of foam left, Lexa smiled at the camera.

"All summer, I have tried to learn how to two-strand twist. So tomorrow, I hope you join me as I meet up with a stylist, and she's going to walk us through how to get the perfect twist."

She applied the conditioner and let it set as she answered the questions popping up on the screen. She chewed on her lip as someone commented, 'I used to play ball but when I was diagnosed the pills made me not able to move as well.'

"So, someone shared that they stopped playing ball due to the medication prescribed to them after being diagnosed with bipolar disorder."

Lexa studied her face in the camera before she responded. Thought of standing on the sideline of Sylvia's court, staring at the hoop. The doctors in the treatment facility had told her to give up basketball and said she wouldn't be able to keep up. It was part of why she'd left with Kayla. But Sylvia put the ball back in her hands. Told her she'd been watching her play, and knew she could go pro. A dream the doctors had tried to drown with water and meds was once again a possibility.

She couldn't tell this person that they would be able to do what she did. A part of her knew if Sylvia hadn't taken over managing her routine and perfecting her cocktail over the years, she wouldn't have made it as far as she did.

"I take meds to regulate, but I will admit that the first year it was awful. Sylvia was definitely my anchor at the time because I felt like I was walking around in a fog. Lethargic and so thirsty. I do have to drink more water than my teammates, and when I first joined the Devils, the girls used to joke because by half time I had to pee so bad that I would be dancing on the court."

A smile spread over her face. "I really can't sit here and say that you can play ball if you're medicated. I know this girl. She's pretty awesome and when I hit the bottom, I expected her to vanish, but she told me that the chaos in my head wasn't something I had to be ashamed of. She said I was just built differently, and it was okay. It was okay to take the meds that made me feel more in control of my life."

Lexa scanned the question scrolling across the screen. She grabbed the bottle of water from the counter and took a long drink before she answered.

"I regret cheating on my wife. I regret hurting her and making her feel like she wasn't enough for me, and being bipolar isn't an excuse. I used it as an excuse for a long time, to the point I think she started to believe it was an expectation. But it's not.

"The reality is mania can cause you to make impulsive decisions. For me, it was typically related to sex and thinking women wanted me more than they really did. But there was, like, this voice in my head that convinced me I was invincible, and I could fix whatever happened. It also had a way of really making me think what I did wasn't that bad until I dropped, and then everything would be so bad."

Lexa fought the urge to run her fingers through her hair that was still sitting with the conditioner.

"Here's the thing I think everyone who is dating someone with bipolar disorder should know. We don't know when we are manic that we aren't superhumans. We have so much going on internally, we just don't realize we are breakable or anyone else is breakable unless we want them to break. And you should never accept our impulsive decisions as just part of the course. You deserve to be treated with respect, and you deserve to have our promises kept to you."

She took a deep breath as she saw Sylvia's name on the screen as a viewer. She'd seen the woman had watched all of her videos as she scanned through the list of viewers in the hope of seeing Charleigh's name appear.

"I will never be able to apologize to my former wife and have her truly believe I mean it when I say I'm sorry because I said it too many times before and then did it again. She deserved the vows I said to her to be honored, so when she told the world our divorce was our fault, it was a lie. It was a lie because the only person who was at fault was me.

"I was the one that refused to take my meds, even though I knew if I didn't, I would spend my nights at the bar and I would go home with someone else who didn't deserve to be treated like a side chick."

With another deep breath, she looked at the camera.

"This wasn't exactly my plan when I started this Live, but I figured while some of you were here, I would just be honest because I haven't been very honest over the last year. I owe a lot of people my life. I owe the waitress at Coach's bar for slapping some sense into me when I tried to pretend I was important. I owe Sylvia for having the courage to say enough and not let me continue to pretend that I was fine and nothing was wrong with how I treated her. Emma Deangelo for literally picking me up off the ground and taking away the scissors when I tried to recreate her hairstyle on my head. I can't pull off short hair the way that woman can. Danaya Tanzon for telling me that she wanted to be friends with Tomorrow Lexa. I am not sure if I am there yet, but each tomorrow gets me a little closer to the human she deserves to play next too, and I'm excited to see her again next season.

"Lastly, I owe so much to the woman who held me above water when I couldn't figure out how to swim. That's what she told me one night when I was hating myself. She said, I just had to learn how to swim, which I knew was possible because I can swim. Like, it was just some skill I needed to practice."

Lexa thought about the swimming lessons she'd gotten from Charleigh. How the woman rarely complained about anything in life besides her own mistakes. There was no stopping the smile as she remembered Charleigh groaning about saying orgasm in class. It fell when she realized she didn't smile when Charleigh told her. She'd gone off her meds again and didn't notice that Charleigh was showing her how to be upset without blowing up. Charleigh had given her so much, and the only thing Lexa offered her was exactly what she didn't want. Used her money to replace Charleigh's things when it was exactly what the blonde had scolded Sylvia for.

"We made a deal that feels like ages ago, I wouldn't mention her ever on social media, so I'm not going to break that promise now. I just want to make sure she knows that I'm learning to swim with the floaties she gave me." Lexa took a breath. "And I hope that she knows if she is getting too tired to swim, that she can call me. That I could hold you if you just need a minute to rest."

She fought back the tears. Swallowed the rest of what she wanted Charleigh to know, including the apology for being another person who was granted access to her heart and didn't realize the care it needed.

Lexa's chin fell, and she looked up at the camera with just her eyes. "And maybe ask her to make sure her sister doesn't try to liquefy me. I kinda like feeling like a lump of obsidian and really don't wanna feel like lava. Ever. Oh, and since Danaya decided to make fun of my hair, I think everyone should know the girl studied geology in school. Like total nerd, so if you see her and you want to make her girl jealous, she loves rocks."

Lexa laughed at how pissed Danaya would be when she woke up the next morning to find she'd been outed as a nerd.

"Well, I'm going to rinse out the conditioner, and I hope tomorrow you will join me as I learn how to twist. And if anyone knows of a good stylist in Melbourne, I'll be there in a few weeks."

She smiled at the camera, hoping someone might take her failures to heart and have the courage not to feel like they had to hide. Then, she turned off the feed and pulled her clothes from her body. As she looked down at the counter, she saw the card Echo had given her.

The therapist had been kind when she'd called for an appointment. Promised to get her in before she left the country so they could have a face-to-face before they started telehealth appointments. But that was a week away and a week after that the extension she'd requested to give her time to see Charleigh would be up.

She'd have to get on the plane whether Charleigh called her or not. She'd have to get on the plane. She'd keep telling herself that, because Sylvia wasn't there to force her to be an adult anymore. She had to manage her career on her own, so she'd be able to show Charleigh she could be trusted to keep her promises when she came back.

38

By 10 PM on Tuesday, most of Echo's customers had moved away from Charleigh's station to the dance floor and patio. With only a group of four women playing a dart match remotely and a creeper that had already pointed out she'd seen Charleigh's tits on the internet, Charleigh wondered how this was supposed to keep her afloat with Joey coming home so soon.

She looked at the therapist making drinks behind the bar, who'd clearly made better life choices than her with her new car parked outside and her stable relationship.

"I'm going to apply for a teaching job with Echo's friend, Victoria. I mean, she knows about the video already, and maybe working at a K-8 won't be so bad. At least Joey could go to school where I work," she told Parker as she leaned over the bar and grabbed an orange wedge from the container Parker just filled.

"Probably a good idea." Bottle caps dinged against the bar. Parker gave her a side-eyed glance as she flicked her wrist and sent another cap in the air. "I've never seen so many beers dropped at once, so many times in a row before."

Charleigh tried to hide the blush on her face with the tray in her hands. "I thought I saw Sylvia, so I was trying to duck. And then people don't like to get out of the way when I am trying to carry them."

As she waited for Parker's sarcastic retort she'd learned to expect, she felt the air stop moving. Parker's eyes grew and she froze with the bottle opener still resting on the cap of the bottle in her hand. Charleigh turned in time to watch Dilynn settling her royal ass into a seat at one of Charleigh's tables.

Parker hummed in disapproval. She ripped her phone from her pocket and tapped against her screen. Setting the device down, she explained, "She never comes in alone, which means Alex dipped again or she is here to pick a fight with you or me."

Charleigh knew Parker called for backup, but this was her job now. No matter what Dilynn had in store for her. "I'll go. Even if she's mad at you, she'll see me and find something to lose her shit over."

With the tray against her chest to cover the display of cleavage Parker had adjusted for her, Charleigh made her way to the woman. She stood across the table and asked politely, "What can I get you?"

Dilynn didn't look up. Her fingertips pressed together until her knuckles popped as she scanned the room. "Vodka coke," she said. Then added, "On ice."

Charleigh took the lack of greeting as the sign that for once the woman was more pissed at someone else. Without a word, she retreated to the bar.

She called the order to Parker, pronounced her annoyance the woman had felt the need to tell her a vodka coke needed ice, and retrieved another orange slice from behind the bar. Parker smacked her hand with the bottle opener, but Charleigh smiled and pushed the fruit into her mouth. She'd forgotten how much she liked oranges.

"She's coming for you," Charleigh said. "Never have I gotten out of her sight without being lashed with her words, so whatever you did, I would start thinking how to undo it. I mean, she needs a new scapegoat, and that car payment has to be heavy."

"Echo said just drop off the drink," Parker instructed when she slid a glass of brown liquid bubbling around the ice cubes to Charleigh. "She'll head over in a few minutes."

Charleigh didn't have to be told twice. She set the drink down without a word, then took another order from the dart players. Her ass was smacked by the creeper when she passed, but she kept walking to the bar where she got another orange while she waited for the drinks.

In the time it took Parker to make the order, Dilynn finished half the glass in a single swallow. Her eyes squinted at the remaining liquid, and she pursed her lips. The weight of something pushed Dilynn toward the table where her breasts rested on the surface, and she spun the glass in her hand.

"You want me to take her next drink?" Parker asked, looking over Charleigh's shoulder at Dilynn.

Charleigh sighed and her head fell back. The regret she'd known would come from leaving behind the check settled in her throat. She tried to swallow it, but it wouldn't budge so she forced the words out around it.

"I got it."

Tucking her hair behind her ear, Charleigh approached the table after dropping off the dart players' orders. She cradled her shield against her once more, covering her breasts from Dilynn's disapproving gaze. The ice queen wouldn't understand the new expectations of her to show more and smile more to sell more.

Calling over the music whose volume had increased, Charleigh asked, "Round 2?"

The watery remnants of the drink shook slightly. Dilynn didn't look up at the disaster across from her, but her disappointment dripped from her words.

"I don't know why I thought you'd show up at the board meeting tonight. I know you said you weren't going to fight. I just thought you'd come."

Customers flooded the dance floor as "The Wobble" started. Echo made her way through the crowd with her phone in hand. She recorded herself with her customers moving in step with the instructions. Smiles and shouts tried to melt the ice around them, but nothing could make the goose pebbles on Charleigh's skin disappear.

"I promised you I would disappear."

It was a promise she'd intended to keep. One even Echo respected by not scheduling Charleigh on nights she'd gotten wind that Dilynn would be coming in. But she'd been too afraid to reach out to follow up with Sylvia, Alex, or Marcus.

"Sylvia said she wouldn't sell the property. If she doesn't call you, then I can go see her." Charleigh dreaded the idea of seeing Sylvia again. "But she promised me she wouldn't sell it."

"She called. Said you changed her mind and that I owed you. There were a lot of other things she said, but... she was right. I should have fought Grace for you. Never should have let her on campus." Dilynn tapped the table and shook the drink. "I knew she wouldn't sell, but Alex... Alex said she just might be angry enough with me to actually do it. That you'd told her how terrible I was to you... that the day in the yard wasn't the first time you'd told them I hated you. That they couldn't believe it until they saw it themself how awful I was. How I.... Was I really that bad?"

Charleigh looked down. She tried to remember a single time since coming back to the school when Dilynn treated her halfway decently, but she came up with nothing. Thinking about it made her angry, and she wanted to list out every time Dilynn publicly tore her confidence apart. Vengeance was never her oath in all her fractured tales because she wanted redemption. She wanted them both to have a moment where they didn't suck. Just a few minutes of reconciliation they could prove to the other that they weren't liars. She was tired of being a liar.

"It doesn't matter. It's done. The school is safe. Marcus, Mona, and Parker's jobs are safe. Kinsley gets to graduate. And none of the kids lose their beds. Everything is how it should be."

"Mona quit," Dilynn stated like Charleigh wouldn't already know that. "All my kids are pissed at me."

She looked Charleigh straight in the face. "*All* of them. Lyra wants to sell her house to Echo because Parker hates me. Evie and Landon are even moving because Mona said she wanted nothing to do with me, so now they are all moving out. Sadie isn't talking to me. And you... you have every reason to hate me. I gave up on ever knowing you, and so you don't know. You don't know that I worked so hard to keep this family together, and you... you don't know the sacrifices I made for all of them. For you."

A group of friends in shimmery blouses crowded around a table in her station. Charleigh tapped her fingers against the wooden top Dilynn leaned against, still staring at the glass.

"I'll get you another drink. Sounds like you could use it."

"The kids came to the board meeting," Dilynn said, raising her gaze from the glass. "Your kids. They came with signs and a chant. Kinsley organized a rally on your behalf."

A smile tugged at the corners of Charleigh's lips. "She's a lot like Mona. All fight. She even tried to punch Sylvia in the face. If she makes it through college without getting pregnant, she's going somewhere in life."

She tucked her hair behind her ear, then decided to share her fear. "I hope, even if she does get pregnant that you'll still help her go to school. She's not as fucked up as me and they have, like, family housing now so she wouldn't have to give up the baby if that happened."

"She's going to school," Dilynn stated. "I changed a lot of things since you, so her college fund is already secured."

"Good." Charleigh looked back at the table of women now glaring at her.

"They caused quite the scene, your kids. The meeting took an extra two hours because we sat through seventy-eight testimonials." Dilynn licked her lips. "They scared the shit out of the board. Kept talking about how it's their responsibility to remind the board where the line between villains and heroes lies, and that power used to strip someone who already was violated is and I quote 'barbaric customs of the dying patriarchy.'"

The corners of Dilynn's lips curled upward. "The board is mainly women, and being equated to men did not sit well with them. Ended in a four to three vote."

Charleigh's eyebrows cinched in the middle. "Vote for what?"

"To reinstate your contract, effective immediately."

Charleigh nodded to the women at the table, trying to flag her down. "I'm sorry they pissed off your people, but at least the kids got to feel accomplished at swaying three people to their side and you still won."

"I did win. I won when they showed up for you. Means I was smart to hire you to begin with. And I won because they forced the board into a tie and as head of the school, I got to be the tiebreaker, so you got your job back... if you still want it."

Charleigh's jaw dropped open. A hundred words flooded her mouth, so she snapped it shut quickly to keep any from falling out.

"I mean, you may need it because you're a terrible server." Dilynn drained the rest of her drink. She pointed to the table of women glaring at Charleigh. "They're about to go to the bar for their drinks."

"You voted to give me my job back?" Charleigh asked instead of pointing out that Dilynn was the one keeping her from getting a tip at the other table.

"I don't hate you. I could never hate you. Never wanted to give you up. I just.... You need to know that I never hated you."

Dilynn swiveled the glass of ice in her hand. Her blue eyes rose to look at Charleigh for the first time since sitting down.

"I hate *me*. Always have. And every time I saw you, it's like looking in a fucking mirror." Dilynn waved her hand in a circle at Charleigh. "It's like watching a rerun of my past. I started drinking after my dad died and my mom was angry and always fighting with me. So, when Marcus and Alex brought you to the school, I was already depressed and I saw you, I thought okay I did the right thing. Opening this school was the right thing because you were the first we tried to save. You were supposed to be like saving Alex, and then everything was so wrong. It's why seeing you in Alex's jacket was too much because they're mine and... I know. I know they would never cheat on me... but I have been left for a younger woman before and it just brought up all those memories. And I didn't know."

Dilynn shook her glass, then her head.

"I looked for you in every kid, and when I first saw you, my heart went into overdrive. I couldn't breathe, and... and I just wanted to hold you. I wanted to hold you because I only had a day with you before they took you away. I left school after you walked into my first period class. I had to leave because I had rushed into the office demanding Alex pull your file. It had to be you. My duplicate with my daughter's name, but it had never been you before, so I was sure it wasn't you again. And I never looked at your file because I couldn't play pretend. I made Evie a promise when I opened the school that I wouldn't bring any more kids home. And Alex had the file held out, but I knew I couldn't look. I couldn't handle it not being you again. Jesus, I was so stupid. I missed all your birthdays because I always took that day off. I couldn't deal. Have never dealt with having to give you up."

The table of women moved to Parker at the bar with Charleigh's potential tip. The Tuesday night crowd thinned quickly as Dilynn's confession continued.

"I shoulda brought you home with Joey, but I was afraid of hurting you more since I already failed you. Alex and I never thought Mona and you would split up. We thought her moving to the school was the best idea since I voted no to Mona coming to live with us. I told Alex we couldn't. I had a promise to keep to Evie and... and... I'd fucked up so much with our girls. I mean, they grew up to be strong women, but I hurt them so much when I lost the baby and said it was because I wasn't supposed to be a mom. They thought it was because of the baby but it was because we got in an accident after we went to visit Sadie in the rehab facility. We had failed her, and the anorexia had gotten so bad because I said we could fix it, and then we couldn't. So, we were coming home, and the car hit us, and Lyra was in surgery and Evie was in shock and Tyler, our baby... she died in Alex's arms because she came too early. And I felt like it all happened because I had failed. I failed at being the mom any of them deserved because if I had gotten Sadie help earlier, then we never would have been there and.... Jesus, you don't need to hear all this."

Each sentence, even the fragments, were pieces of Charleigh's story she'd spent years yearning for. Every word filled in one of the blank pages of her life; answers to plaguing questions. She wanted Dilynn to descriptively disclose every detail from the moment she'd known. Tell her the tale of her name; describe the moments they shared before separation.

The tremble of her lower lip stopped her from asking for more though. She couldn't cry even though Dilynn wiped the tear from her face before it had a chance to fall to the table.

"I just want you to know that I know. I know it was my fault. Everything. I should have brought Mona home, and then you two would have still been together and you wouldn't have been... brutalized. I mean we brought you to the school to be protected and instead... I'm sorry, Charleigh."

It was the first apology she'd ever gotten from Dilynn but for the wrong action. Making Mona a Greyson wouldn't have stopped Joey from being born, but knowing that's what Dilynn wanted made the unshed tears vaporize. She didn't regret Joey being born like Dilynn regretted her. Given the chance to do it again, she knew nothing would have changed because Kyle had bore into her psychologically and physically before Mona even considered breaking up with her.

She'd lied to herself and to others for so long. The meds for depression she'd countered with uppers and booze masked her sorrows when her idol took her birthday off each year. Her pain didn't justify how she'd ruined countless lives by letting Kayla and the boys in the bomb shelter cover up her desire for her mother's love. Allowed for Kyle's promise to teach her how straight girls did things as just a way to go back to the only mother she'd ever known. And the lies were heavier than her limbs felt.

"May I sit?" Charleigh asked, praying the woman wouldn't walk away once more.

Dilynn wiped her nose with her sweater sleeve. "Yeah."

Charleigh's feet thanked her as they lifted from the ground. There wasn't a great place to start because she'd been lying for so long, that she wasn't even sure when she'd become the villain of her own story.

"It wasn't your job to be my mother, just like it wasn't Marcus's job to be my dad," was where she decided to begin. It was the truth, and she was going to tell the truth. "You had the right to give me up for adoption. I don't blame you for that, and I know that being a teen mom is terrifying. You and Trikru and your family are the thing every kid in your school looks up to. You love your kids no matter who they choose to be, so maybe stop beating yourself up so much."

"That's really easy to say," Dilynn said. A heavy breath rushed out of her. "But when they do things that you know are going to hurt them, you can't help but ask yourself what you did wrong. Like you. Why are you with Sylvia? She's too old for you and... look, I know BDSM. Everyone enjoys different things, but she shouldn't ever, I mean *ever*, hit you in the face. She was never like that when we met, and I don't understand what that woman did to her, but that is a line that she never should have crossed."

Charleigh glanced back at Parker. She was still making drinks, but her eyes were constantly looking up at them. She had to get out her truth before Echo or Parker came to save her like a princess in distress. She always knew she wasn't a princess, but she'd have to make amends to stop being the villain.

"I'm not with Sylvia. She just thought if you thought we were together you wouldn't fire me. And I think you should know that I hit her first. She's just way stronger than me, so when she hit me back...." Charleigh shook her head and laughed. "It fucking hurt like hell, but then she offered me a check for a lot of money and gave me a house that I can't figure out how to give back to her. She said she threatened to sell the school to remind you that you made a deal with her, and you didn't keep up your end."

"But I saw her car in the parking lot. The SUV," Dilynn argued.

Charleigh shook her head again. "That was Lexa. Lexa and I were seeing each other for the past several months. She gave me rides to work before I borrowed Danaya's car."

"Then, who made the video?" Dilynn asked.

"Kayla. She made it to hurt me, and--"

Dilynn sucked her teeth. "I should have pressed charges against Kayla for what she did to you."

Glancing around the bar, Charleigh considered what would have changed if she'd made a different choice. The repercussions of her actions would have changed so many lives. Existence as they knew it would be entirely different, but she knew some things for sure. Specifically, she knew Kayla, Lexa, and Sylvia's lives would have been different because if Kayla hadn't gotten expelled then Lexa and Kayla may never have met. Kayla wouldn't have taken Lexa home to Sylvia, who never would have helped Lexa get treatment for so long. Their paths wouldn't have crossed, and Charleigh would probably still be pretending Grace and Dilynn were the reason Joey wasn't with her. She'd still be lying to herself, so she recommitted to stop lying.

"No one wanted to look at me when you were all deciding what to do. None of you ever asked me what happened." She waited until Dilynn looked at her. "You can stop blaming yourself. I knew what I was doing, and I stayed too late so Mona would come get me and I let everyone think I was raped because everyone was too afraid to ask me any questions. I was already pregnant, and the father wanted me to get an abortion to cover his ass, so I made it look like Joey was someone else's. That's why I was there."

The ice in the glass was mostly melted, but Dilynn shook it anyway. A heavy sign rushed over the table, but Dilynn looked up from the drink once more.

"I knew for sure when Joey was five months old, and her eyes were too blue to be any of the boys that went with you that day, who her father was." Dilynn looked up at the ceiling. "I fucked up so badly that even when you came to me for help, you didn't feel like you could tell me that you were being abused in the place we put you to keep you safe. You just took all the responsibility while he got to walk away without anyone thinking any different."

"I always thought Mona would figure it out," Charleigh said, ducking her head. "I guess not ever getting to meet her made it easier for Mona not to know. Marcus too."

"Whatever happened with Kyle shouldn't have happened. I think you should know that Marcus knows too. But I knew Kyle had to be Joey's father and I knew you didn't tell me or Alex or Marcus because of what happened with Mona."

"How did Marcus...?" Charleigh couldn't finish the sentence.

"He said he heard Kyle threaten you right before you went into labor, and he blamed himself for letting it happen. That's why he wasn't at the hospital with you and why Mona couldn't get there," Dilynn explained. "He went on a binder. Called Alex, too drunk to make words beyond that you needed a fresh start. Kyle was his biological son, and he was too ashamed to tell me or Alex that he'd been so blind. He only told me the truth when I confronted him about it when your mom showed up and tried to take custody. I yelled at him that he could go to court and fight for custody. I even threatened to fire him, but he said if you wanted him in Joey's life, you'd have told him. And... he was worried about what would happen if Kyle had access to Joey since he got another girl pregnant right after you had Joey. And Marcus's ex-wife and that crazy cult you were raised in made that girl marry him."

"Yeah, I heard the girl he married finally asked for a divorce," Charleigh whispered.

"Good for her." Dilynn nodded to herself. "Look, Marcus said when you were ready, you would tell him he was a grandfather, but you should know.... After you left, he broke down. He had a heart attack, but he's going to be okay. But, he told me that I was right, that he should have fought because now he'd never get to meet her, and he'd never get to tell you how sorry he was."

Dilynn took a deep breath.

"He wants so badly to meet Joey. We all do. Grace wouldn't let any of us see her. Wouldn't let us come to her first birthday, or any birthday. We got one Christmas before she sent DCS to our house and we couldn't provide the updated guardianship paperwork."

"I figured once I told you that we're related you would have already been at the courthouse fighting for custody," Charleigh confessed.

"Well, my lawyer is marrying my daughter and refused to represent me," Dilynn sucked her teeth. "And the daughter I put through law school told me she is representing the state. And I mean, Sylvia got Simmons to represent to you. And Alex said... well, Alex had a lot to say. More words were put into sentences that I think they have ever compiled at once. They even had note cards to make sure that I understood they too are pissed at me. But they basically said that you made it clear years ago that you didn't want me raising your daughter. That's why you didn't come back to sign the papers."

Charleigh closed her eyes. She'd seen the calendar reminder, but she couldn't bring herself to ask Mona to take her back to the mansion. Seeing the life Dilynn gave Joey after knowing she'd been given away had been too much.

"I... I was depressed. I... I went to the courthouse. I asked for my adoption records because I was going to find my birth mom. I was going to find out if it was worth it. If I should give her to you, and I.... That's why I didn't come to sign the papers." Charleigh squeezed the tray against her chest. "I hadn't seen her since Trikru left the hospital with her. I couldn't see her in your arms because... because I was angry with you and... and... and I was scared I would tell you to keep her, but that you wouldn't want her because you didn't want me. You'd realize she was part of me and you didn't want me around. That she would grow up to look like me and you would hate her as much as you hated me. I have convinced myself that you were raped and that's why you couldn't stand looking at me."

Dilynn's tears felt like waves washing over Charleigh. They didn't stop falling, even as she gave Charleigh more pieces of her story.

"I wasn't raped. Your father... Jax. His name was Jax, and he wasn't a bad guy. He was a kid like me, and he passed when I was twenty. He had a liver disease, and he... he wanted you as much as I did, but my mom convinced me adoption was my only option."

Charleigh let the new information settle. She briefly wondered why she felt like mourning the man she'd never met. However, a piece of her heart was being sewn back together. Knowing she'd not been unloved when she was born was something she'd never thought she would feel.

Reaching into her bag, Dilynn pulled out a thick stack of papers. There was no way it could be a teaching contract, and Charleigh looked at the single line across the top page.

"I don't process like normal people do," Dilynn whispered, pushing the stack toward Charleigh. "I couldn't talk to you over the last few weeks because I didn't know how to say I'm sorry. I didn't know how to tell you that everything you saw from me wasn't how I felt. So, I wrote it down. I started at the beginning, so you would know that there is more than what you saw."

Charleigh's fingers ran over the title of Dilynn's newest novel.

"*Out of the Ashes?*" Charleigh asked, looking up at Dilynn.

"Fractured fairytale," Dilynn offered. She drank some of the melted ice from her glass. "You always loved them when you were a kid. Always wanted to talk about the villain's side of the story, so I thought maybe it was a story you wouldn't mind being a protagonist in."

"Am I the villain?" Charleigh asked, flipping to the first page.

"No, that would be me," Dilynn whispered. "I'm the evil ice queen, as Mona called me, and you're the lost princess who found her way back to the castle. To a kingdom, no one knew you belonged in. But you do belong, Charleigh. I could have.... I should have seen you and I should have fought Grace because then you would have come home. You would have come home, and she wouldn't have been—"

"Did Sadie tell you she's coming home?" Charleigh asked.

Dilynn licked her lips. "I called in a favor. Asked her supervisor if she could reassign your case. I shoulda done it a long time ago, but I was angry. I figured if you saw some hope, then... then maybe you'd have the courage to leave Sylvia. Besides the fact she's too old for you, we were together for seven years. She proposed to me. It's just... not okay."

There was no stopping the laugh that burst from Charleigh. It was so loud it startled Dilynn, but Charleigh had to get it all out before she said, "I told her she better not kiss me in her skit at the school because she'd had her tongue in my mother's birth canal."

Dilynn looked ready to throw up. Covering her mouth, she shook her head.

"And she kissed me anyways," Charleigh said, then bobbed her head from side to side. "And I kissed her back, which was weird, but I get why Echo is obsessed with her. She is a good kisser."

"Nope," Dilynn said, waving the words away. "No. Not okay. I get why Alex doesn't want to ever talk to you girls about romance. I mean, the last time they tried Alex signed us all up for therapy."

They sat at the table both looking at one another. Therapy was probably what they needed at another moment. Not now though. They needed the minutes passing by to make up for lost years. Charleigh stayed still when Dilynn moved a seat closer. Let the woman's hand cup her cheek once more and closed her eyes to imagine a different life where Dilynn's personality and heart had been as warm as this touch.

Dilynn was crying again though. Her tears plunked against the tabletop even as Charleigh took her hand.

"When Joey comes home, she's going to need more than me. I know. I know I'm a fuck up, and I fucked up so much, but she hasn't and I would really like her to have grandparents. I just don't want her to be all alone, so I know it's asking too much again, but—"

"Yes." Dilynn squeezed Charleigh's fingers tightly in her own. "Please, yes. Let me be in her life. Be in yours. I have waited 24 years to be in your life."

"You've known me since I was fourteen."

"I have a garage of presents for you."

Charleigh's eyebrows cinched together. "A garage?"

"Every birthday and every Christmas." Dilynn shook her head. "They kept your whole name."

She pointed to herself. "Diana-Lynn. I named you as my father named me. I... I was told they named you Charlotte. Jax's mom was Charlotte. My mom is Leigh. You can meet her if you want to. She isn't who she used to be because Lyra made her come to her senses after Evie screamed at her until she went into cardiac arrest. But she's different now, and she'd want to know you."

"My dad hated Charlotte. He always called me Chucky, and I think it was to piss Grace off."

"Where did Charleigh come from?" Dilynn asked.

"You."

"Me?"

She pulled at the top of her tank top to cover her breasts some. This wasn't the version of herself she wanted Dilynn to know. She wanted the woman to think about the teacher she'd been. The one she'd learned from Dilynn.

"You were what I wanted to be when I grew up. I thought your name was cool because it wasn't girly like Grace tried to make me. You were gay and you had a boy name but spelled it like a girl, and I... I told everyone I was Charleigh so I could be like you."

There seemed to be an endless well of tears in Dilynn's body. They streamed from the puffy, bloodshot eyes, down flushed cheeks, and fell on the sweater as she made promises Charleigh prayed for once would be true. Promises to make up for the years of holding Charleigh away from her. Omes to make up for all the times she'd hurt her.

"Charleigh, I hired you to be charming, not to make the customers cry," Echo called out as Dilynn's tears splashed against the table.

Echo handed Dilynn a stack of napkins. Then took the tray from Charleigh. "You didn't hit her with the tray, did you?"

"No, boss," Charleigh said with a roll of her eyes.

"Come back to work," Dilynn commanded through the tears and snot. "Please. The kids miss you and I'll be better. I'll be different. I promise, and you don't have to do it alone."

"No! No! No!" Echo yelled pointing at Charleigh. "You got a job. A good job. One where you get to hit people with a tray when they're assholes."

Echo held out the tray to Charleigh. "You can even hit Dilynn if you want to, but you can't hit teenagers when they talk shit, can you?

When Charleigh didn't look away from Dilynn, Echo turned to the woman wiping away tears. "You can't come in here poaching my employees, D! Come on, don't do me like that. I gave you Parker. It was like a trade."

Dilynn waved her hand at Echo dismissively. "She's my daughter so she needs to be a part of the family business. And, she was my employee first, so you're the poacher. Plus, she's a terrible server. I ordered a vodka coke, and she brought me coconut rum in diet."

Charleigh looked at the drink. "I didn't fuck it up."

She took the glass from the table and smelled the rum. Her eyes flew back to Echo, "I swear, I said, 'Vodka Coke, and the bitch said on ice like I don't fucking know a Vodka Coke has ice.' And Parker laughed at me and I told Parker that she's here for her. And I stole an orange slice, and Parker gave me the drink. I swear, I didn't fuck it up. I didn't even drop it!"

Echo laughed, then shook her head. "I know you didn't fuck it up. Parker did. She texted me to come over here when she was making it. Something about revenge for buying another house that Lyra is trying to get her to move into because Evie said she's moving away and at least one of them needed to be nearby."

"Well, they gave away the first one I bought to you," Dilynn smiled at the glass, then held up a hand before anyone else could speak. "Which, I am very grateful for because what Simone did was inexcusable, and if I see her on my street, then I can run her over with my car because, yes, I did buy the actual private street so I could trespass anyone I want to. Fucking cheating bitch. You know, I never liked her. And I hated her for you. You were always so sweet and such a good mom. I am just happy that we—"

"Stop trying to kiss my ass when we both know you're trying to steal Charleigh. Like come on, I waited my turn. I didn't officially employ her until after you fired her," Echo said with a straight mouth that wavered as she tried to hide her smile.

Dilynn looked at Charleigh. "Come back to work. If not for me, then for your kids."

"No," Echo said again. "Remember I was the one that came to Sylvia's and rescued you, so you could throw away 200 grand."

"I didn't come to Sylvia's, but I can tell you that working nights isn't conducive to having a six-year-old at home. The childcare costs will eat up all your tips," Dilynn reasoned.

"No," Echo said again. She moved her body between Charleigh and Dilynn. "I swear I will never serve you again if you steal the third point of the Unholy Trinity. She finally stopped dropping drinks and women come here to see her and Parker in their tiny tank tops. Like, so many customers and I'm a single mom now."

Charleigh leaned over the table to look at Dilynn. "You have to fix the girls' bathroom, so it doesn't smell like flower-covered shit anymore."

Echo scoffed and threw up her hands. She looked down at Charleigh, "At least ask for a raise."

"Okay, over the break we will redo the plumbing in the bathroom." Dilynn held out her hand to Charleigh.

"And a raise," Echo whisper-yelled at Charleigh. "Get a raise."

Charleigh started to hold out her hand but pulled it back. She raised a finger in the air. "No more yelling at me."

"And a raise," Echo said again.

"No more yelling at you besides the normal way I yell at everyone," Dilynn promised and extended her hand. "And Joey and you come to every major holiday. Thanksgiving, Christmas, and birthdays. I get to throw her birthday parties. I love throwing parties and I have six years of parties to make up for missing. Bounce houses and cake. Oh, I have to throw her a welcome home party."

Charleigh took Dilynn's hand, "Deal, but no flowers or pink. She hates flowers and pink. Purple and sparkles."

"Are you allergic to money?" Echo demanded. With her head thrown back, she groaned, "You know what, Dilynn? You can have her. I need someone more cash-hungry than charming."

"I'm glad all this worked out," Parker said as she slid a drink in front of Dilynn. "And since you're over here making deals and shit, you gotta stop trying to get me and Lyra to move across the street. It's weird and creepy."

"Mona and I always called it a cult," Charleigh chimed in. "And I was raised in a cult, so I know a little something-something about them."

Parker slapped the table and pointed to Dilynn. "Yes! That's it. It's like a cult, and nope. I am not joining a cult or drinking Kool-Aid."

Echo looked between the women, then at Dilynn. She leaned in closer to Dilynn and asked, "You serve Kool-Aid at your place and never told me. Rude, D. Just rude."

39

The schedule on Lexa's safety plan no longer needed to be referenced. She'd lived the routine for enough days in a row she moved automatically into thinking about what she would do that would be deemed productive. Packing to leave for Australia was productive but depressing. She'd never packed her bag before, always spent the time begging Sylvia not to make her go this time while her wife carefully folded her things so everything could fit. Lexa had to make things fit this time, and she just didn't want to. After staring at the open suitcase for two days, Lexa shut it and shoved it off the couch.

She thought about texting Sylvia. Asking why she always had to leave. Why did the woman never want her around besides during the summer? But Sylvia's truth thus far had done nothing but strip away the good things she'd remembered from their marriage. The fake marriage Sylvia had given her, just like she'd offered to Charleigh.

Inside was too much, so Lexa grabbed a trash bag and made her way out to the Range Rover. Since it would be going to storage while she was away, she might as well clean it out.

Starting on the driver's side, she pulled out the collection of Starbucks straw wrappers from the compartment in the door, then the ones that had fallen between the console and seat. When she went to the other side of the car, she found a fourth of an Ego lodged between the seat and the console. A part of her wanted to be angry but she remembered it had fallen because Charleigh was throwing shade at Danaya. That was when she almost cried once more over missing Charleigh's witty quips.

It took her a moment to breathe through the pain. Fighting the urge to make emotional pain real had been one of the first things she'd begun working on with the therapist. She was supposed to breathe when she was sad instead of working out. Growing up in team sports, coaches had always challenged her to use her anger to fuel her progress. Dr. Rose had rolled her eyes at that, then explained working out when angry only exhausted her. It would never allow her to think about the emotion, so she would never learn how to deal with feeling that emotion again without the need to hurt.

Missing Charleigh made her sad. She'd spent several hours on Dr. Rose's couch talking through the different types of sadness Lexa had when she thought about Charleigh. The Ego made her feel sadness associated with loss. It was her mind grieving Charleigh's absence. This was different from the sadness of thinking about Charleigh going to Sylvia's without calling her. That sadness had been associated with not being trusted. Grieving sadness and trust sadness were different, so Lexa reminded herself, "Grieving can't be fixed. It has to be felt until it peaks, then the wave will end."

She let the tears fall without trying to hold them back. Crying didn't make her weak, just like pretending things didn't bother her wouldn't make her strong. She took deep breaths as the tears slowly rolled down her cheeks. With each momento Charleigh left in her life being slowly uncovered, she learned Dr. Rose wasn't an idiot. The waterworks accompanying her sadness didn't feel like flash floods anymore, and this one passed even faster than the last.

When she returned to the car, she found another piece of the woman. Well, several pieces. The collection of blonde hair grossed Lexa out, and she tossed it into a bag. She loved the woman, but at no point would she become crazy enough to cherish the hair littering every crevice of the passenger's side of the car.

She pushed her hand under the seat, her fingers finding a crumpled-up piece of paper with purple handwriting. Lexa's lips curled up into a smile. This had brought her back to Charleigh. The only reason she'd gone to the school. She'd never read the letter— forgotten all about it after she'd left Greyson Academy's parking lot— but she still had it.

She sat in the chair and smoothed away the wrinkles from the page. A small flicker of hope ignited in her chest that maybe this was a sign Lexa was ready to go find Charleigh. If she read it this time, there might be a way to make their paths cross once more without bulldozing through Charleigh's boundaries. A word she wished would be erased from the English language because it had kept her from going to Charleigh's house to check on her.

Pushing up the glasses on her nose, Lexa read:

Dear. Ms. Lexa Jenson,

I am writing to you in hopes that you could help me honor my English teacher on her birthday. She is a huge fan of yours and has never missed a game. I know that you are extremely busy, and I know that the playoffs are about to start. (BTW, congratulations on making it to the playoffs.) Marshall is a very special person.

You see she saved my life. Not in the way you may think. She didn't stop a school shooter or do anything that someone would really think of heroic. She doesn't swoop in and spend a bunch of money to like buy you a happy ending. I think she would, if she ever had any money, but since she's a teacher, she's poor and does things like sew her own backpack back together.

Lexa snorted, then covered her mouth. She checked the parking lot to see if anyone had heard her grunt like a pig but found no one. Dropping her eyes back to the letter, she continued.

Marshall saved me because she taught me to read when everyone else had given up on me and that made it so I have a future. I know what you are probably thinking: how did I get to fifteen and not know how to read? You see I've been in foster care my entire life, and once you get to a certain age, you just know you're never getting out. I been moved to six different group homes since my last foster family got tired of being a foster family, and I had just made it to the seventh when I met Marshall. When you been to as many schools as I have, it's really easy to make it so people don't know you can't do anything. ~~So~~ When I met Marshall, I didn't know how to read well. I could sound out the words, but nothing made sense, so school was like a prison, and I just got into fights until they kicked me out. I got kicked out of two schools by the time I was ~~a~~ fifteen.

After the last fight I got into, my case manager sent me to ~~this last chance school~~ a charter school. ~~Like~~ No one else wants you so they send you there, but the school was just there to make money. I hated it and what I hated more was the stupid security dude that was always staring at me. ~~Well~~ One day they had all these people coming in to talk about college and careers. Marshall came to talk about this scholarship she won that paid for her to go to college. I knew I wasn't going to college because you have to be smart and at that point I knew I wasn't smart. I knew my best chance at any type of life was going to let someone like the security guy get me pregnant, so he'd have to take care of me, but that day when he was talking to me, Marshall got in the middle of our conversation. At first, I was mad. She didn't get that this was how things worked for people like me, but then I realized she knew him. She knew him because they lived together when she was a foster kid and she didn't like him at all. She didn't like him so much that she told him if didn't leave me alone that she was going to call their dad and tell about what he did to her when they were kids, then she told the principal that he was being inappropriate with me and they fired him.

She could have just left after that, but instead she made a phone call. I thought she was calling the security guy's dad like she said she was going to, but she didn't. She called her boss. You see I didn't know at the time that she worked at a school. I thought she was just there to talk about the scholarship, but she called her boss and they came to my charter school and they talked to me. I say they because they are nonbinary and we treat people right at Greyson's because we respect who they are not who society says they should be. I learned that from Marshall before her boss got there, and before I knew what was what they were asking if I wanted to go to Greyson's. They got me a room at Marshall's old foster dad's house and he promised his stupid son with his big ugly nose was not allowed at the house. He knows what that jerk did to Marshall but said she didn't want him to know so he just doesn't talk to him very much. That's off my point. The big deal is they all kept their promises. Like they said they were going to make it safe, and I wouldn't have to move anymore and that's what happened. You see no one has ever made me a promise they didn't break before.

This is really long but I need you to know that Marshall could have been done then, but she wasn't. She realized like the week I got there that I couldn't read so she got her boss to give me a class with just her and three other kids, and when I wasn't doing well, she stayed after school every day to keep helping me. I now read stuff that Marshall didn't see until college, and I am going to go to college. I'm going to apply for the scholarship she got next year and I'm going to have a real life, and maybe I'll grow up to be a teacher like her or maybe I'll go into sports management like your agent, Phyllis. She said she'd get you this letter and I hope she does. She's good people, her and her wife. We met at an adoption event a few months ago at Greyson's. They said they liked how well I talked about my goals and where I wanted to go with my life, and none of that would have been possible without Marshall. So she saved my life because I wasn't going anywhere before I met her, but now I'm going to have an education and two families. One with Phyllis and one with Marcus. So I just really want to do something big for her. The only thing she likes more than teaching is watching you play basketball, and I know she'd be so excited to meet you.

So if you have time, I would really appreciate it if you would come to the school on her birthday and meet her. A lot of the adults are really mean to her because she was pretty wild as a teenager when she was sent here, and I think she doesn't think many good things about herself because of that since no one ever gave her a second chance like she gave me. So I want to celebrate her and how much she's changed our lives. And I think if you came, she'd not feel so invisible. Phyllis has the date and the address. You don't have to stay all day, but please come. I won't say anything in case you are too busy, but it would mean a lot to her.

Sincerely,

Kinsley Hernandez

Lexa wiped the tears from her face before any could hit the page. She'd caused not only Charleigh to lose her job, but also this kid to lose her idol. So many kids that the woman loved like Neveah, who lost her coach right before their season started. Too many people were being punished for her choice to not take her meds.

She checked the phone for the time. She'd promised to give Charleigh the space she needed to sort through all the changes in her life, but that didn't mean she couldn't fight for her behind the scenes. Sylvia had tried and failed, but Sylvia didn't love Charleigh as she did.

Lexa put the letter on the seat and got in the car. If she drove fast enough, she could make it to Greyson Academy before it closed. She'd meet this Dilynn Greyson woman, and she'd make that bitch understand firing Charleigh was the worst mistake she could have ever made. She'd get her to see Charleigh deserved a second chance.

The campus parking lot was nearly empty when Lexa pulled in. She put the car in park and hopped from the vehicle with the letter in one hand and her phone in the other just as a blonde woman exited the office with a Mikel Kors purse slung over her shoulder. She was walking toward the Audi Lexa had seen last time she was here, and since Charleigh made shit money there was no way this bitch couldn't be the boss with ass-beating fantasies.

"Hey, you Dilynn Greyson?" Lexa called out.

The woman's face rose from the phone she was staring at, and she froze. She looked at the Range Rover, then back at Lexa.

"Yes, and you must be Sylvia's ex-wife. The woman disrupted my school and caused one of my teachers to be dismissed because you filmed her having terrible sex with you." Dilynn raised an eyebrow at Lexa. "How is it that you were married to Sylvia and don't know how to work a strap?"

Lexa opened her mouth, not sure how to respond. "How do you know my ex-wife?"

"Before she married you, she proposed to me," Dilynn stated coldly. "So, I know Sylvia probably better than you do because you don't know me."

With a twisted stomach, Lexa gagged. Her hand came up over her lips as she realized the blonde Sylvia had told Charleigh about was the boss that wanted Charleigh's ass.

"What do you want?" Dilynn snipped.

"I need to talk to you," Lexa said, remembering why she'd come. She closed the distance between them. "You fired Charleigh because of something that she had nothing to do with, and I need you to read this."

Lexa held out the letter and waved it in the woman's face. "I know about Sylvia threatening to close the school and that Charleigh fixed it so that wouldn't happen, but you can't fire her. She means too much to the kids here and you need to read this. This kid goes to your school, and she wrote me a letter because she knew that no one here ever appreciated how much Charleigh did for this place. She's a good fucking teacher and it wasn't her fault that the video was posted. It was my fault, and you know that. And I can't let you ruin her life because—"

Dilynn took the letter. Her eyes scanned over the page, front and back. She studied the last couple of paragraphs carefully. Then she handed it back to Lexa.

"I already gave Charleigh her job back," the woman stated. She pulled the straps of the bag up her shoulder.

"You did?" Lexa looked over the letter. Then the woman stared at her with her arms crossed over her chest. "Uh... Okay, well, don't fire her again for me coming back here. Don't even tell her—"

The phone rang, pulling her attention from the sentence she hadn't finished. She looked at the scrunched-up face of her blonde on the screen.

"She's calling me," Lexa whispered.

"Then you should answer," Dilynn stated. "And ask her to dinner so she can tell you all about her first week back."

Lexa stared at the screen. "You're not going to—"

"I don't like you. I don't like what you did to Sylvia. And I don't think you're good enough for my daughter. However, I think if you are willing to show up here and fight for her, then maybe you're not the monster I thought you were. So, answer the phone."

It wasn't a promise not to tell Charleigh, but Lexa didn't have time to argue with the woman walking away from her. Not to mention, there was the whole part about Charleigh and this woman being mother and daughter, which was something Lexa felt like she should have probably known. So, she hit accept and said the first thing that came to her mind.

"I missed you so much that I came to the school to yell at your old boss, who is also your mom, which I didn't know. But I came to make her give you your job back. But she said she already gave it back to you, so I want to hear about it. Every class discussion and who put their name in Kahoot wrong." Lexa sucked in as much air as possible and didn't give Charleigh a chance to say goodbye yet. "I want to take you to dinner because I know you haven't eaten anything besides mac and cheese from a box, but you need real food with vegetables and protein, and I need to see you. Please, let me come get you and feed you, and you can yell at me then. I just need to see you."

She'd run out of air, and she sucked in all the breath she could as she prepared all the other promises she'd keep so Charleigh knew she could depend on her.

The phone beeped in her ear. She pulled it away to see the Facetime request, so she accepted. Charleigh stood outside and held the phone up to the house behind her.

"I'm standing outside your new place," Charleigh told her. "Well actually, we're standing outside your place."

Charleigh moved the camera, and she was no longer alone. Joey bounced into view with a bouquet of roses flopping around the screen.

Joey's eyes grew wide as she screamed, "Mommy, it's hers. Its really hers." Then, her attention turned back to the camera, and Joey waved the roses against the lens. There was some rustling before Joey's little bouncing face was back on the screen.

"Can yous comes home, Ms Jenison? We's here to takes yous on a date. Mommy dressed us up ins ours sparklist clothes and we comes to take yous on a date so I can tell you about how I gets to comes to Mommy's forever. I gets to lives with my Mommy and she says when you comes home from playing the bounceketball you's going to lives with us too."

Tears fell down Lexa's face as she smiled at the camera. She looked up to see Dilynn watching her from the other side of the car.

The older woman called out, "What you waiting for? Go before I run you over for hurting my ex-girlfriend and my kid."

Lexa looked back at the carbon copies staring at her through the phone.

"I'm coming, Joey," Lexa promised. "Tell your mommy, I'm coming and I'm never leaving."

40

The Greyson-Trikru mailbox sat across the street from the Range Rover parked behind the U-Haul Landon was loading. Charleigh's plan had been simple. Surprise Dilynn, Alex, and Marcus simultaneously at their monthly Saturday meeting with the granddaughter they'd all been eager to get settled enough to meet her extended family. She'd verified Marcus had arrived from Mona, then she and Lexa tag-teamed trying to get the child fed and dressed to meet the extended family she'd been denied relationships with.

Second chances brought them to the street, and it should have been simple. But Mona didn't know the shiny silver blue Porsche matched the color of Sylvia Winters's eyes.

Charleigh took Lexa's hand, entwining their fingers together.

"It's okay if you don't want to go. I can do this next week, and maybe she won't be here then," Charleigh offered.

"Why is she here though?" Lexa asked, hitting her head against the seat.

"Money," Charleigh stated simply. An evil grin spread over her face as she looked at Lexa. "Or they are having an O-R-G-Y, but Marcus is in there and he doesn't strike me as any of their types."

Lexa's eyes grew huge as her lips curled up her teeth. Then she gagged on the air in the car. "Oh my god, I can't."

"Did you know about her and them?" Charleigh asked. "I heard Sylvia used to throw parties. Parties that didn't include bounce houses."

"No. It was just me and her," Lexa lied.

Charleigh rolled her head against the seat and looked at Lexa. She waited for the woman to swallow the remnants of the lie. "Okay, me, her, and a few others, but never them."

Joey ripped off her headphones and waved an iPad at Lexa. "It won'ts plays," she whined. "I wanna watch Bluey but it won'ts plays, Lek-sa."

Charleigh narrowed her eyes at Lexa and grumbled under her breath, "I can't believe you bought her an iPad."

"How am I supposed to FaceTime her when you are sending me across the world, Athena?" Lexa asked. She took the tablet from Joey and made the video play.

Charleigh groaned at the fifth attempt for a new label. With a roll of her eyes, she said, "Athena?"

"She was not a princess or a good girl," Lexa stated proudly. "So, it fits you. Badass woman I would follow into battle any day of the week."

"I guess it's better than Aphrodite." Then Charleigh asked, "We going to do this battle?"

"Yes," Lexa stated. She pushed the button to shut down the car. "There's gonna be a family picture, and I want to be in it since I have to get on the freakin' plane tonight."

They got out and Lexa moved to the back seat where Joey was fixed into the most expensive carseat Lexa could buy. "Xena, we gotta leave the iPad in the car."

Joey stuck out her lower lip and looked at Lexa with her puppy eyes. "But do I have to?"

Lexa failed the first test of manipulation, and they left the car with the iPad. Charleigh wiped the remnants of the granola bar from her daughter's Phoenix Devils t-shirt. Then she took the iPad and the headphones and chucked it back into the car.

"You can't let her wrap you around her little finger," Charleigh reminded Lexa as they made their way across the street.

Charleigh pressed the doorbell and then stood behind Joey with her hands on her shoulders. She looked up to make sure Lexa hadn't run away.

"Who the fuck is ringing the goddamn mother fucking doorbell," Dilynn yelled from within.

"Probably the solar salespeople again," Alex answered. "Keep swearing and I bet they'll run away."

"Don't even think those words," Dilynn yelled. "I swear to God, you walk out of this house and I'm going to be the next person going viral with Via's tongue down my throat."

Charleigh scraped her tongue against her teeth. Never would she see the woman and not think about the fact Sylvia kissed her with the same tongue she'd gone done on her mother with.

"Do we really need family this bad?" Lexa asked.

Charleigh could hear the footsteps coming toward them, so she elbowed Lexa in the gut. "Shut up, and smile."

Charleigh didn't have a chance to say anything else before the door opened. Alex's eyes crinkled in a smile when they landed on Charleigh, "Hey Charleigh, we weren't expecting..."

Their mouth fell open and the rest of their sentence hit the ground. They dropped to their knees as they looked at Joey clinging to Charleigh's hand on her shoulder.

"Oh my," they whispered. "You're so big, little estrella."

Joey looked up at Charleigh, "Is this the gamma, the gandpa, or the obigee?"

Charleigh smiled at Alex's questioning eyes. "I wasn't sure what to tell her when I said we were going to meet her grandparents today. I remembered Sadie calling you Obi, so I kinda played off that. I hope it's okay. If you want to choose a different label, then we can."

Alex didn't have time to answer before Joey wrapped her arms around their neck. "My mommy says yous loves mes very much buts the means gamma didn'ts lets you comes to my birthdays."

"I do," Alex whispered, pressing their face into the blonde curls. "I love you so much and I am so happy to see you again. I'm ObiG and I'm never going to miss another birthday again."

They picked the girl up in their arms, still holding the child like she would vanish.

"Who the fuck is it?" Dilynn yelled from down the hall.

Alex turned to the woman making her way toward them. The Starbucks cup in her hand dropped to the floor, sending latte splatter all over the entryway. She opened her mouth, then closed it as she wrapped her arms around Alex and the child.

Lexa held Charleigh tightly around her chest as they gave the new grandparents time to hold the little girl who'd been stolen from their arms but never their hearts.

"Yous squeezings the airs from me," Joey said with a giggle.

Alex released the child into Dilynn's arms who continued to hold her tightly. The older woman's eyes raised to Charleigh, "Why didn't you tell me you were coming? I would have thrown a party."

Tucking a lock of hair behind her ear, Charleigh smiled. "I wanted it to be a surprise and not a huge thing. Mona said she'd bring over Evie and Landon later, and Parker, Lyra, Echo, and her kids will stop by in a while. We can't stay too long because we have to take Lexa to the airport."

"Come in," Alex said. "Please, come in."

They followed Dilynn and Joey into the huge house where Sylvia and Marcus looked up from the table covered in large sheets of blueprints. Their words also ceased to exist as they looked between Dilynn, Joey, and Charleigh.

Lexa wrapped her arm around Charleigh when Sylvia's eyes stopped scanning and centered on them. Charleigh knew it was a claim being staked, but she didn't pull away. She wanted Sylvia to know she'd made up her mind, and Lexa was her choice.

Dilynn set Joey to the ground only after she smothered the child's face in kisses.

"Gamma yous gives too much kisses," Joey protested, but gave Dilynn just as many in return.

The girl looked at the other people in the room. Her eyes grew huge as she hopped in place.

"Sylveria!" Joey cried out. "You're here! You're here! And yous knows my gamma and my gobi!"

"Is it bad I like Gobi even more?" Alex whispered to Charleigh. "Makes me sound like a monster killer."

"Makes you sound like a troll," Dilynn quipped. With a smirk, the woman added, "Which is fitting."

Sylvia dropped to one knee as Joey ran to her. Charleigh offered her a smile because she didn't know what else to say to the woman. Not that she needed to say anything because just like the last time Sylvia and Joey met, Joey babbled about getting to play basketball on a real team soon and being a Devil when she grew up.

Marcus walked over to Charleigh. His gait was a little smoother and it was clear he'd been taking better care of himself. He wiped the sweat from his brow, and said, "You did it, kiddo."

"I did it," she echoed. "Joey, come here, please. I have someone important I want you to meet."

Joey's arm was up in the air from showing Sylvia her shot. She turned to look at Charleigh but there was no doubt who her favorite person in the room was. Charleigh knew Lexa would be grumbling about it for the next month.

"I's gots a bounceketball hoop next to Leksa's. Yous comes over and I's shows you with my reals ball that I makes a good shot."

Lexa whined quietly to Charleigh, "I thought I was her favorite."

"You are," Charleigh promised.

"I would love to come play basketball at your house," Sylvia said, looking back at Lexa with a smug grin. "While Lexa is away, I'll teach you how to make a jump shot. I taught her after all."

With an excited fist in the air, Joey ran to her mother. "Mommy, can Sylveria comes to my bounceketball games? I shows her then hows goods I's ams. And we can Facetimes with Lek-sa so she cans sees me too."

"I would love to come to your game," Sylvia stated.

"I don't wanna go," Lexa whined but stepped back into a private conversation with Alex looking very serious.

Lexa's chin dropped, nodding occasionally. Alex crossed their arms over their chest and appeared to be giving Lexa the cheat on her and I'll bust your face open speech.

Charleigh scooped Joey up and onto her hip, turning her attention back to Marcus. She held out her hand and took his.

"This is my dad, Joey."

Joey looked at the man. Her lips crinkled along with her eyebrows into her thinking face. "He doesn't looks likes the pictures at Gamma's."

"You don't have to," he said to Charleigh. "She doesn't have to call me grandpa."

"No, I should have done this a long time ago. You shoulda known from the beginning," Charleigh stated. Then she turned back to Joey. "I have two daddies. My daddy in the pictures at my mom's house died a long time ago, but this daddy, he took care of me when Gamma couldn't anymore. He's where you get your second name from. Josephine Marcia Marshall."

Joey turned back to Marcus whose eyes had filled with tears. "You named her... after me?"

"I named her after both my dads," Charleigh said. "You two were the only people who had ever been there for me. Loved me for me and didn't try to make me into anyone else."

"You're my PaPa," Joey whispered. She reached out and touched his face. "Mommy says I's gets my stinky feet and mys dancing from you. She gots me a tutu and shes says my first dances class ons Tuesday. You can comes to my dances class because yous likes to dance too. Dos you wants to comes to dance class withs me?"

Marcus's grin spread across his face. "I would love to take you to dance class, Joey. Every Tuesday. It can be our Joey-PaPa day."

Joey wrapped her arms around Marcus's thick neck, and she let the man hold her. He looked at Charleigh as he clung to the little human in his arms.

"I'm sorry," he whispered. "I'm so sorry that I wasn't stronger. I thought you didn't want me to know, and I wanted to respect what you wanted."

She shook her head. "No, I'm sorry. I'm sorry I never told you and you missed so much. They would have let you see her if I had told them. I was just scared."

Marcus let the little girl down as she took notice of the playhouse where Dilynn and Alex's daughter, Levi, looked out through the window at them.

"Yous my sister?" Levi asked. "I have lots of sisters, but you can be my sister too."

Joey ran over to the playhouse and smelled the fake flowers. Then she looked at the girl. "No, but I cans bes if you wants mes to bes. I's be your bigs sister and your bestests friend and wes grows old together like my mommy and my auntie, kay?"

"Otay," Levi announced. "I's a big girl. I be free soon. Yous comes to my birthday."

"I's bes seven. Threes not big, big but I helps you knows how to bes the big girl and I teaches you how to play the bounceketball so we can be Devils and play on Sylveria's Devil teams."

With Dilynn and Marcus fawning over the girls who'd decided to be best friends and Alex still giving Lexa the lecture of her life, Charleigh approached Sylvia.

"I didn't know you were coming, or I would have given you space," Sylvia said softly. "I also shouldn't have told you about the scholarship. After you left, I realized how much that must have hurt you, and I have made it one of my life's goals to protect you from any more hurt."

Having found some words, Charleigh said, "If you hadn't shown up that day, I would have given up. I never would have gone home. I would have found a bottle or ten and drank myself into a coma or drove Danaya's car off the highway. I only didn't because you told me to come over and you offered me a life with her that I didn't think I deserved. And you did so much but I was so angry, and I was so rude to you, and I said some really hateful things. I need you to know that I do appreciate that you stepped up for me even when I was a kid you'd thought had been assaulted. One day though, I'll prove to you that I shoulda got that scholarship without it being rigged."

Sylvia looked down at the plans. "You already did."

Charleigh studied the blueprints. Just from the shape of the courtyard, she knew they were for the school. "Are you guys going to build the gym I wrote the grant for?"

Sylvia wrapped her arms around herself. "That and a few other things."

Looking over the plans, Charleigh counted the buildings. It wasn't just a gym, but several new structures were being put in. "You guys are expanding?"

"Dilynn," Sylvia beckoned. "You should be the one to tell her about the changes we're making since none of your other kids have any interest in the school. This one is the legacy, so come show her what you are building."

The blue eyes shot up from the couch where Dilynn sat. She said something to Marcus before she moved quickly to the plans Charleigh looked over.

Dilynn pointed to the large block-shaped building. "We are putting the sports facility here behind Parker's art studio. It's going to have two basketball courts and volleyball courts. We're going to put softball and baseball fields behind your classroom. Then we are going to put a teenager-sized playground here where the girls' bathroom is now. I figured most of these kids missed out on their childhood so why not give them a playground they could enjoy."

Then, she tapped another space on the blueprint. "This is where we are going to put the upgraded girl's bathroom that I promised you. Oh, and you can tell Echo that a raise was written into your contract."

"You didn't have to do that," Charleigh said.

"Well, if you decide to move into your Scottsdale house, then you can use it for gas," Dilynn said.

"Stupid fucking house," Charleigh grumbled.

Sylvia rolled her eyes. "Or you could sell it and buy something closer."

Gesturing toward the street, Dilynn said, "Or you could... I have three houses here, but I know you said you won't move here. But if you moved here then Mona wouldn't move, and all of the kids could grow up together."

"You and your commune," Sylvia snickered. "It's weird Dilynn. Like crazy mother shit."

"Says the woman who lived with Daddy instead of me for seven years," Dilynn snapped.

Charleigh changed the subject by tapping the other new building alongside the office. "Is this more housing?"

"Yeah," Dilynn said, pulling her glare from Sylvia.

"Are we getting a new program?" Charleigh asked. "Like, what classroom is going there?"

"It's actually going to be a preschool and childcare facility," Dilynn said. "For while parents are working or getting their education. With you coming back to work and Mona and Evie having babies. Not to mention Levi. We need a space to ensure our employee's salaries are not being eaten up in childcare costs."

She shifted the pages until the plans for the building were atop the others. "And the upstairs will be built differently than the rest. We are upgrading from dorms to miniature apartments. Each apartment will have a private living space, bathroom, and two bedrooms for teen moms. They'll still have to share a communal kitchen, but it meets all DCS requirements for teen moms to be housed with their child or children."

Charleigh looked up at her, then at Sylvia.

"No woman should have to choose between her education and her child," Sylvia stated. "Why we didn't consider that when we made the initial plans was a serious oversight, and we are correcting it."

Dilynn pulled out a digital mockup of the finished building. The outside was lined with a wraparound porch like the others on campus. A decent-sized playground lay behind a small, fenced area. Above the door, a sign was displayed. Charleigh ran her finger over the name.

"It's going to be called Marshall House," Dilynn stated. "If you're okay with it, I mean."

41

The party began with Mona slapping the front door open for the flood of friends and family to welcome Joey home. Alex only left their conversation about Lexa being a better partner than they had ever been to stop Mona at the entrance to the great room.

"Arms up, Ramirez," Alex commanded.

Mona's chin lifted and a cocky grin spread across her face. She turned out her pockets and lifted the legs of her pants. "You think I'm going to set off a smoke bomb in your house?"

"I think you most definitely would set off a smoke bomb in my house if it meant pissing off my wife," Alex stated. "I'm still trying to figure out how you got them to go off with no one around."

"Different lengthened fuses," Landon stated, earning himself an elbow to the stomach.

"You're about to be cut off from me and your girl," Mona hissed. "A month of nothing but just watching."

Alex's face went pale, and they shoved their fingers in their ears. "LA LA LA."

"She'll save the smoke bombs for work," Evie contributed as she carried her stomach into the room. "Thank God you hired Charleigh back so this one would go back to her classroom. I need some fucking quiet before I go to work, and she wouldn't stop plotting how to remotely detonate elephant toothpaste in the courtyard."

Parker pushed past them with bags of food and Echo at her heels with more. She announced, "I brought the food, so Dilynn doesn't try to kill anyone with pasty chicken and water tonight."

"I made you soup because you were dying, and this is how I am repaid?" Dilynn gawked.

"You tried to poison me after I had already thrown up the contents of my body for two straight days, Mommy Dearest," Parker said, thrusting a plate into Dilynn's hands.

"Oh shit, the heathen actually referred to you as Mom," Evie announced. "Guess you should buy her a house next door and start printing out the wedding invitations."

"Don't you fucking dare," Parker said. She dug through the bags, pulled out a plate, and pushed it to Sylvia. "Echo said you're a fucking vegan and this was the only thing on the menu that fit the requirements. Why are rich people so fucking weird?"

"Oh, you didn't have to," Sylvia said, taking the container and staring at it.

Lexa sucked in her lips to avoid laughing. She'd never seen Sylvia eat anything from styrofoam before and could see the uneasiness buried under the smile.

"Don't worry about it," Parker said and then glared at the door. "Who invited you?"

Lexa turned to the woman standing alongside the wall. Awkwardness seemed to drip from her being as she pushed her hair back from her face.

"She's my best friend and she came to help me move unlike your rude ass," Evie announced. With a hand holding her swollen belly, she turned to the woman. "Zoe, don't flirt with the red-headed demon or my sister, okay? I already claimed rights over the throuple title, so stay away from them."

Parker licked her fangs as Sadie ducked into the room. The younger sister waved at Zoe who started to wave back before Evie scowled at her.

"I said no flirting with my sister!"

"I thought you meant the one I already dated," Zoe said, her eyes scanning over the room until they fell on Sylvia.

Lexa watched the two women look each other over. Her eyebrows scrunched together when the dark-haired woman straightened her shirt and smiled. Lexa didn't like the look of the woman's smile and wanted her to go back to smiling at the skinny sister who had made her way over to the woman, only to be awkwardly ignored.

"Fix your face before I start to believe you are jealous over your ex noticing another woman," Charleigh said, wrapping her arms around Lexa's middle.

"Who is she?" Lexa asked, still watching as Zoe made her way over to Sylvia.

"Well, she's a hotshot ADA who tried to lock Echo's kid up for murder. And I believe, I heard she was secretly dating Lyra, Parker's girlfriend. But before that Parker and Zoe were together in college, and I guess Zoe was, like, head over heels in love with Parker. Like, she still shows up to every shift Parker works at the bar."

Lexa remembered the Heineken bottle taunting her. Recalled Parker's rage about her ex coming to work. Smiling down at Charleigh, she said, "So normal lesbian stuff. Way more normal than Via's mother-daughter fantasies."

Echo approached the couple with her hands buried in her pockets as Charleigh was still landing slaps to Lexa's chest. "Never thought I'd say I'm happy to see you two together."

Lexa held out her hand. "Thanks for looking out for her. I heard you busted some bitch's nose for putting her hands down her pants."

Echo held up the bandaged elbow. "It's a good thing Dilynn gave you your job back," Echo said. "I think you being in my bar is way too dangerous for me. I mean in six months, I had to beat up two fuckers and that's more than I ever had to hit for Parker."

"We have to leave in twenty minutes," Charleigh said. "I'm going to start saying my goodbyes and get Joey."

"Okay."

Echo leaned against the wall Lexa was holding up. She ran her fingers through her hair, then pushed the hat back on her head.

"The nausea stop yet?"

Lexa nodded. "Yeah. I stubbed my toe this morning and it felt like the world was collapsing, so I think it's safe to say the dosage has hit its mark."

"You better be good while you're there, or I'm going to steal your girl." Echo's lips spread into a sly smile.

Lexa didn't even bat an eyelash as she watched Sylvia pick up Joey in her arms and wrap her and Charleigh in a hug. Licking her dry lips, she said, "Pretty sure you'd have to fight off Via, and to be honest if she ever decides she truly wants them, I don't think either of us can compete."

"She is a beast in bed," Echo said.

Lexa stopped breathing just for a moment as she shifted her gaze from her ex to Echo.

With a shrug, Echo said, "You all just left me that night at her house, so we made the best of a shit situation and fucked until the sun came up."

"I coulda lived without knowing that," Lexa grumbled.

"I know, but I felt like telling you was the price for you fucking up my bar and my face." Echo pushed off the wall. "See you in a few months."

"See ya."

The room buzzed with excitement. Promises were made to get together again for pizza on Wednesday night. The sisters Charleigh now had talked shit to each other and Charleigh, razing each other like they'd always been under the same roof. It was a whole family, something Lexa had never been a part of.

For the first time, Lexa realized what Charleigh meant when she said she didn't belong in Lexa's world. Lexa's world was small and surrounded by ball players who scattered across continents only to come together and share their stories. She had a place there; but in Charleigh's world of sisters, schools, and kids, she had nothing to offer.

She scanned the room again. Everyone there had a spot on the roster of the team Lexa wasn't even sure how to try out for. She had nothing to give anyone;

her only possessions were in a couple of bags Charleigh had already packed for her in the car for the flight to Australia. The wasn't time to linger on not being enough for Charleigh though.

The minutes were counting down to her departure, and a new uneasiness twisted up her tummy as she realized she was going to miss all the important things. The first dance class and Joey's first basket in a game. She'd miss the first Christmas while all of these people she didn't know got to shower her girls in presents.

"Okay, you ready?" Charleigh asked with Joey in hand.

"Yeah," Lexa lied.

The family followed them out. A picture was taken on a cellphone and promised to be shared. Then, they waved until Lexa turned off the private drive onto the main road.

Their drive to the airport was quiet. Joey kicked the back of Lexa's seat as she watched *Bluey*, and Charleigh held Lexa's hand until they got to the parking garage.

Lexa handed the ticket to Charleigh. "Use the debit card I gave you to get out," she instructed.

Joey pulled the suitcase for her as Lexa lugged the oversized bag on her shoulder.

"I set up my paychecks to go into that account and it will automatically factor in the exchange rate. I want you to use it for groceries and not just mac and cheese. You have to buy real vegetables besides just green beans."

"I know," Charleigh said.

"And use it for gas for the Range Rover. It's bigger." She held up the hand. "And I know you can barely reach the peddles, but it's safer than the Charger. Plus, it can better handle the curbs you like to hit."

While they stood in the ticket line, Lexa grumbled with each step about having forgotten to check in early to the woman who didn't even hit her for the short joke. Charleigh had ignored her completely, tapping away on her phone and rolling her eyes at Lexa's whining.

"You're going on an adventure," Charleigh stated, sliding the phone in her pocket. "Stop whining about your rich people problems."

A short woman waved at them before Lexa could explain the difference between rich people's problems and tall people's problems. When they made it to the counter, Joey helped Lexa put the suitcase onto the scale.

"Ms. Jenson, here is your ticket. You are boarding first class, so you will be in the first boarding group," the ticket lady said with a plastic smile.

Her eyebrows scrunched together as she studied the ticket. "I didn't book first class."

"I did."

Charleigh and Lexa turned as Joey jumped into Sylvia's arms. Sylvia lifted the child on her hip like having a little human was natural for her.

"I didn't get a chance to tell you before you left," Sylvia said. She looked at Charleigh. "This part is really hard, and I didn't want either of you to have to do it alone."

"How did you get here so fast?" Charleigh asked as they left the ticket counter.

Joey held up the iPad for Sylvia to see, but the woman took it from the girl and tucked it into her oversized purse. "We have to be present for important events. When you're a grown-up, you're going to be very important and you're going to have to always show people they are important to you by paying attention," Sylvia told the child. "I'll give you back the iPad when we are ready to leave."

Then Sylvia turned back to Charleigh like she hadn't just been providing the woman's child a lesson on manners. "Lexa always drives like a grandma when she leaves."

"I do not drive like a grandma," Lexa stated. "I have a child in the car, and I want to be safe."

"She drives, like, ten miles below the speed limit now," Charleigh said. "I'm pretty sure an actual grandma flipped us off on the way to Joey's school yesterday."

"Wait until she asks you to have another baby. She's going to wrap you in bubble wrap," Sylvia stated.

"You's goings to haves a baby?!" Joey asked with wide eyes.

"Ha! Ha! Ha!" Charleigh said, taking her daughter from the woman. "You're so funny. We are still trying to figure out how to manage having one child. Plus, there's no more room."

Sylvia rolled her eyes and held her hands back to Joey, who gladly moved back to her idol. "You own a six-bedroom house that could fit plenty of babies if you'd stop being so stubborn. Or Mommy Dilynn would gladly put you up in a house on her commune. You're the one choosing to rent that shack on my property."

Charleigh looked up at Lexa and demanded, "Tell her to take that house back." She stopped smacking Lexa's arm only to turn back to Sylvia. "What the fuck do you mean you own my house?"

Lexa was too busy smiling at the thought of Charleigh round with her child to care about Charleigh huffing and puffing. Maybe next year they'd be in a place where she could bring up IVF. She wouldn't push it, but she could hope Charleigh would want to carry a child, maybe one who looked a little like her and she could teach that kid to love the skin they were born into. Break some cycles.

She took Charleigh's hand and walked with her toward the escalator where Sylvia and Joey had already escaped the blonde's grunting and groaning. The escalator had always been her nemesis because, once at the top of it, she'd have to say goodbye.

"Should I be worried about this whole, I'm going to be an auntie thing, your ex has going on?"

Lexa hummed for a moment. "She gave you a house for a reason. Pretty sure she's chosen Joey as her heir since you threw her money on the floor. So, you can demand Sylvia never sees her, but of all the people in our lives... she really is the one person who always showed up to help. I think that is someone you want Joey to have."

"I really hate that I think you're right," Charleigh whispered.

The line through TSA was long, but the first-class ticket bought Lexa a shorter path. She looked at it, then back at the blondes.

"I don't wanna go," she said.

Sylvia nudged Charleigh forward. "This is the hardest part. Tell her to get on the plane."

"I don't want you to go," Charleigh said instead.

"Literally, the opposite of what I just said," Sylvia growled. "Sometimes I think you just like to be difficult."

Joey's little head fell on Sylvia's shoulder. "I's don'ts wants yous to goes, Leksi."

Sylvia leaned her head against the top of the blonde braids, then she looked at Lexa. "I never wanted you to leave, but this is your career. They won't call you the goat if you don't play everywhere. You'll end up like me, just someone who plays but no one knows, and you're better than that."

It wasn't an apology for all the secrets. Didn't fix the fact Sylvia hadn't married her because she loved her, but it healed a small part of Lexa's sense of self. The part that made her hate herself enough to always stop taking her meds when she got off the plane. Knowing Sylvia wasn't just sending her away to not deal with her made her feel just a little better, and she was going to do better.

"She's right," Charleigh said. She stepped into Lexa's bubble. "This is part of basketball life. Emma told me I had to prepare for it, and I am. It doesn't make me not miss you already, but you have to get on the plane."

Lexa watched the line moving as Charleigh gave her one of her tightest hugs.

"Promise me you won't leave me for her while I'm gone," Lexa pleaded. "And don't let her adopt my baby."

"I promise," Charleigh said, looking up at her. "Promise me you won't find someone that thinks they're your biggest fan?"

"I promise."

Sylvia set Joey down so she could say goodbye.

Lexa met the girl at her level and pressed kisses to her face. "You make sure Mommy Facetimes me at every practice. I will call you at breakfast and dinner every morning"

"Oh-kay," Joey said with a sniff. "Will yous brings me backs a Jenison jersey from the Aussitrailia?"

"Of course I will." Lexa kissed the little nose. "And I'll try to catch you a little joey and bring it back to you. Do you think Rexa would like a sister?"

"No, silly," Joey said. "I'm the only Joey."

"You are." Lexa stood up and pulled Charleigh and Joey into another hug. Then Charleigh scooped up the teary child in her arms and gave her one of her best hugs.

"Did you pack your meds?" Sylvia asked, pulling her purse straps up her shoulder.

"Yeah." Lexa played with a twist between her fingers. "I already spoke to the team doc out there. They have my records and have set up my script to be refilled in three weeks. And I... I spoke with the team doc. He's going to meet with me every morning and I'm going to take my meds in front of him, so someone is holding me accountable. In case... in case, I let the paranoia convince me otherwise."

"Good." Sylvia ran her hand down her ponytail to smooth away any stray hairs.

"Don't steal my girl while I'm gone, okay?" Lexa asked. "I know you're better than me. You always will be, but I'm going to do what I shoulda done with you. I'm going to stay away from the bars and the girls."

"If you do that, then I'll have no reason to," Sylvia stated.

"I'm not going to marry you," Charleigh hissed. "No matter how good the rewards are."

Sylvia's head fell to the side as a blush ran up Lexa's cheeks. "But I give very good rewards, don't I, Lexa?"

"Don't fucking answer that," Charleigh warned.

"According to Echo the rewards are impressive," Lexa said, hoping it would deter Charleigh from taking interest in either of the women.

Sylvia's lips tightened in a straight line as Charleigh's eyes grew wide. "Damn, you did all my bosses?!"

"I did your parents, your girlfriend, and your boss," Sylvia stated. "Technically, you're all that's left to do."

Announcements scratched over the elevator music. The words grumbled together as Lexa clenched her passport and ticket in her hand.

"If you get on the plane, I'll fly us out over Christmas break to see you," Sylvia promised.

Lexa checked the time on her phone and then glanced at the line. She nodded to Sylvia, then stepped to Charleigh for one last kiss.

"I'll be back," Lexa said, cupping the tear-stained face in her hands. "And apparently Sylvia is going to fly you on her fancy plane to come see me, which means she loves you more than she ever loved me because she never flew me anywhere."

"It's called living humbly, Lexa," Sylvia stated. "And humility was something you always lacked."

"We'll be here waiting," Charleigh promised. She glanced at Sylvia, holding onto Joey's head that was buried in her linen pants. "Apparently all of us, which is a little weird and feels a little throuplish. Maybe we'll bring Zoe the lawyer with us, so Sylvia can find someone else to propose to."

"Not completely opposed to her coming along. Very fit that one was," Sylvia said before taking Joey off to the side to look at the airplane taking off at the window.

"Very fit that one was," Charleigh mimicked. "Fuckin' weirdo."

Lexa pressed her lips to Charleigh's, stealing away any other commentary. Their lips danced together, softly sealing their promises of betterment until they could no longer survive the shared air between them.

She walked through the elastic strips toward the body scanning machine. Every other time she'd walked toward a new team, Lexa refused to look back. This time was different though. She turned to see Charleigh and Joey waving at her.

"I love you," Charleigh called out. Her fingers wrapped in a little heart over her chest.

Lexa made her own heart and sent it up in the air like a three-point buzzer beater. Charleigh held her hands out like a net, then threw them in the air as she cheered for Lexa's successful imaginary shot. Joey bounced as kisses were shot from her little hands for Lexa to catch with her own hoop. She too bounced and cheered for the child.

She didn't stop looking back until she went through TSA and her bag got pulled to the side. When she glanced back, she found Charleigh and Sylvia standing at the end of the lane. Charleigh held up the contested cell phone with its camera angled at Lexa.

Lexa closed her eyes as the frumpled female TSA agent performed a pat down on her body, commenting on how muscular Lexa's legs were.

The lanky man with a scruffy chin pulled out a horse-sized dildo from the duffle with a gloved hand. He dangled it in the air, and told the scanner, "Not a bomb, but another giant schlong."

Lexa's phone rang when the man tried to zip the bag with the silicone head protruding out of the top. She waved at the guy as she pressed the accept button.

"Seriously, just throw it away," Lexa begged. "It's not even mine."

"Miss, we can't have a giant penis sticking out of the trashcan," the woman who'd patted her down said. "We see them all the time. You don't have to pretend it's not yours. We're not here to judge the size of your boat, but maybe go for something a little smaller next time. Most girls got six inches of space, so unless you are planning on doing a horse, think in more moderation."

Lexa looked down at the video conference call to see Emma and Danaya in one little square and Charleigh and Sylvia in the other. All of their faces were laughing at her to the point the sound didn't even come through until they all calmed down.

"You guys fucking suck," Lexa growled, ripping the dick from her bag and shoving it into the nearest trash can. "You fuckers are seriously going to get me banned from Sky Harbor Airport."

"That was fucking priceless!" Danaya called out.

"I can't believe you managed to get it in her bag without her realizing," Emma stated.

"It wasn't that hard, since she refused to pack her stuff," Charleigh said. "Apparently, someone mommyed her so hard she doesn't know how to fold her own clothes."

"True," Sylvia offered. "I was always able to throw in the most random items because I had to pack it for her or it wouldn't get done. One time I only packed her pink crop tops and Daisy Duke jeans."

"How could you do this with Joey right there?" Lexa whined.

Charleigh moved the camera to the child with her headphones on and her face buried in the iPad. "Since you provided her with the perfect distraction, it wasn't like it was hard," Charleigh stated.

Lexa narrowed her eyes at the screen. "You fucking told her you did this at the party didn't you?" she hissed at Charleigh. Then she looked at Sylvia. "And you pretended you came because you gave a damn."

Sylvia shrugged and smiled. "I could not miss the first time my replacement pranked you. It was well worth the first-class ticket to ensure we would be able to get it all on camera."

"I think this calls for a schlong song," Danaya announced.

Lexa plugged in her earbuds so the whole of the airport could miss her friends and girlfriend remixing Sir Mixalot's song in an off-key harmony. And while she was positive at some point TSA would put her on a no-fly list because of the horse dicks she seemed to frequently carry with her, it made the trip to the gate a little more bearable.

Questions for Discussion

The story mentions that Charleigh has a history of being with Lexa Jenson. How does the past relationship between Charleigh and Lexa influence their interactions and the story's plot?

How does Charleigh feel about wearing Lexa Jenson's jersey? What does this choice symbolize for her?

Charleigh forgives Lexa Jenson even though it may not be the truth. What motivates her to do so, and what might be the consequences of this forgiveness?

How does the atmosphere of the basketball game contribute to the story's tension and emotional dynamics?

Mona brings up the idea that Lexa Jenson might be more of a "catchphrase" than a genuine person. How does this reflect Mona's perspective on fame and relationships?

What are your initial impressions of the protagonist, Lexa, and her current state of mind as described in the passage?

How does the author use Lexa's actions and thoughts to convey her frustration and inner conflict?

What do you think is the significance of the basketball and Lexa's difficulty in making the shot? How does it reflect her current situation?

What do you think Lexa's wife, Sylvia, might feel or think when she learns about Lexa's intentions regarding the two blondes she mentions?

How does the author establish the character of Charleigh through her actions, thoughts, and circumstances in the passage?

What challenges does Charleigh face in her life, and how does she handle them, particularly when it comes to her daughter Joey?

The text touches on gender stereotypes and societal expectations, especially concerning women's participation in sports. How does Charleigh address these issues with her daughter Joey, and what message is she trying to convey?

The text highlights Charleigh's struggles with addiction, as indicated by her one-year sobriety token. How do you think her past challenges with addiction might affect her current life and relationships?

Charleigh expresses a desire to "dosss the hard things" so that Joey can come home. What might these "hard things" entail, and what do you think Charleigh's future goals and challenges will be?

In this text, how does the author explore themes related to motherhood, gender expectations, and the pursuit of personal dreams and goals?

What are the main emotions and conflicts presented in chapter 21? How do the characters, specifically Lexa, Charleigh, and Sylvia, contribute to these emotions and conflicts?

Charleigh seems to have made a confession about her feelings and intentions. How does this confession affect the dynamics between the characters, especially Lexa and Charleigh? What do you think Charleigh's true motivations are?

What role does Lexa's wealth and Charleigh's social background play in the unfolding of the events? How do these factors influence the characters' decisions and perceptions of each other?

Lexa's realization about Sylvia's actions and the loss of her house and financial assets appears to be a turning point. How do you think this will impact Lexa's character and her relationships with Charleigh and Sylvia moving forward?

Emma's intervention with Lexa's medication highlights the importance of mental health in the story. How does Lexa's mental health relate to the unfolding events, and how might it impact her future decisions and relationships?

Reflect on the themes of trust, betrayal, and forgiveness in this passage. How do these themes manifest in the characters' actions and dialogue?

Chapter 21 ends with Lexa taking a pill to ease her emotional distress. What does this moment reveal about her coping mechanisms, and how do you anticipate it will influence her in the future?

In what ways do you see this passage setting the stage for further developments and conflicts in the story? What predictions can you make about the characters' futures based on these events?

How does Charleigh's past impact her present circumstances, and how does she cope with the challenges she faces?

Chapter 32 highlights the power dynamics and conflicts between different characters. How do power and control play a role in this scene, and how do characters like Sylvia, Dilynn, and Alex wield their influence?

Charleigh's decision to go along with Sylvia's demands is a significant turning point in Chapter 32. How do you think this decision will impact the story's plot and Charleigh's character development?

In your opinion, who is the most morally complex character in this scene, and why? How do their actions and motivations contribute to the overall intrigue of the story?

Acknowledgements

I wish to thank my wife for her patience as I withdrew into a game she couldn't see. Her unwavering support and understanding gave me the space and time to delve into the intense, heart-wrenching exploration of Charleigh and Lexa's challenging connection, much like a coach trusting a player to find their stride.

To my dear friend Tara, whose problem-solving skills and willingness to dive into the emotional depths with me were like a teammate ready to tackle the toughest challenges on the field. Our nightly talks were akin to strategizing sessions in the locker room, filled with the residue of our shared struggles. Her collaborative spirit played an indispensable role in navigating the complexities of Charleigh and Lexa's difficult journey.

In the creative arena, I find myself indebted to Robin, Carrie, Wendy, and Leigh. Their dedication to tirelessly navigating the emotional, tear-stained pages of this story was like a team persistently pushing through the most challenging game. Their commitment to the evolving narrative was like the echo of a crowd's support, their feedback a crucial play-by-play analysis of our work's progress. Their encouragement was an essential boost, instrumental in refining and polishing this tale into a powerful, visceral experience.

To these remarkable collaborators, each of you has made an indelible mark on the challenging course of this creative process. Your contributions, support, problem-solving, and relentless dedication to repeated readings have shaped this narrative into a profound and poignant story that now carries the raw essence of our collective efforts.

As I release this heartfelt work into the world, I carry with me a deep sense of gratitude, filled not only with the shadows of our struggles but also with the unspoken commitment and passion each of you has invested. May this story resonate with readers like a haunting anthem of sorrowful triumphs, reflecting the shared dedication and support that brought it to life.

About the Author

Chelsey Blue Spicer is a trailblazing author with a deep commitment to amplifying the voices and experiences of the LGBTQ+ community, much like a sports coach committed to nurturing diverse talent. From a young age, Chelsey, with the tenacity of an athlete, embarked on her writing journey, inspired by her mother's own published autobiography. She understood the power of words to spark conversations, challenge norms, and create positive change—much like a game-changing play in a crucial match.

Chelsey's novels stand out for their fearless exploration of post-coming out narratives within the LGBTQ+ community. Driven by a passion for representation akin to a champion's drive for victory, she confronts and dismantles harmful stereotypes, particularly the "bury your gays" media trope that has plagued LGBTQ+ storytelling for years. Chelsey's stories break free from the conventional narratives, showcasing everyday life and celebrating the diverse experiences of LGBTQ+ individuals without resorting to violence or relegating characters to stereotypical roles, much like a player breaking through the defense to score.

Frustrated by the lack of nuanced representation, Chelsey Blue Spicer writes with a mission—to provide models of life for LGBTQ+ individuals after they come out. Her narratives go beyond the struggles, offering glimpses into the joy, resilience, and triumphs that define the everyday lives of the LGBTQ+ community, much like a team's journey to victory.

Chelsey is not just an author; she is a voice for those whose stories have often been overlooked or misrepresented. Through her work, she aims to create a literary landscape where everyone can see themselves reflected, celebrated, and understood. Chelsey Blue Spicer invites readers to join her in breaking down barriers, fostering understanding, and embracing the diverse and beautiful spectrum of human experiences within the LGBTQ+ community, much like a team united in the pursuit of a common goal.

www.chelseybluespicer.com

Turn the page for a preview of Chelsey Blue Spicer's new novel

Available Thanksgiving 2024

Meet Victoria

Victoria's finger circled the rosy bulb, pinching and twisting occasionally. Her body melded against the cushion that complied with her will. The woman across from her couldn't hear the drumming in her head. A smooth tongue peeked out as the woman's speckled star-blue eyes gazed downward. Victoria's lip pulled back between her teeth as her fingers traced the delicate details surrounding the bulb.

"So, you've been out as a lesbian woman for approximately six months. You've moved to Arizona and established yourself. You got the new job as an Assistant Principal," the woman's eyes had wandered back up to Victoria. "How do you feel now?"

The pillow in Victoria's arms shielded her from the therapist. She hated that she loved how the maroon, rose, and pink stitching felt like the pillows on her mother's couch. She leaned back with the pillow still clutched against her chest.

"Lonely," she confessed.

"So, you still haven't had any contact from your family?" Dr. Rose probed, even though they both knew it was the case.

Victoria sighed and looked up at the ceiling tiles. The dim lighting of the room made it seem as though the stars had all combusted in the panels of universes. She searched the divots of the panels looking for constellations, another reminder of the small-town life she'd left the year prior.

"Victoria." Dr. Rose's voice pulled her back from the blankets covering the Utah lawn. From her childhood surrounded by giggling sisters and cousins as they gazed at the heavens. The promised land was now dark at her defiance of the words and her place.

"No. And I won't." Manicured fingers dug into the cloth-covered cotton. "I knew that it would be like this."

The flesh on the inside of Victoria's lower lip bled from her constant chewing. She'd been working at the same spot since she'd arrived at the office. She scraped the metallic taste off her tongue with her teeth, then swallowed the evidence of regret. "It doesn't make it easier though."

A fan burred on the Ikea desk, fluffing Dr. Rose's mein with each oscillation. Her pale thin hand ran over the notes page on her obnoxious yellow pad. She scratched another line to the weekly confession. She looked over the 1980s nerd glasses that had fallen toward the tip of her nose.

"How have you been managing loneliness?"

Victoria's eyes rolled as her head fell back against the wood-paneled wall behind her. "How does one manage to be lonely?"

"What do you do to distract yourself from feeling lonely?"

Victoria sucked her teeth and connected six divots into the little dipper. "I downloaded the TikTok app because I wanted to be prepared for the new school challenges I would potentially be seeing when I start next week. That was a rabbit hole that started with a lot of lumberjacks and somehow, I am now on lesbian TikTok."

"Do you enjoy social media apps?"

"No. I closed down most of my accounts after I saw the wedding photos of my niece. We'd been close her whole life, and I didn't even know the wedding was happening."

"What else have you done?"

"I signed up for one of the meet-up adventure days with other gay people, but then... I chickened out and just stayed home. I couldn't fit into my work clothes, so I joined a CrossFit gym but haven't really spoken to anyone other than basic greetings. I also started to sign up for a dating app, but I had to fill out the 'about me' section and I couldn't think of anything to say."

"Why not try the basics? Things you like to do. Food you like to eat," Dr. Rose suggested.

"I tried." She put the pillow down, then leaned forward. "I don't know what I like anymore. Every part of my life has been flipped upside down. I never used to have time to just do things. There was always church. Some niece or nephew or brother or sister's birthday party to attend. After work, I had to cook dinner, or go to the store, or clean the house. I never realized how much time I spent cleaning up after Michael, until it was just me and now dinner is leftovers for three nights and laundry goes into the actual bin, so I don't have to tidy anything.

"Is it nice not having to clean up after your ex-husband?"

Victoria's lips turned up slightly at the corners. "I had spent every Saturday morning scrubbing pee off the floor and the toilet since I was nineteen. Can I just tell you how amazing it is not to choke on shaving cream stench every time I use the toilet?"

Dr. Rose reciprocated the smile. With a nod, she said, "I can imagine that must feel very liberating."

"Yes." Then Victoria shrugged. "I mean, I guess it is."

Dr. Rose made another note. Victoria wondered what type of archive someone could read someday about the mundane details of her life Dr. Rose found interesting enough to write down.

"So, you mentioned starting the dating profile. How do you feel about dating a woman?"

"Terrified." The word had catapulted from her lips before she'd even had the opportunity to weigh the confession. Shaking her head, Victoria said, "I bet that sounds stupid."

"Does being terrified of something new seem like something that should be deemed stupid?"

"No." She thought about how many times she'd listened to a student justify their actions with fear. "It's just... I mean... I left my husband because of my feelings for women. Now, I'm too scared to date a woman."

"Let's talk about the aspects of dating a woman that you find scary. Is there something in particular?"

Victoria's hand pressed against her eyes and down her face. "Who asks who out?"

"Can you explain?"

Victoria looked up with only her eyes at the therapist. She didn't know how to explain the obvious. The more options her brain provided her tongue, the more she realized though, it wasn't obvious. Not to the therapist who had known she was a lesbian since she was a teenager.

"I guess it is stupid. I know women are equal and blah blah blah. But girls wait for boys to ask them out. It's not something girls do."

Dr. Rose set her pen down. "I can assure you I have been asked out by women before."

Victoria's hand shot up. "Yeah, but you are very clearly a feminine female."

She hated the way Dr. Rose's eyebrows crinkled in the middle. Hated how she tilted her head when the therapist looked at Victoria. Hated how it felt like she was a picture hanging just enough off-center to draw attention to her lack of straightness.

"Do you feel masculine?"

"I'm not the sundress-wearing Barbie, but I am not about to cut all my hair off and start wearing baggy clothes," Victoria spat.

"Then, is that the type of woman you find attractive? Someone more masculine?"

Twisting her head to the side, then back, and then the other side, the tension in her neck popped twice. "No."

Dr. Rose's pen was between her teeth. "Do you feel a feminine woman would not ask you out?"

Victoria's empty stomach fluttered, the air pushing its way into her throat. She swallowed the excess saliva hoping to sedate the hunger at having again forgotten to eat before her dinnertime session.

"I don't know if she would ask me out. I don't know if I could gather the courage to ask someone out myself." She took a deep breath, clenching her stomach to stop the flutters.

Pen scratched to paper. "You said *she*. Is there a woman you are interested in, but you are worried about asking her out?"

"No. Well. No, but yes." Victoria leaned back once more. She didn't have to close her eyes to see the smooth biceps of the brunette woman deadlift. The thick thighs bound only in the thin spandex that stretched as the muscles flexed.

"There's this girl at my gym. She has the rainbow lanyard and the "Lexa Deserved Better" sticker on her water bottle. I know she's gay. I mean I guess she could be more on the masculine side but that's because she is tall and thicker framed and I know she's beautiful, but if I ask her out then I don't know what to do. I have never planned a date in my life. And if I did plan a date, and it went well, and we kept dating then we would get to the point of... you know." She looked up at Dr. Rose. The blue eyes didn't suggest knowing anything, and Victoria wondered briefly if the woman took a class on appearing flat and clueless. "You know," Victoria lowered her voice to a whisper, "the sex part."

Victoria sucked her teeth, then shut her mouth. She didn't want to watch the pen detail another shred of her incompetence as evidence.

"So, what I hear you saying is you are attracted to an identifiably gay woman at the gym. You would like to possibly go on a date with her, but you are nervous about planning a date and if the time came having a sexual relationship with her."

"Yes."

"What type of experiences can you think of that you have had planning other outings?"

"You mean like dinner?" Victoria asked.

Dr. Rose nodded.

Victoria studied the wall above Dr. Rose's head.

"I used to choose the restaurant for my monthly outing with Micheal. Sometimes, I would suggest we see a movie. Simple things. I would inform Michael of the dress code of the venue. That's about it."

"So, you are comfortable choosing a place to eat for yourself and a companion. You have previously chosen movies to see. Possibly even arranged to attend one of those small-town festivals or something. You were able to communicate attire suggestions so your companion at the time would not feel under or overdressed."

Victoria huffed. "You're saying I know how to plan a date."

"Technically, you said so." Dr. Rose scribbled another note on the paper and Victoria found herself leaning forward with the hope she'd be able to make out what was on the page. "Since you are capable, then possibly the real fear is what happens when you plan an amazing date, and she would like to take the evening to the bedroom."

The pillow pressed against the front of Victoria again. Her fingers found the bulb on the pillow, and as she twisted it, she realized how pornographic the whole thing must look. She slapped her hand over the nipple-shaped protrusion. "I don't know what to do with a woman's body," she practically shouted.

Victoria bit into the same spot on her lip, extracting another dose of sobering corporeality. She closed her eyes.

"It's like I'm walking through the temple again and no one ever said anything about what was about to happen. Yes, I'd heard about sex in high school, but I didn't know how it worked and good sisters did not ask those kinds of questions."

"Victoria, have you explored your own body?"

Victoria's eyes shot open. "You mean like masturbated?"

Dr. Rose's lips smooshed together, and then she nodded. "That is one method, yes."

"No. I wouldn't even know what to do."

The therapist got up from her chair, letting the pages of the notepad flop against the fading leather. She rifled through the folders on her desk until she held up a pamphlet. "I would like to refer you to a colleague."

Victoria dropped her eyes to the floor. She scanned over the familiar laminate boards chaotically shoved together. The familiarity of the pillow felt like it too was being torn from her grasp and the stiff couch seemed to tilt, sliding her off it.

"Victoria, come back to me," Dr. Rose called through the tunnel of another place no longer safe. Dr. Rose held the shiny trifold out to her. "I am not saying that I want to stop our weekly sessions. The referral is not for a therapist, but rather a coach."

A single eyebrow rose on Victoria's face. "Like a life coach?"

"Sort of, but no."

Victoria took the thick page, the glossy texture felt good between her fingers. She looked at the front, then flipped it over. "An intimacy coach." She'd never heard of intimacy coaching, but when she opened the pamphlet, her eyes grew. "Is she a prostitute?"

Dr. Rose laughed. "No. Sarah is not a prostitute. Consider her like a health teacher at a high school but instead of STDs and abstinence lectures, she teaches anatomy and how to successfully pleasure a partner."

Victoria looked at the woman settling back into her chair. "She can teach me how to give a woman an orgasm?"

The smile on Dr. Rose's lips rose to her cheeks to her eyes. "She can teach you how to give a woman or even yourself an orgasm. And her service is completely tax deductible as a medical expense since she is being referred by a medical professional. I would like you to reach out to her. Next week, we can talk about how you felt about the conversation and go from there."

"I don't have to do it if I don't like the conversation," Victoria checked.

"You don't have to reach out to her at all. However, I have worked with Sarah for a long time. She is very professional and very, very good at helping individuals and couples improve their confidence in sexual intimacy."

Dr. Rose checked the watch on her wrist before she pulled the pages on the pad down until all the details of Victoria's life were lost in the pile. "Our time is up."